# GOD'S MEN

# GOD'S MEN

Pearl S. Buck

**WHITE LION PUBLISHERS LIMITED**
London, Sydney and Toronto

First published in Great Britain
by Methuen & Co.Ltd. London 1951

Copyright © 1951

White Lion Edition 1976

ISBN 7274 0216 1

Made and printed in Great Britain
for White Lion Publishers Limited,
138 Park Lane, London W1Y 3DD
by Hendington Limited,
Lion House, North Town, Aldershot, Hampshire

A MARCH morning in the year of our Lord, 1950, and the wind so high that on the top floor of a skyscraper in the city of New York William Lane felt a tremor under his feet. He stood by the immense plate-glass window set into the wall behind his desk. The city spread like a carpet before him, and over its horizon he saw the glimmer of hills and sea.

In his fashion he was a man of prayer, and he began his crowded days with these few moments of silence before his window and the world beyond. He had no petition in his heart nor did he ask anything of God. Prayer was an affirmation of himself and what he believed he was, a man of power for good, unmatched at least in his own country. Upon the streets below, so distant that he saw them as grey paths whereon there moved creatures insect-small, were the people whose thoughts he directed, whose minds he enlightened, whose consciences he guided. That they did not know it, that only a few people knew it, increased his power. Long ago he had given up the dream of being a popular leader. He had not the gift of winning popular love. Compelled at last to know that his looks, dark and grave, inspired fear rather than faith, he had immured himself in this great building. From here he had spread over the nation the network of his daily newspapers. For this he bought the services of men and their highest talents. There was no one, he believed, though without cynicism, who could not be bought. Nothing would persuade him, on the other hand, to buy a talent he did not want or which he could not mould to the shape of his own doctrine. The greatest writers found no space in his pages if they did not believe as he did. There were a few, not more than five or six, who were not tempted by fifty thousand dollars. There was only one who had not been tempted by twice that amount. None, he was sure, would refuse as much as he could offer, if he thought it right to offer it. What he bought was not only the fluid flow of men's words. He bought also the quality of their spirits. A man hitherto incorruptible was valuable when he yielded, though only for a while, because he sold also the faith of the people in him.

Upon this March morning, while William thus communed with himself and God, he felt the tremor beneath his feet. He knew that a rigid building, unable to sway slightly before the winds of a storm, might have been overcome. Yielding only a little, the building was safe. Nevertheless, he did not like the tremor. It reminded him of other things that had once made him tremble.

Long ago in China, when he was a boy, he had seen a mob in the streets of Peking, a mob of angry common people who hated him not for what he was, for his white skin and light eyes, but for his kind. His insecurity, the insecurity of his kind on that day, had thrown him into a panic which, though it assailed him no more, he was never able to forget. Any crowd of people, any mass of commonplace faces above dingy clothing, made him remember, although he was no longer afraid, for he had nothing to fear. He was richer than anybody he knew and his friends were some of the richest men in the Western world. Among them he was unassailable, a man of rigid goodness in his personal life. That he had divorced his first wife to marry his second could not be counted a fault, as soon as one saw Emory. She was a creature as delicately pure as a frost flower; her English beauty, her grace combined with her goodness to make her irresistible. Compared to Candace, his first wife, Emory was spirit opposed to earth.

As he thought of his wife the door opened behind him. He did not turn. No one except his secretary dared to enter uncalled, and he waited until her timid voice spoke.

'I'm sorry to disturb you, Mr. Lane.'

'Well?' he said in his dry voice.

'I wouldn't have come in except that it's your brother-in-law, Mr. Miller.'

'Does he have an appointment?'

'No, he doesn't, Mr. Lane, and I reminded him of that, but

2

he said he guessed you would see him anyway, because he has a big idea.'

He would have liked to say quite sharply that he was not interested in any big ideas that Clem Miller might have, but he did not like to give Miss Smith cause for gossip among the lesser staff. They would call him hard, as he knew he was often called, merely because on principle he did not believe in confusing justice with mercy. Nevertheless, it was outrageous for Clem to walk into the offices on a busy morning and expect to be given time for some crank idea. He did not like to remember that Henrietta's husband, too, was a successful man. Clem had grown wealthy by the most absurd methods, so absurd that he believed the fellow, or almost did, when he said that he had never planned to make money. It was hard to believe that Clem did not want to be rich, although the way he and Henrietta lived was strange enough. In spite of wealth, they lived in a frame house on a side street of a town in Ohio. What Clem did with his money no one knew.

'Tell my brother-in-law I can give him exactly fifteen minutes. If he stays longer than that, get him out.'

'Yes, Mr. Lane,' Miss Smith breathed. Her name was not Smith but William Lane called all his secretaries Smith. They resented it but were paid so well that they did not dare to say so.

When he heard the door shut, William turned away from the window and sat down in the great chair behind the semi-circular desk. Against the vast rectangle of light his domed head, his figure, slender but strong, square shouldered and tall, stood forth as though it were chiselled in stone. He sat immobile and waiting, looking at the door.

Thus Clem, coming through that door with his quick and nervous step, faced the mighty man. If he felt the slightest terror before William's eyes, as grey and green as lichen, he did not show it. He was a small thin man, sandy-haired, and his very skin was the colour of sand. Into this general insignificance were set his eyes, a quick, kingfisher blue.

'Well, hallo, William,' Clem said in a high cheerful voice. 'Your help out there is certainly for you. I could hardly get in here.'

3

'If I had known you were coming——' William began with dignity.

'I didn't know I was coming myself,' Clem said. He sat down, not in the chair across the desk from William and facing him, but in a leather-covered chair near the window. 'Nice view you have here—I always like to look at it. How's your wife?'

'Emory is quite well,' William said.

'Henrietta is well, too,' Clem said. 'She's gone to see Candace today.'

'What are you doing here?' William asked. He was accustomed to this husband of his sister's, who jumped about the earth like a grasshopper. Only the coolness of his voice might have betrayed, and then only to Henrietta herself, his displeasure with his sister's continuing friendship with his former wife.

'I got an idea and ran down to Washington,' Clem said. 'The Food Minister in New Delhi wrote me there was a lot of hoarded wheat over there. I wasn't sure he knew what he was talking about, sitting in an office in New Delhi. I guess he did, though. There is considerable wheat put away in India, from what I hear. I don't hardly think it's in the hands of dealers. It's hidden by the peasants themselves, the way you or I might tuck away a bank account against a rainy day.'

William did not answer. He could not imagine himself tucking away money, nor could he imagine a rainy day. But Clem was incurably common.

Clem scratched his pale chin and went on talking. 'If I could persuade these food hoarders of our own in Washington to let up a little and get some wheat over to India, of course it would bring out the wheat over there, and the price would go right down so the people could buy food. I don't know as I can do anything in Washington, though—I don't understand governments, least of all ours.'

'Upon that you and I can agree,' William said. 'I thought that what we had in the White House during the war was bad enough. What we have now is worse.'

4

'Yeah,' Clem said, ruminating. 'Don't matter to me, though. I'm no politician. I just want to pry some wheat loose.'

'What did they say in Washington?' William asked.

'Oh, the usual patter—it would be interfering with internal affairs in India—meaning that if the people get food they might support the present government.'

'Don't they like Nehru?' William asked this with some interest. He had not known what to make of that composite man upon his one visit to America.

'Sure they like him as far as he goes,' Clem said. 'He don't go far enough for some of our Republicans. They want him to swear eternal vengeance on the Russians and eternal loyalty to us. Nehru won't swear; no sensible man would. But that don't interest me, either. What interests me is getting people fed, if for no reason except that starvation is a shame and disgrace to the world and totally unnecessary in modern times. I don't believe in using food, mind you, to manipulate people. Get everybody fed, says I—then you start even. Once all bellies are full, people won't have to vote this way and that so as to get a meal. That's democracy. We ain't practising it.'

Food and democracy were Clem's themes, and long ago William had become bored with his brother-in-law. He saw dreaminess creep into Clem's brilliant blue eyes, a tensity lifted the thin almost boyish voice, and he recognized both as signs of what he called Clem's fanaticism.

'I do not want to hurry you,' he said in his carefully controlled voice, 'I do, however, have a business meeting of unusual importance within the next fifteen minutes.'

Clem brought back his eyes from the world beyond the window. The dreaminess vanished. He got up and went over to the chair facing William and sat down and leaned his elbows upon the desk. His square face looked suddenly sharp and even acute. 'William, I get letters from China.'

William was startled. 'How do you do that?'

'Somebody I used to know in Peking.'

'You'll get yourself into trouble mixing with Communists,' William said sternly.

'I guess I won't,' Clem said. 'The Old Boy knows.' The

5

Old Boy, in Clem's language, was always the President of the United States.

'What does he say?' William asked.

'Just told me he didn't approve,' Clem gave a sharp cackle.

William did not make a reply, and, as he foresaw, Clem went on without it. 'William, there's a mighty famine over yonder in China. You remember? Rivers rising, dikes crumbling away into the water.'

'A good thing,' William said. 'It will teach the Chinese people that Communists cannot save them.'

'That ain't enough, though, William,' Clem said with insistent earnestness. 'That's only the half of it. We got to get the other half across to them. We got to get food over there. What the Reds can't do, we gotta do, or the people will think we can't do it, either, and so what's the use of giving us a try?'

'People ought to be punished for making the wrong choice,' William said grimly.

Clem saw the grimness with detached pity. 'You oughtn't to take pleasure in punishing people, William. I declare, it's not worthy of such a big man as you are now. It's kind of an Old Testament way of thinking that was done away with when the New Testament came along.'

'I will not discuss my religion with you,' William said with some violence.

'I don't want to discuss religion, either,' Clem said. 'I wouldn't hardly know how to say what I believe, and it's your business if you want to be a Catholic, and I told Henrietta so. I don't mind what a man is, if he's a good man—that's what I always say. My father believed in faith, but it certainly didn't save him, and I wouldn't recommend it. I'm not really interested in religion. All I say is if a man don't have a full belly——'

'I know what you say,' William said with weariness. 'Let's get to the point.'

Clem came to the point instantly. 'William, I can get the food to send to China, and to India, too. We're so stuffed with so much food over here that my buyers can get it by the hundreds of tons without bothering Washington at all. I can get

6

my hands on ships, too. Even the Old Boy don't have to do anything—just sit there and look the other way. But I need you, William.'

'What for?' William asked warily.

The light of gospel came into Clem's blue eyes. He held up his right hand in unconscious gesture.

'William, I want you to get behind the idea with your newspapers, so that I won't be hampered by any senators and the like! Everybody reads your papers, everybody over this broad land. There's millions of people reads your newspapers that don't read anything else. Even senators are still afraid of millions of people. I want to tell the people that if we get our extra food over there to Asia it's worth any number of bombs, atom bombs—hydrogen bombs, even——'

'Impossible!' William's voice rang hard with anger. 'If this is your wonderful idea——'

'My idea is to get food to the starving, William! I don't ask you to do it. I've got my ways of getting into places. I've got my friends. I only ask you to explain to our people.'

'Your friends must be Communists!'

'I don't care what they are, any more than I care what you are, just so they get our food to the starving. People will ask, where is the food coming from? America! Don't you see? America don't even ask if people are Communists. Good old America just feeds the starving. It's the greatest advertisement for our democracy——'

'Impossible!' William said bitterly. 'Sentimental, absurd! Clem, those people won't ask anything. They'll just eat. Most of them will think that it's the Communists who are giving them food. You are too naïve.'

Clem refused to yield. 'Even if they do think it's the wrong party, they'll be stronger to see tyranny in the end, won't they? A starving man can't see right or wrong. He just sees food. You've got no judgement when you're hungry. You can't even rebel.'

Clem watched William's face for a waiting second. It did not change. 'You've never been hungry, have you, William? I have.'

7

William did not need to answer.

Miss Smith opened the door softly. 'I'm sorry to interrupt, Mr. Lane, but the gentlemen are waiting in the Board Room.'

Clem got up. 'You don't need to use fancy methods with me, lady. Just tell me it's time to go. Well, William——'

'I wouldn't think of doing what you suggest,' William said. 'I don't agree with you in any particular.'

Clem stood looking down on him. 'Let 'em starve, eh, William?' he said after an infinitesimal pause.

'Let them starve until they confess their folly,' William said firmly and got up. 'Good-bye, Clem. Give my love to Henrietta.'

'Good-bye,' Clem said, and turning he left the room.

Neither of them had put out a hand to the other, but William did not notice it. He seldom shook hands with anyone. He disliked the contact, but more than that in recent years there were twinges of neuritis in his hands which made it painful to suffer the vigour of Clem's grasp. He took out his handkerchief and wiped his forehead and poured himself a drink of ice cold water from the silver thermos bottle on his desk. The strangest touch of fate in his strange life was the fact that Clem Miller was his brother-in-law, Clem, whom more than half a century ago he had first seen on a Peking street and never thought to see again—Clem, that pale and hungry boy, the son of the Faith Mission family, living in a cheap alleyway, a hutung in the poorest part of the city, Clem, whom even then he had despised. How had it come about? Half a century ago. . . .

Young William Lane, leaning back in his mother's private rickshaw, perceived a short quarter of a mile ahead a knot of people. This in a Peking street meant some sort of disturbance. Possibly it meant only amusement. The people of the imperial city, accustomed to pleasure, were never too busy to pause for an hour or two and watch whatever passed, from the entourage of a court lady on her way to the Summer Palace to the tumbles of a trained bear and the antics of a shivering

8

monkey. Since the season was spring it might now be a troupe of street actors, fresh from their winter in the south.

William leaned forward. 'Lao Li, what is yonder?' he asked the rickshaw puller.

His Chinese was pure and somewhat academic, although he was only seventeen. Actually he was not proud of speaking good Chinese. It revealed too clearly that he was the son of a missionary. At the English boarding school in Chefoo where he spent most of the year, the aristocrats among the boys were the sons of diplomats and businessmen and they were careful to show no knowledge of the language of the natives. Among white people in China missionaries were distinctly low class. At school William spoke pidgin English to the servants and pretended he did not understand them when they replied in Chinese. Now, however, he was at home for the Easter holidays, and since he had been born and had grown up in Peking, no pretence was possible.

'Something strange, Young Master,' Lao Li replied. He snatched his cotton jacket from his shoulders as he ran and wiped the sweat from his face. Foreigners were heavy—this young master, for example, though still growing, was already heavier than a man. He could remember when he had pulled him as a child. The years passed. He dared not slacken his pace. A rickshaw puller must not grow old. A steady job in a white man's family could not be lost, however heavy the children were.

He snatched at a hope for rest. 'Shall I not stop so that you can see for yourself?'

William's haughty head was high. 'What do I care what street people look at?'

'I only asked,' Lao Li muttered.

He tried to quicken his pace as he drew near to the crowd and then William's shout startled him so that he nearly fell between the shafts.

'Stop!'

William, seated high, could look over the heads of the people. In the centre of the crowd he saw a horrible sight. A white boy was locked in struggle with a Chinese boy. The onlookers were not laughing. They were intensely quiet.

9

'Let me down,' William said imperiously.

Lao Li lowered the shafts and William stepped over them and strode through the people.

'Let me pass,' he said to them in the same haughty voice. The Chinese parted mutely before him until he reached the centre. There in silence the two boys were struggling together, the brown face, the white face, equally grim.

'Stop it, you,' William said loudly in English.

The white boy turned. 'What business is it of yours?' he demanded. He was small and pale, his frame undernourished, and his grey cotton garments, shrunken by many washings, clung to his bones. Nevertheless there was a certain toughness in his square face, and under his sand-coloured hair his eyes were a bright blue.

'Of course it is my business,' William retorted. He felt his own contrast. His English tweed suit had been made by an excellent Chinese tailor, and his shoes were polished every night by the house coolie—his boots, as he had learned to call them at school. To his horror, he saw that the other boy wore Chinese cloth shoes, ragged at the toes.

'It is degrading for a foreign chap to fight a Chinese,' he said severely. 'It makes them look down on all of us. You have no right to behave in such a way as to bring discredit on us.'

The pale boy blinked rapidly and clenched his fists. 'I'll fight anybody I like!' His voice was high and ringing.

'Then I'll have you reported to the Consul,' William declared. He allowed his somewhat cold eyes to travel slowly up and down the boy's slight figure. 'Who are you, anyway? I've never seen you before.'

'I'm Clem Miller.'

A faint movement of William's lips was not a smile. 'You mean the Faith Mission Miller?'

'Yes.' The bright blue eyes dared William's scorn.

'In that case——' William shrugged his handsome shoulders. He turned as though to go and then paused. 'Still, as an American, you might think of the honour of your country.'

'My father says the world is our country.'

To William Lane, the son of an Episcopal missionary, an aristocrat of the church, nothing could have been more sickening than this remark. He wheeled upon the pale boy. 'As if it could be! You're American no matter what you do, worse luck for the rest of us! What are you fighting this Chinese boy for?'

'He said my father was a beggar.'

'So he is, in a way,' William said.

'He is not!' Clem retorted. He clenched his fists again and began to whirl them toward William's face.

William took one step backward. 'Don't be a fool, you! You know as well as I do that your father's got no proper mission board behind him, no salary or anything.'

'We've got God!' Clem said in a loud clear voice.

William sneered. 'You call it God? My mother says it's begging. She says whenever your food's gone your father comes around and tells us so. He tells everybody you have nothing to eat, but the Lord will provide. Actually who does provide? Well, my mother, for instance! We can't see Americans starve. It would make us lose face before the Chinese.'

He felt a small strong fist just under his chin, and against all his sense of what was decent for a gentleman, he kicked out with his right foot. His shoe was of excellent leather, sharp at the edge of the sole, and it caught Clem under the knee-cap with such pain that he dropped into the thick dust. William did not stop to see what happened next. He turned and strode through the waiting crowd again and took his seat in the rickshaw.

'Go on,' he said to Lao Li.

Behind his back the crowd murmured. Hands were put out to lift up the fallen boy, and the Chinese lad forgot the quarrel.

'That big American boy ought to die,' he declared. 'You are the same kind of people, both from outside the seas. You should be brothers.'

Clem did not reply. After a few seconds of intense pain he limped away.

'Foreigners have bad tempers,' the crowd murmured. 'They are very fierce. You see how they are, even with each other.'

A few turned upon the Chinese boy with advice. 'You son of Han, be careful next time. Naturally a human being does not like to hear his father called a beggar, even though he is one.'

'We were really talking about the foreign god,' the boy explained. 'His father asked my father for one of our loaves. He said they had no bread and my father being a baker, he said that the foreign god had told him to come to our house. My father gave him three loaves and the foreigner said his god always provided. But I said, "How is it he does not provide from among your own people?" This foreign boy was with his father and he heard me say these words, and he told me to follow him, and when we were alone he began to hit me, as you saw.'

To this the crowd listened with interest and there was a division of opinion. Some thought the boy had spoken well enough and others said that silence was better than any speech where foreigners were concerned.

'Nevertheless,' said one man, who by his long robe was a scholar, 'it is strange that the Jesus people are all rich except this one family who live among our poor.'

'Who can understand foreigners? There are too many of them here,' a butcher said. He carried yards of pig entrails looped over his bare arm, and they had begun to stink faintly in the sun and reminded him that he should be on his way. Slowly the crowd parted, and soon there were only the footprints in the dust to tell of the scuffle.

William Lane paused at the front door of his home and waited. He had tried the door and found it unlocked, but he would not go in. In spite of his instructions the house-boy was not waiting in the hall to take his hat and topcoat. He wished that he dared to carry his malacca stick here as he did at school, but he did not quite dare. His sister Henrietta, two years younger than he, would laugh at him, and there was nothing he dreaded more than laughter. He pressed the bell and waited again. Almost instantly the door opened and

Wang, the house-boy, smiled and gestured to him to enter, at the same time taking his hat. 'It is the day your mother, the *t'ai-t'ai*, sits at home,' he said in Chinese. 'So many ladies have come that I have been too busy.'

William did not answer this. Wang had been with the family for many years, and William took pains now to make him feel that the old days of childish comradeship were over. A young gentleman did not chatter with servants. 'Where is my father?' he asked.

'The Teacher has not come home yet from the big church,' Wang replied. He smiled affectionately at the tall boy whom he remembered first as a baby, staggering about these very rooms. 'Little Lord,' the servants had called him. Now he was called Big Little Lord. Sad it was that the family had no more sons, only the two girls.

'Where is my younger sister?' William asked. Of his two sisters he preferred Ruth.

'She is with your mother, and also your older sister,' Wang replied. 'Forgive me, young sir. You would be surprised at the speed with which the foreign ladies eat and drink.'

He hung William's hat upon a large mahogany hat-rack, put his coat into the closet under the stairs and hastened smoothly back into the drawing-room.

William hesitated. The noise of women's voices, subdued only by the closed door into the wide hall where he stood, both tempted and repelled him. Most of the women were the middle-aged friends of his mother, who had known him from babyhood. Yet there might be a stranger or two. Peking was full of foreigners these days, tourists and visitors, and his father was one of the most liberal among the missionaries. His mother, he knew, often declared that she herself was not a missionary, she was only a missionary's wife, and she would not pretend. Privately she had often complained to her son that it was a tragedy that his father had ever chosen to be a missionary in so repulsive a country as China, so distant from New York, where her home was.

'Your father could have been anything,' she told him often. 'At Harvard he was brilliant and handsome. Of course

13

everyone thought he would be a lawyer, like his father. Yours is a good family, William, and I do hope that you will remember it. I don't want you to waste yourself.'

His mother fed him a good deal of private heresy to which he did not make reply but which he stored in his heart. Certainly he would never be a missionary. The English boys at school had seen to that. A merchant prince, perhaps, or a diplomat, he did not yet know which. Although he dreamed of America, he could not see himself living anywhere except in China. It was comfortable here for a white man. He did not like the stories he heard of missionaries on furlough having to do their own cooking and cleaning. Here he never entered the kitchen or servants' quarters—at least, not now that he was practically grown. When he was small and often lonely and bored, since he was not allowed to play with Chinese children, he had gone sometimes to the servants' quarters for companionship. Wang had been young then and afraid of the cook, and he had welcomed William's friendship. Sometimes Wang had even taken him on the street secretly to see a Punch-and-Judy show or to buy some sweets.

That, of course, was long ago. Remembering the sweets, William decided suddenly to go into the drawing-room. The cook made irresistible cakes for his mother's 'At Homes', two golden ones iced with dark chocolate, two snow-white ones layered with fresh coco-nut. More than mere food tempted him. Since he had come home only a few days ago, many of his mother's friends would not have seen him for several months, and he could exhibit his extraordinary growth. He had added inches to his height even since the long Christmas vacation and was well on his way, he hoped, to six feet, his father's height. There were times he feared he would not reach it for his hands and feet were small. Just now, however, he was feeling encouraged about himself.

He opened the door and went in, holding his shoulders straight and his head high. Upon his face he put his look of stern young gravity. For a moment he stood with his back to the door, waiting.

His mother glanced at him. 'Come in, William,' she said in

14

her silvery company voice. 'Leave the door open, please; it's a little warm.'

Her stone grey eyes, set somewhat near together under somewhat too heavy dark eyebrows, grew proud. She looked around the room where at half a dozen small teapoys the ladies were seated. 'William is just home from school,' she announced. 'Isn't he enormous? It's his last term.'

It was a comforting scene to William. The big room was warm and bright. Upon the polished floor lay great Peking rugs woven in blue and gold, and the furniture gleamed a dark mahogany. The pieces were far more valuable than mahogany, however. They were of black-wood, heavy as iron, Chinese antiques, stolen from palaces and pawned by hungry eunuchs to dealers. The houses of Americans in Peking were crammed with such tables and screens and couches. Scattered among them were comfortable modern chairs padded with satin-covered cushions. Today sprays of forced peach blossom and two pots of dwarf plum trees provided flowers. Among these pleasant luxuries the ladies sat drinking their tea, and just now turning their faces towards him. Their voices rose to greet him.

'Why, William—how you've grown! Come and shake hands with me, you big boy.'

He went forward gracefully and shook hands with each one of ten ladies, ignoring his two sisters. Ruth sat upon a hassock by the grate fire of coals. Henrietta was eating a sandwich on the deep window-seat. She did not look at him but Ruth watched him with her pleasant light blue eyes.

'Sit down, William, and have some tea,' his mother commanded. She was a tall woman, lean and large boned, and he had his looks from her, although she was almost ugly. What lacked delicacy in a woman made for strength in a man.

Once he had settled on a chair beside her, Wang handed him sandwiches and cake and in silence he proceeded to feed himself heartily. The ladies began to talk again. He perceived at once that they were talking about the Faith Mission family and saying exactly the sort of things with which he could agree. Mrs. Tibbert, a Methodist and therefore not quite the equal of Episcopalians and Presbyterians, although better than a

15

Baptist, was redeemed by being the wife of a bishop. She was a small pallid woman, bravely dressed in a frock copied by a Chinese tailor from a *Delineator* model, and she had lost a front tooth and had a lisp.

'It's stupid, really, talking about trusting God for everything and then collecting, really, from all of us. We can't let them starve, of course. I wonder if a petition to the Consul——'

'The way they live!' Mrs. Haley exclaimed. She was a Seventh Day Adventist, and even less than a Baptist. It was confusing to the Chinese to be told that Sunday was on Saturday, although immersion, upon which Baptists and Seventh Day Adventists insisted, the Presbyterians and Episcopalians declared was the most confusing of all doctrinal practices. Ignorant Chinese tended to be impressed by much water, and sprinkling seemed stingy, especially in hot weather.

Mrs. Henry Lodge, the wife of the leading Presbyterian minister, was charitable, as she could afford to be, since her house was one of the handsomest in Peking, and her husband the highest paid among the missionaries, besides being related to the Lodges of Boston. 'I feel so sorry for the little children,' she said gently. White-haired and pretty and gowned in a soft grey Chinese crepe with rose ruching, she made a picture which the other ladies, though Christians, were compelled to envy. William looked at her with appreciation. So a lady ought to look, and to call her attention to himself, he decided to tell the story of his own recent experience.

'Mrs. Lodge, perhaps you'd like to know. As I was coming home today——'

He told the story well and was sensible enough to be modest and merciful toward the ill-dressed boy whom he had publicly reproved. When he had finished he was rewarded.

'I am glad you helped him, William,' Mrs. Lodge said. 'That was Christian of you—and brotherly. "Unto the least of these," our dear Lord tells us——'

'Thank you, Mrs. Lodge,' William said.

Clem Miller had walked away from the crowd as quickly as he could. He would have liked to run, but his clumsy cloth

16

shoes and his sore knee made this impossible. What he remembered about William Lane were his shoes, those strong and well-fitting shapes of brown leather, protecting the tenderness of soles and the ends of toes. A good kick from such a shoe would leave its proper mark.

'Yet it will never be I who will have American shoes,' he muttered.

His articulate thoughts were always in Chinese, not the fluid tonal Chinese of Peking, but the scavenger Chinese, the guttural coolie vernacular of treaty ports where boat people lived. His first home had been on a boat, for his father, anxious to follow in the exact footsteps of Jesus, had preached from the waters of the dirty Whangpoo in Shanghai to those who gathered upon the shores to listen. There had been more staring than listening, and respectable Christians had come by night to reproach his parents for bringing shame upon them by such beggarly behaviour.

They still lived like beggars. Clem, scuffling through the Peking dust, could not deny the accusation which William had made. He had looked more than once through the gate of the compound in which William lived, and by the standards of those who made their homes in big houses of grey brick, roofed with palace tiles of blue and green, the four rooms in a Chinese alley, where he lived with his parents and his sisters, were beggarly. His mother, uncomplaining and of a clinging faith, had nevertheless refused to live on the boat any more after the baby Arthur had fallen overboard into the river and been drowned.

There had been long argument over it between his parents. 'Mary, it will look as though you couldn't trust God no more, because of trial,' Paul Miller had told his weeping wife.

She had tried to stop her sobs with a bit of ragged handkerchief at her lips. 'I do trust. It's only I can't look at the water now.'

Arthur's little body had not been returned. They had searched the banks day after day, but the river had clutched the child deep in its tangled currents. So after weeks they had given up this search and had come north to Peking. Paul

17

Miller had taken to God the matter of the dollars necessary for third-class train fare, and then he had gone to the other Shanghai missionaries to bid them farewell, as brothers in Christ. They had responded with sudden generosity by collecting a purse for him, and the missionary women had met together and packed a box of clothing for Mrs. Miller and the children.

'See how the Lord provides when we trust him!' Thus his father had cried out, his mild blue eyes wet with grateful tears.

'Clem, your father is right,' his mother said, 'we've always been provided for, though sometimes God tests our faith.'

Clem had not answered. At this period of his life he was in a profound confusion he dared not face, even alone. The world was divided into the rich who had food and the poor who had not, and though he had been told often of the camel and the eye of a needle and how hard the rich would find it to enter heaven, yet God seemed indulgent to them and strangely careless of the poor. The poor Chinese, for example, the starving ones, God who saw all things must also see them, but if so He kept silent.

Pondering upon the silence of God, Clem himself grew increasingly silent. There were times when he longed to leave his family and strike out alone across the golden plains, to make for the coast, to find a ship and get a job that would see him across the Pacific to the fabulous land where his parents had been born. Once there he would go straight across on foot to his grandfather's farm in Pennsylvania.

Yet he could not leave his pitiful family, though now past his fifteenth birthday, and he troubled himself much about his future. Such thoughts he kept to himself, knowing that were he to speak of them, his parents, incorrigible in their faith, would only bid him put his trust in God. That was well enough, but who was going to teach him Latin and mathematics and English grammar? He had bought a few old English text-books in a Chinese secondhand bookshop, paying for them by teaching English to the bookseller's ten-year-old son. These books he studied alone, but he felt sorely the need of a teacher. And he could not beg. Though he ate the food his parents somehow got, he could not ask of the prosperous missionaries anything for himself. Today, on the way home from Mr. Fong's bookshop, he had seen his father at the baker's, and then had come the fight, after his father had gone on.

Otherwise the day had been fine, though the evening air was now laced with a cold wind from the north-west. He loved the city at this hour. The people were kind enough to him, even though he had fought that one impudent boy. He was sorry for it now. From how the boy looked at it, he had been right. The Miller family, though they trusted in God, were beggars.

He entered the door of his home with so bitter a look upon his face that his mother, setting the square Chinese table with bowls and chopsticks for supper, stopped to look at him. Pottery bowls and bamboo chopsticks were cheaper than plates and knives and forks.

'What's wrong with you, son?' Her voice was childishly sweet and her face was still round and youthful. Her hair, once of the softest red gold, was now a sandy grey. In spite of his adolescent doubts of her he loved her, so soft was she, so tender to him and to them all.

For the moment, nevertheless, he hardened his heart and blurted his thoughts. 'Mama, somehow I'm beginning to see it, we're really beggars.'

She leaned on the table upon her outspread hands. 'Why, Clem!'

He went on unwillingly, hardening himself still more. 'A Chinese boy called us beggars, and I lit into him. Now don't look at me like that, Mama. William Lane came by at that moment, and he—he helped me to stop. But he thought the boy was right.'

'I tremble for you, darling. If we lose our faith, we have nothing left.'

'I want more faith, Mama.' His brain, honest yet agile, was seeking proof at last.

'I don't see how Papa could show more faith, Clem. He never wavered, even when we lost little Artie. He sustained me.'

Her voice broke, and her full small mouth quivered. The tears always waiting like her smile, ran from her golden brown eyes.

'He could have more faith,' Clem said.

'But how, dear?'

'If he wouldn't go and tell people when the bread is gone— at least if he wouldn't tell the missionaries.'

He lifted his eyes to hers, and to his amazement he saw clear terror. Her round cheeks, always pale, turned greenish. She did not deceive him, and for this his love clung to her always. She held out her hands in a coaxing gesture, and when he did move, she came to him and knelt beside the bamboo stool upon which he sat, her face level with his.

'Son, dear, what you're saying I've said, too, in my own heart, often.'

'Then why don't you tell Papa?' he demanded. He could not understand why it was that though he loved her so much he no longer wished to touch her or be touched by her. He dreaded a caress.

She did not offer it. She rose and clasped her hands and looked down at him.

'For why you can't do it, neither,' she said. 'It would break his heart to think we had doubted.'

'It's not doubt—it's just wanting proof,' he insisted.

'But asking God for proof is doubt, my dearie,' she said quickly. 'Papa has explained that to us, hasn't he? Don't you remember, Clem?'

He did remember. His father, at the long family prayers held morning and evening every day, had taught them in his eager careful way, dwelling upon each detail of God's mercy to them, that to ask God to prove Himself was to court Satan. Doubt was the dust Satan cast to blind the eyes of man.

'And besides,' his mother was saying, 'I love Papa too much to hurt him, and you must love him, too, Clem. He hasn't anybody in the world but us, and really nobody but you and me, for the children are so little. He has to believe in our faith, to keep him strong. And Papa is so good, Clem. He's

20

the best man I ever saw. He's like Jesus. He never thinks of himself. He thinks of everybody else.'

It was true. Though sometimes he hated the unselfishness of his father, though his father's humility made him burn with shame, he knew these were but aspects of a goodness so pure that it could not be defiled. He yielded to its truth and sighed. Then he rose from the stool and looked towards the table.

'Is Papa home?'

'No—not yet. He went down to preach in the market-place.'

Paul Miller had left the market-place where he had gone to preach the saving grace of Jesus, for the people were busy and indifferent. On the way home he met Dr. Lane, returning from his Wednesday afternoon catechism class in the church. Ordinarily the tall handsome missionary, settled comfortably in a rickshaw, would have passed the short figure plodding through the dust with no more than a friendly, though somewhat embarrassed, nod. Today, however, he stopped the rickshaw. 'Miller, may I have a word with you?'

'Certainly, Brother Lane.'

Henry Lane winced at the title. Brother he was, of course, spiritually, to all mankind, for he hoped he was a true Christian. But to hear it shouted thus cheerfully in the streets by a white man who wore patched garments was not pleasant. He did not encourage his wife or his son when they criticized the Faith Mission family. Indeed, he reminded them that Christ could be preached in many ways. Now, however, he had to conceal feelings that he was too honest to deny to himself were much like theirs. It was humiliating to the foreign community of Peking to have the Millers there. It was even worse that they were missionaries of a sort, preaching at least the same Saviour. The Faith Mission family had caused wonder and questions even in his own well-established church.

. On the street Chinese began to gather about the two Americans, the immediate crowd that seemed to spring from the very dust. Henry Lane took it for granted that no Chinese spoke English and ignored them.

'Miller, it occurs to me that I ought to warn you that there is very likely to be trouble here against foreigners. I don't like the talk I hear.'

He glanced at the crowd. In the pale and golden twilight the faces were bemused with their usual quiet curiosity.

'What have you heard, Brother Lane?' Paul Miller asked. He rested his hands on the fender of the rickshaw, and admired, as he had before, the delicate spirituality of the elder man's looks. It did not occur to him to envy the good broadcloth of the missionary's garments or the whiteness of his starched collar and the satin of his cravat. Dr. Lane lowered his voice.

'It is reported to me by one of my vestrymen, whose brother is a minister at the Imperial Court, that the Empress Dowager is inclined to favour the Boxers. She viewed personally today an exhibition of their nonsensical pretensions of inviolability to bullet wounds and bayonet thrusts. That is all she fears— our foreign armies. If she is convinced that these rascals are immune to our weapons she may actually encourage them to drive us all out by force. You must think of your family, Miller.'

'What of yours, Brother Lane?'

'I shall send them to Shanghai. Our warships are there,' Henry Lane replied.

Paul Miller took his hands from the polished wooden fender. He looked at the watching Chinese faces, pale in the growing dusk. 'I put my faith in God and not in warships,' he said simply.

Henry Lane, good Christian though he was, felt his heart sting. 'It is my duty to warn you.'

'Thank you, Brother.'

'Good night,' Henry Lane said and motioned to the rickshaw puller to move on.

Paul Miller stood ankle deep in the spring dust and watched the rickshaw whirl away. His face was square and thin, and his skin was still pink and white, although it had been twenty years since first he heard the call of God at a camp meeting in Pennsylvania, and leaving his father's farm, to the consternation of that old man, had gone to China, as the only heathen land of which he had heard. Faith had provided the meagre means for himself and Mary to cross the continent in a tourist coach, and the Pacific by steerage. Neither had been home since. He did not feel it fair to ask God for furloughs, although other missionaries took them every seven years. He was living by faith.

His mouth trembled and his eyes smarted. Until now he had never faced the possibility of death. They had been hungry often and sometimes sick, and the sorrow over Artie continued in him, though he tried not to think about it. But death at the hands of cruel men, his Mary and his little ones, this he had not dreamed of, even in the nights when Satan tempted him with doubt and with homesickness for the sweet freshness of the farm life he had long ago lived. He was often homesick, but he no longer told Mary. At first they had cried themselves to sleep with homesickness, he a grown man. His mother had written to him now and again until she died, ten years ago, but he had never had a letter from his father. He did not even know if he lived.

There in the darkening Chinese street, amid the dim lights of oil lanterns and candles of cows' fat, listening to the sounds of coming night, mothers calling their children in from the streets, a sick child crying, an angry quarrel somewhere, the slam of wooden doors sliding into place in front of shops, a wailing two-stringed violin, the howl of the rising night wind, he was overcome with terror. He was a stranger and in a strange land. Whither could he and his little family flee? He thought of his wife's tender looks, the gentleness of the two pale little girls, his son's growing manhood. These were all he had, given him by God, and what did they have? He had robbed them of their birthright upon the farm, the safety of their own kind about them, a roof secure above their humble heads. If evil men killed these for whom he was responsible he could believe no more in God. In the darkness he stretched his hands towards heaven. The cold and twinkling stars above him. There was no moon. None could see him, and he fell upon his knees, even here in the street, and he cried out to God. Then clenching his hands upon his bosom he lifted his face up and shut his eyes against the laughing stars.

'Oh, God,' he whispered. 'Thou who at this moment maybe art looking down upon my dear old home, which I left, dear God, thinking it was what Thou wanted. Thou canst see into all hearts and knowest whether it is true that evil men are seeking our lives. Humbly I say I have noticed some difference myself in the Chinese in the last months. Our landlord wants us to move without reason. I have kept him paid up, though it has been hard to find the money always on time. But Thou dost provide. Save our lives and keep us safe, I now pray, and especially those dear ones whom Thou hast given me, and yet I say Thy will be done, and I will not love them above Thee.'

His head sank upon his breast and his chin rested upon his folded hands. He waited for the tide of faith to swell into his heart.

It came at last, warming the blood in his veins, strengthening his heart like wine, convincing him that he was doing what was right. 'Fear not, for I am with thee always——' He could hear the words he knew so well.

'Amen, God,' he replied with reverence. He rose and plodded along the empty street towards the four small rooms where those whom he loved awaited him. Yes, he struggled constantly not to love them too well. They were not, he told himself, all that he had. For he had the immeasurable love of God.

In less than half an hour he opened the door of his home and saw the sight which always gladdened him. The table was set for the evening meal. Mary sat beside the lighted oil lamp mending some garment, and Clem was studying one of his books. The two little girls were playing with a clay doll which a kindly Chinese woman had given them.

They looked up when he came in, and he heard their greetings. For some foolish reason he could not keep the tears from his eyes. Mary rose and came towards him and he was glad the light was dim. Even so he closed his eyes when he kissed her lest a tear fall upon her face. Then he stooped to the little girls and avoided the eyes of his son.

Only when he had conquered his sudden wish to weep did he speak to Clem. 'What's the book, son?'

'A history book, Papa. I got it today at Mr. Fong's shop.'

'What history?'

'A history of America.'

He scarcely heard Clem's voice. He was savouring his relief, the assurance God was giving him. They were all here, all safe. He would not tell them about the danger. There was no need. It was gone. 'I will put my trust in the Lord.' With these silent words he bade his heart be still.

'

The lamps in the mission house were all lit, and Dr. Lane was upstairs dressing for dinner. He did not encourage his wife's ideas to the extent of wearing evening clothes every night as the English did, but he put on a fresh shirt and changed his coat. When he had left college, twenty years ago, he had been what he now called a dreamer. That is, he had believed in asceticism for the man of God. The stringency of war years had shaped him, although in his father's house no one had actually joined the army. But they had sheltered slaves from the South, had spent a good deal of money helping them to settle and find work, and his father had been a leader in the Episcopal church in Cambridge. When he had announced his call to the mission field, however, his father had been plainly angry.

'Of course we must send missionaries to heathen lands,' he had declared to the young Henry, 'but I don't feel that we must send our best young men. My father didn't want me to go to war, and I didn't go.'

'God didn't call you to go to war,' Henry had replied.

The struggle with his father, wherein he had not yielded, had helped him when a few months later he fell in love with Helen Vandervent at Old Harbour. She was then the handsomest girl he had ever seen, a creature built on a noble scale even in her youth. He was tall but she was well above his shoulder, and proud and worldly, as he soon knew. He had gone on his knees to God, asking for strength to tame her, not for strength to give her up. Even so she had not yielded to him

25

for nearly two years. She loved him, and she told him that she did, but his belief in her love was chilled by her unwillingness to share the life he felt must be his. This she had denied.

'I don't ask you to give up being a minister,' she had said. 'Surely there are souls to be saved here at home.' Twenty years ago she had said it and he could still remember how she had looked, a tall handsome girl in a bright blue frock and coat. Even her hat was plumed with blue, but a frill of white satin lined the brim. She was queenly in youth, imperious in confidence, and his heart had staggered under the impact of her will.

'Ah, but I must serve God where he bids me go,' he had told her, summoning the reserves of his own will.

She had shrugged her shoulders and maintained her love and wilfulness for nearly six months more, while by day and by night he prayed God for strength in himself and deepening in her love, that she might be softened. Strength he got, but he saw no softening in her and so he tore himself away from her one dreadful summer's evening by the sea at Old Harbour. He had gone thither for one last trial of her love. It was an evil chance. She was surrounded by other young men, who were not beset by God and therefore were free to please her. He got her away at last and on the edge of the cliff above the beach he faced her.

'Helen, I am going to China—alone if you will not come with me.'

He was not sure that she believed it. She had shaken her head wilfully and he had left her and come ahead to China not knowing whether she would follow him. Only when she was convinced that in Peking she could live a civilized life had she written at last that she would marry him. He had yielded enough to give her Peking. The first two years he had spent alone in an interior town, where life was primitive. In her heart she had never yielded, that he knew, although she believed that she was a Christian. In her way she was, he also believed. She kept his home comfortable, managed the servants with justice, and carried out her ambitions for the children.

He worried secretly about his son. There was something

hard and proud in the boy. William laughed too seldom, he fell into a dark fury at any small family joke made at his expense, even in affection.

Sometimes, musing upon this dear only son, he remembered a foolish thing his wife had done. She had taken the boy, when he was only nine years old, to an audience with the Empress Dowager. Once a year the Old Buddha gave a party to the American ladies. Somehow upon that occasion Helen had told the chief lady-in-waiting that she would like to bring her son to pay his respects to the Empress. The lady had laughed, had said something to the Empress, who was in one of her unaccountable moods, alternating between childishness and tyranny. Then the lady had said, 'Our ancient Ancestor says she would like to see a foreign little boy. Please bring him on the next feast day, which is the Crack of Spring.'

Upon a cold day William had gone with his mother to the Imperial Palace and had waited hours in an icy ante-room. At the hour of noon a tall eunuch had summoned them at last into The Presence. William had walked behind his mother and at the command of the eunuch had bowed very low before the spectacular old woman sitting on a glittering dragon throne. It was understood even then that no Americans were required to prostrate themselves.

The Empress was in a good mood. The brilliant and still wintry sun streamed across the tiled floors and fell upon her gold encrusted robes and upon her long jewelled hands lying over her knees. William saw the embroidered edge of her yellow satin robe, and then lifting his eyes higher, he saw the fabulous hands and then the ends of her long jade necklace and so his eyes rose at last to the enamelled face, to the large shining eyes, to the elaborate jewelled head-dress. Eunuchs and ladies, seeing the boldness of this child, waited for the royal fury. It did not fall. In the eyes of the young handsome American boy the Empress saw such worship, such admiring awe, that she laughed. Then everybody laughed except William, who stood gazing at her without response. Suddenly the mood changed. The Empress frowned, waved her encased finger-tips, and turned away her head.

The Chief Eunuch stepped forward instantly and hurried them away.

'Why did the Empress get angry with me?' William asked his father when at home he was once again warmed and fed.

'Who can understand the heart of the Empress?' he replied.

Mrs. Lane hastened to speak. 'William, we must remember that you are the only American boy who has ever seen the great Empress Dowager of China. That's the important thing, isn't it?'

Dr. Lane had not liked this.

'Helen, in the sight of God, all are alike,' he had reminded his wife.

'Of course, I know that,' she replied. 'But we aren't God, are we? The Empress is still the Empress and there is no use in pretending that William has not had a great honour, for he has. It's a wonderful thing and I must say that if I hadn't had the courage to push forward and ask for it, he would not have had the chance.'

Dr. Lane, thinking now of his son, sighed as he often did, without knowing it. Helen had not changed very much. Sometimes, although she observed quite carefully all the outward forms of religion, he feared that at heart she was nevertheless a worldly woman.

William, who had been named for Helen's father, not his, had grown up clever and proud. Whether the boy's heart had ever been touched he did not know. Perhaps a boy's heart was never touched until the dews of young manhood fell upon it. Dr. Lane remembered even himself as a callous youth until suddenly one day when he was almost twenty he had perceived that life was a gift in his hand, to be used or wasted. God had spoken to him at that moment.

The Chinese dinner-gong struck softly, and he turned the oil-lamp low. It was a fine bit of furnishing, something Helen had contrived from a Ming jar. She had a taste for luxury. Outside Peking it might not have been fitting to a minister of Christ who secretly believed in poverty, but in Peking the houses of the diplomats were so much richer that this house was not remarkable. The fantastic extravagance of the

Imperial Court set the atmosphere of the city. Yet the old Empress was conscience-stricken now. The monies which had been collected from the people for a modern navy she had spent upon a huge marble boat, set in the lake at the Summer Palace. While her ministers prophesied disaster from the West and the young Emperor fomented secret rebellion, she was dickering with that absurd secret society of the Boxers. They, excited by her notice, were boasting like fools that they were invulnerable. Neither swords nor bullets, they declared, could pierce their flesh. They had a magic, they told the superstitious Empress, and she might be desperate enough to believe them.

He went slowly down the carpeted stairs, uneasy in his heart, not knowing what to do. Precautions would be taken, of course, by the American Embassy. Yet should he wait for this? William was ready for college, and Helen longed for a summer at home. Home was always America.

He went into the dining-room where his family were waiting for him and took his seat at the head of the oval table. The linen was fine and the Chinese nuns at the Catholic convent had embroidered it with a large heavy monogram. It was the sort of thing, he told himself, which looked expensive but was not. The nuns worked cheaply and he had not the heart to deny Helen beauty of so little cost. After all, she had given up a great deal to become his wife. She missed the New York season every year, music and theatre and parties. She had never enjoyed the Chinese theatre although the finest was here in Peking and this was as well, perhaps, for most of the missionaries were still puritans and he was always conscious of their criticism, unspoken, of his wife. Most of them came from simpler homes than his in America and this did not make them more merciful. Perhaps had she had time to learn Chinese—yet for that he could scarcely blame her. William had been born a scant year after their marriage and the two girls followed quickly. Since her passionate anger with him that day when she found herself pregnant for the third time, there had been no more children.

He folded his napkin and looked about the table at every

face. Ruth was growing very pretty. She looked like his side of the family. William and Henrietta took after their mother, the boy was handsome but Henrietta had missed her mother's distinction. She would have to go in for good works. He was not sure that he wanted any of his children to be missionaries. That was as God willed. He smiled at them.

'How would my family like to go home for this summer?'

Wang, robed in a long white linen gown, was serving the soup. From it rose the smell of chicken delicately flavoured with fresh ginger.

'Why, Henry!' his wife exclaimed. 'I thought you said we couldn't this year because the house at Peitaiho was costing so much.'

Like most of the missionaries they had a summer home at the seashore. A hurricane had torn the roof from the walls during the winter and it had cost some hundreds of Chinese dollars to replace.

'We could let the house,' he replied. 'That would pay something towards the tickets. I don't think we can ask the Board for expenses, since my furlough is not due yet.'

'I don't want to go,' Henrietta announced in a flat voice. She was gulping her soup but Dr. Lane did not correct her. He had a sympathy with Henrietta which he himself could not explain.

'But is William quite ready for Harvard?' Mrs. Lane asked. Her eyes were upon Wang as he served croutons.

'Since he has been taught by English standards, I believe he would have no difficulty,' Dr. Lane replied. He disliked soup, and he helped himself well to the crisp croutons.

'I'd like to go,' William said. The thought of having no more to face the arrogance of English boys, who still called all Americans rebels and missionaries yellow dogs, cheered him. He began to eat with sudden appetite.

Ruth was silent, her mild blue eyes stealing from face to face.

'I had better tell you the truth,' Dr. Lane decided. 'I do not at all like the way things look. Something is seething in the countryside. The young Emperor is in difficulties again with the Old Empress and she has locked him up. The gossip is that she is determined to kill his tutors for encouraging his Western ideas. But she will have to do something to satisfy her ministers. They are outraged with the new foreign concessions she has been compelled to give the German Government. If she should take it into her ignorant old head to exterminate all foreigners, I don't want my family here.'

He tried to speak humorously, but they saw that he was anxious. His quiet rather delicate face, always pale, now looked white above his clipped grey beard and moustache.

'I've always said the Chinese hate us,' Mrs. Lane said.

'I don't believe they hate us,' he said mildly.

'They've killed those German missionaries,' she argued.

He put down his soup spoon. 'That was an accident, as I've told you, Helen. The bandits just happened to attack a town where the Germans were.'

'Even bandits have no right to kill foreigners,' she retorted. No one paid any heed to Wang until she said almost violently, 'Wang, take away the soup plates!'

'I don't think Wang hates us, Mother,' Ruth said when he had left the room. Her voice, soft and timid, was different from the other voices. Even Dr. Lane, accustomed to many years of preaching, spoke with an articulate clarity which was almost forceful.

'That's because he gets paid,' Mrs. Lane replied.

Dr. Lane felt obliged, for the sake of the children, to pursue truth. 'If the Chinese feel anti-foreign, it is the result of the way Germany has behaved. To seize ports and demand the use of the whole bay, besides all that indemnity, just made an excuse for the murder of the missionaries. Then Russia, then England, then even our own Government—all this is at the bottom of these so-called anti-foreign outbreaks. Naturally the Chinese don't want to see their country sliced away.'

Mrs. Lane interrupted. 'Oh, of course, Henry, you always think the Chinese are right!' She went on, repressing his attempted reply. 'If there is any danger, I want to go away at once. But I won't go without you. I will not allow you to sacrifice yourself for these people. Your first duty is to the children and to me.'

31

'I don't think I can go,' he replied. 'I don't think I ought to go. The Chinese Christians will expect me to stay. The Boxers will be against them as well as us, if things break loose. Of course the Legation soldiers will protect us, but I don't want you and the children to face a siege, if it comes to that. But it would not look well for me to run. It would not be possible for my conscience. My duty to God comes first.'

The children fell into silence. By the patient firmness with which their father spoke they understood that he was determined to go through an argument with their mother. Usually she won, but when their father brought God into the conversation thus early, they guessed the end. Alone he might lose, but under that divine leadership, he would prevail even against her.

Yet only a few days later Mrs. Lane was ready to go and at once. It was Saturday and Dr. Lane was working on his usual Sunday sermon. He had chosen a text strangely inept for the times. 'The wicked flee when no man pursueth,' and he was weaving his thoughts, divinely directed, about the profound meaning in these words, when he heard Mrs. Lane's voice crying aloud his name. Almost immediately the door of his study opened, and he saw William. The boy's garments were covered with dust, his face was ashen and there was a cut on his forehead. He stood there speechless.

Dr. Lane cried out, rising from his chair. 'William! What has happened to you?'

William's lips moved. 'The—the people—a mob——'

'What?' Dr. Lane exclaimed. He hurried into the hall and there found his wife sitting upon one of the carved Chinese chairs, looking faint.

'Helen, what——'

'There was a mob!' she cried. 'I thought we couldn't get away. If it hadn't been for Lao Li—William and I crowded into the same rickshaw.'

'Where was this?' Dr. Lane broke in.

'At that tailor shop on Hatamen Street, where I always go for William's clothes. He needs a new suit——'

'What did William do?' Dr. Lane demanded. Instinctively

he knew that someone had done something. Mobs did not gather without cause.

Mrs. Lane sobbed. 'Nothing—I don't know! There was a man sleeping against his rickshaw when we came out—a beggar. William pushed him with his foot; he didn't kick him. The people sprang at us from every door. Oh, Henry, I want to get right out of here—all of us!'

He soothed her gently, directing Wang meanwhile to make some tea. 'Helen, I quite agree that you should go. The people are very touchy. Don't go out again, my dear. There might be a real incident.'

'It was an incident!' she insisted. 'If you'd seen their frightful faces—where's William? Henry, you must find William! They pushed him down into the dust, and if Lao Li hadn't helped him, they would have trampled him to death.'

'Go into the living room and wait for your tea,' Dr. Lane said. He was very much disturbed, but it would not do to show it. He had told William often, never to touch a Chinese. They considered it an indignity to be touched. Once, he remembered, in a New Year's crowd upon the street when he had taken the children out to see the sights, William in six-year-old impatience had pulled the queue of a tall old gentleman standing in front of him, and the man had turned on them in a fury. Dr. Lane had been compelled to apologize again and again, and only William's youth had saved them from serious trouble.

He searched for William and found him upstairs in his room, changing his clothes. He had put a bit of gauze and some sticking plaster on his forehead.

'Did you disinfect that cut?' Dr. Lane asked.

'Yes, sir, thoroughly,' William said.

The boy's face was still white, Dr. Lane noticed. 'You had better go downstairs and have some tea with your mother. You look rather shaken.'

'I do feel so, a bit.'

'Never touch a Chinese. Do you remember?' Dr. Lane said with unusual sternness.

'It was a beggar, leaning against the rickshaw.'

33

'Never mind who he is or what he is doing. Never touch a Chinese!' Dr. Lane repeated more loudly.

'Yes, sir.'

William turned his back on his father and began tying a fresh tie. His hands were trembling and he stood so that his father could not see him. The people had turned on him, ignorant common people who did not know his name! He American and white, the son of privilege, had been beset by poor and filthy people. He would never feel safe again. He wanted to get away from Peking, from China, from these hordes of people——

'You might have been killed,' his father said.

William could not deny it. It was true. He might have been trampled upon by vile bare feet. Lao Li had lifted him up and shielded him until he could get to the rickshaw where his mother was shrieking. They had clung together in the rickshaw while Lao Li, bending his head, butted his way through the crowd and William had stared out at the angry people, pressing against the wheels. He would never forget the faces, never as long as he lived.

The next week with his mother and sisters he left Peking.

The northern spring drew on. The dust-storms subsided, the willow trees grew green and the peach trees bloomed. The festival of Clear Spring was observed with the usual joy and freedom. People strolled along the streets, the men carrying bird-cages and the women their children, and over the door-ways of houses were hung the mingled branches of willow green and peach pink. The Imperial Court made great holiday of the feast and the Old Empress ordered special theatricals. Outwardly the city was as calm, as stable, as it had been for hundreds of years, and yet every Chinese past childhood knew that it was not so.

The Empress had expressed her feelings in December, when the two German missionaries had been killed in the province of Shantung. The foreign governments had demanded that the provincial governor, Yu Hsien, be removed. The palace news trickled through the city, through eunuchs and servants.

Everybody heard that the Old Buddha, as they called the Empress, had at first refused to withdraw Yu Hsien. Her ministers had surrounded her, telling her the size of the foreign guns and the number of soldiers already in the foreign legations. She would not believe that foreigners could prevail against her, but she had been compelled by her ministers. Yet when she had withdrawn Yu Hsien and had appointed Yuan Shih K'ai in his place, as her ministers had recommended, she had given the huge inner province of Shansi to Yu Hsien. In a rage she had set him higher than before, and the people had laughed in rueful admiration. 'Our Old Buddha,' they told each other, 'our Old Buddha always has her way. She is a woman as well as ruler.' They were proud of her, though they hated her.

The spring had never been more beautiful. The Americans in the city were reassured by the warmth of the sun, by the blossoming fruit trees, by the amiability of the crowds upon the streets. The guards sent the year before to strengthen the legations had been withdrawn again, and the murder of the missionaries had been paid for. Shansi was far enough away so that Yu Hsien, though as high a governor as before, seemed banished, and life in the wide streets went on as usual.

Nevertheless the consuls had warned all Westerners to stay off the streets during the festival, lest some brawl arise which might make cause for fresh trouble. But the day passed in peace, and in the afternoon the foreigners came out of their compounds and walked about. In the morning the farmers had brought in fresh young greens from outside the city, turnips and radishes and onions and garlic from their new fields, and the people, surfeited with the bread and sweet potatoes of winter, ate to renew their blood. The hundreds of the poor who could not buy went outside the city gates to dig the sweet clover and shepherd's purse to roll in their rounds of baked bread. Children played in the sunshine beside their mothers, shedding their padded coats and running about barebacked.

Clem Miller, pursuing his daily round, felt no difference upon the streets. Since the day when William Lane had stopped the fight he had spoken to no white person outside his own family. His father, he knew, was disturbed and uneasy, but then he was always anxious lest their food be short and always trying to deny anxiety even to himself, lest perchance God, whom he yearned to believe was tender and careful of His own, be made angry by the unbelief of Paul Miller and so refuse to supply food to those who depended upon him. Clem himself had no direct experience of God. Though he prayed as he had been taught, night and morning and sometimes feverishly in between, on the chance that it might do good when their food was low or when there was no cash to pay the landlord, he was still not sure that God gave such gifts. He wondered if his father, too, was not sure and if uncertainty were the cause of his father's uneasiness. He loved his father and felt something childlike in him and he asked no more for proof of faith, only eating the less at home. It was easier to declare himself not hungry, and he filled himself on the sweetmeats that were always on the table when he went to teach Mr. Fong's eldest son at the bookshop.

For Mr. Fong, observing the American boy's thin body and hollowed cheeks, had taken pity. He said to Mrs. Fong, the mother of his children, 'See how the young foreigner eats up the sweets! He does not get enough food. Put some small meat rolls in the dish tomorrow, and boil eggs and peel them and set them on the table.'

Mrs. Fong was a Buddhist and ate neither meat nor eggs herself, but she did not believe that foreigners would go to heaven anyhow, and since she would gain merit for her soul by feeding one who could make no return, she obeyed her husband. Each day, therefore, Clem found some sort of hearty food waiting, and his pupil Yusan urged him to eat, having been so bidden by his mother. Clem ate, thinking that perhaps this also was God's provision. Yet it was hard to believe that God used heathens to perform his mercies. In confusion he believed and did not believe, and meanwhile his growing body would have starved without the food.

No one spoke to him of the Empress and her whims or of the demands now of Italy as well as Germany. Italy was a place

36

of which he had never heard except that Christopher Columbus had come from there. No one told him either of the warships steaming into Chinese harbours from Britain, Germany, and France. His world was in the dust of Peking, and when he dreamed it was of a farm in a place called Pennsylvania. How big Pennsylvania was he did not know, except that it was more than a city. He had learned when he was quite little not to ask his parents about it because it made them both sad and sometimes his mother wept.

The festival ended. One spring day followed another and May passed into June. People were eating big yellow apricots and one morning Mrs. Fong set a dish of them on the table.

'Eat these, little brother,' she bade Clem. 'They cleanse the blood.'

He ate two and against his sense of decency hid two in his pockets to give his sisters when he went home after the lesson. These he bade them eat in secret, lest their father discover in Mrs. Fong a new source of food and go there to beg in God's name. Ever since he had heard William Lane's voice of scorn Clem could not think of his father asking a Chinese for food. Yet when he saw the eagerness with which his younger sisters seized the fruit he brought home to them, he could not refrain the next day from hiding a few cakes in his pockets and then two of the meat rolls. It was a sort of stealing, his ready conscience told him, and was it better to thieve than beg, and was he not worse than his father? 'At least I do not take the food in the name of God,' he told himself, and continued to take it.

But guilt made him anxious one morning when Mr. Fong came into the sunlit brick-floored room. Mr. Fong sat down and drew his rusty black silk gown up over his knees. He was a tall man, a native of the city, and his smooth face was egg-shaped. Today, since it was warm, he had taken off his black cap. He had been freshly shaved and his queue was combed and braided with a black silk cord.

'Eh,' he began, looking at Clem. 'I have something to say to you, Little Brother.'

'What is it, Elder Brother?' Clem asked, and was much afraid.

37

'While I talk, you eat,' Mr. Fong said kindly. He clapped his hands at his eldest son, looking at him with always fond eyes. 'Yusan, you go away and play somewhere.'

Yusan, pleased to be free, tied his book in a blue cotton square, thrust it in a drawer and left the room.

'Drink some tea,' Mr. Fong said to Clem. 'What I am about to say does not mean that I am angry.'

Clem could neither eat nor drink upon these words. What would he do if kind Mr. Fong wanted him to come no more? There would be an end of books and food.

Mr. Fong got up and shut the door and drew the wooden bar across it. Then he sat himself down so near to Clem that his voice could pass into his ear.

'The Old Empress is about to command that all foreigners leave our city—even our country.' These were the horrifying words Clem now heard.

'But why?' he gasped.

'Hush—do you know nothing? Has your father not been told? You must go quickly or——' Mr. Fong drew his hand across his throat.

'What have they done?' Clem demanded.

It did not occur to him for the moment that he himself was a foreigner, and the word 'they' came to his tongue instead of 'we'.

That his parents were foreign, he well knew. They were foreign even to him, whose birth and whose memories were only of the Chinese earth. They had no money to go away. But where could they hide? Who would dare to take them in? He could not believe that the proud missionaries would shelter them, nor could he ask Mr. Fong to risk the lives of his own family.

Meanwhile he felt cold and his knees began to tremble.

Mr. Fong cleared his throat, stroked his bare chin and began again his guttural whisper. 'The foreign governments, you understand, are cutting up our country like a melon. This piece is for the Ying people, this piece is for the Teh people, this piece is for I-Ta-Lee, this for the wild Ruh people to the north.'

'My parents are Americans,' Clem urged.

Mr. Fong rolled his head around rapidly on his shoulders. 'Your Mei people I know. They do not slice with a knife, but they come after the slices are cut and they say to us, "Since you have sliced to these other people, we too must be given some gift." True, true, you Mei people are better. You are against slicing, but you also wish gifts.'

'I have heard nothing,' Clem said doggedly.

'There is no time to tell you everything now,' Mr. Fong said. 'Listen to this one word, Little Brother. Go home and tell your parents to flee to Shanghai. The times are bad. Do not delay lest the way be closed. I have a relative who works in the palace. I fear what is about to happen.'

'My father will not go,' Clem said sadly. 'He believes in God.'

'This is no time to believe in God,' Mr. Fong replied in a sensible voice. 'Tell him to save his family first.'

He rose, and opening the drawer he removed the blue cotton square from his son's book and filled it with cakes and fruit. 'Take this with you. Remember I do not hate you. If I dared I would ask your family here. But it would do them no good and my family would only be killed with them. We have been warned. Come no more, Little Brother, alas!'

So saying he thrust Clem out of a small back door. Clem found himself in an alleyway. On the street it seemed impossible to believe that doom hung over the city. It was a morning as mild as summer. The people of the city had risen from their beds, had washed themselves, had eaten, had set their faces to seem the same as on any other day. Clem as usual left home very early, before the shops had taken down their boards, for Mr. Fong believed that the human brain was most active at sunrise. Often when Clem hurried on his way he met straggling rows of sleepy schoolboys, their books wrapped in blue cotton squares under their arms, already on their way to school. This morning, he remembered now, he had met none, and had wondered that he was so early.

Now hurrying on his way he knew that schools should be open and yet he saw not one schoolboy, and surely the shops must have taken down their boards, and yet they had not, although the sun was high. He made his way through strangely silent streets towards his home. Yet before he could reach it, at some signal he neither saw nor heard, the city began to stir, not to its usual life, but to something new and frightful. Good people stayed inside their gates, but the evil came out. Clem, clinging to walls and hiding in doorways, heard a bestial shouting, a rising roar, near the very quarter where the foreign legations were. There, too, the wealthy missionaries lived, the princes of the church. He hastened on toward his own. Perhaps they might be safe hidden among the houses of the poor. Perhaps God had some purpose, after all, in sheltering those who bore a cross.

At this moment Mr. Fong was looking up and down the street. He too saw that this day was different from any other and he knew why. His cousin had visited him about midnight and had told him what had taken place in the palace. Doubtless half the people in the city now knew. Many families had relatives inside the palace, women servants and court ladies, eunuchs who held offices from cooks to ministers, and these sowed among the people outside the Forbidden City the sayings and doings of those within. There was nothing the people did not know about their rulers.

Mr. Fong, remembering the agitated hours of last midnight, now decided to put up the boards of his shop and cease business for the day. Whatever happened he did not want to seem to know anything about it. He was a brave man but not a foolhardy one. He knew that the Old Woman would certainly lose but that she would be desperate and arrogant before she knew herself lost. Mr. Fong had read too much Western science. He knew that the Boxers could not possibly survive iron bullets. Still, it would take time to prove this. The Old Woman was so stubborn that she would have to see foreign armies marching into the city before she believed it could happen. He sighed in the semi-darkness of his shop and was glad that he had had the prudence to buy up two months' supply of millet and wheat. In the back court his wife had eleven hens and he had planted in another corner away from the chicken coop a small patch of cabbage. They would not starve.

He did not, however, feel strong enough to join his family for an hour or so. He wanted to be alone and as his usual pretext he drew out his account books and opened his ink boxes and uncovered his brushes. His wife never disturbed him when he was thinking, as she supposed, about money matters. Actually his mind went over all that his cousin had told the night before.

The city, his cousin had said, was full of Boxers. They were now bold enough to enter at every gate. Indeed they were wholly fearless ever since Prince Tuan had persuaded the Empress to let them come even into her presence and show proof of their magic powers.

'But are they magic?' Mr. Fong had asked his cousin with anxiety. In the midnight silence his reason was not so strong as by day.

'They are flesh and blood,' his old cousin had replied scornfully. This cousin was only a scribe in the palace but he was a man of sense and learning.

On the ninth day of the month, the cousin then went on to say, the very day when the Empress had returned to the city from the Summer Palace, some Boxers had gone to the racecourse three miles west of Peking and had set a fire, and they had thrown a Chinese Christian into the flames to burn to death. Inside the palace the Empress was telling her ministers that she would drive the foreigners from the city.

On the eleventh day, the cousin said, the Chancellor of the Japanese Legation was murdered outside the walls of the city. He had gone to the railway station to discover perhaps when the trains would run again to Peking. No trains were running now.

After telling all this, the cousin had gone away, drenched in gloom.

Mr. Fong sat another hour over his figures and then he closed his books, put them in the drawer and locked it. He went back into the inner courts where his family waited. They were all quiet, even Mrs. Fong. She was getting the noonday meal ready.

41

'Put more water into the millet from now on,' he commanded her. 'We will drink soup instead of eating porridge.'

'Eh,' she sighed. 'If we only live——'

He did not answer this. Having nothing else to do, he went to his room and began to read the Book of Changes, in which he often said all was foretold if one had the wit to understand.

After this silent meal, at which he strictly forbade any one of his family to go into the street and commanded the children to play quietly in the innermost court, he went to bed and to sleep for the afternoon. He rose only to eat once more at dusk and then he went to bed. There was nothing he could do, he told his wife, and he had better save his strength for the days to come.

At midnight he woke abruptly to hear his wife screaming in his ears.

'Fong-ah!' she was calling. 'Fong-ah, wake up.'

He had buried himself so deep in sleep that it was a minute or two before he could grunt a reply.

'Eh—what——' he muttered.

'The city is on fire!' she screamed.

He woke then and shuffled into his slippers lest a centipede sting him and ran into the court and looked up. The sky was red and the night was as light as day.

The children were awake now, and all were crying with fright and he turned on them fiercely when he came back into the house. 'Be silent!' he commanded them. 'Do you want the neighbours to think you are weeping for the foreigners?'

They fell silent instantly and he crept to his shop and opened the boards to the central door two inches, enough so that he could peer into the street. Twenty fires lit the sky and he knew what they were. The houses and churches of the Christians were burning. He closed the boards again and went back to his family. They were gathered in a small huddle in the gloom of the main room.

'Go back to bed,' he told them. 'Fortunately we are not Christians and we will survive.'

Clem had waked his father after a moment of not knowing what to do. The fires were not near the hutung where they lived. They were nearly all in the better part of the city, near the Legation Quarters. He had not gone into the street since Mr. Fong had given him the warning. Even his father had gone out only by night—to beg, he supposed, at some missionary door, for he had come back with three loaves of foreign bread and some tinned stuff. One tin held Australian butter. Clem had never tasted butter. That night they had each eaten a slice of bread spread with the yellow butter and he had savoured it curiously.

'We made our own butter on the farm,' his father said suddenly. Clem had been about to ask how when his mother said in a heart-broken voice, 'Paul, don't talk about the farm!'

Clem went to bed as soon as evening prayer was done, and had slept until the light from the red sky had wakened him in his corner of the small centre room where his bed stood, a couch by day. He had got up and gone out into the court and then fearfully into the narrow street. There was no one in sight but he hurried through the gate again and barred it. Then because he was afraid and lonely he felt compelled to wake his father.

His father opened his eyes at once, silent and aware, and Clem motioned to him to come into the other room.

'Fires in the city!' he whispered.

His father came barefoot and in his underpants and they stared at the sky together.

'Don't wake your mother or the girls,' his father whispered. 'It's a terrible sight—God's Judgement. I must go into the streets, Clem, to see what I can do. People will be suffering. You stay here.'

'Oh, Papa,' Clem whispered, 'don't go. How shall I find you if something happens to you?'

'Nothing will happen,' his father said. 'We will pray together before I go—as soon as I get my clothes on.'

Quickly his father was back again, dressed in his ragged cotton suit. 'On your knees, dear boy,' he said in the same ghostly whisper.

43

For once Clem knelt willingly. He was helpless. They were all helpless. Now if ever God must save them.

· 'God who hearest all,' his father prayed, 'Thou knowest what is going on in this city. I feel I ought to be about my business and Thine. Probably there are a good many suffering people out there we ought to be looking after. Fires bring suffering as Thou knowest. Protect my dear ones while I am gone and especially give strength to my dear son.'

His father paused and then in his usual firm voice he added, 'Thy will be done, on earth as in heaven, for Thy Name's sake. Amen!'

They got up and his father shook Clem's hand strongly and was gone.

It was nearly dawn before Clem, sleepless upon the board of his bed, heard his father's footsteps carefully upon the threshold. He sat up in bed and saw his father at the door drenched with sweat and black with smoke.

'I must clean myself before your mother sees me,' he said. 'Get me some water in the basin—some soap if we have any. I'll wash here in the court. Has your mother awakened?'

'No,' Clem said and got out of bed. He went to the old well in the little courtyard and let down the wooden bucket. A bit of soap was hidden where he had left it above a beam, his own bit of soap, still left from a yellow bar his mother had managed to give him at Christmas. He stood beside his father while he stripped and began to wash.

'The Boxers are in the city,' his father said in a low voice. 'The Old Empress has given us up. We are in the hands of God. The persecution of the Christians has begun.'

'What about the other foreigners?' Clem asked. For the first time he knew that his place must be among those who had rejected him. William Lane, that proud boy——

'I went to Brother Lane's house,' his father was saying. 'Of all of them, Brother Lane is the kindest. He gave me the food I have brought back and a little money. A man of tender heart! He is alone in his compound. He has sent his family away to Shanghai. They went before the railways were broken. He

44

has been sheltering Chinese Christians but now they are leaving him. It is safer for them to be among their own people.'

Now Clem was really afraid. If the railways were broken Peking was cut off.

His father looked at him tenderly. 'Are you fearful, Clem? Don't be so, my son. The Lord is the strength of our lives. Of whom shall we be afraid?'

Clem did not answer. They were alone among enemies. He sent his own angry prayer towards the sky, where sunshine and smoke were in combat. 'God, if you fail my father, I will never pray again.'

Then he turned and went into the house and heard his sisters talking softly over their clay doll while their mother still slept.

Mr. Fong knew upon each day what had happened in the palace. His old cousin stole out by night to report the doings of the Empress whom he now called the Old Demon.

'A mighty struggle is going on,' he declared to Mr. Fong in the depths of the night. The two men sat in the shop in darkness. The cousin would not allow a candle to be lit, neither would he allow the presence of Mrs. Fong. His hatred of the Empress had become so violent that he trusted no woman. Yet his family feeling was such that he felt obliged to tell Mr. Fong of all possible dangers in order that the Fong clan might be kept safe.

Mr. Fong dared not tell his cousin of their one real danger, which was Clem. Neighbours had seen the foreign boy coming day after day to the house.

'Proceed,' Mr. Fong said to his cousin.

'Prince Ching has been dismissed. He was the only reasonable one. She has appointed that blockhead Prince Tuan and three others who understand nothing. This is to prepare for her open union with the foolish Boxers.'

On the sixteenth day of this month the cousin reported that the Empress had called a meeting of her clansmen and then of the Manchus to whom she belonged and the Chinese whom she ruled. To these she spoke long of the evils the foreigners had done. She said the Manchus wanted war.

'Then she was confounded,' the cousin whispered, 'for even among the Manchus there was Natsung, a man of sense, who told her she could not fight the world. He was upheld by a Chinese, Hsu Ching-cheng. The young Emperor, as her nephew, also begged her not to ruin the country. Upon this the great quarrel burst forth. That fool Prince Tuan spoke for the Boxers, though Prince Su spoke against him, saying that it was madness to believe that these ignorant men could not be shot to strips of flesh.'

On the eighteenth day the cousin told Mr. Fong that the Empress had seen the Boxers prove their powers, and she had decided to join with them.

'When the young Emperor heard the Old Demon declare this,' the cousin said, 'he began to weep aloud and he left the room. It is now too late for us to hope. Prepare yourself, Elder Brother, and prepare our family for what must come, for we are lost. The forts at Tientsin have already fallen to the foreign armies but our people do not know it. Neither do the foreigners here in the city know it, since they have no word from the advancing armies sent to rescue them. And the Old Demon puts her faith in these monsters, the Boxers! To-morrow, before the foreigners can hear of the loss of the forts or of their own coming rescue, she will demand that they leave the city. But how can they go, hundreds of them with women and little children? They will not go. Then the Boxers will try to kill them all. For this our people will be cruelly punished when the foreign armies reach the city. Prepare—prepare, Elder Brother!'

On the twentieth day of that month Clem was wakened by his mother in the early morning. He opened his eyes and saw her finger on her lips. He got up and followed her into the court. There were times when between his parents he felt he had no life of his own. Each made him the keeper of secrets from the other, each strove to bear the burden of danger alone, with only Clem's help.

'Clem, dear,' his mother said in her pretty coaxing voice. In the dawn she had a pale ghostlike look and he saw what he had seen before but today too clearly, that she was wasting away under this strain of waiting for lonely death.

'Yes, Mama,' he said.

'Clem, we haven't anything left to eat. I'm afraid to tell Papa.'

'Oh, Mama,' he cried. 'Is all that bread gone?'

'Yes, and all the tins. I have a little flour I can mix with water for this morning. That's all.'

He knew what she wanted and dreaded to ask him and he offered himself before she spoke.

'Then I will go into the streets and try to find something, Mama.'

'Oh, Clem, I'm afraid for you to, but if you don't Papa will, and you can slip through the hutungs better than he can. He'll stop maybe to pray.'

'I won't do that,' he said grimly.

'Then put on your Chinese clothes.'

'I'd better not go until after breakfast, Mama, or Papa will notice.'

'Oh yes, that's true. Go after breakfast when he is studying his Bible.'

'Yes.'

His mother's soft eyes were searching his face with anxious sadness. 'Oh, Clem, forgive me.'

'There isn't anything to forgive, Mama. It's not your fault.'

He saw the tears well into her eyes and with love and dreadful impatience he stopped them.

'Don't cry, please, Mama. I've got all I can bear.' He turned away, guilty for his anger, and yet protecting himself with it.

He was silent during the meagre breakfast, silent when his father prayed longer than usual. The food was hot. They were out of fuel but he had torn some laths from a plaster wall. Their landlord did not come near them now. They were only grateful that he did not turn them into the streets.

After breakfast Clem waited for his father to go into the inner room and then he got into the ragged blue cotton Chinese garments and put them on where the girls could not see him and know that he was going out. Not bidding even his mother good-bye, waiting until she was in the small kitchen, he climbed the wall so that he would not leave the gate open and dropped into the alleyway.

Where in all the vast enemy city should he go for food? He dared not go to Mr. Fong. There was nowhere to go indeed except to Mr. Lane, alone in the compound. He had given them food before and he would give again, and Clem did not mind going now that William was not there. So by alleyways and back streets, all empty, he crept through the city towards the compound. None of the compounds were in the Legation Quarter, but this one was nearer than the others.

The gate was locked when he came and he pounded on it softly with his fists. A small square opened above him and the gateman's face looked out. When he saw the foreign boy, he drew back the bar and let him in.

'Is the Teacher at home?' Clem asked safely inside.

'He is always at home now,' the gateman replied. 'What is your business?'

'I have something to ask,' Clem said.

In usual times the gateman would have refused him, as Clem well knew, but now he refused no white face. These foreigners were all in piteous danger and he was a fool to stay by his own white master, but still he did. He had no wife or child and there was only his own life, which was worth little. Thus he plodded ahead of Clem to the big square house and knocked at the front door. It was opened by Dr. Lane himself, who was surprised to see a foreign boy.

'Do I know you?' he asked.

'I don't think so,' Clem replied. 'But I know you, sir. I am Clem Miller.'

'Oh, yes,' Dr. Lane said vaguely. 'The Millers—I know your father. Come in. You shouldn't be out on the streets.'

'My father doesn't know that I am,' Clem replied. He stepped into the house. It looked bare and cool.

'My family is in Shanghai,' Dr. Lane said. 'I'm camping out. Did you know my son William? Sit down.'

48

'I've seen him,' Clem said with caution. He sat down on the edge of a carved chair.

Dr. Lane continued to look at him with sad dark eyes. He had a kind face except that it looked as though he were not listening.

'What did you come for?' he asked in a gentle voice.

'We have no food,' Clem said simply. The blood rushed into his pale face. 'I know you have helped us before, Dr. Lane. I wouldn't have come if I had known where else to go.'

'That is quite all right,' Dr. Lane said. 'I'll be glad——'

Clem interrupted him. 'One more thing, Dr. Lane. I don't consider that when I ask you for food it's God's providing. I know it isn't. I don't think like my father on that. I wouldn't come just for myself either. But there's my mother and my two sisters.'

'That's all right,' Dr. Lane said. 'I have more food than I need. A good many tins of stuff—we had just got up an order from Tientsin before the railway was cut.'

The house was dusty, Clem saw, and the kitchen was empty. Dr. Lane seemed helpless. 'I don't know just where things are. The cook left yesterday. He was the last one. I can't blame them. It's very dangerous to stay.'

'Why didn't you go with William?' Clem asked.

Dr. Lane was still searching. 'Here's a basket. I didn't go because of my parish. The Chinese Christians are having a time of sore trial. I can't do much for them except just stay. Here are some tins of milk and some meat—potted ham, I believe.'

He filled the basket and put a kitchen towel over it. 'Better not carry the tins in the open. They might tempt someone. I wish I could send you home in the rickshaw but of course the puller has gone—a faithful fellow, too. Lao Li was his name. There's only the gate-keeper.'

He was leading the way to the door. 'You'd better get home as fast as you can. Tell your father that he must get your family into the Legation Quarter if any trouble comes. We'll have to stick together. I suppose our governments will send soldiers to rescue us. They may be on the way.'

49

'I'm afraid my father won't go into the Legation,' Clem said. To explain that his father would consider such retreat a total loss of faith, might hurt Dr. Lane's feelings.

But Dr. Lane knew. 'Ah,' he said, 'it takes more courage than I have for such faith. For myself, I can—but not for my son.'

They were at the door now and the old gateman was waiting.

'Good-bye, Clem,' Dr. Lane said.

'Good-bye, sir.'

The gateman stared at the basket, and he went into his little room and brought out some old shoes and put them on top of the towel. 'Let it seem rubbish,' he said, 'otherwise you will be robbed.'

The gate shut behind Clem and he was alone in the street, the basket heavy upon his arm. It was mid-morning, and the sun was beginning to be hot. There were a few people about now, all men, and he saw they were soldiers, wearing the baggy brightly coloured uniform of the Imperial Palace. He tried to escape their notice, and had succeeded, he thought, for their officer was laughing and joking and did not notice him. They were looking at a foreign gun the officer held. Then they did see him and they started after him. He began to run. On another day, at another hour, he might have shown better sense by stopping to talk with them in their own tongue. Now he wanted only to keep his face hidden from them, his face and his pale foreign eyes. He ran out of the alleyways into Hatamen Street, the eastern boundary of the Legation. Perhaps he could get into the Legation gate. He turned and was stopped by a small procession of two sedan chairs and their outriders. In the sedans he looked into two foreign faces, arrogant, severe, bearded faces he had never seen before. Before he could slip away into an alley again, he was caught between the Chinese soldiers and the foreigners in their sedans. The soldiers blocked the street so that the bearers were forced to set the sedans down.

Now the curtain of the first sedan lifted and the foreigner put out his head and shouted fiercely to the soldiers, 'Out of the way! I am Von Ketteler, the German Ambassador, and I go for audience with the Empress!'

50

The second sedan opened and he heard a guttural warning. It came too late. The Chinese officer raised his foreign gun and levelled it at the German. Clem saw a spit of fire and the Ambassador crumpled, dead. Clem crawled behind the sedan, and clutching his basket, he hurried as fast as he could from the dreadful spot.

Homewards he ran through streets now filling with people. It was hopeless to escape them. Hands reached out and tore away the coverings of the basket and revealed the food. Dirty hands fought for the tins and emptied the basket in an instant, and then he felt hands laid upon him.

'A foreigner, a foreign devil——' he heard voices screaming at the sight of his face. He burrowed among legs and forced his way through, agile with terror, and hid himself inside an open gate, looking this way and that until he saw a woman's angry face at a window and then he darted out again. Now he was near home and the crowd was surging in the opposite direction to see the murdered German. He was safe for a moment but what would he do without the food? He began to sob and tried to stop because his sobs shook him so he could not run, and then he had no breath to run and so he walked, limping and gasping, down the hutung to the small gate. He would have to knock; he was too weary to try to climb the wall. Ah, the gate was open! He stopped, bewildered, and then saw something bright in the dust of the threshold at his feet. It was blood, brightly red, curling at the edges in the dust. A new more desperate terror fell upon him. He could not think. He ran through the gate and into the meagre courtyard. The paper-latticed doors of the little central room were swinging to and fro, and he pushed his way through them.

There he stopped. Upon the rough brick floor his father lay, resting in his own blood which flowed slowly from a great gash in his throat, so deep that the head was half severed. His arms were flung wide, his legs outspread. Upon the quiet face, though bled white, he saw his father's old sweet smile, the greeting he gave to all alike who entered this house, to strangers and to his own, and now to his son. Under the half-closed lids the blue eyes seemed watching. Clem gazed down at his father unable to cry out. He knew. He had often seen the dead. In winter people froze upon the streets, beggars, refugees from famine, a witless child, a runaway slave, an unwanted new-born girl. But this was his father.

He choked, his breath would not come up, and he tried to scream. It was well for him that no sound came, for in the silence he might have been heard, and those who had gone might have come back. He gave a great leap across his father's feet and ran into the other room where his mother's bed was. There he saw the other three, his mother, his two sisters. They were huddled into the back of the big Chinese bed, the two children clinging to the mother, but they had not escaped. The same thick sword that had cut his father's throat had rolled the heads from the children. Only his mother's long blonde hair hid what had been done to her, and it was bloodied a bright scarlet.

He stood staring, his mouth dried, his eyes bulging from their sockets. He could not cry, he could not move. There was no refuge to which he could flee. Where in this whole city could he find a hole in which to hide? He thought for one instant of William Lane and the security of that solid house enclosed behind walls. The next instant he knew that there was no safety there. The dead might be lying on those floors, too. No, his own kind could not save him.

He turned and ran as he had come along the high walls of the alleys, by lonely passages away from the main streets back again to Mr. Fong's house.

In the central room behind the shop Mr. Fong was sitting in silence with his wife and their children. News had flown around the city from the Imperial Palace that two Germans had fired on innocent Chinese people and that a brave Chinese soldier had taken revenge by killing one of the Germans and wounding the other. Mr. Fong doubted the story but did not know how to find out the truth.

'The wind blows and the grass must bend,' he told Mrs. Fong. 'We will remain silent within our own doors.'

He was troubled in mind because his eldest son could speak

English and he feared that it might cause his death. Not only foreigners were to be killed. The Old Buddha had commanded today at dawn, at her early audience in the palace, that all who had eaten of the foreign religion and all who could speak foreign languages were also to be killed.

Mr. Fong had just finished quarrelling with his wife, and this was another reason for the silence of the family. The quarrel, built upon the terror of what was taking place in the city, of which rumours were flying everywhere, had been over the very matter of the eldest son speaking English.

'I told you not to let our Yusan learn the foreign tongue,' Mrs. Fong had said in a loud whisper. Sweat was running down the sides of her face by her ears. Though she fanned herself constantly with her palm-leaf fan nothing dried her sweat this day.

'Who could tell that the Old Empress would put the Young Emperor in jail?' Mr. Fong replied. 'Two years ago everything was for progress. Had all gone well, the young Emperor would now be on the throne and the Old Woman would be in prison.'

'The gods would not have it so,' Mrs. Fong declared.

Nothing made Mr. Fong more angry than talk of gods. He read as many as possible of the books he sold, and among them he had read the books of revolutionary scholars and other books which they had translated from foreign countries. Thus he knew many things which he concealed from Mrs. Fong, who could not read at all. Through his cousin he had learned much that happened in the Forbidden City. He had long known that there was a certain troupe of actors who, a few years before, had been summoned from Shanghai to play before the Imperial Court. Among the actors were the two famous rebel scholars, Liang Ch'i Ch'ao and T'an Tzu-t'ung, and they were responsible for informing the young Emperor that times had changed and that railways and schools and hospitals were good things. What a pity that all their efforts now had failed! That man at court whom they had trusted, that Yuan Shih K'ai, though pretending sympathy with them, had betrayed them to the chief eunuch Jung-lu, because the two had long ago sworn blood brotherhood, and Jung-lu had told the Old Empress, and so she had won after all. Liang had escaped with K'ang Yu'wei, the young Emperor's tutor, but T'an had been killed. Since then the Old Demon, as Mr. Fong called her in his private thoughts, had gone from worse to madness.

There was no use in telling Mrs. Fong all this. He heard her voice complaining against him still, though under her breath, and being frightened and weary and more than a little fearful that she was right, he squared his eyebrows and opened his mouth and shouted at her.

'Be quiet, you who are a fool!'

Mrs. Fong began to cry, and the children not knowing which way to turn between their parents, began to wail with their mother.

In the midst of this hubbub which, having aroused, Mr. Fong now tried to stop, they heard a stealthy beating upon the back door. Mr. Fong raised his hand.

'Be quiet!' he commanded again in a loud whisper.

Instantly all were still. They could hear very well the sound of fists upon the barred gate.

'It is only one pair of hands,' Mr. Fong decided. 'Therefore I will open the gate and see who it is. Perhaps it is a message from my cousin.'

He rose, and Mrs. Fong, recalled to her duty, rose also, and with her the children. Thus together they went into the narrow back court and inch by inch Mr. Fong drew back the bar. The beating ceased when this began, and at last Mr. Fong opened the gate a narrow way and looked out. He turned his head towards Mrs. Fong.

'It is Little Foreign Brother!' he whispered.

'Do not let him enter,' she exclaimed. 'If he is found here, we shall all be killed.'

Mr. Fong held the gate, not knowing what to do. Against his own will he heard Clem's voice, telling him horrible news.

'My father and mother, they are dead! My sisters are dead! Their heads are off. My father lies on the floor. His throat is gashed. I have nowhere to go.'

Against his will Mr. Fong opened the gate, allowed Clem to come in, and then barred it again quickly. The boy had vomited and the vomit still clung to his clothes. His face was deathly and his eyes sunken, even in so short a time.

'Now what shall we do?' Mrs. Fong demanded.

'What can we do?' Mr. Fong replied.

They stood looking at each other, trying to think. Clem, past thought, stared at their faces.

'We must consider our own children,' Mrs. Fong said. But she was a kind woman and now that she saw the boy and the state he was in she wished to clean him and comfort him, in spite of her fright.

'Why should they kill your family?' Mr. Fong demanded of Clem. 'Your father was poor and weak but a good man.'

'It is not only my father,' Clem said faintly. 'I saw them kill a German and another only barely escaped though he was shot in the leg.'

'Did the Germans not shoot into a crowd?' Mr. Fong demanded.

Clem shook his head. 'There was no crowd. Only me.'

'Who shot then?'

'A soldier.'

'Wearing what uniform?' Mr. Fong asked.

'That of the Imperial Palace,' Clem said. Clem was telling the truth, Mr. Fong saw by his desperate honest boy's face.

'The Old Empress has gone mad,' Mr. Fong said between set teeth. 'Can she turn back the clock? Are we to return to the age of our ancestors while the whole world goes on? She has made us the laughing stock of all peoples. They will send their armies and their guns, and we shall all be exterminated because we listened to an old ignorant woman who sits on a throne. I will not fear her!'

So saying he seized Clem by the ragged elbow of his jacket and led him into the house, and behind him the family followed.

'Take off his garments and let me clean them,' Mrs. Fong said.

'Go into the inner room and get into the bed there,' Mr. Fong said. 'After all, we are an obscure family. We have no enemies, I believe. If anyone comes to ask why we had a foreign youth here to teach our son, I will say it is because the foreigner was only a beggar.'

Like a beggar then Clem went into the dark small inner room, and taking off his outer clothes he crept under the patched quilt on the bed. He was dried to the bone. There were no tears in him, in his mouth no spittle. His very bladder was dry and though his loins ached he could make no water. The palms of his hands and the soles of his feet itched. Tortured by this drought, he lay under the quilt and began to shake in a violent and icy chill.

Clem was hidden thus for how many days he did not know. Nor did he know what went on in the city. Not once did Mr. Fong or any of his family pass through the boarded doors of the shop. The cousin came sometimes at midnight, and through him Mr. Fong knew what was happening. Thus he knew that the Old Demon, in her wrath, had set the fourth day after the murder of the German as the day when all over the empire foreigners were to be killed.

There were other edicts. Thus on the seventh day of the seventh month the 'Boxer Militia' was praised and exhorted to loyalty, and such Chinese as were Christians were told to repent if they wished to stay alive.

Mr. Fong, who was not a Christian, knew, too, from his cousin that all the foreigners in the city were locked into the Legation Quarter, and that a battle was raging against them. He had heard continuous shooting, but he did not dare to go out to see what it was. In his heart he tried to think how he could convey Clem secretly into the fortress of his own kind and so rid his household of the danger, but he could think of nothing. He did not dare tell even his cousin of Clem's presence in the house, for if it were discovered that the cousin was at heart a friend of the young Emperor and therefore an enemy to the Old Empress, he might be arrested and tortured, and to save himself he might get grace by telling about his own relative who was shielding a foreigner. Mr. Fong said nothing and listened to everything.

To Clem day and night were alike. The door to his small inner room was kept barred and was opened only by Mrs. Fong bringing food, or sometimes by Mr. Fong coming in to feel the boy's wrists for fever. Clem lay in a conscious stupor, refusing to remember what he had seen, neither thinking nor feeling.

Then one day, and at what hour he did not know, he felt himself unable to keep from weeping. The gathering strength of his body, too young to accept continuing sleep, roused his unwilling mind, and suddenly he saw clearly upon the background of his brain the memory of his dead family, hacked and hewed by swords, and he was strong enough for tears. His numbed spirit came back to life, and the tears flowed. From tears he rose to sobbing which he could not control, and hearing these sobs Mr. Fong hastened into the room. Clem had struggled up and was sitting on the edge of the bed, clutching his chest with his hands.

'There is no time to weep,' Mr. Fong said in a whisper. 'I have been waiting for this awakening. You are too young to die of sorrow.'

He went to a chest that stood against the wall and brought out a short blue cotton coat and trousers.

'I bought these at a pawnshop two nights ago,' he went on. 'The madness in the city has abated somewhat. It is said that the foreign armies are very near. I prepared the garments against this moment. They will fit you. We have made black dye for your hair and there are shoes here. Put these on, and eat well of the meal my children's mother is cooking. She has baked loaves and wrapped salt fish and dried mustard greens into a package for you and put them into a basket such as country boys carry.'

Clem stopped sobbing. 'What am I to do, Elder Brother?' he asked.

'You must make your way to the sea, to a ship,' Mr. Fong said in a whisper. His smooth face, usually so full, looked flat and his eyes were sunken under his sparse stiff brows. He had not shaved for days, and a stubble stood up on his head and his queue was ragged. 'Now hear me carefully, Little Brother. All those of your kind who are not dead are locked behind walls in the foreign quarter, and a fierce battle has raged. We shall lose as soon as foreign soldiers with guns arrive at the city. Our stupid Old Woman will not know she has lost until she has to flee for her life. We can only wait for that hour, and it is not far off. But our people are not with her. You will be safe enough among the people. Avoid the cities, Little Brother. Stay close by the villages and when you pass someone on the road, look down into the dust to hide the blue colour of your eyes.'

Clem changed into the Chinese garments and though his legs trembled with weakness, the thought of escape gave him strength. He ate well of the strong meat broth and bread and garlic which Mrs. Fong set before him, all this being done in silence. When he had eaten she brought a bowl of black dye, such as old women smear upon their skulls when the hair drops out, and with a strong goose feather she smeared this dye upon his sand-coloured hair and upon his eyebrows and even on his eyelashes.

'How lucky your nose is not high!' she whispered. When she had finished she stood back to look at him and admire the change. 'You look better as a Chinese!'

Mr. Fong laughed soundlessly and then pressed the basket on Clem's arm and together they took him to the small back door. 'You know your way to the South Gate,' Mr. Fong whispered. 'The wind now is from the south. Follow it and walk for three days, and then turn eastwards to the sea. There find a ship that flies a foreign flag, and ask for a task of some sort upon it.'

Clem stood for one instant beside the door. 'I thank you for my life,' he stammered.

'Do not thank us,' Mr. Fong replied. 'The stupidity of the Old Woman has not made us enemies. Return to the land of your ancestors. But do not forget us. Take this, Little Brother. If I were not so poor I would give you a full purse.' He put a purse into Clem's hand and Clem tried to push it away.

'You must take it for my own ease of mind,' Mr. Fong said. So Clem took it.

Even Yusan, his childish pupil, must give him a last gift. The boy did not understand why Clem must be hidden or why be sent out in secret, but he clung to Clem's hand and gave him two copper coins. Mrs. Fong touched the edge of her sleeves to her eyes and patted Clem's arm once and then twice, and Mr. Fong opened the door and Clem went out.

It was night, at what hour he could not tell, but the darkness was deep and the city was silent. He stood listening, and he heard the soft sound of the wooden bar as Mr. Fong drew it against the inside of the door. Still listening he heard in the distance the cracking of guns, a volley and then another. He could only go on, and feeling the dust soft beneath his feet, he lifted his face to the wind and let it guide him southwards.

II

UPON a sea as blue as the sky above it a British ship shone as white as a snowbank. William Lane, pacing the deck after a solid English breakfast, held his head high, aware of the glances which followed him as he went. Ladies were arranging themselves in the deck-chairs, and only a few minutes earlier he had helped his mother with her rug, her cushion, her knitting, her book. Henrietta was writing letters in the saloon, and Ruth was playing shuffleboard. When he felt like it he would join her, but just now he wanted to walk his mile about the deck.

Upon his father's direction they had taken passage on the first ship that left Shanghai. Only the assurance of the Consul-General had persuaded them to leave.

'You cannot possibly help anyone by remaining here,' the Consul-General had said irritably to Mrs. Lane, when they had gone to him for advice. 'Your husband is as safe as we can make him in the Legation Quarter with all the other foreigners. They are in a state of siege, of course, but they have plenty of food and water, and relief is on the way. It is only a matter of days.'

'Why should we go then?' Henrietta had asked in her blunt voice.

The Consul-General had stared at the plain-faced girl. 'Merely to get on your way,' he retorted. Merely to get out of my way, he meant.

Mrs. Lane decided the matter abruptly. 'We had better go, or we may not get away for months,' she told William. 'I will settle you in college and Henrietta in boarding-school, and we will have the summer together with your grandfather at Old Harbour. If things are quiet in Peking by autumn I will go back. If not, your father will come home. We all need a rest and a change. I am sick of China and everything Chinese.'

So they had taken passage. Since British ships docked at

Vancouver, their course was northerly and the weather was cool and fine.

William Lane tried not to think of his father and a good deal of the time he succeeded. He was feeling many things at this age, everything intensely. Above all, he was heartily glad that he would never again see the English boarding-school where he had been so often unhappy. He was ashamed and yet proud of being American, ashamed because to be American at the school had kept him second-class, proud, because America was bigger than England. The consciousness of an inferiority which he could not believe was real had clouded his school-days. He had isolated himself both from the Americans and from the English, living in loneliness.

He was altogether ashamed of being the son of a missionary. Even the children of English missionaries were secondary. The son of the American ambassador alone had any sort of equality with the English boys, and seeing this, William had often bitterly wished that his father had been an ambassador. Men ought to consider what they were, he thought gloomily, for the sake of their sons. He hated Henrietta because when she came last year to the school she had immediately joined the Americans and had foolishly declared that she did not care what her father was. Thus William and Henrietta had been utterly divided at school and their division had not mended. She had taken as her bosom friend a girl whom he particularly despised, the daughter of an American missionary who lived in an interior city and was of a lowly Baptist sect. The girl was loathsomely freckled and her clothes were absurd. She should never have been at the school, William felt, and to have her the chosen friend of his own sister degraded him. In his loneliness he developed a grandeur of bearing, a haughtiness of look, which warned away the ribald. He avoided Henrietta because she was not afraid of him. Sometimes she laughed at him. 'You look like a rooster when you prance around like that,' she had once declared in front of their schoolmates. Shouts of laughter had destroyed his soul.

'I say,' the cricket captain had cried, 'you do look like a cock, you know!'

61

Well, that was over. He need never return to the school. Yet he did not and would not acknowledge how profoundly he would like to have been English. The most that he allowed himself was to dream occasionally as he walked the decks, his head high, that people who did not know him would think he was English. Lane was a good English name. His accent, after four years at school, was clearly English. The most fortunate youth he had ever met was the son of an English lord who spent a day at the school once when his father was visiting on shore from an English battleship in the Chinese harbour.

He passed his sister Ruth at the shuffleboard. 'I wish you'd play with me now, William,' she said in a plaintive voice.

'Very well, I will,' he replied. He paused, chose his pieces and the game began. He played much better than she did. The only fun he found in playing with her at all was to allow her to seem to win until the very end when, making up his mind that it was time to stop, he suddenly came in at the finish with victory.

'Oh, William!' she cried, invariably disappointed.

'I can't help it if I'm better than you,' he replied today and sauntered away, smiling his small dry smile.

He did not like to play with Henrietta. She was a change-able player, losing quickly sometimes and again winning by some fluke that he could not foresee. He never knew where he was with her.

There were no boys on the ship whom he cared to culti-vate, but there was one young man, English, some five or six years older than he, to whom he would have liked to speak, except that the chap never spoke first, and William did not want to seem American. At school the chaps always said Americans were so free, rushing about and speaking first to everybody.

He would have been considerably bored had he not thought much about the future and had there not been so many meals. Just now the morning broth was being served on little wagons, pushed by white-robed Chinese table boys and deck stewards. He approached one of the wagons, took a cup of hot beef broth and a handful of what he had taught himself to call biscuits instead of crackers, and sat down in his deck-chair beside his mother. She had already chosen chicken broth as lighter fare. She complained about the plethora of food and yet, he noticed, she ate as they all did. It cost nothing more, however much one ate, but none of them would say such a thing aloud except Henrietta.

'Henrietta seems to have picked up a young man,' his mother now remarked.

She nodded towards the upper deck, and William saw his sister leaning against the rail, the wind blowing her black hair from her face. She was talking in her earnest abrupt fashion to the young Englishman. A pang shot through his heart. He renounced the friendship he had craved. Whoever was Henrietta's friend could never be his.

'Henrietta will speak to anybody,' he told his mother. 'I noticed that at school.'


Clem plodded his way across the Chinese countryside. He was shrewd in the ways of the people and no human being was strange to him. Mercy he expected of none, kindness he did not count upon, and when he did not receive these, he blamed no one.

He walked by night and slept by day in the tall sorghum cane that grew in the fields at this season. When he saw no one ahead on a road as he peered out of the growth, he took advantage of this to cover as many miles as he could of those miles still between himself and the sea. The canes cut him from the sight of any farmer working in the fields and he had only to look ahead, for he walked faster than anyone coming from behind.

One day he fell in with an old country woman. She had long passed the age of concealing herself for modesty's sake and she had paused to relieve herself by the road. Comfort was now above all else. Clem came upon her about noon on a lonely country road and for a moment he thought her part of a bandit group. When the canes are high it is the season of bandits and often a gang of men will carry with them an old woman as a decoy.

The old woman laughed when she saw his start. 'Do not be afraid of me, boy,' she said in a cheerful voice while she tied her cotton girdle about her waist.

She spoke a country dialect which Clem understood, for its roots were the same language he had heard in Peking and so he said, 'Grandmother, I am not afraid of you. What harm can we do each other?'

She laughed at nothing as country women will. 'You cannot do me any harm,' she said in a voice very fresh for such a wrinkled face. 'Thirty years ago perhaps but not now! Where are you going?'

She fell into pace beside him and he slowed his step. It would be well for him to be seen with this old woman. He might be taken for her grandson. 'I am going east,' he said.

'How is it you are alone?' she asked.

He had tried to keep the dangerous blue of his eyes away from her, but when he stole a look at her, he saw that he need not take care. She had cataracts on both eyes, not heavy as yet, but filmed enough to see no more of him than his vague outlines.

'My father died in Peking,' he said truthfully, 'and I am going to find my grandfather.'

'Where is your grandfather?' she asked.

'To the east,' he replied.

'I am going eastward, too,' she said. 'Let us go together.'

'How far east?' he asked with caution.

She named a small city at the edge of the province.

'How is it you are alone?' he asked in his turn.

'I have no son,' she replied. 'Therefore I have no daughter-in-law. But I have a daughter who is married to an ironsmith in the city and I go there to ask for charity. My old man, her father, died last week and I sold the house. We had two-thirds of an acre of land. Had I a son I would have stayed on the land. But my fate is evil. My twin sons died together in one day when they were less than a year old.'

She sighed and loosened her collar as though she could not breathe and so her wrinkled neck was bare. Clem saw around it a dirty string on which hung an amulet.

64

'What is it you wear on your neck, Grandmother?' he asked.

She laughed again, this time half ashamed. 'How do I know what it is?' she retorted.

'Where did you get it?' Clem asked.

'Why do you want to know?' the old woman asked suspiciously.

Now the amulet was a strange one for a Chinese woman to wear. It was a small brass crucifix wrapped around with coarse black thread.

'It looks Christian,' Clem said.

The old woman gave him a frightened look. 'How does a boy like you know what is Christian?' she demanded, and she buttoned her coat.

'Are you a Christian?' Clem asked softly.

The old woman began to curse. 'Why should I be a Christian? The Christians are bad. Our Old Buddha is killing them. You come from Peking; you ought to know that.'

'The cross is good,' Clem said in a whisper.

She stopped in the middle of the road and heard this. 'Do you say it is good?' she asked.

'My father believed the cross was good,' Clem said.

'Was your father one of Them?'

Now Clem decided to risk his life. 'Yes, and he is dead. They killed him.' All this he said without her knowing that he was not Chinese.

He saw her mobile wrinkled face grow kind. 'Let us sit down,' she told him. 'But first look east and west and see if there is anyone in sight.'

No one was in sight. The hot noonday sun poured down upon the dusty road.

'Have you eaten?' the old woman asked.

He had been walking for four days and his store of bread was gone. He had still some of the dried mustard wrapped in the cotton kerchief. 'I have not eaten,' he said.

'Then we will eat together,' the old woman told him. 'I have some loaves here. I made them this morning.'

'I have some dried mustard leaves,' Clem said.

65

They shared their food and the old woman prattled on. 'I asked Heaven to let me meet with someone who could help me on the road. I had not walked above half the time between sunrise and noon when you came. This is because of the amulet.'

'Why do you say Heaven instead of God?' Clem asked.

'It is the same,' the old woman said easily. 'The priest said I need not call the name of a foreign god. I may say Heaven as I always have.'

'What priest?' Clem asked.

'I can never remember his name.'

'A foreigner?'

'Foreign, but with black hair and eyes like ours,' the old woman said. 'He wore a long robe and he had a big silver cross on his breast. He prayed in a foreign tongue.'

Catholic, Clem thought. 'What did this priest say the amulet meant?' he asked.

The old woman laughed. 'He told me but I cannot remember. It means good, though—nothing but good.' She looked so cheerful as she chewed the steamed bread, the sun shining on her wrinkled face, that she seemed to feel no pain at being alone.

'Did he teach you no prayers?' Clem asked.

'He did teach me prayers, but I could not remember them. So he bade me say my old O-mi-to-fu that I used to say to our Kwanyin, only when I say it I am to hold the amulet in my hand, so, and that makes the prayer go to the right place in Heaven.'

Wise priest, Clem thought, to use the old prayers for the new God! He had a moment's mild uncensuring cynicism. Prayers and faith seemed dream stuff now that his father was dead.

The old woman was still talking. 'He is dead, that piteous priest. If he had been alive I would have gone to find him. He lived in a courtyard near his own temple—not a temple, you understand, of our Buddha. There were gods in it, a man hanging on a wooden shape—bleeding, he was. I asked, "Why does this man bleed!" and the priest said, "Evil men

66

killed him." There was also a lady god like the Kwanyin, but with only two hands. She had white skin and I asked the priest if she were a foreigner and he said no, it was only that the image was made in some outer country where the people are white-skinned, but if the image had been made here the lady would have skin like ours, for this is her virtue that wherever she is, she looks like the people there. The man on the cross was her son, and I said why did she not hide him from the evil men and the priest said she could not. He was a wilful son and he went where he would, I suppose.'

'How is it that the priest is dead?' Clem asked with foreboding.

The old woman answered still cheerfully. 'He was cut in pieces by swordsmen and they fed the pieces to the dogs and the dogs sickened and so they said he was evil. I dared not tell them that I knew he was not evil. It was the day after my old man died and I had no one to protect me.'

They sat in the sun, finished now with their meal, and Clem hearing of the priest's dreadful end felt shadows of his own fall upon him. 'Come,' he said, 'let us get on our way, Grandmother.'

He decided that he would keep his secret to himself. Yet as the day went on a good plan came to him. He could pretend to be blind, keep his blue eyes closed, feel his way, act as the old woman's grandson, and so they could walk all day more quickly and safely than by night. Then too he could use the money which Mr. Fong had given him, which until now he dared not use at an inn. Yet to make the pretence it was needful to tell the old woman who he was and she was so simple that he could not make up his mind whether he dared to trust his life into her hands.

When night drew near and a village showed itself in a distant cluster of lights, he thought he could tell her. He knew by now that she was good and only what she said she was, and if he were with her he might keep her awake to danger. If by chance she betrayed him as not Chinese, then he must make his escape as best he could.

So before they came to the village he took her aside, much

to her bewilderment, for she did not know why he plucked her sleeve. Behind a large date tree, where he could see on all sides, he told her.

'Grandmother, you have been honest with me, but I have not told you who I am.'

'You are not a bandit!' she exclaimed in some terror.

'No—I am someone worse for you. My father was a foreigner, like your priest.'

'Is it true?' she exclaimed. She strained her eyes and then put up her hand to feel his face.

'It is true,' he said, 'and my father and mother and my sisters were killed as the priest was killed and I go to the sea to find a ship to take me to my own country.'

'Pitiful—pitiful,' she murmured. 'You are not very old. You are not yet grown.'

'No,' Clem said. 'But I am alone, and so I am glad that you met with me.'

'It was the amulet,' she said. 'Heaven saw us two lonely ones walking the same road and brought us together.'

'Grandmother,' he went on, 'you cannot see my eyes, but they are not black as the priest's eyes were.' ·

'Are they not?' she asked surprised. 'What colour are they, then?'

'Blue,' he told her.

'Blue?' she echoed. ''But only wild beasts have blue eyes.'

'So have many of my people,' he said.

She shuddered. 'Ah, I have heard that foreigners are like wild beasts!'

'My father was not,' Clem replied, 'and my mother was very gentle. You would have liked her.'

'Did she speak our tongue?'

'Yes,' Clem said, and found that he could not tell more of his mother.

'Ai-ya,' the old woman sighed. 'There is too much evil everywhere.'

'Grandmother,' Clem began again.

'I like to hear you call me so,' the old woman said. 'I shall never have a grandson, since my sons are dead.'

68

'Will you help me?' Clem asked.

'Surely will I,' she replied.

And so he told her his plan and she listened, nodding. 'A half-blind old woman leading a blind grandson,' she repeated.

'We can go to the village inn there and sleep under a roof. I have slept every night in the canes, and two nights it rained.'

'I have some money,' she said, fumbling in her waist.

'I also,' Clem said. 'Let us spend mine first.'

'No, mine.'

'But mine, Grandmother, because when I get to my own country it will be no use to me.'

She was diverted by this. 'How can money be no use?'

'We have a different coin,' he replied.

They began to walk again and planned as they went. Far from being stupid as he had thought her, she was shrewd and planned as well as he did. All her life she had been the wife of a small poor man compelled to evade the country police and tax gatherers and she knew how to seem what she was not and to hide what she was.

An hour later Clem was walking down the village street with her, his eyes shut, holding in his hand one end of a stick the other end of which she held. She led the way to the inn on the single street and asked for two places on the sleeping platform for herself and her grandson, and the innkeeper gave them without more questions than such men usually ask of those they have not seen before. The old woman told a simple story, much of it true, how her husband and son were both dead together of the same disease and how she had left only this grandson and they were returning to her old city where she had been reared and where she might find her daughter married to the ironsmith.

'What is his name?' the innkeeper asked.

'He is named Liu the Big,' the old woman said.

A traveller spoke up at this and said, 'There is an ironsmith surnamed Liu who lives inside the east gate of that city and he forged me an iron for a wheel of my cart, when I came westward through there. He has the finger off one hand.'

69

'It is he,' the old woman said. 'He lost the finger when he was testing a razor he had ground. It went through his finger like flame through snow.'

Clem passed the night lying among the travellers on a wide bed of brick overlaid with straw and slept in spite of the garlic-laden air because for the while he felt safe again.

Nights and days Clem spent thus, always as the grandson of the old woman, and each day she grew more fond of him. She told him many curious tales of her early childhood and she asked him closely about his own people and why he was here instead of in the land where he belonged and marvelled that he knew nothing at all of his ancestors.

'You foreigners,' she said one day, 'you grow mad with god-fever. There is something demon in your gods that they drive you so. Our gods are reasonable. They ask of us only a few good works. But for your gods good works are not enough. They must be praised and told they are the only gods and all others are false.'

She laughed and said cheerfully, 'Heaven is full of gods, even as the earth is full of people, and some are good and some are evil and there is no great One Over All.'

Clem did not argue with her. There was no faith left in him except a small new faith in the goodness of a few people. Mr. Fong and his wife had been good to him and so now was this old woman good, and he listened to her as they walked over the miles, side by side unless they came among people when he took the end of the stick she held and pretended to be blind. From her lips he learned a sort of coarse wisdom as he went, and he measured it against what he had learned before and found it true. Thus, the old woman said, the great fault with Heaven and whatever gods there were was that they had not arranged that food could fall every night from the sky, enough for everybody to eat so that there could be no cause for quarrel.

'If the belly is full,' she said, 'if we could know that it would always be full, men would be idle and laugh and play games like children, and then we would have peace and happiness.'

70

These words, Clem thought, were the wisest he had ever heard. If his father had needed to take no thought for food, then his faith might have been perfect. Assured of food, his father could have preached and prayed and become a saint.

Thus talking and thinking, sleeping in inns at night, Clem and the old woman reached the city where she must stop. He had noticed for a day or two that she seemed in an ill humour, muttering often to herself. 'Well, why should I not?' this she asked herself. Or she said, 'Who cares whether I——,' or 'My daughter does not know if I live.'

Before they got into the city, on an afternoon after a thunderstorm during which they had taken refuge in a wayside temple where there were gods but no priests, the old woman came out with what she had been muttering to herself.

'Grandson, I ought to go to the coast with you. What will you do if I leave you? Some rascal will see your eyes and think to gain glory with the Empress and he will kill you and take your head to the capital to show for prize money.'

Clem refused at once such kindness. 'Grandmother, you are old and tired. You told me yesterday that your feet were swollen.'

They made an argument out of it for a while and at last the old woman said, 'Come with me at least to the door of my daughter's house. We will see what Big Liu says.'

To this Clem consented, and when they came to the city the old woman would not enter until just before the gates closed so that people could not see them clearly. As night fell they joined the last people crowding to get inside the gate and walking quietly along mingled with the people, they came to the house of Liu the ironsmith.

Clem's first sight of the ironsmith all but overcame him. The forge was open to the street, and there the mighty man stood, his legs apart, his right arm uplifted and holding a great iron hammer, his left hand grasping thick tongs which held a red-hot piece of metal. Upon this metal he beat with the hammer and the fiery sparks flew into the night with every blow. The ironsmith was black with smoke and his lips were drawn back from his teeth so that they showed very

71

white, and so white, too, were the whites of his eyes, above which were fierce black brows.

'That is he,' the old woman whispered.

She went in boldly and called out above the din. 'Eh, Big Liu! Is my daughter at home?'

Big Liu put down the hammer and stared at her. 'It is not you, mother of my children's mother!' This he shouted.

'It is I,' the old woman said. Then she wiped her eyes with her sleeves. 'My old man, her father, is dead.'

Big Liu still stared at her. 'Come inside,' he commanded. When he saw Clem following he stopped again. 'Who is this boy?' he asked.

'He is my foster grandson,' the old woman said and then she went on quickly. 'A poor orphan child he is, and I an old lonely woman and we fell in along the road and the gods sent him, I swear, for he took such care of me that I know he is no common child but some sort of spirit come down. His eyes are the eyes of Heaven and his heart is gentle.' Thus talking very fast while Big Liu stared the old woman tried to make Clem safe.

But Clem shook his head. 'I will tell you who I am,' he said to Big Liu. They went into the inner room and all talk had to wait until the old woman and her daughter had cried their greetings, had exclaimed and wept and hugged the three small children. By this time Big Liu had taken thought and he knew that Clem was no Chinese and he was very grave. He got up and shut the doors while the women talked and wept, and at last he made them be silent and he turned to Clem.

'You are a foreigner,' he said.

'Yes,' Clem said. 'I cannot hide it from you.'

Then he told him his story, and the old woman broke in often to tell how good he was and how they must help him, and if Big Liu did not think of a way, she must go with Clem herself to the sea.

Big Liu was silent for some time and even his wife looked grave and gathered her children near her. At last Big Liu said, 'We must not keep you here for a single day. Were it known that there was a foreigner in my house you would be killed and we would all die with you. You must go on your way, as soon as the East Gate opens at dawn.'

Clem got up. 'I will go,' he said.

Big Liu motioned with his huge black hand. 'Wait—I will not send you out to die. I have an apprentice, my nephew, a lad older than you, and he shall lead you to the coast. Since you are here, wash yourself, and I will give you better garments. Then lie down to sleep for a few hours. My children's mother shall make you food. Have you money?'

'He has no money,' the old woman said. 'He would use his money on the way and so I will give him mine.'

Big Liu put out his hand again. 'No, keep your money, good mother. I will give him enough.'

So it all happened. Clem obeyed Big Liu exactly as he had spoken for this big man had a voice and a manner of command, though he spoke slowly and simply. Clem washed himself all over with a wooden bucketful of hot water, and he put on some clean garments that the apprentice brought, who stared his eyes out at Clem's white skin under his clothes.

Clem ate two bowls full of noodles and sesame oil and lay down on a bamboo couch in the kitchen while the apprentice lay on the floor. But Clem could not sleep. He knew that the ironsmith sat awake, fearful lest someone discover what was in his house, and although the old woman bade Clem not to be afraid, she could not sleep, either, and she came in again and again to see why he did not sleep and to tell him he must sleep to keep his strength. As for the apprentice, he did not like at all this new task, but still he had never been to the coast nor seen a ship, and so he was torn between fear and pleasure.

Before dawn broke Big Liu came in and Clem sprang up from the couch and put on his jacket.

The apprentice was sleeping but he got up too, and yawned and wrapped his cotton girdle about himself and tied his queue around his head under his ragged fur cap and so they crept to the door.

'Come out this small back gate,' Big Liu said. 'It lets into an alley full of filth, but still it is safer than the street.'

One moment the old woman held Clem back. She put her arms about his shoulders and patted his back and then sighed and moaned once or twice. 'You will forget me when you cross that foreign sea,' she complained.

'I will never forget you,' Clem promised.

'And I have nothing to give you—yet, wait!'

She had thought of her amulet and she broke the string and tied it around his wrist, and the small cross hung there.

'I give this to you,' she said. 'It will keep you safe. Only remember to say O-mi-to-fu when you pray, because the god of this amulet is used to that prayer.'

She wept a little and then pushed him from her gently, and so Clem left her and went on his way with the apprentice.

To the lad he said very little in the days that they travelled together, which days were fewer by half than those he had already come. They walked by day, the lad silent for the most part, too, and they slept at night in inns or sometimes only on a bank behind some trees for shelter, for the apprentice was fearful whenever they passed swordsmen. But never were they stopped, for Clem wore his old hat like any farm-boy and kept his eyes downcast.

When they came to the coast they parted, and Clem gave the apprentice nearly all that was left of his money. There were several ships in the harbour, and he would not let them go without finding one which would take him aboard. He was no longer afraid here, for it was a port and he saw policemen and he saw white men and women walking as they liked and riding in rickshaws and carriages. He went near none of them for he did not want to be stopped in his purpose, which was to cross the sea and find his own country. But he did hear good news. Listening in an inn where he sat alone after the apprentice had left him, he heard that the Old Empress had been forced to yield to the white armies. She had fled her palace, leaving behind a young princess who had thrown herself into a well, and the foreign armies had marched into the city, plundering as they went and killing men and raping young women, so that all China was mourning the suffering which the Old Empress had brought upon them.

74

This Clem heard without being free to ask more about it. He wondered how the Fong household did, and whether they had shared in the suffering, and whether they in turn had been killed even as his family had been. But nothing could he know. When he had eaten he went to the docks and loitered among some sailors and on that same day he was able to find a ship and go aboard as a cabin boy. As for the apprentice, after staring half a day at the ships and wandering about the city, he left again for home.

On the American freighter Clem made his way still eastwards. The ship had brought ammunition and wheat to China and had taken away hides and vegetable oils. The hides, imperfectly cured, permeated the ship with their reek, and Clem, racked often with sea-sickness, wished sometimes that he too was dead. Yet the wish never lasted. Upon rolling grey seas the sun broke, the winds died, and the waves subsided. Then, eating enormously in the galley with the thirty-odd men who made up the crew, he wanted to live to reach the farm.

The men knew his story. They had heard it first on the pier at the port when, approaching one of them, he had asked timidly for a job on the ship.

'We don't want no Chinks,' the sailor had replied.

'I am not Chinese,' Clem had said.

'You ain't?' the sailor had said, unbelieving.

Clem had pointed to his eyes. 'See, they are blue.'

'Damned if they ain't,' the sailor had agreed after staring at him a moment. 'Hey, fellows, anybody ever seen a blue-eyed Chink?'

'When is a Chink not a Chink?' a sailor had inquired. 'Why, when his ma is somethin' else!'

'She wasn't,' Clem had declared, with indignation. 'She was good and so was my father and they were American and so am I.' But English felt strange upon his tongue after the many days when he had spoken only Chinese.

The men had gathered about him, delaying the pleasures they planned for their brief hours ashore, and with pity and wonder they had listened to his story which he had poured out. Looking from one coarse face to the other, he found himself telling everything to save his own life. Even the things he had not allowed himself to remember he told, and he began to sob again, trying not to, his fists clenched against his mouth.

The men listened and looked at each other, and one burly fellow took Clem's head between his hands. 'It's all over, see! And we believe you, sonny. And you come with us, if we have to smuggle you. But the old man is soft enough. He'll let you on board.'

They had dragged him before a little sharp-faced captain and made him tell his story all over again, and then he had been hired as a cabin boy. With the captain he held long conversations.

'Reckon you'll never want to be going back to no heathen country after this!' the captain said.

'I don't know,' Clem replied. He had mixed a whisky and soda, and set it before the captain. 'I might have felt that way except that Mr. Fong saved my life. And people were kind all those days I tramped. I can't forget the old grandmother.'

No, he could never forget. In the night, lying in his hard and narrow berth, tossed by the sea, he remembered the long days of tramping across the Chinese country, beside the old woman. Summer had ripened the fields, and the lengthening shadows of the green sorghum, high above their heads, gave them good shelter. Big Liu, too, had been kind. It would have been easy to tell the local police about a foreign boy and for the telling to have received a reward. Big Liu was poor enough to value money and Clem was a stranger. None would miss him if he died, but Big Liu had not betrayed him. Wonder and gratitude at the goodness of common men and women filled Clem's heart with faith, not the faith of his father but a new faith, a faith which bound him to the earth.

The sailors, too, were kind, although they were rough and of an ignorance he had never yet seen. They were mannerless, coarse, drunken when they could get drink, lewd in act and speech, easily angry, always ready to fight. He thought of them as men half made, left unfinished, never taught. They knew no better than they did.

Were the people of his country all like these? He had none to judge by, never having known his own kind, except his father who he felt vaguely was a man peculiar. The delicacy of the Chinese was soothing and comfortable to remember. Here on the ship, though he knew the men were friendly to him, yet for some fault, or no fault except that a man might be surly from too much drink the night before on shore leave, he might feel his ears jerked or his head cuffed, or a blow between his shoulders might fell him. He learned it was useless to be angry, for immediately the man would joyfully urge him to fight, and he was no match for any of the men, short and slender as he was. Once he complained to the captain, but only once.

'You don't think I'll defend you?' the captain had said.

'No, sir,' Clem said, 'except maybe to tell them to leave me alone.'

'Do they hate you?'

'No, sir. I don't think they do; it's like play, maybe.'

'Then put up or shut up,' the captain said.

Yet the long journey over the sea was good for Clem. An endless roar of command sounded in his ears. He was at the beck and call of all of them. Twice the ship stopped for coal, once in Japan, once again at the Hawaiian Isles, but he had no shore leave. He gazed across the dock at strange lands and unknown people and saw sharp mountains against the sky. At night he helped drunken sailors to bed, staggering under the load of their coarse bodies leaning on his shoulders, smelling the filthy reek of their breath. When one or another vomited before he could reach the rail, Clem had to clean the mess before the captain saw it. By morning all had to be ship-shape, and sometimes there was little sleep for Clem. He loathed the coarseness of the men and yet he pitied it. They had nothing to make them better. They hated the sea, feared it, cursed it, and yet went on living by it, for they did not know what else to do. In a storm they were filled with blind terror. Clem felt old beside them, old as a father, and sometimes like a father he tended them, pulling off their sodden

77

shoes when they slept before they could undress, bringing them coffee at dawn when they were too dazed to take watch. They were kind to him in return, half ashamed because they knew him only a child, and yet helpless before him. He remained a stranger to them, aloof even while he served them. Pity prevented his blame, and his pity made them often silent when he came near them. But this he did not know. For himself he felt only increasing loneliness, and he longed for the voyage to end that he might find those who were his own.

The sea voyage ended at last and one day he went ashore into a country which was his and yet where he was still a stranger. The crew collected a purse for him, and he would never forget that. It meant that he could travel to the east on a railway, instead of tramping the miles away as he had done across the country in China. He had not minded doing it there because he knew the people and there was the old woman at his side, but here where he did not know the people or the food it would have been different.

So though the sailors were so evil, they were good, too. On the first day ashore in San Francisco they went together to a shop and bought Clem a suit of clothes. It was too big for him, but he rolled up the trousers and sleeves. They bought him two clean shirts and a red tie, a hat and a pair of shoes, and three pairs of socks and a pasteboard suit-case. Then they took him to the railway station and bought him a ticket to Pittsburgh on the day coach. There was not quite enough money, for they would not let him spend the ten dollars they had given him, and one of them had pawned a gold thumb-ring he had bought in Singapore. They clapped him on the back, embraced him, and gave him good advice.

'Don't talk with nobody, you hear, Clem?'

'Specially no women.'

'Aw, he's too runty for women.'

'You'd be surprised if you knew women like I do. Don't talk to 'em, Clem!'

'Don't play no cards, Clem!'

'Send us a postcard once in a while, Clem, will ya?'

The train pulled out and he stood waving his new hat as they receded until he could see them no more. So he was alone again, riding in a train across his own country. He had a seat to himself, opposite a red-faced man in a grey suit who slept most of the time and grinned at him vaguely when he woke. 'Don't speak to nobody on the train,' the sailors had told him. 'Shore fellows will take your money away from you.' He kept quiet and his wallet was in his breast pocket where he could feel it against his ribs every time he took a deep breath. When he needed money to spend on food he went into the men's room and there alone he took out a dollar at a time, keeping his change in his hip pocket against the back of the seat.

Hour after hour, in every hour of daylight, he stared from the window, seeing a country he could not comprehend. It seemed empty and without people. Where were all the people? The mountains were higher than he could have imagined, the deserts wider and more desolate, their emptiness terrifying. To his amazement, many times at the stations he saw white men doing coolie work, and in the few fields between mountains and on the fringe of deserts he saw men and women more ragged, more poor, though white, than any he had seen in China. Where was the land of milk and honey his father used to call home?

One night while he slept upright in his seat, they rolled into green plains. When he woke at dawn it was to another country. Green fields and broad roads, big barns and compact clean farm-houses charmed his eyes. This was Pennsylvania, surely!

Long before Clem had begun his voyage William had reached America. The white English ship docked at Vancouver, and Mrs. Lane, brisk and experienced, bullied the courteous Canadian customs officers and found the best seats on the train that carried them across Canada to Montreal, where they changed for New York.

It was a smooth journey, and William enjoyed it with quiet dignity. He kept aloof from his mother and sisters, staying most of the time in the observation car where behind a

79

magazine he listened to men's talk. There was no difficulty in Montreal, and in New York his mother took them at once to the Murray Hill, where he had a room to himself because he was a boy. It was high ceilinged, and the tall windows had red velvet curtains held back by loops of brass. The luxury of the room and its bath pleased him. This then was America. It was better than he had feared.

They ate in a dining-room where fountains played and canaries sang, and he enjoyed this, too.

'I believe in the best,' his mother said. 'Besides, Papa and Mama always stayed here when we came to town.'

His mother kept him with her in New York for a week while she smoothed his path towards college, but Henrietta and Ruth she sent to her parents at Old Harbour. She did not take him at once to the office of the Mission Board. Instead she toured the best stores, asking to see young men's clothing. When she found something she liked she made William try it on. She bought nothing, however, merely making notes of garments and prices.

With these in a small note-book in her handbag she went on the morning of the fourth day to the Board offices and there was received with a deference which was balm to William's pride.

'Ah, Mrs. Lane,' a rosy-faced white-haired executive said, 'we've been expecting you. We had a cablegram from Dr. Lane. What can we do for you?'

'I have a good deal of shopping to do for my son's entrance into Harvard,' Mrs. Lane said. Her voice and look were equally firm.

The plump elderly executive, a retired minister himself, looked doubtful. 'We have special arrangements with medium-priced stores to give us ten per cent discount.'

Mrs. Lane interrupted without interest in the medium-priced stores. 'I want to see the treasurer immediately.'

'Certainly, Mrs. Lane—this way, please,' the white-haired man said.

'You stay here, William,' Mrs. Lane commanded.

While William waited, his mother had a long interview with

the mission treasurer which left him looking dazed and certainly left him silent. William had stayed in the reading-room because his mother wanted, she said, to be alone with the finances. He had sauntered about, reading pamphlets impatiently. They were religious and full of hopeful accounts of the hospitals and schools and orphanages and churches with which he was entirely surfeited. He wanted to get away from everything he had known. When he entered college in the autumn he would not tell anyone who his father was or that he came from China.

'There now,' Mrs. Lane said when she emerged from the inner office. 'I have everything all arranged. You'll be able to get along nicely.' She held her long skirts in one hand and over her shoulder she said to the little mission treasurer, 'Thank you, Mr. Emmons, you've been very helpful.'

Mr. Emmons broke his silence. 'You do understand, don't you, Mrs. Lane, that I haven't made any promises? I mean— I'll have to take up these rather unusual requests with the Board—evening clothes, for example——'

'I'm sure they'll see that my son deserves some special consideration, after all we've been through,' Mrs. Lane said in her clear sharp voice. 'Come, William, we can get the noon train after all.'

He had followed her, holding himself very straight and not speaking to the shabby little treasurer.

When they reached his grandfather's house at Old Harbour, he was pleased to see it was a large one. It was old-fashioned and needed paint, but it stood in large, somewhat neglected grounds.

'Papa doesn't keep things up the way he used to, I see,' his mother said. They had taken a hack at the station and now got down. She handed him her purse. 'Pay the man his dollar, William,' she told him.

'Grass needs cutting,' she went on. 'I suppose Papa can't afford a gardener all the time, now he's retired.'

The hack drove away, and William looked at the suit-cases the man had set down in the path. 'We'd better take what we

can,' his mother said with some embarrassment. 'I **don't**
know how many servants Papa has now. We used to have a
houseman and three maids.'

She picked up two suit-cases, and much against his will he
took the other and followed her to the house. The door stood
open and when they entered they were met by Henrietta and
Ruth, dripping in bathing-suits, and by a carelessly dressed old
gentleman whom he recognized, though with extreme discomfort, as his grandfather.

Mrs. Lane swooped down upon him. 'Well, Papa, here I
am again!'

'You've grown a little older,' he said, looking at his tall
daughter.

Mr. Vandervent was no longer imposing. He was a pot-
bellied, mild-looking man, and he seemed timid before his
tall grandson.

'How do, William,' he said, putting out a round little hand.

William clasped it coldly. 'I'm very well, sir,' he replied
correctly 'I hope you are, too.'

'So so,' Mr. Vandervent said. 'The sea don't really agree
with me, but your grandma likes it.'

'What we've been through——' Mrs. Lane began.

She was interrupted by a loud scream. A tall fat woman
burst through a swinging door, an apron tied about her waist.

'Helen, my goodness!'

It was her mother They embraced and kissed. 'I was just
stirring up one of my chocolate cakes, thinking that William
would probably—we only have two maids now, Helen—why,
William, this isn't you, never! Isn't he the image of your
father, Robert? Your great-grandfather was a real handsome
man, William.'

Henrietta had disappeared and through the window William
saw her walking along the shore. Ruth was standing on one
foot and then another.

'William!' she now whispered. 'Do get into your bathing
suit. The ocean is wonderful.'

It gave him an excuse and he seized it.

'May I, Mother?'

'Go on,' his grandmother said heartily. 'You'll have time before supper.'

Supper! The word chilled his spine. He had heard it among the commoner missionaries, the Seventh Day Adventists, the Primitive Baptists, the Pentecostal people. At the English school the evening meal was always called dinner and since at his own home it had been so, too, it had not occurred to him that it could be anything else here.

He mounted the stairs with laggard steps and was arrested by his mother's voice. 'Here, William, since you're going up, you might as well take some of the suit-cases.'

He stopped, not trusting his ears, and looked at his mother. She laughed, but he discerned embarrassment in the steel grey eyes she kept averted from his. 'You may as well realize that you are in America, son,' she told him. 'You'll have to do a lot of waiting on yourself here.'

He stood still for one instant; then with a passionate energy he turned and ran downstairs and loaded himself with the bags and staggered upstairs again. Once he glanced over the banister to see if they were looking at him, but nobody was. His mother was talking about the siege, and they had forgotten him.

No one had told Clem to telegraph to his grandfather, and he would have been reluctant to spend the money. When he got off at last at Centerville, there was no one to meet him, but he had expected no one. Carrying his suit-case, he approached a fat man who was staring at the train and scratching his head.

'Can you tell me where Mr. Charles Miller lives?' Clem inquired.

The man had started a yawn and stopped it midway. 'Never heard of him.'

'He lives on a farm,' Clem said.

'Your best bet would be that way,' the man said, nodding towards the south.

'Thank you,' Clem said.

The man looked surprised but said nothing and Clem began

walking. His days on the sea had made his feet tender although they had once been horny from long walking on rough Chinese roads. But his muscles still were strong. The heat here was nothing to that in China, and the air was sweet with some wild fragrance. He did not see anyone after he left the small railway town, and this was strange. Were there no people here! It occurred to him that it was nearly noon, and they might be having a meal. Even so, where were the villages? As far as he could see there was no village in sight. The fields rolled away in high green waves against a sky of solid blue. They were planted with corn, he saw with surprise. Did the people here eat only corn?

After another hour he was tired and hungry and he wished that he had stopped to buy some food. Five miles had seemed nothing in his excitement. He sat down beside a small stream and drank and rested, and while he sat there a wagon came by, pulled by two horses as high as camels. A man drove them, seated on a bench in the wagon. 'Hi, there, feller,' he called down. 'Wanta ride?'

Clem was cautious. Why should a stranger offer him a ride? Might not the fellow be a bandit? 'No, thank you,' he replied.

The man drew the wagon to a stop. 'You look like a stranger.'

Clem did not reply. The barber on the ship had clipped his hair close to get rid of the dyed hair, and he was conscious of his baldness.

'Where you goin'?' the man asked.

'To Mr. Charles Miller's farm,' Clem replied.

The man stared at him, his jaw hanging. He was a dirty fellow, clad in a sweat-soaked shirt and blue cotton trousers. Through the unbuttoned front of his shirt Clem saw a chest woolly with repulsively red hair.

'Old Charley Miller is dead,' the man said.

The sunlight glittering upon the landscape took on the sharpness of dagger points, springing from the edges of leaves, the tips of grass, the points of fence rails. Clem's eyes blurred and weakness laid hold upon his knees.

'When did he die?' His mouth was full of dust.

84

'Coupla years ago.' The man prepared for the story. He spat thick brown spittle into the road and pushed back his torn straw hat.

'Fact is, the old man hung himself in his own barn. Disappointed that's what. He'd been tryin' for ten years to get a job with the Republicans, and when they got in that year they give him the sheriff's job. He had to put somebody off a farm the very first day—mortgage couldn't be met. He was too soft-hearted to do it—he was awful soft-hearted, old Charley was. He just hung himself the night before—yeah.'

The man shook his head and sighed. 'Wouldn't hurt a flea, Charley wouldn't. Couldn't kill a fly. Lived all alone. He had a son somewhere, but he never come home.'

'His son was my father.' The words escaped Clem like a cry.

The man stared, brown saliva drooling down his chin. 'You don't say!'

Clem nodded. 'He's dead, too. That's why I came to find my grandfather. But if I haven't anybody—I guess—I guess I don't know what to do.'

The man was kind enough. 'You get up here along of me, sonny, and I'll take you to your grandpop's farm, anyway. There's folks livin' there. Maybe they'll lend a hand.'

For lack of any directing thought Clem obeyed. He lifted his suit-case and gave it to the man and then stepping upon the axle he crawled into the seat. There in the hot sunshine he sat, his suit-case between his knees, and in silence the man drove two miles and put him down before an unpainted gate set in a decaying picket fence lost in high weeds. The wagon went away and Clem stared at a small solid stone house.

This, then, was the place of which he had dreamed as long as he could remember. The grass grew long and unkempt even in the yard. Over the house leaned an enormous sycamore tree. Under this tree he saw some ragged children, two boys and two girls. The boys were about his own age, the girls younger, or at least smaller.

They were eating dry bread, tearing at hunks of it with their teeth as they held it. When they saw him they hid the bread in their hands, holding it behind them.

85

'What you want?' the bigger boy asked in a gruff voice. He had a thin freckled face and his hair grew long into his neck.

'Who lives here?' Clem asked.

'Pop and Mom Berger,' a girl said. She began to chew again at her bread. 'You better go 'way or they'll set the dogs on you.'

'Are you their children?' Clem asked. Where could he go in a strange country where nevertheless he belonged?

The thin boy answered again. 'Naw, we're Aid children.'

Clem looked at them, comprehending nothing. 'You mean— Aid is your name?'

They looked at each other, confounded by his stupidity. 'Aid children,' the girl repeated.

'What do you mean?' Clem asked.

'We're Aid children. Children what ain't got nobody.'

Clem gazed and his heart began to shrink. He, too, had nobody. Then was he, perforce, an Aid child?

Before he could reply to this frightful question, a short stout man ambled from the open door of the house and yelled: 'Here, you kids—git back to work!' The children fled behind the house, and the man stared across the tumbled grass at Clem.

'Where'd you come from?' he demanded.

'I thought Charles Miller, my grandfather, was here,' Clem said.

'Been gone two years,' the man said. 'I bought the place and took over the mortgage. I never heard he had no grandson.'

'I guess my father didn't write. We lived a long way off.'

'Out West?'

'Yes.'

'Folks still there?'

'They're dead. That's why I came back.'

'Ain't none of your folks around here as I know of.'

He was about to go back into the door when something seemed to occur to him. 'How old are you?' he asked.

'Fifteen,' Clem said.

86

'Undersize,' the man muttered. 'Well, you might as well come in. We was just thinkin' we maybe could do with another Aid boy. The work's gittin' heavy.' He jerked his head. 'C'mon in here.'

Clem took up his suit-case. He had nowhere else to go. He followed the man into the house.

'I'll report you to the Aid next time she comes,' the man said.

William Lane was walking solitary along the beach. He had to be solitary a good deal of the time, for he had met no boys of his own age and it was intolerable to him to be with his sisters. Occasionally he went swimming with Ruth, but only at a time when the beach was not crowded. He had supposed of course that the beach was private since his grandfather's house faced upon it, and on that first day of his arrival when he had gone for a swim with Ruth he had been shocked to see at least fifty people in or near the water.

'Does grandfather let all these people use our beach?' he had asked Ruth.

Before she could answer he heard Henrietta's horrid laughter. She came swimming out of the sea, her long straight hair lank upon her shoulders. 'Nobody has private beaches here, stupid,' she had said in a rude voice.

Ruth had reproached her as usual for his sake.

'How can William know when it's only his first day?'

'He'd better learn quick, then,' Henrietta had retorted and returned to the sea.

Now of course he knew the truth. The beach belonged to everybody. Anybody at all could come there. They were all Americans he knew, and yet they were of a variety and a commonness which made him feel the loneliest soul in the world. He longed for his English schoolmates, and yet he was cut off from them forever, because he did not want to see them any more. He did not want them to know that America was exactly what they had said it was, a place full of common people.

He lifted his head with a resolute arrogant gesture which

was almost unconscious but not quite, since he had caught it from the boy who had been the captain of the cricket team last year, a fair-haired tall young man, whose father was Sir Gregory Scott, the British Consul-General. Ronald Scott had been all that was splendid and fearless. Why not, when he had everything?

At least, William thought, his grandfather's house was better than some of the others facing the beach, and there were the two maids. He had felt slightly better when he discovered that most of the other houses had no servants, although in China women were only amahs for younger children. The two maids were old and badly trained. He had put his shoes outside his bedroom door the first night and they were still there the next morning, but not polished.

'I say,' he had asked his mother, 'who does the boots in this house?'

She had given him a curious smile. 'We do them ourselves,' she said smoothly and without explanation. This was another thing that made him solitary. In Peking he had always been able to count on his mother, but here he did not know her as she was. She took his part when they were alone, but in front of other people he felt she did not. When he left his hat and coat in the hall for the maid to hang up his mother hung them up and his grandmother had been sharp about it. 'William, don't let your mother wait on you,' she had exclaimed.

'Oh, never mind,' his mother had said quickly.

'Now, Helen, don't spoil the boy,' his grandmother had retorted.

'He'll be going to college in just a few weeks, and then he'll have to look after himself.' This was the feeble answer his mother had given. He had looked at both of them haughtily and had said nothing.

The air today was as clear and cool as a June day in Peking, and the sea was very blue. He had left the house after luncheon and seeing the beach crowded, he had walked straight away from it and towards the other part of Old Harbour, the best part. It had not taken him many days to find that the place where the really rich people lived was there. Great houses set in plenty of lawn faced wide bright beaches almost empty of people. Now almost every day he came here, always alone, too proud to pretend that he belonged here and yet longing to seem that he did before a chance passerby.

At this hour of early afternoon no one was to be seen. The heat of the sun was intense, though the air was cool, and the people were, he supposed, in their great houses. He was walking along the edge of a low bluff and suddenly he decided to climb it. The ascent was not difficult. He had only begun when he saw a flight of wooden steps and was tempted to use them. It would be degrading to him if he were discovered trespassing, and yet his curiosity compelled him. He compromised by not using the steps and scrambled up the sandy rock ledge until he had reached the grass at the top. There he found himself still alone. For a quarter of a mile the lawn sloped back towards a knoll, and hidden behind masses of trees he saw a vast house. His imagination hovered about it. Had his grandfather lived there and had he belonged there, how easily he might have been proud of his country!

He threw himself down upon the grass and buried his face in his arms. The sun beat upon his back and he felt suffocated with despair. He longed for the summer to be over so that he could leave his family and be alone at college. Yet how could he be successful there when it now appeared that his grandfather had no intention of helping him with any money? His mother had asked his grandparents outright if they could help him so that he could spend all his time in studying, and his grandfather had said, 'Let him work his way through, as much as he can. It'll be good for him.'

His mother had told him this with curious hesitation. 'I suppose in a way it would be good for you,' she had said thoughtfully. 'But in another way I know it wouldn't. Work classes you here, actually, as much as it does in China. I wish we'd sent you to Groton.'

'Why didn't you?' he had asked violently.

'Money,' she had said simply. 'Just money. Everything goes back to that.'

'Does grandfather have no money?' he had demanded.

'He seems to have enough for himself but nobody else,' his mother had replied. Then she had one of her inexplicable changes. 'Why do I say that? He's feeding us all—four of us —I suppose that's something, week in and week out.'

William would have wept had he not been too proud. He continued now to lie like stone under the sun, his flesh hot and his heart cold. His disappointment was becoming insupportable. Of all that he had seen, nothing in his country was what he had hoped it would be, nothing except this spot where the great houses stood facing the sea from their heights of green, and here he did not belong.

At this moment he heard a voice.

'What are you doing here, boy?'

He lifted his head and saw an old gentleman leaning on a cane. A loose brown tweed cap hung over his forehead and he wore a baggy top coat of the same material. His face was brown too, against the white of his pointed beard and moustache.

'Trespassing, I'm afraid, sir.' William sprang to his feet and stood very straight. He went on in his best English manner, instilled by the headmaster in Chefoo. 'I couldn't resist climbing the bluff to see what was here. Then I was tired and wanted to rest a bit.'

'Do you like what you see?'

'Rather!'

He felt some sort of approval in the old gentleman, and he held his black head higher and compelled his grey gaze to meet the sharp blue eyes that were staring at him. Then he smiled, a slow cautious smile.

The old gentleman responded at once and laughed. 'You sound English!'

'No, sir, I'm not. But I've just come from China.'

The old gentleman looked interested. 'China, eh? Where?'

'Peking, sir.'

'Been a lot of trouble over there.'

'Yes, sir, that's why we came away—all of us, that is, except my father. He is in the siege.'

The old gentleman sat down carefully on a boulder placed

for the purpose. 'It is very nasty, all those Americans locked up there. The Chinese will have to be taught a good lesson, especially as we have always been decent to them—the Open Door and so on. What's your father doing in Peking?'

It was the question he had been dreading. He toyed for an instant with the idea of a lie and decided against it. 'I hope you won't think it strange, sir, but he's a missionary—Episcopal.' He wanted to explain but could not bring himself to it, that being Episcopal meant at least a Christian aristocracy.

He averted his eyes to avoid the inevitable look of disgust. To his astonishment the old gentleman was cordial. 'A missionary, is he? Now that's interesting. We're Christian Scientists. What's your name?'

'Lane. William Lane.'

He was as much disconcerted by approval as he might have been by rebuff. Before he had time to adjust himself the old gentleman said in a dry, kindly voice. 'Now you come on up to the house. Mrs. Cameron will want to look at you. You can talk to her about your father. She's interested in foreign travel. I'm pretty busy, myself.'

He stumped ahead of William, panting a little as the lawn rose towards the house. Behind him William walked gracefully, almost forgetting himself in his excitement. He was to enter this house looming ahead in all its white beauty.

'I have a son,' Mr. Cameron was saying. 'He isn't as strong as we wish he was and we have him here trying to get him ready for Harvard in the autumn—freshman.'

'I'm going to Harvard, too,' William said.

'Then Jeremy will want to see you,' Mr. Cameron said.

He paused on a wide white porch and William was compelled to stop, too, though his feet urged him to the door. Mr. Cameron's sharp small blue eyes roamed over the sea and the sky and fixed themselves upon the horizon.

'No storm in sight,' he murmured.

He turned abruptly and led the way through the open door into a wide hall that swept through the house to open again at the back upon gardens of blooming flowers.

'I don't know where anybody is,' Mr. Cameron murmured

again. He touched a bell and a uniformed manservant appeared and took his cap and coat, glanced at William and looked away.

'Where is Mrs. Cameron?'

'In the rose garden, sir.'

'Tell her I'm bringing someone to see her. Is Jeremy with her?'

'Yes, sir.'

'Very well.'

The man went silently towards the end of the hall and Mr. Cameron said to William, 'It is always warm in the gardens. Come along.'

He strolled towards the door and William followed him. His eyes stole right and left, and he saw glimpses of great cool rooms furnished in pale blue and rose. Silver-grey curtains hung to the floor at the windows, and flowers were massed in bowls. Here were his dreams. He lifted his head and smiled. If such dreams be real he would have them, someday, for his own.

The smell of hot sunshine upon fragrant flowers scented the air of the gardens as they reached the open doors. He knew very well from the garden about the mission house in Peking that only workmen could bring about the high perfection of what he now saw. Formal flower beds as precise as floral carpets stretched about him. A path of clean red brick led to an arbour a quarter of a mile away, and the arbour itself stood in a mass of late-blooming roses. The manservant emerged from the arbour and stood respectfully while Mr. Cameron approached.

'Mrs. Cameron is here, sir. I am to bring tea in half an hour, sir, if you wish.'

'Oh, all right,' Mr. Cameron replied carelessly.

They entered the vine-hung arbour, and William saw a slender pretty woman, whose hair was greying, and a boy of his own age. She was sitting by a table filling a wicker basket with roses. The boy was stretched on a couch, a book turned face down on his lap. He was tall, with light hair and pale skin and pale blue eyes.

'This is William Lane, my dear,' Mr. Cameron said. 'I found him lying on his stomach on top of the bluff, and he says he comes from China.'

'Do you really?' Mrs. Cameron exclaimed. 'How interesting!' She lifted large sweet brown eyes to William's face.

'I do, Mrs. Cameron,' William replied. 'I'm glad if it interests you.'

'This is Jeremy,' Mr. Cameron said.

The two boys touched hands.

Mr. Cameron sat down. 'I have a daughter somewhere, too. Where is she, my dear?'

'Candace?' Mrs. Cameron was busy again with roses. 'She went to the village to buy something or other. I begged her to wait and get it in town, but you know how she is.'

Mr. Cameron did not answer this. He looked at his son. 'Well, Jeremy, William is going to Harvard, too. Coincidence, eh? You'll have to get acquainted.'

Jeremy smiled. His mouth cut deep at the corners, was sweet and rather weak. 'I'd like to—but imagine China! Did you find it exciting? Do sit down. I'd get up, only I'm not supposed to.'

William sat down. 'It didn't seem exciting because I've always lived there.'

'Does it seem strange to you in America?'

'Not here,' William said.

'The Chinese love flowers, I suppose,' Mrs. Cameron said.

William considered. 'I didn't see very much of the Chinese, really. I grew up in a compound, and my mother was always afraid I'd catch something. But we did have chrysanthemums, and I remember the bowls of lilies our gardener used to bring before Chinese New Year.'

He felt he was not doing very well and his anxious instinct urged him to frankness. 'I suppose I should know a great deal about the Chinese, but one doesn't think much when one is growing up. The common people are rather filthy, I'm afraid, and the others are fed up with Westerners just now and didn't want to mix with us. There was even real danger if they did— the Old Empress didn't favour it.'

'A wicked old woman, from all I hear,' Mr. Cameron said suddenly. 'Trying to stop normal trade!'

'I do hope your parents are safe,' Mrs. Cameron sighed. 'What we've read in the newspapers has been dreadful. So shocking! As if what we were doing wasn't for their good!'

He was diverted from answer by hearing a clear young voice. 'Oh, here you all are!'

A very pretty yellow-haired girl was coming towards them. She was all in white and she had a tennis racket with low-heeled white shoes tied to it. At the viney entrance she paused, the sunshine catching in her hair and making a nimbus about her pleasant rosy face. She looked like Jeremy and she had the same sweet mouth but her lips were full and red.

'Hallo,' she said in a soft voice.

Jeremy said, 'Come in. This is William Lane. William, this is my sister Candy.'

She nodded. 'Do you play tennis?'

'I do, but I haven't my things.'

'Come along, we have plenty.'

'Candace dear—perhaps he doesn't want to——' Mrs. Cameron began.

'I'd like to, very much,' William said.

He rose. Tennis he played very well indeed. He had chosen it instead of cricket and his only chance for pleasurable revenge had been when a cricketer opposed him upon the immaculate coolie-kept courts at Chefoo.

'Come back again,' Jeremy said, his smile wistful.

'Do come back,' Mrs. Cameron said warmly.

Mr. Cameron was silent. Leaning against the back of the cushioned wicker chair, he had closed his eyes and fallen asleep.

Beside the girl William held himself straight and kept silent. His instinct for dignity told him she was used to much talk and deference. To his thinking all American women were pampered and deferred to far too much. Even the maids at his grandfather's house were sickening to him in their independence. In China an amah was not a woman—merely a servant.

94

'I hope you don't mind cement courts,' Candace said, as she gave him tennis shoes and a racket from a closet in the great hall. 'Ours are frightfully old-fashioned, but my father won't change them. I like grass but of course grass isn't too easy at the beach. Though my father could, if he would—only he won't.'

'I shan't mind,' William said.

'How old are you?' Candace inquired, staring at his handsome profile.

'Seventeen.'

'I'm sixteen.'

'Are you going to college?'

'No, of course not—Miss Darrow's-on-the-Hudson, for a year, and then I'm to come out.'

He had the vaguest notions of what it meant for a girl to come out, but now that he knew he was a year older than she, he felt more at ease. 'Shall you come out in New York?'

'Of course—where else?'

'I thought perhaps in London.'

'No, my father is frightfully American. I might be presented at the court of St. James, later. The man who was once my father's partner is the American Ambassador there.'

'I knew a lot of English people in China.'

'Really?'

'I didn't like them. Very conceited, as though they owned the country. Their merchant ships ply all the inner waters and their men-of-war, too. If it hadn't been for us, they'd have made a colony out of the whole of China.'

'Really? But don't they do that sort of thing very well?'

'They've no right to hog everything,' William said stiffly.

Candace mused upon this. 'I suppose not, though I haven't thought about such things. We've always been in England a lot—Mother and Jeremy and I. My father has no time.'

'What does your father do?'

'He's in the Stores—and in Wall Street—and that means he's in everything.'

They were at the courts now, two smooth wire-enclosed rectangles surrounded by lawns set with chairs and big umbrellas. No one else was about.

95

'It's too hot to play, and that's why no one is here,' Candace said carelessly. 'Two hours from now the place will be jammed.'

'I mustn't stay,' William said quickly.

'Why not?'

'In bathing things and a jacket?'

'It doesn't matter. We'll all bathe before sundown. There's a dance tonight. Do you like to dance?'

'Yes.'

He danced badly, never having had lessons, and he made up his mind to speak to his mother about it. Before he went to Harvard he must have lessons.

They were playing now, and he found within a few minutes that he could beat her, not easily, but surely. She played well, for a girl, her white figure flying about the court opposite him, though she served carelessly.

'I don't see how you hit the ball standing still,' she called to him at last with some irritation.

'I don't actually stand still,' he called back. 'I was taught not to run about; the sun was hot in China.'

'It's hot here, too.'

She flung down her racket at the end of an hour and came to the net to shake hands with him formally.

'There, that's enough for one day. You do play well. I have to go now and change. People are coming, and I'm dripping. You can leave the shoes and racket here.'

She did not again suggest his staying to tea and he withdrew, deeply wounded. 'Good-bye, then, I'd better be getting along.'

She waved her racket at him and smiled and left him to find his way alone. He ought not to have played so well, he supposed. For his own sake he should have allowed her to win. American girls were spoiled. Then he lifted his head. He would always play his best and he would yield to no one.

He went across the wide lawn and down the steps to the beach and turned homeward, his jacket over his arm and the sun beating down on his shoulders. The water was rippling over the sand and he walked in the waves curling in tendrils from the sea. At his grandfather's house he went in, carrying

96

plenty of wet sand upon his feet. Millie, the lesser of the maids, came out with a broom.

'Oh, look at those feet,' she exclaimed. 'Just after I've swept, too! I declare, Willum——'

They were alone and he turned on her with the fury of a young tiger. 'What do you mean by calling me Willum?' he hissed at her through white set teeth. 'How dare you? You have no more manners than a—a savage!'

He left her instantly and did not turn to see her shocked face. Half-way upstairs, he heard a door slam.

After a little while his mother tapped at the door of his room.

'Come in,' he said listlessly. He had bathed and put on fresh clothes and had sat down at his desk to write, toying with some verses.

'William,' his mother began. 'What did you say to Millie?'

He whirled on his chair. 'What did she say to me, you had better ask. She called me Willum!'

'Hush, William. Don't be so angry. She comes from Maine and everybody——'

'I don't care where she comes from. She can call me Master William.'

'She wouldn't call anybody master.'

'Then she needn't speak to me.'

'William, it's not easy living with all of us in this house. The maids aren't used to children.'

'I am not a child.'

'I know, but——'

'Mother, I simply do not intend to be insulted by servants.'

'I know, dear, but they aren't our servants.'

'Any servants.'

His mother sat down in a rocking-chair. 'In some ways it is really easier to live in Peking, I admit. But we are Americans, William, and you must get used to it.'

'I shan't allow myself to get used to that sort of thing.'

He was aware of her admiration behind her distress. She was proud of his spirit, proud of his looks, proud of his pride. She rocked helplessly for a few minutes and then got up. 'I'll give Millie something, this once.'

She went out of the room, and he was alone again. He was not writing verses to Candace. He was not attracted by her. He was writing something about a man's soul finding its own country, but he could not satisfy his fastidious taste in words. His poetry was not good enough and he tore the sheets into bits and threw them into the waste-paper basket.

The farm in Pennsylvania was as remote from the rest of the world as though it were an island in the sea. Nothing else existed. No one came near and the inhabitants never went away. The five children, of whom Clem was now one, made a human group, solid because they were utterly alone and at the mercy of two grown people, a man and a woman, who were cruel.

To Clem the memory of his dead parents and the two little girls who had been his sisters grew vague and distant. They had been killed by men he had never seen, a violence as inexplicable as a typhoon out of the southern seas. But here in this enchanting landscape the cruelty was mean and constant. There was no escape from it.

The man and woman, as he called them always in his mind, his tongue refusing to call them Pop and Mom, were animal in their cruelty, snarling at the helpless children, striking them in fatigue or disappointment. Thus when the spotted cow had a bull calf instead of a heifer, Pop Berger pushed Tim.

'Git out of my way!' he had bellowed.

Tim stepped back to escape the man's upraised fist but it struck him and he fell against the corner of the stone wall of the barn.

Clem saw all and said nothing. His watching eyes, his silence, the strangeness of his unexplained presence, kept the Bergers shy of him. They had not yet beaten him. His swiftness at work, his intelligence, superior to any in the house, gave them no excuse, and while with the other children they needed no excuse, with him they still searched for one. He rose at early dawn and went out and washed himself in the brook behind the house, 'the run' it was called, and then he went to the milking. He could not drink milk however hungry he was, and he was always hungry. The warm sweetish animal smell of milk sickened his stomach, the thick coarseness of the cows' teats in his hands disgusted him. Yet he treasured the stuff and learned to get the last drop from a cow, enough so that he dared to give the children a secret cupful apiece. The cup he hid behind a loosened stone in the barn wall. The children learned to come to him one by one, as soon as he began the milking, before Pop got out of bed. The cup of fresh milk stayed their lean stomachs until the breakfast of cornmeal mush. And the day went on in harshest labour, the thoughts of all of them dwelling always upon food.

Clem, always until now pallid and small, suddenly began to grow. His bones increased in size and he was obsessed with hunger. He would not steal from these strangers into whose midst he had fallen and therefore he starved. He imagined food, heaping bowls of rice and browned fish and green cabbage. In China God had given them food, and he had eaten. His hunger all but drove him back to praying to God again as his father had done. But his father had gone out to other people who had answered the prayers for God. Here there were no such people that he knew. It did not occur to him that God would work through such people as the Bergers.

He was stupefied by these human beings among whom he found himself. Who were they? Where were those to whom they were kin? No one came near the farm-house, neither friends nor relatives. In China all persons had relatives, a clan to which they belonged. These, the evil man and woman, the desolate children, belonged nowhere. Clem had no communication with them, for they said nothing to him or to each other except the few necessary words of work and food. The silence in the house was that of beasts. Nothing softened the hopeless harshness of the days, there was no change except the change of day and night.

Yet as one glorious day followed another Clem felt there must be escape. This was a net into which he had fallen, a snare he had not suspected. He must simply leave it. Whatever lay outside could not be worse than this. The desolate children seemed never to dream of escape, but they had no dreams of any kind, he discovered. Their hope went no further than to steal something to eat when Mom Berger was not looking, to stop working when Pop's back was turned. They were ignorant, and he soon found, depraved as well. When he first discovered this depravity he was sick. His own parents had been people of pure heart, and from them he had inherited a love of cleanness. Mr. Fong had been clean in speech and act. Though Clem had seen a simple naturalness in the behaviour of men in the countryside about Peking, it had been clean. Birth was clean, and the life of man and woman together was decent. There was nothing about it which he did not know as he knew life itself. But what he found here was indecency; the furtive fumbling of boys and girls who were animals. Pop grinned when he saw it, but Mom Berger yelled, 'Cut that out, now!'

She was a thick-set woman, her neck as wide as her head, her waist as wide as her shoulders, her ankles as big as her calves. She wore a shapeless dress like a huge pillow-case without a belt. Except sometimes when she went to town with Pop, she was barefooted. Clem had never seen the feet of a woman before. Chinese women always wore shoes on their little bound feet and his mother had worn stockings and shoes. In China it was a disgrace for a woman to show her feet. And so it should be, Clem told himself, avoiding the sight of those fleshy pads upon which Ma Berger moved.

For the first few days he had lived in complete silence towards the children. There was no time for talk, had he been so inclined. Pop took him upstairs into a filthy room where there was a wide bed, a broken chair, some hooks upon the plastered wall. On the hooks hung a few ragged garments. Pop scratched his head as he stared about the room. 'Reckon that bed won't hold five of you,' he had rumbled. 'You'll have to have a shakedown, I guess. I'll tell Mom.'

He went down the narrow circular stairs and left Clem alone. This was his return. He walked to one of the windows, deep set in the heavy stone wall, and gazed out of it to see the countryside beautiful. Long low hills rolled away towards the horizon and fields lay richly between. He had never seen such trees, but then he had seen very few trees. The northern Chinese landscape was bare of them, except for a few willows and a date tree or two at a village. This was a country fit for dreams, but he knew that whatever had been the dreams once held in this house, there could be no more. He tried to imagine his father, a boy perhaps in this very room, hearing the voice of God bid him go to a far country. Oh, if his father had not listened to God, he, Clem, might have been born here, too, and this would have been his home. Now it could never be that.

He heard heavy panting on the stairs, and Mom Berger's loud voice cried at him.

'Come here, you, boy, and help me with these yere quilts!'

He went to the stair and saw her red face staring at him over an armful of filthy bedding.

'Am I to sleep on this?' he demanded.

'You jes' bet you are,' she retorted. 'Lay 'em to suit yourself.'

She threw the quilts down and turned and went downstairs again, and he picked them up and folded them neatly, trying to find the cleanest side for sleep. He would have to sleep in his clothes until he could get away, for of course he would go within the next day or two, as soon as he found the name of a town or of a decent farm.

But he did not go. The misery of the four children held him. He had no family left, and in a strange reasonless sort of way he felt these pull upon him. He would go, but only when he had given them help, had found their families, or had found some good man to whom he could complain of their plight. His wandering and his loneliness made him reliant upon himself. He was not afraid, but if he left them as they were, he would keep remembering them.

In silence on that first day he had made his pallet and put his locked suit-case at the head of it. Into the suit-case he folded his good clothes, and put on instead the ragged blue overalls. Then he went downstairs.

The big kitchen was also the living-room. Mom Berger was

cooking something in a heavy iron pot, stirring it with a long iron spoon.

'Pop says you're to go out to that field yonder,' she told him, and nodded her head to the door. 'They're cuttin' hay.'

He nodded and walked out to a field where he saw them all working in the distance. The sun was hot but not as hot as he had known it in Peking, and so it seemed only pleasant. The smell of the grass and the trees was in his nostrils, a rich green fragrance of the earth. What was hay? He had never seen it. When he got near he saw it was only grass such as the Chinese cut on hill-sides for fuel.

He waited a moment until Pop Berger saw him.

'Hey you, get to work there! Help Tim on that row!'

Clem went to the sandy-haired boy. 'You'll have to show me. I've never cut hay.'

'Where'd you come from?' Tim retorted, without wanting to know. 'You kin pitch.'

Clem did not answer. He watched while Tim's rough claws grasped a huge fork and pitched hay upon a wagon pulled by two huge grey horses. It looked easy but it was hard. Nevertheless he had continued to pitch doggedly until the sun had set.

From that day on his life had proceeded. The work changed from one crop to another, but the hours were the same, from dawn to dark for them all. The girls worked in the house with the woman.

He became aware, however, of a certain day, dim in the minds of the children when he first came, which became more probable as the months dragged on. They expected a visit from what they called the Aid. What this Aid was Clem could not find out. He put questions to Tim, the eldest and most articulate of the boys. To the girls he did not speak at all. He felt a terror in them so deep, a timidity so rooted, that he thought they would run if he called their names, Mamie or Jen.

'Aid?' Tim had repeated stupidly. They were raking manure out of the barn. 'Aid? It's just—Aid. It's a woman.'

'Why is she called Aid?'

Tim considered this for a full minute.

'I dunno.'

'Does she help you?'

'Nope—never did. Talks to Pop and Mom.'

'What does she say?'

'Axes things.'

'What things?'

'Different—like does we work good, does the boys and girls sleep in one room—like that.' Tim grinned. 'They're scared of her.'

'Why don't you tell her?'

'Tell her what?'

'That you don't get enough to eat—that they hit you.'

Tim's wide pale mouth was always open. 'We're only Aid children.'

'What is that?' Clem began all over again.

'I tole you,' Tim said patiently. 'We ain't got no folks.'

'You mean you don't know where your parents are?'

Tim shook his head.

'Are they dead?' Clem demanded.

'Bump never had none,' Tim offered.

Bump was the second boy, now bringing the wheelbarrow to fill with manure.

'Bump, haven't you any kin?' Clem asked.

'What's 'at?' Bump asked.

'Uncles and aunts and cousins.'

'I got nawthin',' Bump said. He was spading up the manure that Clem had put into piles.

'Doesn't anybody come and see you?'

'Nobody knows we're here lessen the Aid tells,' Bump said.

'Then why do you all want this Aid woman to come?'

''Cause Mom gets a big dinner,' Tim said with a terrible eagerness. 'She don't say nothin' neither when we eat. Don't dast to.'

Clem threw down the fork he was using. 'If you'd tell the Aid woman they're mean to you, maybe she'd put you somewhere else.'

There was silence at this, then Tim spoke. 'We're used to

103

it here. We been here all of us together. Maybe Bump would get somewhere way off, and we're used to Mamie and Jen, too. They're scared to go off by themselves. I promised we wouldn't never say nawthin'.'

Clem perceived in this a fearful pathos. These homeless and orphaned children had made a sort of family of their own. Within the cruel shell of circumstance they had assumed with one another the rude simplicities of relationship. Tim, because he was the eldest, was a sort of father, and the others depended on him. Mamie, the older girl, so lifeless, so still, was nevertheless a sort of mother. As the days went on he perceived that this was the shape they made for themselves, even in depravity. The man and woman were outside their life, as unpredictable as evil gods. They suffered under them, they were silent, and they were able to do this because they had within themselves something that stood for father and mother, for brother and sister. Because of the family they had made for themselves out of their own necessity, they preferred anything to separation.

Clem asked no more questions, and judgement died from his heart. Something almost like love began to grow in him towards these children. He wondered how he could join them and whether they would accept him. He had held aloof because they were filthy and unwashed, because their scalps were covered with scales, because they had boils continually. He had thought of leaving them as soon as he could. But as weeks went on he knew he could not leave them—not yet. They were all he had.

He pondered upon their solitude. In China, whence he had come, all people being set in their natural families, there were no solitary children, except perhaps in a time of famine or war when anyone might be killed. If parents died of some catastrophe together, there were always uncles and aunts, and if these died, then there were first cousins and if these died there were second and third and tenth and twentieth cousins, all those of the same surname, and children were treasured and kept within the circle of the surname. But these children had no surname. He had inquired of Tim, and Tim had said after his usual moment of thought. 'It's writ down in the Aid book.'

'But what is it?' Clem had insisted.

'I—disremember,' Tim had said at last.

As the day when the Aid was to come drew near Mom Berger became more irritable. 'I gotta get this house cleaned,' she said one morning in the kitchen, when the children stood eating their bread and drinking weak, unsweetened coffee. 'The Aid'll be here come Tuesday week. You girls better git started upstairs this very day. Everything's gotta be washed—clothes and all.'

From that day until the Tuesday which was dreaded and anticipated there was no peace in the house or in the barn. Even the barn had to be cleaned.

'That Aid woman,' Pop snarled, 'she ain't satisfied to stay in the house. No, she's liable to come snoopin' out here among the cows. I'm goin' to tell her that's why I need more help, Clem. I'm goin' to tell her if I have to clean this yere barn I gotta have another boy. That's what I'm goin' to tell her.'

'How often does she come?' Clem asked with purposeful mildness.

'The law claims once in three months. She don't get round that often though—may be oncet, twicet a year. Always tells us before she comes. I git a postcard a month or so ahead.'

On the day before, they took baths. The woman heated kettles of hot water and in the woodshed the boys washed one after the other in a tub with soft home-made soap.

'You ain't hardly dirty, Clem,' Tim said with some admiration, staring at Clem's clean body.

'I wash in the run,' he replied.

'What'll you do come winter?'

'Break ice—if I'm still here.'

They all glanced at the door at these words. Tim whispered, his eyes still on the latch, 'You wouldn't go an' leave us, would you?'

Bump paused in the scrubbing of his piteous ribs. 'Clem, don't you go and leave me!'

'I don't belong here,' Clem said simply.

'You belong to us,' Tim said.

'Do I? How?' Clem felt a starting warmth in the inner desolation of silence.

Tim had one of his long pauses, shivering and naked. His shoulder bones were cavernous, and between his sharp hip bones his belly was a cavity. Pale hairs of adolescence sprouted upon his chest and pelvis. 'You ain't got nobody, neither.'

'That's so,' Clem said.

Tim made a huge effort of imagination. 'Know what?'

'What?'

'Sposin' we lived by ourselves on this yere farm—— You could be the boss, say, like you was our father.'

The woman's fist pounded on the door. 'Git out o' that, you fellers!' she yelled. 'The girls gotta wash.'

They hurried, all except Clem. He took the pail of cold water and doused himself clean of the water in which the others had bathed.

'Maybe I'll stay,' he said to himself. 'Maybe I'd better.'

In the night, in a bed cleaner than he had slept in since he came, he began to think about his strange family. Food was what they needed. He recalled the boys' bodies as he had seen them today naked, their ribs like barrel staves, their spines as stark as ropes, their hollow necks and lean legs. Food was the most precious thing in the world. Without it people could not be human. They could not think or feel or grow, or if they grew, they grew like sick things, impelled not by health. Everybody ought to have food. Food ought to be free, so that if anybody was hungry, he could simply walk somewhere not very far and get it. Food should be as free as air.

He began to dream about himself grown and a man, rich and independent. When he got rich he would see that everybody would have food. 'I won't depend on God, like Papa did,' he thought.

The Aid came just before noon. They had all been waiting for her through an endless morning. The barn was clean, the house was clean. Whatever had not been washed was hidden away until she was gone. The girls were in almost new dresses which Clem had not seen them wear before. They had on

106

shoes and stockings for the first time. Pop was in his good clothes, but he had taken off his coat, lest it seem that he did not work.

'Put it on when you sit down to table, though,' Mom ordered.

'You don't have to teach me no manners,' Pop said.

She sat all the time because she too had on shoes and stockings and her feet hurt. The girls had to bring her anything she wanted. She had on a grey cotton dress that was almost clean. Clem had put on his good clothes that the sailors had bought him. They sat about the kitchen smelling the food on the stove, their stomachs aching with hunger.

'Here she comes,' Pop cried suddenly.

Through the open door they all stared. Clem saw a small thin woman in a black dress come down from a buggy, which she drove herself. She tied the horse to the gate and came up the path carrying a worn black leather bag. Pop hastened to her and Mom got up on her sore feet.

'Well, well!' he shouted. 'We didn't really know when to expect you and we just went about our business. Now we're goin' to set down to eat dinner. I'd ha' killed a chicken if I'd been shore you was comin'. As it is, we only got pork and greens and potatoes. New potatoes though, I will say, and scullions.'

'That sounds good,' the woman said. She had a dry voice, not unkind, and she stood in the doorway and looked at them all. 'Well, how's everybody?'

'Pretty good,' Mom Berger said. 'The children look a little peaky on account of a summer cold. They like to play barefoot in the run, and I hate to tell 'em not to. You know how children are. Come and sit down while I dish up.'

'It's been a hot summer,' the Aid woman sighed. She sat down and took off her rusty hat. 'Well, I see they're growing.'

'That's another reason for their peakiness,' Ma Berger said. 'I keep tryin' to feed 'em up, but they don't fatten no matter how I do. Their appetites is good, too. You'll see how they eat. But I don't begrudge 'em.'

'I'm sure you don't,' the Aid said absently. She was searching through some papers in her bag. 'I guess I'd better begin checking now. I have to get on right after dinner. The territory is more'n I can manage, really. Let's see, you have five children. Why—the book says four!'

Pop began hastily. 'This yere Clem is a new boy. Just turned up one day and I kep' him, because he hadn't nowhere to go. I was goin' to tell you.'

'Boy, where do you come from?' The Aid was suddenly stern.

'From out West,' Clem said. He was standing, as all the children were. He had told none of them that he came from China. They would know nothing about China and he could not begin to tell them.

'You can't just come here like that,' the Aid declared. Indignation sparkled in her little black eyes. 'You should have stayed where you was. The state can't take charity cases from other states. It's going to make a lot of trouble for me.'

'I thought my grandfather was still alive,' Clem said. 'He used to live here.'

'Old Charley Miller,' Pop exclaimed. 'Him as hanged himself when he got to be sheriff.'

The Aid stared at Clem. 'You're his grandson?' she demanded.

'Yes.'

'Say, "yes, ma'am" to me,' she said sharply. 'Where's your proof?'

'I haven't any,' Clem said.

'He's Charley's grandson all right,' Pop said quickly. 'He's got the same kind of a face and his eyes is just the same colour and all. I'll guarantee him.'

'I don't know what to do,' the Aid sighed. She had a thin washed-away face and a small wrinkled mouth. Behind her spectacles her eyes were dead when the small flare of anger was gone. There was no wedding-ring on her hand. She had never been married and she was tired of other people's children.

'Why don't you just mark down five?' Pop coaxed her. 'It'll save you trouble.'

'I could do that,' she mused. 'One of the children in the last house died. I could just transfer the money from that one to this one.'

' 'Twould save you trouble,' he said again.

So it was done. Clem took the place of the dead boy.

They all sat down to dinner. On the table a platter of pork and greens was surrounded by boiled potatoes and by dishes of sweet and sour pickles. There were apple-pies to be eaten, too, and the children had milk from a pitcher, all except Clem who took water.

'You must drink milk, boy,' the Aid said. 'That's why it's so good for children to live on farms.'

'I don't like milk,' Clem said.

'Say ma'am,' the Aid reminded him. 'And it don't matter what you like. You make him drink it, Mrs. Berger.'

'I certainly will,' Mom promised.

There was no time for any talk. At the table there was only time for eating. The children ate desperately until they could eat no more.

'I see what you mean,' the Aid said. 'At this age they just can't be filled up.'

'I do my best,' Mom said.

When the meal was over the Aid rose and put on her hat. 'Everybody looks nice, Mrs. Berger,' she said. 'I'm always glad to give you a recommend. I don't believe I'll bother to go upstairs. I can go through the barn on my way out, Mr. Berger—though you always—the children are real lucky. Better off than in their own homes. What's that?'

Some noises coming from Tim stopped her at the door. He looked helplessly at Clem.

'He wants to know what his last name is,' Clem said for him.

The Aid's empty eyes suddenly lit, and she stepped towards him. 'Will you say ma'am when you speak to me?'

Clem did not answer, and Pop broke in quickly. 'I'll shore learn him before you git here next time.'

'Well, I hope so,' the Aid replied with indignation. She forgot Clem's question and went on briskly towards the barn.

The conscience in Clem's bosom was as concrete as a jewel and as pure. He felt its weight there day and night. It had grown with his growth and now had facets which were strange to him. Thus while his father's too simple faith had been its beginning, it had taken on accretion not of faith but of doubt, mingled with suffering, pity, and love, first for his father and mothers and sisters when they were hungry, and now after their death, pity for hunger wherever he found it. He, too, was hungry here on his dead grandfather's farm, but his hunger only hastened the growth of his conscience and made it more weighty. If he were hungry, what of these others, these children? For he perceived that Tim, though older than himself and inches taller, was and would always be only a child. Others must feed him as long as he lived and he would always be at the mercy of any man with a measurable brain. Mamie, too, was meek and mild, and Jen was an aspen of a child, trembling always with terror remembered and terror about to loom again. Bump was stolid and silent and he followed Clem like a dog. At night with dumb persistence he insisted upon sleeping beside Clem's pallet.

How could anyone know what was in any of them? They were obsessed with hunger. They dared not steal bread from the bread-box or left-over bits in the cupboard, but they did steal from the dog. Mom Berger scraped the bottoms of pots and the cracked bones and heaped them upon an old tin pie plate outside the kitchen door. There Clem, coming suddenly from the barn one day, found the four children, as he thought of them, waiting for the mongrel dog to eat its fill. They dared not snatch from the beast lest it growl and Mom Berger hear. But they were using guile. Bump, for whom the dog had a fondness, was coaxing him, though in silence, from his plate. When the dog looked up to wag his tail, Tim and Mamie snatched handfuls of the refuse. When they saw Clem's eyes fixed upon them they shrank back as though he might have been Pop Berger. This caused the conscience in him to burn with the scintillating flame he knew so well, a fire at once cold and consuming. He did not love these ragged children, he was repelled by their filth and their ignorance. The language they spoke was, it seemed to him, the grunting communication of beasts. Nevertheless, they did not deserve to starve.

Seeing them with the dog's food clutched in their hands,

staring at him in fear, he turned and went back to the barn. There he sat down again to his task of husking the last of the corn. Pop Berger lay asleep upon the haymow. Thinking of the work to come, Pop had yawned heavily after the midday meal. 'Reckon you kin finish the corn,' he had said and had thrown himself on the hay. Clem had gone to the house after an hour to get a drink. The pork and cabbage they had eaten had been very salty, but he had forgotten his thirst. His mind burned with the determination to escape.

'Of the thirty-six ways of escape,' Mr. Fong had once told Clem, 'the best is to run away.' It was an ancient Chinese saying, and it came back to Clem's mind now. He was Chinese in more ways than he knew. The early wisdom of people who had long learned what was essential had seeped into him from the days when he first began to know that he was alive. Courageous though he was, and with a tough natural courage, he knew that the first wisdom of a wise man is to stay alive. Only the dead must be silent, only the dead are helpless.

His father's conscience, too, was his inheritance—yes, and his grandfather's also. There were times when Clem went alone into the barn to stand and gaze at the beam that Pop Berger had pointed out to him.

'That there's the one he hung himself on.'

'Why did he do it?' Clem had once asked.

'Softhearted,' Pop had answered in accusation. He had added details later. 'The ole feller took a new rope he'd bought a couple days before to tie up a calf with. He had some kinda crazy notion if good men could git into the gov'-ment they could straighten things out. He didn't want the sheriff's job, though—wanted to give it up right away, but the party boss told him he had to keep it for the sake of the party, like. First thing ole man had to do was to close the mortgage on that there farm, yander.' Pop Berger's thick forefinger pointed next door. 'He wuz softhearted, like I said. He said he'd ruther die. Nobody took him serious, like. Doggone if the old man didn't mean it. Next day somebuddy found him hangin' dead.'

Clem never answered. Pop Berger could not comprehend the

only answer that he could have made. Of course his grandfather would rather die. It had been his way of escape from an intolerable duty. He thought a great deal about his grandfather, searching out about the barn, the house, the farm, the small signs of a conscientious, careful, good old man. The cow stalls, for example, were larger than most. There was room for a cow to lie full length in a stall. Pop fretted at the waste of room. There was a trough outside big enough for all the horses to drink at once. The water ran into it through an iron pipe from the well so that it was always fresh. In the house the step between kitchen and living-room had been taken away and made into a gentle slope. His grandmother had gone blind in her old age, Pop told him.

Heir of the conscience of his fathers, Clem could not be hardened by the miseries of his present life. Instead he felt a constant soreness in his breast, an ache of remorse for sins of which he was not guilty. This discomfort he now tried to heal superficially by helping the children to get more food to eat. It was not easy, and after some struggle within himself he decided, remembering the dog's dish, upon simple theft.

After the Aid woman had gone, not to return he knew for many months, even perhaps a year, he was angered to see how instantly the man and woman fell back into their careless cruelty. The meat was put away and the milk was watered. Yet he dared not complain. He, too, was now in the power of these two, and if they saw his courage they could prevent the escape he planned. His Chinese childhood had taught him never to be reckless even in anger, for anger is no weapon. Anger can give energy to the mind, but only if it is harnessed and held in control. Therefore he locked his anger behind his teeth and, having decided upon theft, he used a deep cunning. He stole food so cleverly that the man thought the woman had eaten some left-over, and she thought the man had taken it. Neither believed the other and they snarled at each other, while the blank faces of the children told nothing. It comforted Clem to know meanwhile that inside Tim's slack stomach there was a piece of boiled beef or a slice of home-cured ham, and that Jen had a lump of butter on a piece of bread. He was

112

just in giving out his booty, saving nothing for himself. At the table he had courage enough to eat more than the younger ones, and since he worked well and was seemingly obedient, Pop gave him more than he might have given. Milk, Clem stole without heed. In the pasture, hidden behind the brow of a hill, the children learned to come to him between meals, and he took a tin can from under a rock and milked a can full from one cow and another, never too much from one. Each child had a can full at least twice a day of the pure milk, warm from the cow's body. When they were strong enough, Clem told himself, they would run away together. It must be before the winter fell again.

When autumn came, he had supposed they would all go to school. Tim had told him that the law said they had to go to free school and even Pop had to obey the law. That would make it easy, Clem planned, for them to run away. They could be a day upon their way before night came and before Pop, finding that they did not come home, could report their escape.

But he had not counted on Pop's cleverness. Pop said one day in the barn, 'They ain't no call for you to go to school, Clem. You're too big.'

Clem looked up from the hay-chopper. 'I want to go to school.'

Pop chuckled. 'Yeah? Ain't nobody knows you're even here.'

Clem stared in silence, waiting. A frightful comprehension was stealing into his brain.

'See?' Pop said. He was picking his teeth after the noon meal and he leaned against a cow stall. 'You jest come here, didn't you? You don't belong nowheres, as I see it. School board don't even know you're alive.'

'I could tell them,' Clem said in a tight voice.

'Just you try,' Pop said.

Clem did not answer. He went on chopping the hay while his mind worked fast. This was the final reason why he had to go at once. He would wait no longer. To grow up in ignorance and loneliness was more than he could do. He had dreamed vaguely of finding people to help him, school-teachers whom he could tell of the misery of the children. Perhaps Pop had thought of that, too.

'We dassent tell the teacher anything,' Mamie had said once. 'Pop says he'd kill us if we told, and he would, too.'

'Yeah, he would,' Tim agreed.

'Well, ain't you goin' to say nothin'?' Pop inquired now.

'No,' Clem said. 'I've never been to school anyway.'

He kept his face averted and Pop saw only his bent, subdued body working at the hay-chopper, and he sauntered away.

But Clem, whose patience was the long endurance of those who have never known better, had suddenly reached the moment of decision. He would run away on Saturday when the man and woman went to the town to do their marketing. He must leave this desecrated house of his forefathers and he must take the children with him, for his own peace, for without him they would starve. Sooner or later they would sicken one by one, and then they would die because they were already half starved, their frail bodies struggling and scarcely able to live even when they were not ill. Where he would go he did not know, nor what he would do with them. Even though he found work, how could he earn enough to feed them?

He looked back on the days in Peking as sweetness he had not known enough to taste while it was in his mouth. He remembered the pleasantness of Mr. Fong's shop, the cosiness of the inner rooms where he had sat at the square table teaching Yusan. It had been a home rich in kindness and his eyelids smarted now when he thought of it. Of his own parents he would not think. He remembered them no more as they had been when they were living but only as he had seen them dead, and this memory he could not endure and he put it from him so far that it had become blankness. He could not remember even their faces. Mr. Fong's he saw clearly, and Mrs. Fong's face he saw always wreathed in smiles as it was when she brought in the cakes and meat rolls. He dreamed of that food.

Slowly, while his conscience burned, Clem made his plans. On Saturday, early, as soon as the man and woman had left the house, he would tell the children. He did not dare to prepare them earlier for they were too childish to be trusted. He would help them to gather their clothes together and tie them in bundles. They would take whatever food was left in the house.

Saturday morning dawned clear and cool. Hateful as his life was to him, Clem had fallen in love with the land. He woke early as usual, even before the heavy footsteps of the man shook the narrow stairs, and he put on his clothes and let himself out from the window upon the roof of a shed below and thence he dropped to the ground. At the stream he washed himself in a small pool below a shallow falls. The stream bed was of rock, slanted in layers so precise that when the falls rose after a rain, slabs came off like great Chinese tiles. He had taken a score or so of them and had laid them neatly at the bottom of the pool and when the sun shone through the water, as it did this morning, the stones shone in hues of wet amber and chestnut and gold.

The stream was out of sight of the house, hidden by a spinney of young sycamore trees, the children of a mighty old sycamore whose roots drove through the hill-side to the sources of water. Behind this wall of tender green, Clem stripped himself and plunged into the water, this morning almost winter cold. Above him the hills rose gently, the woods green but flecked with the occasional gold of autumn. The sky was beautiful, a softer blue than Chinese skies and more often various with white and moving clouds.

Yet where, Clem often asked himself, were the people upon this land, and how could it be that a house full of children at the mercy of a man and woman, ignorant and brutish, remained unknown and unsought? In China it would not have been possible for an old man's house to have been unvisited, or to have been sold after his death in so summary a fashion. He had asked Pop Berger once who had sold the house and had been told that it went for unpaid taxes. But why were the taxes not paid by some kinsman? How had it come to pass that his old grandfather had been so solitary, even though his son had gone so far? And why, and why, and this was the supreme question, never to be answered, had his father left his home and the aging man to go across the sea to a country he had never seen, where the people spoke a tongue strange to him, and there try to tell of a god unwanted and unknown? None of these questions could be answered. What Pop had said was true. There was no one who knew of his existence.

Clem stepped out of the small cold pool and dried himself by stripping the water from his body with his hands and then by waving his arms and jumping up and down. In spite of poor food he was healthy and his blood rushed to his skin with heat, and soon he put on his clothes and climbed the hill to the house. Pop Berger was already out at the barn, and Clem went in; without greeting he took a small stool and a pail and began to milk a brindled cow.

At first, accustomed by the Chinese to greeting anyone he met, he had tried to greet the man and the woman and the children when he first saw them in the morning. Then he perceived that this only surprised them and that it roused their contempt because they thought he was acting with some sort of pretence. He learned to keep his peace and to proceed in silence to work for food.

This morning there was none of the usual dawdling and shouting. Pop Berger harnessed the wagon early and began piling into it the few bags of grain he wanted to sell, and some baskets of apples. He left all the milking to Clem, and stamped away into the kitchen to eat and to dress himself. There the woman, too, made haste, eating and dressing, and within the hour the pair were ready to be gone, leaving the dishes and the house to the two girls.

'You, Clem!' Pop Berger shouted from the wagon seat. 'You can git the manure cleaned out today. Don't forget the chickens. Tim can do whatever you tell him. I told him a'ready to lissen to what you sayed.'

'And I've left the food you're to eat in the pantry, and that's all anybody is to have. Don't open no jars or nothin'!' Mom shouted.

Clem had come out of the barn and he nodded, standing very straight, his arms folded as he watched them drive off. He wondered that he did not hate them, and yet he did not. They were what they were through no fault of their own, their ignorance was bestial but innocent and their cruelty was the fruit of ignorance. He had seen degenerate cruelty sometimes in the streets of Peking. There the people knew, there they had been taught what humanity was, and when they violated what they knew, the evil was immense. But these two, this man and this woman, had never been taught anything. They functioned as crudely as animals. Where had they come from, he often wondered, and were the others all like them? There were no neighbours near, and he had no one with whom to compare them.

He finished milking the cows and carried the milk into the spring-house, where it would be cool. Then he went into the kitchen to find food. There, as usual when the man and woman were gone, nothing was being done. The bare table was littered with dirty dishes. Mamie and Jen sat beside it, silent and motionless in dreadful weariness, Tim slumped in Pop Berger's ragged easy chair. Bump was still eating, walking softly about the table, picking crumbs.

'Got breakfast for me, Mamie?' Clem asked.

She nodded towards the stove and he opened the oven door, took out a bowl of hominy, and sat down at the end of the table.

He looked at them, one and the other. Tim's lack-lustre eyes, agate brown, held less expression than a dog's and his mouth, always open, showed a strange big tongue bulging against the teeth. His body, long and thin, a collection of ill-assorted bones, folded itself into ungainly shapes. Mamie was small, a colourless creature not to be remembered for anything. Jen might die. The springs of life were already dead in her. She did not grow.

'Come here,' he said to Bump. 'I don't want all this. Finish it, if you like.'

He held out his bowl and Bump snatched it, went behind the stove on the woodpile, and sat down in his hiding place. Often the woman lifted the poker and drove him out of it, but today he could enjoy it.

'Listen to me, all of you,' Clem said, leaning on the table.

They turned their faces towards him.

'How would you like to go away from here?' He spoke clearly and definitely, for he had learned that only so did they heed him. Accustomed to the loud voices of the man and woman they seemed to hear nothing else.

'Where?' Tim asked, after a pause.

'I don't know—run away, find something better.'

'Where would we sleep?' Mamie asked.

'We'd take a blanket apiece, sleep by a haystack somewhere until we got ourselves a house, or some rooms.'

'What would we eat?' she asked again.

'I'd work and get money and buy something. Tim could work, too. Maybe you could find a job helping in a house.'

He had expected some sort of excitement, even a little joy, but there was neither. They continued to stare at him, their eyes still dull. Jen said nothing, as though she had not heard. She seemed half asleep, or perhaps even ill.

'Jen, are you sick?' Clem asked.

She lifted her large, pale blue eyes to his face, looking not quite at his eyes, but perhaps at his mouth. She shook her head. 'Awful tired,' she whispered.

'Too tired to come with us—out into the sunshine, Jen? We could stop and rest after we had got a few miles away.'

She shook her head again.

'If Jen don't go, I won't neither,' Mamie said.

'I ain't goin',' Tim said.

Clem stared at them. 'But you don't like it here,' he urged. 'They're mean to you. You don't get enough to eat.'

'We're only Aid children,' Tim said. 'If we went somewheres else it would be just like it is here.'

'You wouldn't be Aid children,' Clem declared. 'I'd fix things.'

'We'll always be Aid children,' Tim repeated. 'Once you're Aid you can't do nothin' about it.'

Clem was suddenly angry. 'Then I'll leave you here. I've made up my mind to go and go I shall. You can tell them

118

when they get home tonight. Say I've gone and I'm not coming back ever. They needn't look for me.'

They stared at him, Jen's eyes spilling with tears.

'Where you goin'?' Tim asked in a weak voice.

'Back where I came from,' Clem said recklessly. He longed unutterably to get back somehow to Mr. Fong's house in the familiar streets of Peking, which he had not known he loved. That was impossible, but to leave this house was possible. For the moment anger quenched his conscience. He had given them their chance and they would not take it. He had said he would take the burden of them on his own back, though he was no kin of theirs, and they had refused him even this hard way to his own freedom. Now he would think only of himself.

He leaped up the crooked stairs and took his suit-case and crammed his clothes into it. He had a little money left from the store the sailors had given him and he had kept it with him always in the small leather bag one of the sailors had made. This bag he had kept tied about his waist, night and day, lest the woman or the man discover it and take it from him. He paused for a moment to decide the matter of a blanket and then revolted at the thought of taking anything from this house. He would not even take bread with him. Alone he would be free to starve if he must.

Down the stairs he went again, carrying his suit-case. They were still in the kitchen as he had left them. None of them had moved. Their eyes met him as he came in, faintly aghast, and yet unspeaking.

'Good-bye, all of you,' he said bravely. 'Don't forget I wanted you to come with me.'

He drew his folded cap out of his pocket and put it on his head.

'Good-bye,' he said again.

They stared at him, still unanswering, and upon the strength of his continuing anger he strode out of the room and across the weedy yard to the gate which hung crooked upon its hinges. He leaped over it and marched down the road, his head high, to meet a world he did not know.

Despair drove him and lent him courage, and then the

beauty of the land lifted his heart. Surely somewhere there were kind people, someone like Mr. Fong, who would recognize him and give him shelter for a while. He would work and repay all that he received and some day he would, after all, come back and see the wretched children he had left in that kitchen.

He had gone perhaps a mile when he heard the sound of feet padding in the dusty road. He stopped and turning his head he saw Bump running doggedly along, and he waited.

'What do you want, Bump?' he asked the sandy-faced, sandy-haired child who blinked at him, panting. The signs of hominy were still about his mouth.

'I'm comin' with you,' he gasped.

Clem glared at him, for a moment resentful of the least of burdens. Then his conscience leaped into life again. Surely he could take this small creature with him, wherever he went, a younger brother.

'All right,' he said shortly. 'Come along.'

III

IN mid-August the newspaper head-lines had announced the end of the siege in Peking, and a cablegram from Dr. Lane brought the news that he intended to stay. The Imperial Court had fled, and the Old Empress had wailed aloud her hardships. She had not even been given time to comb her hair, and her breakfast on the day of the flight had been only a hard-boiled egg.

'Serves her right,' Mrs. Lane said briskly. 'Well, William, it looks as though I'll have to go back to your father. But you'll be able to manage by yourself if I get your clothes ready before I go.'

William went to Cambridge for his final examinations in September. He had missed the preliminaries but Mrs. Lane had herself gone to the dean with a certificate signed by the headmaster of the Chefoo Boy's School. She had so talked and persuaded and demanded that the dean was much impressed and granted her son a certain clemency, and William was admitted conditionally. He was confident that whatever promises his mother had made to the dean, he could in the course of four years fulfil. Indeed, he preferred not to know all that his mother had said and done for him. Thus he did not know, though he suspected, that the admirable arrangement he had made with Mr. Cameron to be Jeremy's room-mate, and when necessary his tutor, had taken shape first in the active brain of his mother.

Mrs. Lane, before she went back to China, had chosen a final Sunday afternoon to call upon Mr. and Mrs. Cameron. She had grown friendly if not intimate with them during the summer when William had gone almost every afternoon to play tennis at the house on top of the cliff. He had asked her to call upon Mrs. Cameron, stipulating that neither of his sisters nor his grandmother was to go with her.

'The Camerons are the kind of people I belong with,' he

had explained. 'I want them to know I have a mother I need not be ashamed of. Nobody else matters.'

Mrs. Lane was touched. 'Thank you, dear.'

The formal call had gone off well, and Mrs. Cameron had explained that she must be forgiven if she could not return it, since in the summer she made no calls. Mrs. Lane and William were, however, invited to dinner within the month. After the evening pleasantly spent by Mrs. Lane's talking about the Empress Dowager and the magnificence of Peking, it had occurred to the indomitable mother that a problem which had been worrying her much could now be solved. In spite of all her efforts, it was clear that William would be compelled to earn money somehow during college, and she could not imagine how this was to be done. She had inquired of the dean, and he had suggested waiting on table or washing dishes. This suggestion she had accepted with seeming gratitude but she knew it was impossible. William would not wait upon anyone nor would he wash dishes. It would be impossible to make him. She remembered the delightful evening in the great seaside house. It was a pity, she had thought, that the heir to all the wealth was only a pale sickly boy. William would so have enjoyed it, would have been so able to spend it well, looking handsome and princely all the while. She had thought deeply for some weeks, and had at last decided to call one last time upon the Camerons. She wrote a short note to Mrs. Cameron, was grateful for all the kindnesses of the summer, mentioned her impending return to China and how she feared to leave her boy so new and friendless here, and asked permission to come and say good-bye. When Mrs. Cameron telephoned her to say they would be at home on a certain Sunday, thither she went, at five o'clock.

The butler ushered her into the drawing-room, where Mrs. Cameron sat doing nothing while Mr. Cameron read the *Transcript*.

'Do sit down,' Mrs. Cameron said, and made a graceful motion with her ringed left hand.

'Thank you,' Mrs. Lane replied.

She had spent a good deal of thought upon her costume for

this occasion. It should be plain, but not poor. It must convey good taste and a civilized mind.

Knowing the ready impatience of the rich, she had begun upon her theme as soon as Mr. Cameron put down his paper to greet her.

'Don't let me interrupt your reading,' she said. 'I have come for a very few minutes to say good-bye—and for one more purpose. It is about William.'

'What's the matter with William?' Mr. Cameron inquired.

'He has always done very well in school,' Mrs. Lane said. 'We expect that. His father was graduated from Harvard *summa cum laude*. No, the concern is in my own heart. William is so young, so lonely. He has no one to take his parents' place. His grandparents, my father and mother, are old and they can scarcely understand him. They have the responsibility of the girls, too. My husband's parents are dead and the family scattered. If I could feel that William would be able to look to you and Mrs. Cameron for guidance—through Jeremy——'

'He can always come here,' Mrs. Cameron said in a mild voice. 'I'm sure there is plenty of room here.'

Mrs. Lane sighed. 'Thank you, dear Mrs. Cameron. I dread the long vacations. His father says he must work and earn part of his way, but what does William know about such things?'

'It won't hurt him to work,' Mr. Cameron said.

Mrs. Lane agreed quickly. 'That is just what his father says, and I am sure you are both right. Please, Mr. Cameron, for the first summer at least, could you help to find something suitable for my boy, something that will not lead him into bad company? He doesn't know his own American people yet.'

'Oh, well,' Mr. Cameron said. 'I can do that. There are always jobs waiting for young men, if they are the right sort. I supported myself entirely after I was fifteen, as a matter of fact.'

Mrs. Lane proceeded bravely to the most difficult part of her purpose.

'I am going to ask you something really bold, dear Mr.

123

Cameron. Do you think that William could be useful some-how to your son? Could he not perhaps look after him, help him even with his lessons? When—if, of course—he should be ill, William could look out for him, you know—go to his classes and take notes for him—that sort of thing.'

Mrs. Lane was faltering under Roger Cameron's stern eyes, and she looked pleadingly at Mrs. Cameron for relief. To her joy she saw a mild approval there.

'It might be a good idea, Roger,' Mrs. Cameron said.

'William's a proud sort of fellow,' Roger replied.

'Not too proud to help his friend,' Mrs. Lane said. 'William is a Christian boy, Mr. Cameron.'

Roger pursed his lips. 'How much do you expect me to pay him?'

Mrs. Lane knew her battle was over. She shook her head and folded her hands in her lap. 'Please don't ask me that, Mr. Cameron. I trust your judgement—and your generosity. I wish there need be no talk of money—it's so dreadful. Had my husband remained in this country instead of choosing poverty upon the mission field . . . but no matter!' She smiled sadly and changed the subject. After ten minutes of lively talk made up of news from her husband's recent letters, she rose to say good-bye. She clasped Mrs. Cameron's hand between both her own and smiled bravely. 'I cannot tell you how safe I feel now about William. I leave him in your care, dear friends.'

Mr. and Mrs. Cameron bowed, still looking a little bewild-ered. When the door had closed they sat down again exactly as they were before and Mr. Cameron picked up the *Transcript*. Neither of them spoke for a few minutes, and Mrs. Cameron gazed out of the window into the garden.

'It is a good thing that William Lane is so handsome,' she said at last. 'We really won't mind having him about. Candy says he is clever. I do hope he will always be good to Jeremy. Sometimes I think there is something cruel about his mouth. His hands are small for such a tall boy. Have you noticed that? I always think small hands mean cruelty in a man.'

She did not speak often but when she did a little rush of

124

words came from her lips, as though reserve had temporarily been removed.

Mr. Cameron listened, still reading the paper. 'It won't hurt Jeremy to have a strong young fellow around to keep him lively.'

Mrs. Cameron did not reply for some little time. Then she said, 'As for vacations, you must not forget that Candace is also in the house. The two of them, both being so healthy, will want to play games together . . . I shouldn't at all like her to marry the son of a missionary.'

'Candy will marry whom she pleases,' Mr. Cameron said. He loved his daughter and was proud of her, though with steady pessimism. Sooner or later the young always betrayed the old.

'Do keep quiet, there's a good girl,' he went on. 'This Bryan is putting me into a state, even on Sunday. He'll be the death of us all, talking about the Philippines. What does he know about those foreigners over there?'

Mrs. Cameron fell silent, and Mr. Cameron read the paper with fury, chewing the yellowed ends of his moustache.

The examinations were easily passed, for which William was grateful to the hard gruelling of English schoolmasters. He was practical enough to realize that he could also thank his own talents and ambition. It was intolerable for him not to do well and so he did well. When Mr. Cameron had asked him to come to see him, one day after his mother had sailed for China, he went with some excitement within, although with entire calm upon his surface. His mother had told him, not quite truthfully perhaps, what Mr. Cameron would talk about.

'He has some idea that you might be a sort of tutor for Jeremy,' she had said that last day. 'Don't get proud and refuse it, William. Remember the alternative is dish-washing or waiting on the college tables. Besides, no one need know. You will simply be Jeremy's room-mate and you will have the chance to live in those beautiful rooms. I don't think I could get you in there otherwise.'

125

The beautiful rooms, he had already discovered, were on that short and noble street called the Gold Coast. There the sons of the wealthy lived like young princes in suites of rooms with separate bedrooms, a private bath, and a shared living-room. Anything less seemed impossible to William. He made up his mind that he would accept whatever Mr. Cameron offered.

He was pleasantly grateful, then, when the offer was made. 'I leave it to you,' Mr. Cameron said, 'to see how you can help my boy. You know him pretty well now, don't you?'

'I think so,' William said, and he added quite sincerely, 'At least I like him more than any boy I've ever known.'

'That's good,' Mr. Cameron said with more heartiness than usual. 'Then you can help him, I guess. Keep him cheerful, you know—that's very important. We don't believe in medication. It's very important to believe in the power of mind over matter.'

'Yes, sir,' William said.

'Now,' Mr. Cameron went on. 'Will a hundred dollars a month be about right?'

'Whatever you say, sir,' William replied. He was startled by the amount, but he would not show his amazement.

'Well, if you find it isn't enough you can let me know,' Mr. Cameron said. 'And look here, one more thing, what say we keep this little arrangement to ourselves? It might make Jeremy feel queer with you. He's democratic and all that.'

'You mean just you and me, sir?' He thought of Candace. He did not want her to know that her father was paying him.

'Just us,' Mr. Cameron said. 'Of course, Mrs. Cameron knows the general idea, but she won't say anything if I tell her not to, and she isn't interested in details.'

'I'd like it,' William said. 'That is, sir, I'd like to forget it myself, so that I won't be thinking of money in connexion with Jeremy.'

'No, no,' Mr. Cameron said, quite pleased.

'I'll just ask him if he will let me room with him,' William suggested.

'That's right,' Mr. Cameron said. 'You fix it up and on the first of every month there'll be a cheque.'

The outcome of this was that when the two young men entered college, William found himself on the Gold Coast, with a bedroom of his own across the pleasant living-room from Jeremy's. Mrs. Cameron came with them and spent a week furnishing the rooms properly. There was even a small grand piano for Jeremy to use. William, secure in the monthly cheque, spent the money his mother had left him to buy himself a few luxuries that she had not been able to persuade the agitated mission treasurer to include in his necessities, a handsome set of razors, some silk pyjamas, a blue brocaded satin dressing-gown and leather slippers to match.

Thus William began his four years at college. He was reserved, modest, and dignified, and took his work with secret seriousness, though outward ease. He fulfilled exactly his every obligation to Jeremy and was at once kind and stern. He felt sometimes that Jeremy did not like him but he did not allow this to disturb him. The brilliance of his own academic standing was answer enough. Among the hundreds of young men who were matriculated at Harvard that year, William was notable. In prudence he made no close friends as the months passed, but he surveyed the Gold Coast carefully. It did not occur to him to search for friends outside that bright area. He marked here and there men whom he might cultivate as time went on. There was plenty of time.

Nevertheless, by Christmas he had approached a class-mate who attracted him above all others, a handsome fellow who lived in Westmorly, too careless to be ambitious for high marks with his professors, too self-confident to consider marks of first importance. He had already his group of friends, in the upper classes as well as among the freshmen, for he had prepared at Groton. He did many things well. He sang in the freshman glee club, he was a fine oarsman, and he was already marked for those clubs which William exceedingly desired to enter. Franklin Roosevelt was the man, William told himself, that he would like to have been, his father rich and his mother secure in her place in American society. Having everything, the gay and handsome boy could say what he liked, could believe as he felt, behave as he willed. In the election that autumn he was for Bryan, although his own cousin, Theodore Roosevelt, was running for vice-president, and he flouted England by raising money for the Boers. It was this high-handedness that won William's notice. He could not have taken sides against England even though he could not approve the Boers, or disapprove the English, and he envied the ease with which it seemed that Franklin did both, without liking the Boers or disliking the English. For some reason which William could not comprehend, there seemed to be such an overflow in this youth, such a limitless privilege, that he made a habit of believing that the poor, the uneducated, the miserable must be championed, although without hatred of the oppressor.

William knew nothing of South Africa. That he might prove to himself at least that the man he unwillingly admired was wrong he began for the first time in his life to read newspapers and to perceive, though dimly, how omnipotent they were. Even he was dependent upon them to shape his own opinions about the war. He was convinced from what he read that England was right and that the Boers were coarse farmers, ignorant dwellers upon the soil. When he announced this opinion, not to Franklin Roosevelt, but in his presence, he was answered only by loud though pleasant laughter. His opponent refused to argue. He did not care what William believed.

The tall young man did other things more amazing. He helped the men who lived in the Yard, in the cheap dormitories and in even cheaper rooming houses, and the day students, to organize themselves and win the class elections away from the little group that had always won them.

The Gold Coast inhabitants sneered. 'Anything to get himself popular!'

William listened and said little. He was cautious in the world of his own country, still so new to him, and being insecure and unready to take what he felt was his proper part, he hovered near the young Roosevelt who had no doubts and behaved like the prince of a royal house. He made his approach of friendship tentatively slight, a conversation in the dining-room at Memorial Hall, a chance to walk together to separate class-rooms. Roosevelt answered without assuming

128

superiority and was mildly interested to hear of William's birth in China. His own grandfather had made his fortune in China and his grandmother in her twenties had visited the fashionable parts of Hong Kong and Canton.

Upon this slight interest William built his hopes. Of all the young men he knew or saw, this one was most nearly his equal, most fitted for friendship. Why that friendship did not grow, why the hoped-for companionship faded, William never knew. It was a bud that did not bloom. Franklin Roosevelt's greetings were carelessly kind, but he had no time. There was never a time for talk, no time for companionship, and William, too sensitive, withdrew into cold and secret criticism. He was reminded of the English days in the Chefoo school. Because he was not allowed to love, he took shelter again in hatred. The fellow, he told himself, wanted to run the college. When both of them were chosen for the staff of the college newspaper, the *Crimson*, William felt himself freeze towards the young man who was still too happy to notice him.

On a cold day in January in William's sophomore year, his father stood on the balcony of Mr. Fong's bookshop. Dr. Lane knew Peking well, and the day before he had walked along the street judging each house for its view of the Great North Gate, through which on this day, the seventh day of the Western first month, the Old Empress with her Imperial Court was to return to the palace. Dr. Lane did not know Mr. Fong and it was by the merest chance that he saw above this bookshop the narrow balcony to which one must climb by a ladder, since it was merely a façade upon the roof. From it, however, was the best possible view of the great event of tomorrow.

Dr. Lane went into the bookshop and bowed to Mr. Fong, who stood behind the counter reading an old book he had bought from the library of a man recently dead. Since the man had no sons and none of the females of the house could read, there was no more use for a library.

'What can I do for you, Elder Brother?' Mr. Fong inquired. He was polite to all foreigners because, being a good man, he was sorry for everything that had happened. While he could not say that he was glad that his country was defeated, for he put no more trust in foreign governments than in his own, yet he grieved that foreigners and Chinese had been killed.

Especially was he ashamed of the folly of the Old Woman who had put her faith in the society of ignorant men called Boxers. She deserved the catastrophe that had befallen her when she had been compelled to flee the city in such haste, seventeen months ago. So impetuous had been the Court's flight, as Mr. Fong heard, that more people had been killed by the Imperial Guard in getting the Old Buddha out of the city than the foreign soldiers had killed when they came in. It was over at last, to the disgrace of all concerned, and pity to those dead, both Chinese and foreign, and especially the little children, and Mr. Fong was polite at the sight of a foreign face now that it was safe to be friendly.

Dr. Lane replied with equal politeness. 'I wish to rent a few feet of your excellent balcony tomorrow in order that I may see the return of the Empress Dowager.'

Mr. Fong was surprised. 'Elder Brother, are you and the elder brothers of your country pleased to see her return?'

'At least I am,' Dr. Lane said. 'I believe that the people need their government and I have every hope that the Empress will have learned her lesson and that she will allow the young Emperor to put in reforms.'

'Western elder brothers have more faith in women than we have,' Mr. Fong replied. 'Whether Elder Brother is right I do not know and it is always likely that I am wrong. I could not take money for the balcony. Pray use it as though it were your own.'

After some minutes of such talk, Mr. Fong finally accepted two taels of silver, which was not too much since the foreigners were eagerly buying whatever space they could find. Chinese would not of course be allowed to see the royal return. All doors were to be barred, all windows closed, and blue cotton curtains were even now being hung across side streets and alleyways, so that no common eye could look upon the Old Buddha. Foreigners could not be thus controlled since they were the victors in the brief war.

130

'You know, Elder Brother,' Mr. Fong remarked when the transaction was over, 'I feel more than usually unhappy to take silver from you because I had once in this house a clever small brother of your people.'

'Indeed!'

'Yes,' Mr. Fong said, stroking his sparse beard. 'He came to teach my son a foreign language. He did not take money for pay. Instead he asked for my foreign books, of which I have a few. Servants steal such books from their foreign masters to sell for a few coins, and that is how I got them.'

'Who was this foreign boy?' Dr. Lane asked.

'You remember the god-man who was killed, he and his wife and children? The one who was always begging for bread?'

'I do, indeed,' Dr. Lane said. He remembered very well that the Miller family had been found lying in their own blood, but the boy was not there, nor had he ever been heard of, although the American officials had made efforts to trace him.

'The boy was here,' Mr. Fong said solemnly. He tapped his polished wooden counter with his long finger-nail. 'Here he was in my house. He came early to teach my son. Thus he escaped death. Surely there was meaning in it. I have considered it a good omen for my house.'

'What became of him?' Dr. Lane asked with intense interest.

'He came back,' Mr. Fong said. 'And he told me what he had found in his own house. He stayed with us until he was able to escape. Then I told him to go east to the sea and to find a foreign ship and to return to his own land and his father's father's house.'

'That was very good of you,' Dr. Lane said. 'I shall report this to the American officials.'

'Please do not do so,' Mr. Fong said hastily. 'It is better not to tell anyone so long as the Old Woman is alive. She will come back smiling, as you will see tomorrow, but who will know what is in her heart?'

Who indeed could know? Dr. Lane himself would never wholly recover from the long siege within the Legation

Quarters. He had caught dysentery in the heat of that summer and was nearly dead when at last the soldiers from the West came surging into the city. When his wife came back to him from America, after William was safely in college, she had tried to make him give up China.

'Surely, Henry, you have done enough.'

'I have done nothing yet,' he replied. It was the beginning of the long struggle between them over whether China was worth his life.

'See how many foreigners have been killed!' she had cried passionately.

'Hundreds of us have been saved, and by six men,' he had retorted.

It was true. Jung-lu, the favourite of the Empress Dowager, had done all he could to save the foreigners from her fury. Yuan-cheng and Hsu Ching-cheng had deliberately changed the word 'slay', in the royal edict, to 'protect'. Li-shao, Liu-yuan, and Hsu Tung-i the Empress had put to death for opposing the war against the foreigners. And there were the noble host, those whom he never forgot, the thousands of Chinese Christians, more than two score of them of his own church here in Peking, who had refused to give up their faith and who died, martyrs for a god who to them was a foreign one.

No, Dr. Lane told himself steadfastly, it was beyond his wife's power, strong woman though she was, to move him from his own faith, not only in God but in the Chinese people.

'I will be here tomorrow,' he promised Mr. Fong.

Thus, on the next day, Dr. Lane stood upon the balcony, wrapped in a thick quilted Chinese robe inside of which he still shivered. Mrs. Lane had refused to stand there with him, when looking out from the window of their bedroom this morning, she had seen the city shrouded in yellow dust from the deserts of the north-west. A bitter wind was blowing, even then. Dr. Lane had been slightly exasperated to perceive it, for it added to the honour of the Imperial return. It was an ancient tradition in the city that whenever an emperor left his palace a strong wind would go with him, and would bring

132

him back again. Heaven itself seemed to be on the side of the Old Buddha.

While he waited on the balcony in the fury of the cold wind Dr. Lane thought of what Mr. Fong had told him. The Miller boy had doubtless done exactly what his Chinese friend had bade him. He might now be safely in America. He must write and tell William of the possibility. He had reported the story to the American officials yesterday, concealing Mr. Fong's name.

He glanced with concern at the great gate. There was still no sign of the royal entourage. Helen had been wise, perhaps, to content herself with seeing the Empress at the mighty reception which she was to give to her conquerors when she reached the Imperial Palace. Yet he did not want to attend it. He was not dazzled by her arrogant and heathen splendour. He hoped to see her as she came in the North Gate and to discern for himself whether she had repented. He had prayed solemnly that her heart might be softened for the good of the people. He did not honestly know whether such prayers were answered.

Everything was in readiness for the moment at the gate. Across the city the wide street had been cleared of all vendors and stalls and booths. The street had been swept clean and spread with bright yellow sand, yellow, the imperial colour. No common man was on the street. The imperial guard stood waiting, and princes and dukes were ready each with his own banner corps. Here and there down the street foreigners stood at windows, a few opened by permission that the visitors might witness the return.

Mr. Fong's head appeared above the edge of the ladder. He held out a small brass hand-stove. 'Take this, Elder Brother,' he whispered. 'I have put fresh coals in it.'

Dr. Lane took the hand-stove gratefully and before he could speak his thanks Mr. Fong was gone. Now he perceived certain signs. A line of Chinese heads would appear here and there over a roof-top, instantly to disappear again. Word was running through the city that the Old Buddha was near. She had descended from the train. For the first time in her life the

Old Buddha had ridden on a train, and with her, her court. She had not enjoyed it. The dust had been suffocating, the noise insupportable. When the whistle blew she had been terrified and indignant, and when she learned that this was the duty of the engineer she sent word by a eunuch that he was not to blow it without telling her before he did it. The railway from Poating to Peking had been destroyed during the war and rebuilt again under the foreign victors and the foreign soldiers had brought it into the very heart of the city, tearing great holes in the walls. The Old Buddha would not pass through these desecrated walls. She had ordered the court to alight outside and to enter their royal palanquins, that they might return to the city in proper state through the great gate.

Dr. Lane, holding the little hand-stove, heard a rising shout. A small army of eunuchs on horseback galloped from the gate. They wore black caps with red feathers and on the breasts of their robes were huge medallions of red and yellow embroidery. Behind them came the imperial herald, crying in a high voice that the Imperial Court was returned. All those officials waiting on the street fell to their knees and bowed their faces into the dust. Dr. Lane leaned on the frail banisters of the balcony and stared down into the street, and the destiny of this moment was impressed upon him. He watched everything, intent to remember it all, to tell William. He saw the Imperial Guard, followed by military officers. Great flags of yellow satin swirled in the wind, and upon each was embroidered a blue dragon swallowing a red sun. On either side of the flags were the imperial banners embroidered with the imperial arms.

Behind these rode the young Emperor, a sad young man, sitting within his yellow palanquin, which was lined with blue silk. The curtain was up and there he sat, his face unmoved, gazing straight ahead. He sat upon his crossed feet in the position of the Buddha.

'The sacrifice of youth,' Dr. Lane murmured to nobody. Death was already clear upon that tragic face.

But death had nothing to do with the Empress herself. He was indignant to see the redoubtable figure, seated in her great palanquin in the midst of her guards, followed by the young

Empress and the court ladies. Upon that gay and wicked old visage there was nothing but the liveliest pleasure. Seeing the foreigners who were her conquerors, she had put aside the curtains of the palanquin and waved her handkerchief at them. He was the more indignant to see some of the foreign ladies, among them he recognized Americans, too, wave back to the old sinner, laughing as they did so. Thus quickly was all forgotten.

He came down from the balcony and returned the hand-stove to Mr. Fong with thanks.

'How did the Old Woman look?' Mr. Fong inquired.

'She has not repented,' Dr. Lane said grimly.

'Did I not tell you?' Mr. Fong replied and he laughed, though his face was full of rue.

William Lane remembered suddenly in the midst of his preparation for a test in advanced English that he had not read his father's letter. He had got it in the morning with other letters, one of them from Candace, and hers he had read first. He wanted very much to be in love with Candace, and most of the time now he thought he was. The obstacle to his complete conviction was simple enough—herself. She expected from him a quality of attendance, a constant gallantry, which he found little short of degrading. For a woman to be beautiful was entirely necessary in his eyes. He despised his sister Henrietta for her plain face. Candace was beautiful enough to satisfy him, could he subdue her other less-attractive qualities.

At the moment, however, his relation with Candace was puzzling and exciting. He felt at a disadvantage, there was so much he did not know because he had not always lived in his own country. The secret hostility he had always felt towards his father for compelling him to be born the son of a missionary in China was now rising into a profound and helpless anger. In spite of this he loved his father in a strange half-hating fashion, and some of his darkest moods were those in which he brooded upon what his father might have been had he not heard the unfortunate call of God. Handsome in face, winning in manner, a leader of men, there was no reason, William thought when his fancy was rampant, why his father might not have gone into politics and even become the President of the United States. There was nothing wonderful about Theodore Roosevelt. William spent a good deal of time studying that bumptious angular face. Anybody could be President!

He pulled his father's letter from his pocket and saving the Chinese stamp for Jeremy, he tore the envelope and took out the sheets of thin paper, lined closely with the delicate and familiar handwriting. He was quite aware that his father always took pains to communicate with him on equal terms, and especially to tell him constantly what was happening in the land that had been left behind. William was too shrewd not to understand these pains. His father dreamed that the dear only son would come back to China, to be a better missionary than anyone had ever been before, to persuade the changing nation towards God. Some day or other, William knew, he would have to destroy this dream, but he had not yet the courage for it. He did not put it in terms of courage. He told himself that he was only waiting for the moment when it would hurt his father least. Now quickly and carelessly he read what his father had written slowly and with care.

'I told you of the pending return of the Court. Now it has come. It was a strange and barbaric sight, a motley crowd of rascals ruled over by a feminine tyrant, and yet somehow there was magnificence in it, too, a sort of wild and natural glory, the atmosphere which the Chinese can manage so well in whatever they do. The Old Empress is too great a person, in spite of her monstrous evil, to remain ungenerous. She has acknowledged her defeat, if not her fault, and now she sees that she must begin reforms for the people. Even before the return she issued an edict demanding that the officials of the empire immediately learn all about political science and international law. She has given them six months in which to complete this task, upon pain of death. Six months. There speaks the old ignorance and the new!

'Perhaps more exciting, because more practicable, is the fact that she has appointed a commission to draft a public school system, the first that China has ever had. Some day the old examinations will be entirely abolished and China will be modern. It may happen before you finish college, dear boy, so that when you come back it will be to another country altogether, one which you can help to build.

'But I do not wish to speak only of China. Tell me about yourself at college. What you say of Jeremy seems pleasant and good. What fortune to find such a friend! I had feared loneliness for you. The young can be so cruel to those who have not their exact experience. Give him my warm regards.

'Your mother is writing you tomorrow, she says, about the reception which the Old Empress held for all the foreigners. It was a great affair. All the diplomats and their wives went and so far as I can learn from your mother, the Empress behaved exactly as though she had won the war and was graciously meeting her captives and freeing prisoners. So successful was she that a number of ladies capitulated to her frightful charm. I myself refused to go. I could not stomach having to be polite to that female personification of the Evil One. Your mother was not so scrupulous and apparently enjoyed herself.'

His father's letters always took him back to China, however much he might resist. He could see clearly that bold figure of the Old Empress, great enough to accept defeat lightly and so be still imperial, still powerful. There was power in her which William felt was sacred, compelling a quality in himself which might be a similar power. As he grew into manhood to his full height of six feet one, he felt the excitement of his ambition surging into his body and his mind. He was drawn always to the powerful and the proud. Once he had passed the famous president of the university crossing the yard with an enormous water-melon under his arm, and he never felt the same respect again for him. Whatever the genius of Charles Eliot, and William acknowledged genius, it was lessened by the man's lack of pride. Nothing could have persuaded William to carry even a bundle under his arm.

Indeed, few of his professors fulfilled his secret expectations.

It was hard to give high respect to a pudgy philosopher with a big head thatched with rough yellowish-grey hair covered with an old tired-looking hat, or a little man with a high forehead and a shaggy dishevelled moustache. Two men alone satisfied his instinct for dignity and seriousness. One was a great handsome German who looked like the Kaiser and taught psychology with the voice of a thundering god. The other was a tall slender man, a Spaniard, whose eyes were dark and cold. Under George Santayana alone William sat with complete reverence. The man was an aristocrat.

The same absolute and delicate pride he had seen long ago in the Chinese Empress, a quality which could not stoop to common folk. For William democracy meant no more than that from among the common mass a king might arise, a Carlylean hero, a leader unexplained. People tried to explain such persons by many myths of virgin births and immaculate conceptions. Chinese history, he had often heard his father say, was rich with such myths. The unexplained great men, born of ordinary parents must, the people felt, be the sons of gods.

In the dark depths of his emotions William acknowledged the possibility of explanation. How explain himself? There was no one in his family like him. He could not be explained any more than the Chinese Empress could be, for she was born the daughter of a common small military official. Somewhere in the path of the generations, certain genes met to make the invincible combination. He would never forget the haughty face of the indomitable ruler bent above him, a young American boy. It had been his first glimpse of greatness and it remained in him, a permanent influence.

So William created his world in his own image. The sons of gods were the saviours of mankind and they lived upon the Gold Coast, anywhere in the world.

William folded his father's letter and saw on the back of the sheet one further note:

'By the by, here is something interesting. You remember the Faith Mission family Miller, who were killed by the

Boxers. Actually the boy escaped. Quite by accident I met a Chinese who had saved his life and sent him on his way to the coast. From there, if he got a ship, he may have reached America safely—may be there now, under God's care.'

This news did not interest William. That brief and humiliating moment in the dusty Peking street was repulsive even in memory. He crushed the letter in his hand and threw it into the wastepaper basket under the desk.

In William's junior year he reached his final hatred of Franklin Roosevelt when Roosevelt was chosen president of the *Crimson*. William had supposed himself secure for the place and he did not know why he had failed. He was not able to hide his disappointment from Jeremy, always quick to feel suffering in anyone else.

'Sorry, William,' Jeremy said. 'You would have done a magnificent job.'

'It doesn't matter,' William said with a grimace.

'Don't be ashamed of feeling,' Jeremy said gently.

William allowed a few words to escape from his vast inner misery. 'It seems unjust that I shouldn't get it, and that fellow got it so easily.'

He saw Jeremy looking at him with a peculiar and pitying gaze and he averted his eyes.

'I'd like to say something to you, William, if you'll let me,' Jeremy said after a moment.

'Well?' William heard his own voice harsh.

'Perhaps we can't say such things to each other. We never have, somehow. Perhaps if we could we would both feel better.'

'Say what you like,' William said. He sat down abruptly at the desk and pretended to fill his fountain-pen with ink.

'Roosevelt has got everything he wanted because he is warm towards everybody. He is full of a sort of—of love, if you know what I mean.'

'I'm afraid I don't,' William said. 'He is full of loose ideas, so far as I am concerned.'

'I know some of his ideas are crazy,' Jeremy admitted. 'But everything else about him is so right that he can just about think as he likes.'

William dropped the pen and it fell on the floor. His grey eyes were furious under his black brows and his lips tightened. 'I suppose you mean his father is rich, his mother is socially correct, they live on the right street, all the sort of things that I haven't!'

'You know I don't mean that,' Jeremy said. 'We'd better drop it.'

They had dropped it and he was too proud to tell Jeremy that he did know what he meant. For William was beginning to know that he lacked one grace among his gifts. He could not win love from ordinary people. He excused himself by saying that it was because they felt his superiorities, his obvious mental power, his ability to do easily what others did only by effort. The superior man, he told himself, turning the pages of his Nietzsche, must always be hated by his inferiors, but even this hatred could be turned to advantage and used as a tool for further power for good.

'I must expect hatred,' William thought. 'I must accept it as my due because I am not understood. What the common man cannot understand he hates.'

Sometimes he thought even Jeremy hated him. But such moments passed and he was careful to seem kinder to his friend, more quick to help him, more patient with his frailties, his headaches, his manners.

William, relentlessly remembering his defeat, was further disturbed by an editorial in the *Crimson* before the class elections. Roosevelt wrote:

'There is a higher duty than to vote for one's personal friends, and that is to secure for the whole class leaders who really deserve the positions.'

These were the words of a man determined to be a liberal in spite of class and property. While the Gold Coast repudiated them, votes belonged to the many.

William never forgave Franklin Roosevelt. He had already begun to believe that the people anywhere in the world were clods and fools and now he was convinced of their folly. The Boers who fought England were clods and fools. The Chinese he remembered upon the streets of Peking were clods and fools. From now on he spoke to no one at Harvard except those who lived on the Gold Coast.

Yet he heard one day a remark that horrified him again. A pallid professor with long moustaches said these words with an emphasis too fervent for William's taste: 'The American people control their own destiny.'

William began then in earnest the study of the history and government of his own country. He perceived to his dismay that the professor's remark was a true one. Clods and fools though they might be, the American people elected their rulers, laughed at them, despised or admired them, obeyed or disobeyed them, clung to them or rejected them. He began after that to look at the people he passed on the street with consternation and even fear. Out of ignorance apparent upon their faces, obvious in their crude speech, these men chose from among themselves certain ones upon whom they bestowed the powers of state. It was monstrous. For months William felt himself in a den of lions. He tried to talk to Jeremy, who first laughed at him and then tried to explain:

'Americans aren't just people—they are Americans.'

William had no such reverence. What he saw beyond the Gold Coast reminded him ominously of the streets and roads of China. He had feared the common people there. Had they not risen up in all their folly against men like his father? Von Ketteler had been murdered by an ignorant clod. He remembered that dignified German, who at the Fourth of July celebrations at the American Embassy had more than once spoken to him with courtesy. The common people could rise against their betters anywhere and kill them, unless they were taught and controlled.

Yet, how to control these boisterous, independent, noisy jokesters who were the common folk of his own country? They would not tolerate a real ruler. They had no respect for those above them. They delighted to pull down the great and destroy them. Look at Admiral Dewey, a hero for an hour, whose plaster triumphal arch, designed for marble, fell to dust and was carted away by the garbage collectors! The whim of the people was the most frightening force in the world.

Upon this William pondered, knowing now his own lack of charm, that strange senseless power to attract his fellows, the charm which young Franklin Roosevelt possessed as easily as he possessed height, fearlessness, and ready laughter. Without this frail gift, William told himself proudly, he must rely upon his brains and devise a means of teaching and controlling the wild beast of the multitudes. He would lead them wisely, insidiously, charming them through words, himself never seen.

In that third year in college he wrote to his father to say that he would not come back to China. 'I feel I am needed more here than there. The truth is, I am not impressed by American civilization. I intend to start some sort of newspaper, something ordinary people will read, or at least look at, and so do what I can to enlighten my fellow countrymen.'

Some day, William vowed to his own heart, he would be the editor and owner of a newspaper, perhaps even a chain of newspapers, by which he could defeat any man he disliked or disapproved. To dislike was to disapprove. Money, of course, he must have but he would get it somehow. Quite stupid men were able to get rich.

Meanwhile, Franklin Roosevelt did not win the Phi Beta Kappa key, and William felt assuaged when he himself was among the chosen.

Yet the college years, as they passed, were good ones. He became a member of the Cameron family and spent his vacations with them, after brief duty visits to his grandparents and his sisters. It was accepted now that William was independent and different. Henrietta was proudly silent with him, Ruth worshipped him timidly, and his grandparents tried, somewhat in vain, to treat him as an ordinary young man. They knew he was extraordinary. Even Mrs. Cameron saw that now. It was pleasant to have about her a handsome young man who knew how to dress and was always ready to do what she needed done. He paid little attention to Candace, she reflected after each vacation, and he behaved like a strong elder brother to her poor son. She introduced William to the ladies at her Christmas 'At Home' and forgot to mention that his father was a missionary, leaving the impression that he was connected with the diplomatic corps in Peking. William did not correct her.

His dreams hovered about the many happy weeks he spent in the great square house on Fifth Avenue. Each summer he accepted a job that Mr. Cameron offered him. He went to Europe with Jeremy, a combination secretary and guide, and they shared a valet. Together the two young men wandered about old cities and sailed the Mediterranean. It was a matter of course that William would always go home with Jeremy when the journey was over. He had his own two rooms in the vast Cameron house. They opened into Jeremy's suite. From there he seldom wrote to or heard from his sisters and his grandparents, and Peking he had nearly forgotten. The Camerons had become his family.

He thought about the Camerons a great deal, pondering again the question of how, through them, he might reach vague heights he imagined but could not see. Among the many things he discussed with Jeremy this was not one. William was not crude. He had lived too long among Chinese, even though only servants. He felt crudity in his mother and shrank from it, but he forgave her because of her willingness to sacrifice. His mother was 'for' him, as he put it, and when he discovered this quality in any person, he overlooked all else. Nevertheless he was glad that during his college years his mother was remote in Peking. He was still not yet sure that the Camerons were entirely 'for' him, not even Jeremy. This uncertainty made him pleasantly diffident and unselfish in his dealings with each of them. To Jeremy, he gradually became someone always willing to spare him tiresome stairways when he wanted a book from the library, and so he wore away dislike. To William's listening silence Jeremy in vacations talked more freely than at college, uncovering a delicate and poetic mind, racked with questions, and a spirit confounded by conscience. Thus Jeremy spoke on the solid matter of money.

143

'I know that if my father had not been rich I would now have been dead. But I wish I could owe my life to something else.'

'Perhaps you might say that you owe it to your father's being so able as to get rich,' William had suggested.

'I don't know that merely being able to get rich is anything particularly noble,' Jeremy had replied.

'Not everyone can do it, nevertheless,' William said. 'Your father must have had some natural gift.'

A look of aversion came upon Jeremy's pale and too mobile face. 'The gift is only that of being able to overcome someone less strong in the competitive game.'

To this William put up silence, and into the silence Jeremy continued to talk. 'Sons of rich men always complain of their father's riches, I suppose. Yet there ought to be some way of living without stamping all the ants to death.'

Still William made no answer. Jeremy had come to no grips with life. The trouble with Jeremy was that he wanted nothing. He himself wanted everything; success with the newspaper he meant to have, and after that a wife beautiful and wealthy, a mansion to live in, a place in the world where he could be unique in some fashion he did not yet know, and the means to all this, he perceived, was money. He was perfectly sure that money was what he wanted first of all.

In his quiet way he reflected further upon the Cameron family. His brotherly relation to Jeremy he could easily develop. Quite honestly, he liked Jeremy. Candace he would consider as time passed. He was too nearly an intellectual to be in haste for marriage. Mrs. Cameron he understood and did not fear. His thoughts, flying like tentative grey hawks, now lit warily near the image of Mr. Cameron. This man was the central figure, the most important man, the one whom he must approach with real finesse. Mr. Cameron knew secrets. Pondering upon that vague and unimpressive person, William perceived that behind the nondescript face, the long and narrow mouth, there was something immense, a power strong and profoundly restrained. He guessed by some intuition of like mind that Mr. Cameron never told his true thoughts to his family, certainly at least not to women, and probably not to his over-sensitive and delicate son. Into that loneliness William determined to go, not with deceit but with honesty.

'Mr. Cameron,' he said on Easter Sunday, 'I would like to ask your advice about something.'

'Why not?' Mr. Cameron replied. Sunday was a day on which he drowsed. It was now afternoon, however, and late enough for him to have recovered from the immensities of dinner. He had slept, had waked, had walked in the garden with his wife and daughter to see the promise of some thousands of daffodils, and had come in again to re-read the newspaper in the small sitting-room off the drawing-room, which was his favourite resting place. There William had come, after waiting patiently in his own room, from which he could see the prowling among the daffodils. Jeremy and Candace had gone with their mother to see their grandparents.

He sat down at a respectful distance from Mr. Cameron and upon a straight-back chair. His childhood in Peking had taught him deference to elders, and he would not have been comfortable had he chosen one of the deep chairs upholstered in brown leather.

'I would like to talk about my future, sir,' he said.

'What about it?' Mr. Cameron asked. His eyes roved to the newspaper at his feet. The financial section was uppermost and he was disgusted to see that the profits of a rival company had risen slightly above those of his own.

'I want to get rich,' William said simply.

Mr. Cameron's grey eyebrows, bunched above his eyes, quivered like antennæ. 'What do you want to get rich for?' he demanded. He stared at William with something more than his usual careless interest.

'I see that here in America a man cannot get any of the things he wants unless he is rich,' William replied.

Mr. Cameron smiled and agreed suddenly. 'You're damn right!' He kicked the newspaper from his feet, sat back, and felt in his pocket for a cigar. It was a short thick one, and he lit it and puffed out a cloud of blue and fragrant smoke. The vague barrier that stood always between himself and his son's friends fell away. He felt he could talk to William. He had always wished that he could talk to young men and tell them the things he knew. If an older man had talked to him when he was young he would have got along faster.

'I'll tell you.' He shifted his cigar to the corner of his mouth. 'If you want to get rich, William, you'll have to quit thinking about anything else. You'll have to concentrate. You have to put your mind to it.'

'Yes, sir.' William sat at attention, his hands folded upon his crossed knees. They were small hands, as Mr. Cameron remembered his wife had said they were, and they were already covered with surprisingly heavy black hair. William's hair on his head was black, too, in contrast to his light grey-green eyes. An odd-looking boy, Mr. Cameron reflected, though so handsome.

'Have you thought of any special line?' Mr. Cameron asked.

William hesitated. 'Did you, sir, at my age?'

'Yes, I did,' Mr. Cameron replied. 'That's the trick of it. You have to think of something that people want—not a few rich people, mind you, but all the ones who don't have much money. You have to think of something that they must buy and yet that won't cost too much. That's how I thought of the Stores. I was clerk in a general store.'

William knew the Cameron Stores very well. There was one in almost every city. He had wandered about them more than once, looking at the piles of cheap underwear and kitchen utensils and groceries and dishes and baby carriages and linoleum, everything that an ordinary family might want and nothing that Mrs. Cameron would have had in her own house. It was repellent stuff.

'I've thought of a newspaper,' William said.

Mr. Cameron looked blank. 'What about a newspaper?'

'A cheap newspaper,' William said distinctly. 'With lots of pictures so that people will first look and then read.'

'I never thought of such a thing,' Mr. Cameron said. He stared at William, digesting the new and remarkable idea. 'There are already plenty of newspapers.'

146

'Not the kind I mean,' William said.

'What kind do you mean?' Mr. Cameron asked. 'I thought I knew about every kind there was.'

'I suppose you do, sir,' William said. 'What I am thinking of though, is new for America. I got the idea from England— and a little bit, perhaps, from the *New York World*, and then the *Journal*. But I didn't think of doing anything myself until I began to hear about Alfred Harmsworth in England. Have you seen his papers, sir?'

'No,' Mr. Cameron said. 'When I'm in London I always read *The Times*—maybe look at the *Illustrated Times* on the side.'

'My paper,' William said, as if it already existed, 'is what's called tabloid size and it is to have everything in it that can interest the masses. It won't be for people like you, Mr. Cameron. It will have plenty of pictures. I've noticed even in college that most of the men don't really read much but they will always look at pictures.'

'I hope you don't mean yellow journalism,' Mr. Cameron said severely.

'No, I don't,' William said. 'I hope I can do something more subtle than that.' He paused and then went on thoughtfully, his eyes on the patterned carpet. 'I thought, if you approved, I would talk with Jeremy about it and some day we might go in on it together.'

Mr. Cameron was pleased. It might be the very thing for Jeremy, easy work, sitting behind a desk. He had often wondered what to do with his fragile son, but he was too prudent to show approval. 'Well, it would depend on what Jeremy wants. Newspapers cost a lot of money to start.'

William was calm. 'That's why I want to get rich.' He was too wise to repeat what his mother had often told him, even before he went to Chefoo. His mother had sown in him early the seeds of common sense. 'You can't have but so many friends,' she had said. 'And each friend ought to count for something.' He had seen the folly of useless friends in the English school; his speaking acquaintance there with the British Ambassador's son had served him more usefully than the horde of missionaries' children.

At college he had selected from among Jeremy's friends three whom he was transferring to himself, Blayne Parker, Seth James, and Martin Rosvaine. Blayne William still doubted because he was a poet, and Jeremy supplied to him something that William knew was not in himself. Seth and Martin he was resolved to keep. Yet there was no reason why the five of them, Jeremy included, should not stay together after college. Seth's father alone could, if he would, supply the capital they would need. Meanwhile he was getting into their clubs.

'Got it all figured out, eh?' Mr. Cameron said. A look of admiration came over his face, mingled with reluctance. If Jeremy had been this sort of fellow, he would have got him into the Stores. Invitation was on the tip of his tongue. 'How would you like——' He swallowed the words. William would be too smart, maybe, ten years from now when he himself was getting to be an old man. He might not be able to cope with that new young smartness in case it opposed him. It was all right to give young men a chance, but not the whole chance. On the other hand, William might be the making of the Stores, at the time when he needed somebody. If the boy married Candy, for example, it would be almost as good as though he were born into the family. This would take time to think out. He leaned back and crossed his hands on the small paunch that hung incredulously on his lean frame. 'When the time comes,' he said dreamily, 'I might be able to do something myself, William. Only might, that is. I can't tell from year to year, government being what it is in this country.'

William rose. 'I wouldn't think of such a thing, Mr. Cameron,' he said in a firm and resonant voice. 'I'm sure I can stand on my own feet.' It was entirely the proper answer, although he felt that the time would come when he would need Mr. Cameron. Far better to owe money to Mr. Cameron than to the father of Seth James.

Before Mr. Cameron could reply, the door opened and Candace came in looking, her father thought fondly, like the morning star. She was all in rose and silver and wrapped in soft spring furs of white fox. Her cheeks were pink with the wind, for she had insisted on having the carriage windows open, and her yellow hair was curled about her ears and feathered over her forehead.

'Why have you two hidden yourselves away here?' she demanded. 'Mother says please come out at once and be public. We have callers.'

'We've been talking business,' Mr. Cameron said. It was his instinctive reply to any demands from women.

'Nonsense,' Candace said. 'William hasn't any business.'

'He has an interesting idea,' Mr. Cameron said, fitting the tips of his fingers together. 'A very interesting idea.'

Then he got an idea himself. He rose and made haste with his slow step towards the door. 'I'll go, just to please your mother. William doesn't have to be bothered with our friends unless he wants to. I'll bet it's the Cordies, anyway.'

'It is,' Candace said, with dimples.

'Don't you come, William,' Mr. Cameron said. 'They won't remember you next time they see you, anyway.'

Thus he left these two young members of his society together, and went his way inwardly pleased. Candace could be trusted. She wouldn't let even her own husband do the family any damage. He was long used to eating his cake and having it too. The secret of such manoeuvring had laid the foundation of his fortune—that and the resolute ignoring of the misfortunes of others. Maybe when the time came he would help William. He had a lot of loose cash he didn't know what to do with.

Left alone with Candace, William said nothing and she sat down in the chair where her father had been sitting, threw off her fur jacket, and lifted her small flowered hat from her head.

'What have you two been talking about?' she asked.

'Your father asked me what I wanted to do after I finished college and I said start a newspaper,' William replied.

Her very clear blue eyes were sweetly upon him. 'And why a newspaper?'

William shrugged his handsome shoulders. 'Why does one do anything except because it is what one wants to do?'

'No, William, don't run around the corner. Why do you feel so inferior to everybody?'

She had thrust a point into his heart. His blood rushed into his face and he was careful not to look at her.

'Do I feel inferior?' His usually careful voice was dangerously careless.

'Don't you?' she demanded.

'I really don't know myself.'

She refused the responsibility of special knowledge. 'Anybody can see that you never come straight out with answers. You always think what to say.'

'I suppose that is because I have never lived much in America,' he replied. Though he despised his China, he often found it convenient to take refuge there. It gave him a reason, faintly romantic, for his difference from ordinary people.

'You mean the Chinese don't answer honestly?' she asked.

'I think they prefer to answer correctly,' he said.

'But honesty is always right.'

'Is it?' he asked with wisdom gentle and superior.

'Isn't it?'

'I don't know,' he said again.

'But you must think,' she cried with soft impatience.

'I don't always know what to think,' he replied. 'I guess my way a good deal of the time. I meet people every day whom I cannot understand. I have no experience that would help me.'

She considered this for a brief moment. 'Are the Chinese so different from us or are you only pretending?'

'Pretending what?'

'That you are different.'

'I hope I am not too different from you, Candy.'

This was a bold step and she retreated.

'I don't know if you are or not. I can't make you out, William.'

He felt he had gone far enough. 'Nor I you, sometimes, except today you look lovely. We don't have to make each other out as you call it—not yet, anyway. Let's not hurry, eh, Candy? I want you to know me, as I really think I don't know myself. That means time, plenty of time.' He said all this with his cultivated English accent which he had not yet rejected.

She fended him off.

'Why do you keep talking about time?'

He laughed silently. 'Because I don't want someone else to come dashing up on a steed of some sort and carry you off!'

This was very plain indeed, and she dropped her eyes to the pink rose she had fastened upon her white fur muff, and considered. When she spoke it was with mild malice upon her tongue.

'Yet I am sure that you always reach out to take what you want—as soon as you are sure you want it.'

William met this with astuteness. 'Ah, but you see, this time you might not want what I want. And I confess to being Chinese again to this extent: I don't like to be refused, even indirectly. I prefer not to be put in that position.'

'That's your sense of inferiority again.'

'Call it just being sensible.'

'A bad sport, then.'

'What we are talking about is not sport.'

He spoke with such quiet authority that her youth was compelled to respect his. He was only a year older than she, and yet he might have been ten years her senior.

'I don't know what we are talking about,' she said wilfully.

'You and me,' he said gravely, 'though two, or three years, perhaps, from now.'

'I shan't want to marry anybody for a long time yet,' she said.

'That is all I wanted to know,' he replied. He had been leaning against the marble mantelpiece, his hands in his pockets. Now he went over to her and lifted her hand and put it to his lips. She would have pulled it away but he did not give her time. In the same instant he put her hand down and left the room. His lips had been cold and dry but his palm was damp. She took her handkerchief and rubbed her hand; then she thrust it deep into her muff and sat for a long time alone and thoughtful.

151

As the last months of college passed, William was oppressed by fear lest his parents decide to return for his commencement, a fear that he had never acknowledged even to himself until his father had written in April from Peking:

'Neither your mother nor I can be there to see you take your honours, my dear son. This is a real grief to us. We have discussed the matter many times, and at first I was inclined, with her, to use our small savings and ask for leave of absence without salary. Then it seemed to me that I had no right to put personal feelings ahead of God's work. This is a peculiar age in which we now live in China. The opportunity to preach the gospel is unprecedented. Much as I deplore the manner in which we finally brought the Old Empress to her knees, and especially the looting of the city by Western troops, nevertheless it has taught her a lesson. We are given every opportunity now—God works in mysterious ways and we must not lose the harvest. I only wish the old Dowager Empress could understand that she is defeated. Alas, she cannot imagine it.'

Two weeks later his mother had sent pleasantly heart-broken pages:

'My darling William, I cannot see you in all the pride of graduation from Harvard! The girls are costing us so much this year. Henrietta's operation for appendicitis has prevented it. The Board paid for it, of course, as they should do, but when I asked for a brief furlough to see my own only son graduate they refused me, saying that they had already been put to much expense. We cannot blame Henrietta, still it does seem strange it should have happened like this. We could use our savings—such a mite—but I will not do it, for it would give the Board future ideas. They owe us much for just living so far from our homes. Oh, my son, do have many pictures taken of the event! I am sure that you have friends who will, for your mother's sake, make the day visible to me. Do beg dear Jeremy, or Mr. Cameron. Tell them how my heart aches not to be with you and them.'

William had written a suitably sad letter and then, his spirit freed from the possibility of the presence of his preposterous parents, he had set himself to finish his senior year with glory.

One evening in June he was dressing himself for a dance. It was a few days before commencement and Martin Rosvaine's family in Boston was giving him the occasion. The Rosvaines were old Bostonians, proper except that their ancestry was French instead of English. Wealth mended this defeat and Gallic gaiety lingered in their blood and made them enjoy pleasures more lavish than could be found usually among other Bostonians. William was as near complete happiness on this evening as his unfulfilled ambitions allowed. Candace was among the young women invited and she and her parents were staying at the Hotel Somerset until after commencement. He felt a warm anticipation when he thought of her soft and pretty face, and he wondered if he would tell her that his name stood among those few who would receive their diplomas *summa cum laude*. He decided that he would not, because Jeremy had barely passed, in spite of William's unflagging help with higher mathematics and modern languages. Candace was quick to be scornful of boasting and he could not explain to her that the English schoolmasters had grounded him well and had taught him to dig into fundamentals. Jeremy, persuaded by tutors through a delicate childhood, had not known that mathematics must be seized as one seizes a thistle, that German cannot be learned unless it is grappled with and overcome by force, that French can elude mind and tongue with its smoothness and escape memory entirely. Because an English schoolmaster in a Chinese seaport had used a ruler freely upon William's palms, had cracked him over the skull, had tweaked his ears, had poured out the bitterest and most dry sarcasm about upstart Americans who were properly only English colonists, William had learned early how to achieve even his small ambitions. Somewhere in dark and private action there had to be struggle and mastery.

Never having had the advantage of such knowledge, Jeremy had been content to escape failure. He was now lying in bed, dressed in lavender silk pyjamas becoming to his fair hair and

153

pale skin. He had declared himself exhausted by watching the baseball game in the afternoon. Idly he watched William shave clean his strong dark beard with an old-fashioned razor. June sunshine poured through the windows and William stood with his feet in a bright square. His mind was busy with plans that had nothing to do with college. After commencement was over he would take two weeks' holiday with the Camerons, and then he would plunge into the matter of getting money for the newspaper. His first plans for getting money he had given up altogether. He could not beg money from his college mates and their relatives. He would find it himself, get it, if possible, from Roger Cameron, borrow it perhaps, with Roger's backing. Then he could hire Martin Rosvaine and Seth James. But he would do most of the work himself.

'You're thinking about the paper,' Jeremy said suddenly.

'So I am,' William replied. He was putting on his tie, his small fingers expert and supple. 'How did you know?'

'I know that godalmighty look on your face,' Jeremy replied lazily. 'I fear and respect it.'

'I'm no son of a millionaire,' William said with a mirthless smile. 'I have to get out and hustle, the way your old man did. Maybe my son will be able to lie around and write poetry.'

'I can't imagine your son doing such a thing,' Jeremy retorted.

He fell silent at this mention of William's son, for inevitably a son must have a mother, and he knew by now that William wanted to marry Candace. He was in the puzzling position of being the confidant of both his sister and his friend and of being unable to betray to either what the other told him. Each was equally unsure. William had said frankly, only a few days ago, 'I don't know if I am doing wisely in letting myself fall in love with Candy. I like her being your sister, I like the notion of being your brother-in-law, you son-of-a-gun! But she's used to everything, and I shall have a hard row to hoe. I shan't want her running home to papa, either. When I marry I'll be the boss. If I have to eat cornpone, she'll have to eat it and like it.'

William had looked particularly handsome at the moment

when he had so **spoken. They had come back to their** rooms from a stag dinner at their club, and he was wearing new evening clothes presented somehow by his mother. He had gone down to New York to have them fitted.

Jeremy had laughed. 'I'll guarantee you won't eat corn-pone twice yourself,' he had replied. William's taste in food was fastidious and expensive, shaped, Jeremy always said, by his early years of feeding upon shark's fins and bird's-nest soup in Peking.

When Candace had last mused upon marriage in his presence he had warned her that William was hard-hearted.

'He has to be the master,' he had told Candace.

'Has he been that with you?' she demanded.

'No, because he has not got all he wants from me yet.'

'What does he want?'

'He wants power more than anything,' Jeremy said thoughtfully.

'That's because he feels inferior,' Candace said at once. 'He is afraid in his heart. That's so pitiful, Jeremy. He doesn't know that he needn't be afraid of anything or anybody, because actually he's wonderful. He doesn't know how wonderful he is.'

Jeremy grinned in brotherly fashion. 'Doubtless he'd like to have you tell him so. But I warn you, Candy! You'll have to give up to him, once he's got you.' Then, after an instant's silence, 'It makes my flesh crawl.'

This startled her. 'Why?' she demanded.

He shook his head. 'There's no love in him anywhere, for anybody.'

'Maybe he's had nobody to love,' she said simply.

Fragments of such conversations came back to him as he lay watching William dress.

'You're going to be late,' William said, throwing him a sharp look. His light eyes under the dark and heavy brows had a strange metallic quality.

'My family is used to me. They'll wait. Maybe we'll do the waiting. I wish my father had brought an Apperson instead of a Maxwell.'

'The Maxwell is bigger,' William said.

Mr. Cameron had surprised them all by buying an automobile after Easter, and had chosen the Maxwell for touring. It ran by steam, an idea already old-fashioned, but Mr. Cameron was afraid of the new-fangled gasoline cars.

A goose-like honking rose through the open window, followed by a hissing of steam. Jeremy leaped out of bed, put his head out of the window and shouted to the chauffeur, 'Cool her off, Jackson!' He disappeared into the bathroom, snatching towels as he went, soft silky towels embroidered in Ireland with a large and intricate initial.

Left alone, William thought of Candace while he finished his toilet. His finger-nails perfected, his coat adjusted, his tie correct, his hair smooth, he examined himself in the mirror. The dark oval of his face did not displease him, although he did not like the faint resemblance he saw there to Henrietta.

He looked at his watch. It was later than he had thought and he wondered if the florist had delivered the pink rosebuds and blue forget-me-nots he had ordered for Candace. His thoughts played pleasantly about her for a moment. He had made up his mind to marry her, and thinking of it he felt a hitherto vague excitement suddenly focus itself. Why should he not ask her tonight? A warm, fine night, the romantic setting of an opulent house, his own sense of success to be crowned soon with *summa cum laude*—what else did he lack? He was not impulsive, emotion had waxed slowly to this moment, and he would complete this first era of his history by settling the matter of his marriage.

He was so silent and even solemn that Jeremy watched him thoughtfully while dressing. In the car they were compelled to silence, muffled in caps and dusters, while Jackson speeded at more than ten miles an hour across the darkening country-side. There was a rising wind, and when in Boston the door of the huge house opened to them, sustained by a footman, both young men went at once to a dressing-room to wash the grey dust from their faces.

William was separated from Jeremy immediately by Martin, come to find him.

'William—I say!' Martin cried in a low voice of excitement. 'My old Aunt Rosamond is here and she's interested in the newspaper!' He had pulled William into a corner under the vast oaken darkness of the stairs.

'I can't ask people for money,' William muttered.

'Don't be silly,' Martin said. He took William by the elbow and pushed towards the ballroom, where an old lady in black lace and diamonds sat in a high-backed chair against some palms.

'Auntie, this is William Lane,' Martin said.

William bowed.

'So you're the young man,' Aunt Rosamond said in a loud voice. 'Come from China, my grandson tells me. It's an awful country, from all I hear, tying up women's feet and killing missionaries!'

'I hope that is over, Miss Rosvaine,' William said gracefully.

'Don't talk about China, Auntie,' Martin said impatiently. 'Talk about our newspaper!' Over the plumed white head, Martin's eye met William's and winked.

'Why should she care about a picture paper for people who can scarcely read?' William asked.

'Aunt Rosamond is a shrewd woman,' Martin replied. 'Aren't you, Auntie? Why, she tells her own stock-brokers what to buy and what to sell.'

Aunt Rosamond giggled. 'I'm old enough to be their mother,' she said in her harsh, loud voice. 'I'm old enough to be anybody's mother. I could be your great-grandmother, only I'm glad I'm not. Young men are so ribald these days. Is your newspaper going to make money?'

'Piles of it,' William said. 'That's why we're starting it.'

'I hope it's not for any nonsense of doin' good to the masses,' Aunt Rosamond said still more loudly.

'Only good to ourselves,' William said. 'I want to be a millionaire before I am thirty.' He knew now that the only way to interest the rich was to suggest more riches.

'You come and see me,' Aunt Rosamond commanded with quick interest. She turned large black eyes to his face, and he saw with surprise that once she must have been beautiful.

'Thank you,' William said. He turned to Jeremy. 'There is Candace. Do excuse me, Miss Rosvaine.' He bowed and left them because he did not want to seem eager before a rich old woman, and he saw in Martin's face the unwilling admiration which he loved.

Walking across the carpeted floor he stopped to shake hands with Mrs. Rosvaine, a grey-haired, handsome woman in a silver gown, and then with Mr. Rosvaine, who looked like the portrait of his French great-grandfather hanging over the mantelpiece. Then he went to the Camerons and, pretending that he saw Candace last, he shook hands with the two elders before he turned to her. She wore a long filmy white dress and carried the roses and forget-me-nots. She looked as a beautiful girl should look and as he wanted his wife to look, and the deep and secret jealousy of his nature rolled up out of his heart. It was intolerable that anyone except himself should possess this precious creature with all her gifts and graces. He might look the world over and not find a woman so suited to him, who was at the same time attainable.

'You look like a princess,' he told Candace.

'William, don't tell me you're poetic.' She gave him her careless and pretty smile.

'No, just that I'm partial to princesses,' he protested. 'I grew up in the neighbourhood of a palace, in Peking, you know, where princesses lived and played. They're not strange to me.'

Mrs. Cameron overheard and said a little sharply, 'Are your sisters coming to commencement, William?'

Taken aback he, too, spoke more sharply than he knew. 'They're coming tomorrow.'

'You're a silent sort of an ape,' Jeremy put in. 'Why didn't you tell me they were coming?'

'I didn't think you'd be interested,' William retorted.

'Of course I am,' Jeremy insisted. 'You know my sister, and am I not to know yours?'

'Henrietta is quite ugly,' William said with apparent frankness. 'And though Ruth is pretty, I have never discovered anything interesting about her.'

'Men never see anything in their sisters,' Candace declared.

Their interest in any conversation not connected with themselves waned quickly. In the fashion of the rich, William thought.

'It is going to be hot,' Mrs. Cameron said in a plaintive voice.

'You can't possibly be as hot in that outfit as I am in mine,' Mr. Cameron told her.

'I don't know,' she said. 'I have to wear cor——'

'Mother, spare us!' Candace put in.

'I don't mind William,' Mrs. Cameron said. 'He's used to us.'

'Thank you, Mrs. Cameron,' William said. 'Come and sit down. I hope you've made Candace keep the first dance for me. She promised it but she never keeps her promises.'

'She's a very naughty girl,' Mrs. Cameron said with vague indulgence, sitting down.

'I did keep it,' Candace said. 'And I don't break my promises.'

The orchestra began to play and the ballroom seemed suddenly full. William made a smile serve for answer and drew Candace into his arms. He danced beautifully and he was aware of watching eyes. He imagined them thinking of him with admiration, however reluctant. He liked to compel admiration.

Then he looked down and saw Candace's face, calm and beautiful. Her skin was fine and smooth and creamy white, her lips sweet and deeply cut. How fortunate for him if she would marry him soon! Why should they be long engaged? He needed Candace now, for herself and for everything she could bring to him. He would ask her tonight. He could see Jeremy's eyes watching him. It was a man's own business whom he married and when he married. In such dreams, compounded of the many mixtures in himself, he went through the evening, evading Jeremy, dancing with Candace again and again, and when she was not free he asked no one else. Then to his horror he saw her dancing twice with Seth James. Pangs seized him. Seth was one of her kind, the son of a man richer even than her father.

He went to Candace to claim his own last dance. 'I can't let Seth look at you like that,' he said sternly, and he took her in his arms.

She smiled dreamily without answer and he saw her shoulders shining white and her hair gold in the light of the lamps. He imagined that she was withdrawn from him and instantly he wanted to force her attention to himself.

'I won't tell you how beautiful you are,' he said half carelessly. 'I suppose Seth has said all that.'

'Yes,' she murmured.

He imagined that she was holding herself away from him and he drew her closer. 'You are not in rhythm.'

'They're playing the waltz too slowly,' she replied, but she yielded herself, her cheek all but touching his shoulder. Still he was not satisfied.

He stopped and they stood motionless in the whirling crowd. 'Come along outside,' he said abruptly. 'I've been full of something all evening—something I've wanted to say.'

He put her hand in his arm and led her away, looking strangely grim for a young man in love. Jeremy, across the room, watched them go through an open door and since for the moment he was not dancing, he went to find his parents. They were waltzing quietly together in a distant corner and they stopped as he came up.

'I just want to warn you,' he said in a low voice. 'At this very moment William is going to ask Candace to marry him.'

'Oh dear!' his mother exclaimed.

His father looked grave. 'I don't know that we can do a thing about it,' he said after an instant's thought.

Before Jeremy's astonished eyes the two looked at each other and resumed again the slow measures of their waltz. He left them after another moment and then went to pour himself a large glass of whisky and drink it down.

Outside the house, under a wisteria bower in the garden lit by Chinese lanterns, William began his proposal to Candace. He had wondered often how this should be done, and had made some half-dozen plans, none of which he now used. She looked so cool, so full of sweet common sense, that he felt it wisdom to approach her in like mood.

'Candy, I think you have known for a long time that I want to marry you, if you will have me.'

These were the words he spoke almost as soon as she had sat down. She shook out her little Chinese fan. He had given her the fan last Christmas, a thing of silk and sandalwood which his mother had chosen for him in Peking. He smelled the sandalwood now in the warm air of the night, and childish memories stirred, sandalwood and incense and the close sweet smell of old temples in the hills where the American missionary families had sometimes picnicked in the long, bright, northern summers. He turned away from such useless remembrance.

Candace had not replied.

'Well?' he asked a little too sharply.

'I didn't think you would ask me quite yet,' she said.

He was not able to tell from the pure cool tones whether she was glad or sorry. 'I didn't know, either,' he replied in the manner with which he had chosen to present himself to her. 'Perhaps I ought to wait until I have some sort of income. But the last few days I've asked myself why I should wait. I'd rather like to remember some day when I've built you a palace and filled it with slaves that I proposed to you when I was penniless and that you accepted me so.'

She laughed. 'A nice idea!' She waved the fan and once more the scent came blowing against his face. He moved from it half impatiently.

'Then will you, Candy?'

'Will I what?'

'Oh, Candy, don't tease!'

'But you haven't said you love me!'

'Of course I love you.'

It was the first time he had ever spoken the words to any creature and they sat upon his tongue like pebbles.

'How strangely you say that!' she said shrewdly.

'Because it is strange to me. I've never said it before to anybody.'

This touched her, he could see. She looked at him curiously, her lashes lifted and long. He had the usual amount of passion in him, he supposed, though he never tried himself. Jeremy was clean and delicate, and though Martin went about visiting strange places, the young men whom William had cultivated were not often physically gross. Lustfulness was not one of his own natural sins. Yet slowly he felt rise in him a strong desire to touch this beautiful girl and, guided by instinct, he put out his arms and felt her come into them. Beneath and against his cheek he felt her hair.

'Dearest!'

The word rose to his lips of its own accord. He had heard his father use it once or twice to his mother. They had not often been affectionate before others, and the word had clung in his mind.

'Will you be good to me, William?'

'Yes, I will. I swear it.'

He heard her sigh, he felt her lean against him and the fan dropped to the ground. It seemed to him suddenly that he loved her with all the love he ought to have.

Over the grass, in moonlight and lantern-light mingled, a quickened waltz floated upon waves of music and Candace pulled herself away. 'Let's go back and dance!'

'But are we engaged, Candy?' he urged.

She stood up but he would not let her go, his arms about her waist. He wanted to be sure she was his before she went back into the rooms crowded with young men.

'I—I suppose so,' she said, half unwillingly, half shyly.

'We are!'

He stood up and seized her again and kissed her long and hard. When he released her she gave a little cry.

'Ah, you've broken my fan!'

He had indeed. When he picked up the fan it lay in his hand like a broken flower. He had crushed the filigree with his heel, and the scent was strong in his nostrils.

'Never mind, I'll send to Peking for another, ivory instead of sandalwood, and set with kingfishers' feathers instead of silk.'

'Ivory has no scent,' she complained. 'Give me the pieces, William. I shan't ever like a fan so well again.'

He gave them to her, half resentfully, and they walked into the house and began to dance together in silence. He was angry with himself and then with her. The moment that he had wanted to be perfect had ended badly. He had been awkward, perhaps, but she had been unforgiving. Nevertheless he had proposed and had been accepted. They went on dancing.

On commencement day William rose and breakfasted before Jeremy woke, and from the dining-hall he went out and across the Yard to the big elm under which he had agreed to meet his sisters and grandparents. They had reached town early, had taken a hack to a small second-class hotel and there had breakfasted.

He saw them waiting for him now, and for a moment they were as detached, as isolated, as a photograph in a family album.

Henrietta was plainer than ever and his grandparents were more middle class than he had thought possible. Ruth had grown up pretty and gentle and he felt a sudden renewal of affection for her. He need not be ashamed of her. But no distaste showed on his resolute young face. He smiled and shook hands properly with his elders.

'How are you, Grandfather? Grandmother, it's awfully good of you, really—I hope the trip wasn't hard.' He kissed Henrietta's cheek and squeezed Ruth's slender shoulders in his arms. 'Come along. We'll get good seats.'

The Yard was coming to life. Seniors in cap and gown were hastening here and there.

He led his guests into the wide-open doors of the hall where a few people were already gathering, and he took pains to find seats where they could see him receive his honours.

'Ruth shall sit on the aisle, so she can see me when we come marching in,' he said, and caught her smile.

Henrietta had said nothing since they met. She wore a plain dark blue linen suit and a stiff sailor hat that emphasized

163

the angles of her face. Her eyes were brown like their father's, but they were deep set and intense, while his were shallowly set and pleasant. This William saw but he did not notice silence. He was in haste to be off on his own business, to leave them.

'Let's meet again under the elm after this is over.'

He met their solemn, dazed eyes, tried to smile, and hurried away. His rooms were empty. Jeremy was gone. He snatched his cap and gown and put them on, glanced at himself in the mirror, and joined the thickening crowd. He felt them looking at him as he strode towards the Yard but he pretended he did not. Confidence, excitement, the assurance of success, were hid behind his set and handsome face. The honour the day would bring him was only the first step to all that lay ahead, and he knew it. He took his place among his class-mates, and the important day began, the end and purpose of four long and sometimes tedious years.

Then suddenly he lost it as he was to lose so many days from his life. Everything became unreal to him. His mind seemed to leave his body. It raced ahead into the years, planning, fighting, conquering, gaining all that he wanted. When would he have enough? When would he know and what would be satisfaction? He tried to bring himself back to this hour, which now that he had it seemed no more an end but only a beginning. He even felt vaguely that he was losing it and he wanted to keep it. It was a part of satisfaction, the first step at least towards fulfilment, a fragment of his life completed. He tried to think of Candace as he sat among his fellows; he tried to value the sound of his name upon the list of honour men.

'William Lane, *summa cum laude*——'

But he had ceased already to value what he had, so immense was his desire for what was yet to come.

When the long morning was over he went at once to his grandparents and his sisters. They were waiting for him under the big elm, and his grandmother murmured affection as he came to them.

'Your mother will be so proud.' Her eyes misted with the easy tears of the old.

'My father got the same honours,' William said modestly. 'It was harder in his day, I daresay. He took much more Greek than I did.'

Ruth held out a small package, and he took it with affected surprise. 'A chain for your watch,' she murmured. 'It's nothing much.'

'I bought you a book,' Henrietta said, producing a package. 'I wrapped it in red because it's what they do in China.'

'And Grandma and I just have a little cheque,' his grandfather said, giving him an envelope.

'It is all too much,' William said gracefully.

Ruth cried out softly. 'Let's go and see if there are letters from Mother and Father! I know Mother was going to try to have a letter here on this very day.'

'We'll go to my rooms on our way to the hotel,' William said.

When he looked in his box there was no letter from China. A few bills were there, still to be paid, and one letter addressed in a hand he did not recognize. It was a tight scrawl, crude and yet formed in some curious personal fashion. He saw on the envelope the address of a town in Ohio that he did not know, and above it was the name of Clem Miller.

'No letter,' he told his sisters. 'None from them, I mean. Here's a strange one.'

He tore open the envelope. Within it was a single sheet of lined paper, upon which was the same cramped, clear handwriting.

'Dear William,

'You may not remember me. Once you told me to stop fighting a Chinese fellow in Peking. I never saw you after that. I am here at a grocery store. Got a fair job. Wish, though, I had a chance at your education. Am fighting my way up though. I got your address from your father. Wrote to some friends of mine named Fong in Peking but

165

had forgot a good deal of my Chinese and wrote English thinking maybe their son, Yusan, would be able to read print. He showed the letter to your father, and I got a letter that way telling me you were finishing college. I haven't had the chance. Your father told me to get in touch, and I am doing so in memory of old days.

'Yours sincerely,

'Clem Miller.'

'Who is it from?' Ruth asked, as they walked towards the street.

William was looking up and down for a hack. The sun was getting hot. 'You remember that Faith Mission family in Peking?'

Ruth shook her head. 'I can't remember very much about Peking.'

'I remember them,' Henrietta said suddenly. 'Let me read the letter.'

'You may keep it if you like,' William said carelessly. 'There is no reason for me to answer it.'

He saw a hack, called it, and they climbed in, he taking the small and uncomfortable seat although Ruth offered to sit there. 'You are my guests,' he said with his best smile.

The day went on, he living each hour of it grimly and correctly. He showed his family about the college and his grandmother suggested seeing his rooms. He put this off until Henrietta was suddenly cross. 'I think you don't want us to see them,' she declared.

Upon this, with secret anger, he led them to the rooms, dreading the possibility that the Camerons were there. But the rooms were empty, and his grandmother sat down in Jeremy's easy chair and slipped her shoe from her heel. 'I bought new shoes for the big day,' she said in apology. 'You know what they do to your feet.'

He did not reply to this dreadful remark, and was restless until he got them up again. Yet not in time, for at the moment when they reached the door Jeremy came in and William could not refuse introductions. Jeremy, with his usual grace, stood talking to the elders and Ruth joined them. Henrietta waited in her stolid fashion.

It lasted but a moment, and he was leading them on again, now towards the gate and the hack. Then they were gone and he felt exhausted and yet he could not show exhaustion, for men he did not know stopped to congratulate him on his honours. He tried to accept their praise modestly, to seem careless as though honours meant nothing to him, but he imagined that they saw through his pretence, and then he grew brief and proud and he felt hurt and weary. He was hot and he wanted a bath and a few minutes' sleep.

Half an hour later, stretched on his bed in his room alone, the shades drawn to shut out the sun, when he tried to think of Candace he found himself thinking instead of Aunt Rosamond. It might be very easy indeed to get money from an old lady like that, perhaps a great deal of money. Then after some deep thinking of this sort he felt that he would like honestly to be ashamed of it, but he could not be. He had nothing and no one to help him. There was not one person in his own family who could be anything but a hindrance to him, and the sooner he separated himself from them the better. He toyed with the memory of Aunt Rosamond's invitation. It meant nothing. He knew by now that the rich could speak pleasant words as easily as they breathed, with as little significance. It was hard to be the friend of rich men and their sons, but it was the only way to get what he needed for his own independence. Some day, when he had all he wanted, he would let them know how he despised them.

IV

ALONE in her small hot room in the suburban house, Henrietta was writing a letter to Clem Miller. She was desperately tired and as usual, after she had been with William, melancholy wrapped her about. His first glance at her had been enough to tell her that she was still ugly, still all that she did not want to be. It was a sign of greatness in her which she did not recognize that she loved Ruth tenderly and humbly in spite of William's preference. Why, she asked herself again tonight, did it matter what William thought? But she did care and would always care what he thought of her. It had begun in the old days in the mission house in Peking when the amah who had served them all had taught her that girls must always yield to the precious only son of the family.

'You,' Liu Amah had said, 'you are only a girl. Weelee is a boy. Girls are not so good as boys. Men are more valuable than women.'

Henrietta sighed. It was late and she should have been sleeping but she could not. Her grandparents and Ruth had gone to sleep, or else by now her grandmother would have tapped on her door to inquire why her light was still on. Swept by the bottomless misery of youth, Henrietta had reached out into the night and had thought of Clem. His letter was still in her handbag and she read it through twice, carefully and slowly. Then she began to write.

'Dear Clem,

'You do not know me, but I am William Lane's sister. William is too proud to write to you. He has always been a very proud boy and now he is worse than ever, although he is no longer a boy. He considers himself a man. I suppose he is a man since he has finished college. He is very smart. He graduated yesterday with highest honours. I am sorry to say I don't think he will ever write to you. But I think someone should, since you knew each other in old Peking, and so I am writing to you.

'I don't know anything much about you, and so I will tell you about myself. I am eighteen and next autumn I will go to college, I hope. I am not at all pretty—I had better tell you that right away. It is strange, for I look a good deal like William, and he is thought to be very handsome. I suppose it is not the way for a girl to look. My sister Ruth is pretty.'

She paused and realized that she had nothing to say. This was another of her miseries. She felt so much, she was so racked with vague sorrows and longings and infinite loneliness and yet none of this could she put into words to anyone. She and Ruth went to a public school, since all the money had been needed for William, but she had found no special friends there. The girls thought her queer because she had grown up in China. Perhaps she was. She bit the end of her wooden pen and then went on.

'Do you ever think of Peking? I do, often. From the window of my room there in the house where my parents live I used to look out upon a sweet little stubbly pagoda— a dagoba, I think it was called. There were bells on the corners, and when my window was open and I lay in bed I could hear them ringing. Please tell me whether you think of such things. And shall you go back one day? I would like to but I cannot think how to earn my living there, not wanting to be a missionary.'

Beyond this she could not go and so she signed herself sedately, sincerely his. When the letter was sealed it seemed to her that she must post it at once, even though it was now midnight. The small clock on her mantel gave this severe notice to her but she did not heed it. She put a dress over her nightgown, and with her feet slippered she went silently down the stairs and out of the back door to the street, where stood a post-box. At seven o'clock, she knew, the mail was collected and by breakfast time the letter would be on its way to the small Ohio town that seemed as far away as Peking. She heard the envelope rustle softly behind the shutter, and then she went back home and to her room again. Now she could go to bed. She had put forth a hand into the darkness and perhaps someone would reach out and clasp it. Comforted by hope she flung herself upon her bed and fell into a sleep that led her back into childhood dreams of a walled compound in Peking, a big shadowy mission house, where soft-footed brown servants came and went, bringing smiles and gentle encouragement to a shy and plain-faced American child.

When the letter reached Clem he was in the grocery store. It was the middle of the morning, and Owen Janison, the owner and his employer, came in from his daily trip across the street to the post office. Clem's letters were few and until now they had borne Chinese stamps and postmarks.

'You got a letter from some place in New York, looks like,' Mr. Janison said. He was a tall thin man, whose moustaches hung down his chin and joined a faded yellow beard. He wore a grey suit and a stiff white shirt with a celluloid collar.

Clem was shirt-sleeved behind the meat counter. He took the letter and looked at it carefully without opening it. 'Thanks, Mr. Janison,' he said. He slapped a piece of corned beef on the scrubbed wooden counter and trimmed off some porous fat.

'A pound, did you say, Mrs. Bates?' he inquired.

'Mebbe a pound and a half,' the customer replied, hesitating. 'Mr. Bates is terribly fond of the stuff though I don't eat it myself, more'n a bite.'

Clem did not answer this remark. In the years since he and Bump, one weary morning, had walked into New Point, Ohio, he had learned to live upon two levels, the immediate and the real. Mrs. Bates was immediate but not real. Even Mr. Janison, upon whom he and Bump were dependent for their living, was immediate and not real. Real was the past and real was the future, both equally clear to him alone.

To recapture the past he had written to Yusan, Mr. Fong's son, and he had received the letter from Dr. Lane. Yusan had forgotten his English and had given Clem's letter to the missionary. From Dr. Lane had come a friendly letter, mainly about William and only a little about Yusan. Dr. Lane took it for granted that a youth in America named Clem Miller must be interested in his son William.

ʾReading the faintly stilted lines of the letter, for anything Dr. Lane wrote fell inevitably into the shape of a sermon, Clem had felt all the old realities. Yusan at sixteen was betrothed to a girl in the mission school, though the wedding was still far off. He had grown into a sober young man, over whose soul the missionary yearned. Yet Yusan refused to be Christian. Real was the memory of Yusan, the stubborn boy, growing into a young man. Real were the hours Clem had spent with him in Mr. Fong's bare house. Real was the memory of the Peking streets, the wind-driven snows that covered the tiled roofs of house and palace in winter. Real were the fabulous summer skies. Clem remembered every detail of his childhood, the pleasure of owning sometimes three small coins with which he bought a triangular package of peanuts wrapped in hand-made brown paper thick and soft like blotting paper. Real, too, was the joy of a hot sweet potato on a cold morning, bought from a vender's little earthen oven, and real the pleasure of a crimson-hearted water-melon split upon a July day. Real were the caravans of camels padding through the dust, led by a man from Mongolia who knitted a garment as he walked, pulling from the camels the long strands of wool which they shed when the winter was ended. Real were the little apes on chains and the dancing bears, the travelling actors and the magicians, and all that had made the city streets a pleasure place for a wandering foreign child.

Out of the need to bring nearer to him that reality of childhood in the remote land which was still his own but which he could not claim and which did not claim him, Clem had upon an impulse written to William, whom he remembered only as he had looked that day when a Chinese lad had called his father a beggar because he trusted God for bread.

The letter Mr. Janison now brought him was, he supposed, from William. He waited, however, until it was time for his midday meal, which he made by taking a roll of stale bread and cutting off a slice of cheese and eating in the store-room. Mr. Janison went home to noonday dinner and Bump was working on a farm, now that school was over. Clem had been firm about Bump's going to school. He had given up the hope that some day he himself would go to a school somewhere, though not to learn ordinary things like geography and arithmetic, which he could get for himself out of books in his room at night. He wanted to learn large important matters, such as how to feed millions of people. He was obsessed with the business of food, although his own appetite was frugal. A thin, middle-sized boy, he had grown into the same kind of young man. His frame had taken on bony squareness of shoulder, leanness at the hips, without any flesh. Even the square angles of his face remained fleshless and his cheeks were hollow and his blue eyes deep set.

He had discarded the faith of his father, and said no prayers except those he spoke to his own soul. There were, he believed, only a few essentials to a good life, but they were essential to all people, and food he put first, cheap, nourishing food. Bump for example, could not be filled. He sat sometimes watching Bump eat in the small room they lived in together. He always got a meal for Bump at night, a stew or a hunk of boiled beef and cabbage and plenty of bread and butter. His own slender appetite soon satisfied, he enjoyed Bump's bottomless hunger. He had provided the food and this was the pleasure he felt. Nobody had given them anything. He had worked and bought the food. He bought cheap food for it was good enough. He had no desire for fancy eatables and was stern with Bump about cake and pie. If everybody could eat his fill of good plain food, he would tell Bump, then there wouldn't be any more trouble in the world.

He was bringing up Bump himself and by himself, sometimes ruthlessly but on the whole kindly, with the deep paternal instinct with which he viewed the world, though he did not know it. His cure for a drunk coming into the store to beg on a winter's night for a nickel to buy 'a cup of coffee', was to take a stale loaf and slice off two thick pieces and thrust a wedge of cheese between them. 'Eat that and you won't want to get drunk for a while,' he said with young authority.

In the back room, the store empty during the town's midday meal, he now sat down on a crate and took the letter from his pocket. Without wasting time on curiosity, he tore the envelope open and was amazed at the first words. He had never had a letter from a girl, nor ever written to one. He had thought little of any girl, being busy at earning his living and rearing Bump. Now a girl had written to him.

He read the letter carefully and considered it a sensible one and read it again. She remembered Peking, too, did she? He felt excited, not because she was a girl but because she, like him, had been born in another world which nobody here knew anything about. He had learned now to live in America, but there would always be the world for him as well, and other people. He could not talk about it to Americans. They did not want to know about it. The people here were satisfied not to know about anything except what happened in their own streets.

He sat musing until he heard the tinkle of the bell that announced a customer, and then he went back into the grocery store. He would answer the letter, maybe on Sunday, when he had sent Bump off to Sunday School.

Thus two weeks later, on a Thursday morning, Henrietta received the letter for which she had waited and for which she had gone herself every morning to open the door for the postman. The moment she saw it she took it and thrust it into the bosom of her apron. That day she was cleaning the attic for her grandmother, a musty place, hot under the roof and filled with dead belongings. There she returned to read Clem's letter.

'Dear Henrietta,

'It was a surprise of course but I had rather maybe have a letter from you than from William. I am older than you but I know I cannot go to college on account of earning my

173

living. I am an orphan and I have an orphan also to support. I do not even know his whole name, Bump he is called but I am sure it is not his name. He says when he was little he was thought bumptious and so people began to call him that. He cannot remember any family and so was an Aid child. I don't know why I tell you about him. Some day I will tell you how I got him.

'I am a poor letter writer not having much time but I would like you to know that I do remember Peking. It would be nice to talk with you about it as nobody here knows anything about it over there. Who knows, sometime maybe I could come to see you though not until I get Bump educated. I have a great many ideas of what I want to do when that job is done when I can think of myself and my own life.

'I would enjoy hearing from you again. Yours sincerely,
                                                    'Clem Miller.'

Thus began the passage of letters between a small town in Ohio and a suburb of New York. Without seeing each other for two more years, boy and girl wove between them a common web of dreams. So profound was their need to dream that neither spent the time to tell the other the bare facts of their lives; Henrietta that she had graduated from the big bare public high school almost friendless because the other girls thought her too proud to join their chatter of boys and dances, and Clem that he was grinding out his youth behind a counter in a country store. These things neither considered important. They were both weaving together the fabric of the past to make the fabric of the future. It was years before Henrietta learned all the simple facts of Clem's life.

These were the facts. He had turned back that day to see Bump padding through the dust after him. That night they had slept in a barn, taking care not to rouse the farmer and his family, and from it they had set forth again in the early morning.

'Reckon the Aid will chase us?' Bump asked in the course of the next day.

174

'I don't think she'll care what becomes of us,' Clem replied.

The sky was bright above their heads. On that day he began to have his first intimations of his own country. He had walked for endless miles across the Chinese land with an old woman he did not know, linking village to village with his lonely footsteps. Now he walked as many miles with a child who was a stranger to him, across a landscape strange to him, too. Here there were few villages and the farm-houses stood separate and solitary. He avoided them unless he needed food, and then he went to knock upon a kitchen door to ask for work. He was stiff with soft-hearted farm wives who wanted to give them a meal and he demanded that he be allowed to pay for what he got, and he was equally harsh with surly men who declared there was nothing for him to do. Work there must be, he told them, because they must have food.

How many days he walked in that bright autumn he did not count or care. Slowly he learned to love the look of this land, even its uncultivated spaces, its ragged roadsides, its sparsely settled miles. He learned to be wary of old tramps and to choose the back roads they avoided. In the back roads and the remote farm-houses the people he found were good. They were not gregarious, these countrymen of his. They did not live in big families as the Chinese did. Two generations in a house were enough and maybe too much. More often a man and a woman and their children were alone under a roof. The children were usually tow-headed and their faces were burned brown with the wind and sun, and because he was a stranger they ran when they saw him just as the Chinese children had done. He thought of these dwellers on the land as folk half wild and scarcely civilized and yet he kept among them.

'Ain't we goin' to settle down somewheres?' Bump asked, as the days went on.

'Some time soon. You have to get to school,' Clem said.

'Do I have to go to school?' Bump wailed.

'Surely you do,' Clem said sternly.

One day at last they came into a town he liked, though it

175

looked no different from any other. But it was in Ohio, a state that he had come to enjoy in the past days, a place where the people were decent and Bible reading. They made him think of his own Bible-reading parents, mingling kindness with rigid goodness. The streets in the town were clean and there was a school-house of wood frame painted white. The church, the post office, and the general store stood around a green square, in the midst of which was a rough statue of Abraham Lincoln. These were the reasons Clem chose New Point, and he went first to the store. Inside he found the tall lean man who hired him, after some hesitation, and then let him rent a room upstairs as part of his weekly wage. Clem bought Bump a suit of clothes and a pair of shoes and two pairs of socks on credit, and started him at school the next Monday.

At the end of that Monday he had given Bump his first and only whipping. The boy had come back from school gloomy and had gone upstairs quietly. Clem was busy with a customer and as soon as he was free he hastened up the stairs behind the store. There he found the boy packing his clothes into a flour sack.

'What are you doing?' Clem demanded.

Bump scowled at him from under sunburned brows. 'I ain't stayin' with you,' he said in a flat voice.

'Why not?' Clem asked.

'I ain't goin' to no school.'

Clem glared at the boy who had become his whole family. 'Why not?' he asked again.

'I don't like it.'

Rage filled Clem's soul. Not to like to go to school, not to take the chance that was offered, not to accept the gift of sacrifice, seemed to him ingratitude so immense that earth could not hold it nor heaven allow it. He rushed at Bump and seized him by the seat of his trousers and swung him clear of the floor. He flung him down flat and knelt beside him and beat him with his open hands until the boy howled. Upon this scene Mr. Janison hastened up the stairs.

'Lay off!' he bellowed. 'You want to kill that boy?'

Clem turned upon him a face set and white. 'He's going to

take his chance if I do have to kill him,' he replied and finished his punishment. When he let Bump get up he pointed at the flour sack and waited until the weeping boy had unpacked it and put his clothes away again.

Janison waited, too, a quizzical look behind his moustache. Then Clem turned solemnly to his employer. 'I aim to bring this boy up like my own brother. That means he's going to get a good education, the kind I'd give my eyes to have, nearly. He's to be a man, not some worthless son-of-a-gun.'

Mr. Janison pulled his goatee. 'Go to it,' he said. 'That was as pretty a lickin' as ever I see.'

He went downstairs again and Clem sat down on the bed. 'Bump, I hope never to lick you again,' he said gravely. 'I don't believe in it and I don't feel I ought to have to do it. But if you dare to run away and throw out a fine chance like I'm offering you, I will come after you and lick you wherever you are. You hear me?'

'Ye-es,' Bump sobbed.

'Well, then,' Clem did not know how to go on. 'You come downstairs and I'll get you some crackers and cheese—and some liquorice,' he said finally. Food, he thought, was what the boy needed, and something sweet, maybe.

During the next years, as Bump began to grow into a satis-factory boy, Clem wondered often about his beginnings. That he was a child without parents, Clem knew; without parents, that is, except in the simplest animal sense. Mom Berger had told him one night after the younger children were in bed, that they were all love children, 'except that there Bump.'

'What is he?' Clem had asked.

'I dunno what you'd call him,' she had said mysteriously. With an embarrassment which sat ridiculously upon her thick person, she had pursed her lips and remained silent. Pop Berger had taken up the sordid story.

'That there Bump,' he said after some moments of rumina-tion and chewing upon a vast quid of tobacco. 'He's what you might call a rape child.'

Clem had flushed. 'You mean——'

'Yeah,' Pop Berger had said slowly, relishing the evil news.

177

'His paw attackted a girl on the streets of Philly. 'Twas all in the papers.'

'Yeah,' Mom Berger said from beside the stove. 'And I ast you was it real rape. A woman don't rape easy or if she do, it ain't rape.'

Pop took the story away from her again. 'Anyways, it was brought up in court for to be rape, and the raper, that was Bump's paw, mind you, he had to pay the girl a hunnerd dollars.'

'Some women makes their livin' one way and some another,' Mom Berger had said, and had clattered a stove lid to let Pop know that enough was enough.

If the story was true, Clem had told himself with reflecting pity, then Bump had no parents at all, neither father nor mother. By the accident of two conflicting bodies he had been conceived, his soul snared somewhere among the stars. He was not orphaned, for even an orphan had once possessed parents. The boy's solitary creation moved all that was fatherly in Clem's being, and it was most of him.

He had not been alone in what he did either for Bump or himself. With the affection so easily found in any small American town, the citizens observed the solitary and ambitious boy. They knew no more about him than that he was an orphan and they took it for granted that Bump was his brother. That he had run away from an eastern state endeared him to them. Mr. Janison soon began to spread news of Clem's monstrous good qualities. His industry was astounding to the employer. When other young males of the town were crazed with spring and the baseball season, Clem continued behind the counter, even staying to sweep the store as usual when the day was over. His belated arrival on the baseball field and the frenzy of those who awaited him only made him more beloved. For all his medium stature, Clem had long strong arms that could perform wheels in the air and send a ball faster than imagination. 'A good all-round feller,' New Point decided, 'a feller that'll make his way.'

Two persons kept to themselves their thoughts about Clem. Miss Mira Bean, Bump's teacher to whom Clem had gone after the whipping, knew that Clem was more than New Point discerned. She knew it the first evening he had come to her door, clean and brushed and holding his cap in his hand.

'Come in,' she had said with her usual sharp manner to the young.

Clem had come into her small two-room flat.

'My name is Clem Miller.'

'Sit down,' she commanded.

The rooms were small and crowded with furniture and books. There was little space to sit, and he took the end of a haircloth sofa. Miss Bean was like any of the middle-aged women he saw upon the streets of New Point, a lean, sand-coloured shape, washed and clean, straight-haired and grey-eyed.

'What do you want, Clem?' she asked.

'I want to talk to you about Bump,' he said. He had gone on then to tell why he had felt compelled to whip the boy.

'But I can't whip him again,' he said. 'You, Miss Bean, have got to make him like school well enough so he will want to get an education.'

'He's got to stay in school, whether he likes it or not,' Miss Bean said somewhat harshly. 'It's the law.'

Clem had sat looking at her. 'I don't think you ought to take advantage of that,' he said. 'The law is on your side, of course. But even the law can't make a boy get an education. It can only make him sit so many hours a day where you are. He's got to like it before he can get educated.'

Miss Bean was not a stupid woman and she was struck with this wisdom in a youth who was still too young to be called a man.

'You're right about that,' she said after a moment.

She had done her best, not only for Bump, but also for Clem, lending him books, guiding his reading, letting him talk to her for hours on Sundays. For though Clem made Bump go to Sunday School and lectured him about the value of going to church, he himself never went.

'Why'n't you go, then, if it's so good?' Bump grumbled.

Clem, polishing Bump's ragged school shoes, paused to

179

answer this as honestly as he could. 'I just can't get myself to do it,' he confessed. 'What's more, I can't tell you why. Something happened to me once somewhere.'

'What was it?' Bump asked.

Clem shook his head. 'It would take me too long to tell you.'

He never told anyone anything about himself. It would indeed have taken him too long. Where would he begin, and how would he explain his origins? How could he ever tell anyone in this peaceful town in Ohio that he had once lived in Peking, China, and that he had seen his parents killed? There were things too endless to tell. Only to Henrietta was he one day to speak, because she knew at least the beginning.

The church bell came to his aid. 'You run along,' he told Bump briskly. The shoes were polished and he washed his hands in the china bowl. Then he fixed Bump's tie to exactitude and parted his hair again and brushed it. 'Mind you learn the golden text,' he said sternly.

The minister at the Baptist Church was the other person in New Point who kept to himself his thoughts about Clem. He stopped sometimes in the store to see the industrious young man and to invite him to come to the house of God. He was a red-haired, freckle-faced young minister, fresh of voice and sprightly in manner, and there was nothing in him to dislike. But Clem did fear him, nevertheless, though the young minister was persuasive and ardent.

'Come to worship God with us, my friend,' he said to Clem one day at the meat counter. He had come to buy a pound of beef for stew.

Clem fetched out a piece of nameless beef and searched for the knife. 'I don't have much time, Mr. Brown,' he said mildly. 'I really need my Sundays.'

'It costs more time in the end not to be a Christian, more time in eternity.'

Clem smiled and did not answer. He cut the meat and weighed it, and then cut another slice. 'Tell Mrs. Brown I'm putting in a little extra.' This was his usual answer to those whom he refused something. He gave a little extra food.

The store, Clem knew as the years passed, was not his final destination. He was learning about buying and selling, and he was learning about his own people. Living among the kindly citizens of the small town, he began to recover from the shock of the farm and the man and woman who lived upon it. In its way, he sometimes mused, it had been a shock as severe as that he had received when he found his parents murdered on that summer's day in Peking. He was taut with nervous energy, he never rested, and there were days when he could not eat without nausea. Food he held sacred, yet food could lie heavy in his own belly. He could not drink milk or eat butter because he could not bear the smell of the cow, and he disliked eggs. Meat he ate almost not at all, partly because he had been so little used to it. He forgot himself. Around the matter of food his imagination played and upon it his creative power was focused. Under Miss Bean's dry guidance, he read economics and came upon Malthus, and lost his temper. The man must have been one of those blind thinkers, sitting in his study, playing with figures instead of getting out and seeing what was really going on in the world. People were starving, yes, but food was rotting because they could not get it. There was plenty of food, there were not too many people, the trouble was that men had not put their minds to the simple matter of organization for distribution. Food must be bought where it was plentiful and cheap and carried to where the people could buy it.

When this idea first came into Clem's mind, its effect upon him was like that of religious conversion. He did not know it yet, but he was illumined as his father before him had been, not then by the satisfaction of feeding human bodies, but by the excitement of saving men's souls. Clem had no interest in saving souls, for he had a high and unshakeable faith in the souls of men as he saw them, good enough as God had made them, except when the evils of earth beset them. And these evils, he was convinced, rose first of all from hunger, for from hunger came illness and poverty and all the misery that forced men into desperation and then into senseless quarrels. Their souls were degraded and lost because of the clamouring hunger of their bodies. As simply as his father had left his home and followed God's call across the sea, so simply now did Clem believe that he could cure the sorrows of men and women and their children.

He did not want to leave his own country as his father had done. Here among his own people he would do his work, and if he were proved right, as he knew he would be, then he would spread his plan of salvation to other lands and other peoples and first, of course, to the Chinese. Other people would see his success and follow him. If he had money he would not keep it. He would pour it all into spreading the gospel of good food for all mankind.

On Sundays when Bump was at Sunday School and the town in its Sabbath quiet, Clem in his room alone or walking into the countryside beyond Main Street, planned the business of his life. As soon as Bump was through high school he would begin and Bump could help him. Mr. Janison had offered him a partnership in the store in three more years. He would take it. He had to have a centre somewhere. He would make New Point the centre of a vast marketing network, buying tons of food in regions where harvests were plentiful, and supplying markets wherever there was scarcity. Meanwhile he must prepare himself. He must learn accounting and management as well as marketing. He must learn the geography of the country until he knew it as he knew the palm of his own hand, so that he could see what harvests could be expected from every part of it.

A vast scheme, he told himself, and a noble one, and he wanted to tell Henrietta. He clarified his own mind for many weeks afterwards, writing to her every week of his developing ideas.

'Keep my letters, Henrietta,' he told her. 'I haven't time to make copies. Sometime I may want to check with myself and see how well my notions have worked.'

Henrietta kept his letters with reverence. She bought a tin box and painted it red and kept it locked and in the back of her closet. The key she wore around her neck, and when she wrote this to Clem he sent her a strange dirty-looking little amulet on a string and told her how he had come by it from an old woman in China. 'Put it in the box along with my letters,' he told her. 'It might bring us luck.'

William's wedding was in September after his graduation from college. He had not wanted so early a marriage, and he had suggested to Candace that they wait for a year, or even two, until he knew where he was going to find the two hundred thousand dollars he felt was the least possible capital upon which he could hope to start his newspaper. Candace, who could be a laggard when she must decide, had pouted at the idea of delay.

'If it is only money——'

'It is not just money,' William said. 'I must make my plans very carefully. You don't just start a newspaper. You have to have a prospectus and a dummy and you have to get advertising together.'

'You could do all those things as well after we were married as before,' she insisted. 'I'm going to talk to Papa.'

When she said this William was about to forbid her and then he did not. All summer he had worked hard and late in the city and he had worked alone. Through months so hot that one by one Martin Rosvaine and Blayne Perry and Seth James had stolen away to luxurious homes by sea and mountain and lake, William had lived steadily alone in a cheap two-room flat in lower New York, working day and night upon one dummy after another to get exactly the newspaper he wanted. Once a month he allowed himself to visit Candace. Upon such a visit they were now talking.

'I don't want to depend upon your father,' he said at last.

'Don't be silly,' Candace replied with easy rudeness. 'Papa would do anything for me.'

'So would I,' he said, smiling.

'Then let me talk to Papa,' she said.

'Don't ask him for money, please,' he replied. 'I can find it somewhere.'

He was sorely tempted by the old possibility behind her words, for he had felt compelled to delay his marriage while he searched for money. Grimly handsome and determinedly suave, he had made friends wherever he could among the rich. He was not one of them but he knew how to be. Though through this summer he had stripped himself bare as a coolie, a towel about his loins while he sweated at his desk night after night, there had been other nights when his garments were such that he feared no valet as he sallied forth to dine or dance among the wealthy. He did not talk easily but his high-held head and his correct courtesy served him well enough instead. Silence had this value, he found, that when he did talk people listened.

On this next visit, the last before his marriage, Roger Cameron asked him to come into his private library one night after dinner. William knew the room well for he had been made free of it during college vacations. The books were curious and heterogeneous, and they provided a fair pattern of Mr. Cameron's self-education. There was a whole shelf of Christian Science and now, in latter years, another on the religions of India.

'Sit down,' Mr. Cameron said. 'Candace has been talking to me.'

'I asked her not to, sir,' William said somewhat sternly. But he sat down.

'Yes, well, Candy never obeys anybody,' Mr. Cameron replied mildly. 'Now, William, she wants to get married and she tells me you feel you can't for a year or two.'

'I feel only that I should see my way fairly clear before I take on the support of a wife and a house and so on,' William said.

'That's reasonable,' Mr. Cameron said. 'Very right and reasonable. I did no more in my young days. Fact is, I had to wait. Mrs. Cameron's father wouldn't hear to anything else, no matter how she cried or how I got mad. We waited. Well, thinking about that makes me feel I don't want my girl to go through the same thing her mother did. How much money do you need, William?'

William looked reluctant. 'I don't know exactly.'

'No, I know you don't,' Mr. Cameron said with mild impatience. 'I'm just asking.'

'I think I should see two hundred thousand dollars ahead,' William said.

Mr. Cameron pulled his underlip. 'You don't need that all at once.'

'No, but I have to be able to lay my hands on it.'

They were silent for a while. The big room was dark with oak panelling and the lights were lost in the beamed ceiling.

'Suppose you tell me a little more about this paper,' Roger Cameron said at last. 'What makes you want a paper, anyway? Why don't you come into the Stores with me?'

'I appreciate that, Mr. Cameron,' William said very properly. 'I do indeed. But I have set my heart on building up an entirely original sort of newspaper. If it is successful, I shall begin a chain. It will sell for two cents, and it will have more news than two cents ever bought before.'

'You'll have to get a lot of advertising,' Mr. Cameron said.

'That's where the money will be,' William replied. 'But it's not entirely a matter of money.'

'If it's not a matter of money, what is it?' Mr. Cameron asked with some astonishment.

'I want to accomplish more than making money,' William said. He was not afraid to tell Mr. Cameron the truth. His thin erect body, his high head, his small tense hands clasped together were taut with earnestness. 'I look at it this way, Mr. Cameron. Most of the world is made up of common people. They are stupid and ignorant. What they learn in school doesn't help them to think. They cannot think. They have to be told what to think. They don't know what is right and wrong. They have to be told.'

'People don't like to think,' Mr. Cameron said shrewdly.

'I know that,' William said. 'Therefore they act without thought or they listen to Socialists and agitators and they act foolishly and endanger decent people. I propose to do the thinking, Mr. Cameron. That is why I want a newspaper.'

'How do you know people are going to take to your thoughts?' Mr. Cameron asked. He was very much astonished. He did not know himself what to think of this young man with his lichen-grey eyes.

'I won't say they are my thoughts, Mr. Cameron,' William said. 'I shall do exactly what you do in the Stores. You have men whose job it is to find out what sells best and you buy in quantity what you think people want. Actually, you show people what they ought to buy. That is what I shall do. My paper will be full of what people like. There'll be plenty of stories with pictures about oddities, about murders, about accidents. But there'll be events that happen in the world, too, that people ought to know about.'

'Where are your ideas coming in?' Mr. Cameron demanded.

'In the way everything is told,' William said. 'And not told,' he added.

Mr. Cameron shot him a sharp look. 'Smart,' he murmured. 'Very smart. I hope you're always right.'

'I won't be always right,' William replied. 'But I shall try to be.'

It was more than he had told anybody, even his friends. They knew that he was to be the editor for he had always assumed that he would be, but they did not know that he planned to shape every item, every line, decide the news he would not tell as well as what he did. The paper would be a reflection of his mind and the direction that of his own soul. When he had put out his first issue he would take it to big business firms and show it to top men. He'd say, 'Here is your safeguard. Advertise here and help me influence the people towards Us and away from Them.'

'You don't like folks, do you?' Mr. Cameron said suddenly.

William did not know how to answer. Then he chose the truth. 'I have profound pity for them,' he said.

'Pity breeds contempt,' Mr. Cameron said sententiously.

'Perhaps,' William said. 'You feel the same way, though, Mr. Cameron.'

Mr. Cameron was pulling his lower lip again. 'In a way,' he admitted.

'I knew it as soon as I saw the Stores,' William said. 'If you didn't despise people you couldn't sell that stuff to them.'

'Here—here——' Mr. Cameron said sheepishly.

186

'I admire you for it,' William said. 'But I have a little more idealism than you have. I think the people can be guided to better things.'

Mr. Cameron looked at him sideways. 'You may be wrong, William. People are awfully mulish.'

William did not yield. 'They can be influenced towards something or away from it, just as in the Stores. If you should decide that purple was to be the season's colour, you could get people to buy things in purple.'

'I don't care,' Mr. Cameron said. 'It makes no difference to me what they buy.'

'I do care,' William said.

They did not talk much after that, but after another ten minutes Mr. Cameron got up. 'Well, William, whatever your reasons are I'll say this: I'll put away a hundred thousand dollars—half of what you need—and keep it handy, and I want you to go ahead and have the wedding.'

William flushed. 'Nothing would please me better, Mr. Cameron,' he said.

His marriage day dawned as bright as though he had commanded the sun. At that light striking through his open windows he remembered a story his mother used to tell of his childhood. He had wakened once at dawn in the old temple where his family was summering upon one of those bare brown mountains outside the city of Peking. The light was pearly above the horizon and he had shouted, leaping out of bed, 'Come up, Sun!' At that moment, as though in obedience to his command, the sun sprang above the edge of the earth. He could not have been more than four years old.

The sun had come up as suddenly this morning and he lay realizing as much as he could the meaning of the day. Everything was ready and all that he had to do was simply to be the bridegroom that the day demanded. He had no doubt of himself, for he was to be alone. He had struggled for months over the matter of his sisters and his grandparents and then had dismissed his conscience. Both the girls were at college and his grandfather was not well. The old man was recovering

187

slowly from a stroke and one side of his face was askew. William would not have them at his wedding.

When Candace spoke of them he shook his head. 'I don't want them there,' he said. She had looked at him with strange eyes and had said nothing.

The bridesmaids were six of Candace's school-mates and friends. Jeremy was his best man and Martin, Blayne, and Seth were his ushers. He had made everything as he wanted it.

The door opened and the valet came in, a middle-aged man with a careful English accent.

'Shall I draw your bath, sir?'

'If you please.'

'Mrs. Cameron thought you might like your breakfast fetched on a tray.'

'I would, thanks.'

The ceremony was to be at noon and they were sailing for England immediately. Roger Cameron was giving them the trip. He was giving them a house, too. Not a large one, but a pleasant small structure of cream-coloured brick near Washington Square. William had not pretended that either luxury was in his power to provide.

'Someday I'll be able to do all these things for Candy, sir,' he had said, gracefully accepting the gifts.

'Of course you will,' Roger Cameron had replied.

The bath water stopped running and a valet held up a silk robe, his head turned away. William got out of bed and drew it about his shoulders.

'Bring breakfast in half an hour,' he said with the brusque manner he had learned in his childhood towards servants.

The valet disappeared and William went into the bath. He would stay in his room this morning, away from everyone. The rehearsal had gone off well yesterday. There was no detail left for anxiety. Candace was supposed to sleep until just before she needed to dress for the ceremony. He did not want to see Jeremy or any of the fellows. He could do with two hours or so of pure leisure.

There was a knock at the door and he answered. A footman came in with a small wheeled table on which was set a large

188

tray of covered dishes. In the midst of them was a little silver bowl of roses.

'Your breakfast, Mr. Lane,' the man murmured.

'Set it there by the window, Barney,' William replied. The man was young and not much older than William himself. He was Irish, as his somewhat shapeless face declared, and his eyes were innocent and humble as the eyes of the poor and ignorant should always be. William liked him and had sometimes encouraged him to talk.

''Tis a nice day for it, sir,' Barney now said. He arranged the tray by the window, from which could be seen the trees of the park, their green tinged with coming autumn.

'It is, indeed,' William said. He had put on his new dressing-gown, an affair of blue and black stripes, effective with his dark hair and stone-grey eyes. He should perhaps have kept it for tomorrow when he would be breakfasting with Candace, but he felt that magnificence alone had also its special pleasure.

Barney hovered about the table. 'Your eggs is turned as you like 'em, sir, and the toast I did myself.'

'Thank you.'

'Well, sir,' Barney said at last, 'my best wishes, I'm sure.'

'Thank you,' William said again.

Upon such composure Barney retired. When he had eaten William sat for a while, smoking a cigarette and drinking a second cup of coffee. Two hours were left in which he need do nothing. He did not know how to do nothing. He thought of going to bed, but he could sleep no more. He did not want to think about Candace. There would be plenty of time for that. He could not read.

Two hours—a valuable space of time! When would he be alone again? He got up abruptly and went to the desk at the other end of the room and sat down before it. There for the two hours he worked steadily and in silence until the thump upon his door announced Jeremy. It was time to get ready for his wedding.

A perfect wedding, of course, he had expected. Anything less would have surprised and annoyed him. His ushers did

189

their work well and Jeremy was only less efficient. He seemed strangely thoughtful throughout the ceremony and hesitated a long moment when it came to the ring, so long that Candace looked at him with startled ~yes. But the ring was there in Jeremy's waistcoat pocket and he gave it to William with a veiled, beseeching look.

William did not notice the look. He was absorbed in the proper conduct of his own part, and he slipped the ring on Candace's finger and made his promises. Going down the aisle a few minutes later, his steps measured to the music, he held his head high in his habitual proud fashion.

The fashionable church was crowded. He looked at no one, and yet he was aware of every personage there. Beside him Candace walked as proudly as he did, but it was he who set the step. He had begun the stately march of his life.

Clem's engagement to Henrietta took place abruptly and even awkwardly. The first tentative letters that they had exchanged had carried far more than their proper weight of meaning. They were secret communications between two persons completely solitary. Though Henrietta had moved apparently serene through public high school in the comfortable, unfashionable suburb, living with Ruth, their grandparents, and the two elderly housemaids, she knew herself as lonely as though she lived upon a desert isle. Ruth was popular and pretty and might easily have married while very young any of several men, even before she went to college. That she did not do so, that she postponed marriage by going to college, was because she visited more and more often in William's home. Vacations soon meant a few hurried days with Henrietta and getting a wardrobe together suitable for the rest of the vacation, even the long summer, with William and Candace. There was no discussion of Henrietta's going, too. Ruth had learned to live delicately between her brother and sister, conveying to each the impression of apology and greater affection.

'I feel guilty,' she told Henrietta. 'I go flying off and you stay here and take care of the grandparents.'

'It is what I want to do,' Henrietta said.

Ruth paused in the folding of a silky film. 'You would like Candace if you let yourself. Everybody does. She's very easy.'

'I dare say I would like Candace but there's William,' Henrietta replied with her terrible honesty.

'He is your brother,' Ruth persisted, though timidly. She was equally afraid of Henrietta and William.

'I can't help that,' Henrietta replied. 'Don't forget I knew him long before you did—and much better. We had those two years together at the Chefoo school when you were at home in Peking with Papa and Mama.'

Nevertheless, when Ruth was gone, when she had waved to the pretty face under the flowery hat, smiling through the train window, Henrietta knew she was lonely. Like William's the lines of her face were severe and her frame was angular and tall. Inside she was like him and yet how unlike! She was so like him that she could see in herself his very faults. She had no sense of humour, neither had he. But in their spirits there was no likeness. She was possessed with honesty and a depth of simplicity that frightened away all but the brave, and among the young there are few who are brave. Young men feared her and young girls avoided her. There remained Clem, whom she never had seen and who had never seen her. To Clem, in long silent summer evenings, she poured out her feelings almost unrestrained. He answered her letters on Sundays, when he had sent Bump to church. He had no other vacant hour throughout the week. Even on Sundays he had to work on the books for Mr. Janison.

She went to a small girls' college, an inexpensive one, while Ruth had decided to go to Vassar. She did not want to be with Ruth for by then even she could see that Ruth had chosen William and the sort of life he wanted. She listened to Ruth's account of that life, repelled and forlorn. Ruth's flying blonde hair, her sweet blue eyes, her white skin and slender shape were the means whereby she was welcomed in William's life. William was living in a beautiful house, neither large nor small, on Fifth Avenue. Candace had furnished it in pink and grey and gold. There was a great room where they

191

gave parties. It had been two rooms but William had ordered the wall between taken down. William worked fearfully hard and his paper was getting to be successful. Everybody was talking about it.

'We ought to be proud of him,' Ruth said.

Henrietta did not answer this. She sat gazing at Ruth rather stolidly and no one could have known that she was in her heart giving up this younger sister whom she tenderly loved. When Ruth came back from a long summer spent with William, she had been prepared to tell her about Clem. She had planned it in many ways. She might say, 'Ruth, I don't want you to think I'm in love, but. . . .' Or she might say, 'Do you remember the Faith Mission family in Peking? Well, I know Clem again.' Or she might simply choose one of Clem's letters, perhaps the one that explained how he wanted to open a chain of markets, right across the country, in which people could buy good food cheaply, or if they had no money, they could simply ask for it free. 'People don't ask unless they must—that is, most people,' Clem had written. He had a deep faith in the goodness of people. People didn't like to beg or to be given something for nothing. The human heart was independent. Henrietta was moved by the greatness of Clem's faith. In her loneliness she wanted desperately to believe that this was true. But when Ruth talked about William, Henrietta could not tell her about Clem. The two names were not to be linked together.

Then one day she saw something new in Ruth's face, a quiver about the soft lips, a shyness in those mild eyes. Ruth, catching the loving query in Henrietta's look, suddenly collapsed into tears, her arms around Henrietta's neck and her body flung across her sister's lap.

'Why, baby,' Henrietta breathed. She had not used the name since they had been little girls playing house, and she had always been the mother and Ruth her child. She put her arms about the small creature now and hugged her, and felt how strangely long it was since she had offered a caress to anyone. She and Ruth had not been demonstrative in recent years, and there was no one else.

'I'm in love,' Ruth sobbed. 'I'm terribly, terribly in love.'

'Don't cry,' Henrietta whispered. 'Don't mind, Ruthie. It's all right. It's not wrong. Who is it?'

'Jeremy,' Ruth said in the smallest voice.

Henrietta did not release her hold. She tried to remember Jeremy's face as she had seen it when William graduated from college. A nice face, rather thin, very pale, very kind, this she remembered. Then she remembered slow, rather careful movements, as though something inside hurt him, and very pale and delicate hands, bony and not small.

'Does he know?' she asked.

'Yes, he does,' Ruth said. She slid from Henrietta's lap to the floor and leaned against her knee and wiped her eyes with the edge of Henrietta's gingham skirt. 'He told me first—I wouldn't have dared——'

'You mean you are engaged?' Henrietta asked.

Ruth nodded. 'I suppose so—as soon as he dares to tell. Candace knows, but none of us dares to tell William.'

'Why not?' Henrietta said with fierceness. 'Is there any reason why it is his business?'

'It just seems to be,' Ruth said.

'Nonsense,' Henrietta replied.

Her mind flew to Clem. Was not this the moment to reveal that she too was beginning to love? But still she could not speak of him.

'I'll tell William myself,' she declared.

'Oh, no,' Ruth said quickly. 'Jeremy wants to do it. He will, one of these days. I don't know why he thinks William won't like it.'

'I know,' Henrietta said. Her voice was gloomy. 'William doesn't want the people he goes about with to think he has any family at all. Nobody is good enough for him.'

'That's not quite true,' Ruth said. 'William's very nice to me, usually.'

'Because you always do what he says,' Henrietta said.

'Well, usually I don't see any reason why I shouldn't,' Ruth said. 'Anyway, it's to be kept a secret for a while.'

She got up from the floor and went to the mirror and

smoothed her curls. The intimate moment was over. William had broken it as he always did, and Henrietta said nothing about Clem.

The college year began again and the sisters parted.

Clem's Sunday letters reached Henrietta on Wednesday. She had chemistry laboratory on Wednesday afternoons and among her test-tubes she read the long, closely written letter lying between her notes. Then one week there came the letter she had not expected. On Thursday she scarcely ever bothered to go to see whether she had mail, but that day she had happened to pass by the office and, on the chance that there might be a rare letter from her mother, she stopped and found instead another letter from Clem.

'Do I have to be home early?' Bump had inquired.

He was now a podgy boy who had just begun to wear spectacles. Long ago he had given up rebelling against Clem.

Clem looked at his big dollar watch. 'You can stay out till eleven o'clock but you can't play pool.'

'I was going to the nickleodeon.'

'All right.'

Thus Clem had had the room alone that Monday night while he wrote to Henrietta. It might have been the solitude that moved him to ask her now to marry him. It might have been his constant wish to comfort her for loneliness. It was certainly his unchanging feeling of union with her, though he had never seen her face. She was the only person in the world who could understand when he spoke about his childhood, that other world where all his roots were planted so deeply that there could be no uprooting.

'You and I have not met,' he now wrote. 'It may seem ——' he paused here to look up the word in his dictionary— 'presumptuous for me to have the idea. But I have it and I might as well tell you. It seems to me that you and I are meant to get married. I have not seen you nor you me, but I take it we don't care first for looks. There is something else we have together. We understand things, or so I feel. I hope you do, too.'

He paused here a long time. When he went on he wrote, 'I do not like this idea of proposing to you by letter. If you are willing I will come to see you. Mr. Janison owes me some time and I have saved money. Bump can help in the store after school. I could get away a couple of days and have a whole afternoon with you.'

When he had written these words he then went on to tell her the usual news of his life. Bump had got to like school at last and was even talking of college. He'd have to work his way. He himself had given up hope of a real education but he read a lot, Miss Bean telling him what books. He had just finished *The Wealth of Nations*. It was hard going but full of sense. Then he told his big news. Mr. Janison not having any children, had asked if he didn't want to consider taking over the store some day.

Clem chewed his pen a while when he had written this. Then he went on to tell Henrietta again what he felt and what he had never told anyone except her. 'If I do take this store I won't be content just to handle the one outfit. I will likely start up my cheap food stores in other places. I haven't got it all worked out but I believe it can be done like I have told you. Farmers can sell cheap if they can sell direct. Plenty of people need to eat more and better food. I could maybe think out some way even to ship food across to the people in China, or maybe just help them over there, once I learned how here, to get their own food around. It's really a world proposition, as I see it.'

He paused again, frowned and sighed. 'Henrietta, I hope you will understand that I am not just interested in material things. But I feel that if everybody had enough food so they did not need to worry about where their next meal was coming from, then they could think about better things. I have not the education for teaching people but I could feed them. Anyway, to my thinking, food is something people ought to have the way they have water and air. They ought not to have to ask for it or even work for it, for all have the right to live.'

He paused again and closed his letter with these words. 'I hope you will forget your brother William's attitude towards you as you feel it is, and remember that I care enough to make up for it to you, if you will let me.'

Such a letter deserved many readings before it was committed to certainty, and he read it again and again. There was nothing in it to change, he decided finally, although he would have liked to make it more polished in the writing since she was in college. This he did not know how to do and so he sealed it, addressed it, and took it to the corner post-box. There he noticed by the town clock that it was a quarter past eleven. He was just beginning to allow himself to feel severe about Bump when he saw the light come on in the room above the store. The boy was home, then. Everything was all right. He walked down the street towards the store whistling slightly off key a tune whose name he did not know.

This was the letter Henrietta received on Thursday. She kept it with her all night, waking twice to read it over again by the thin light of a candle shaded against her sleeping room-mate. Of course she wanted to marry Clem. No man had ever asked her to marry him, no boy had ever even asked her to a dance. Yet she wanted to go slowly about loving Clem and marrying him because it was her whole romance and there would be no other. It was wonderful to feel his letter in her bosom, a warm and living promise of love. She could trust his love as she had not trusted even the love of her parents or Ruth's demanding affection. Tomorrow, in the library where it was quiet, up in the stacks where she had a cubbyhole because she was doing a piece of original research in her chemistry, she would write to Clem and tell him that if when they met, they both felt the same way. . . .

The next day in the cubbyhole, writing these very words, she was interrupted by her giggling room-mate.

'Henrietta, there's a man wants to see you!'

'A man?' She was incredulous, too.

'A young man, terribly skinny, covered with dust!'

She knew instantly that it was Clem. Without a word more she ran down the narrow iron steps and across the hall, across the stretch of lawn to the dormitory sitting-room. It was early afternoon and no one else was there except Clem. He stood in the middle of the floor waiting for her.

'I had to come,' he said abruptly and shook her hand with a wrenching grip. 'I oughtn't to have put it in a letter. If a fellow wants to marry a girl he ought to come and say so.'

'Oh,' she gasped, 'that's all right. I didn't mind.'

They stood looking at each other, drinking in the detail of the flesh. They were both plain, both honest, both lonely, and one face looking at the other saw there its own reflection.

'Henrietta, do you feel the way I do?' Clem asked. His voice trembled.

Henrietta flushed. Then he did not mind the way she looked, her straight dark hair, her ugly nose and small grey eyes, her wide mouth.

'You might not like me—after you got to know me.' Her voice was trembling too.

'Everything you are shines right out of you,' he said. 'You're the kind I need—somebody to put my faith in. Oh, I need faith!'

She gave a great sigh that ended in a choking gasp. 'Nobody has ever really needed me, I guess. Oh, Clem——'

They put their arms around each other awkwardly and their lips met in the passionless kiss of inexperienced love.

He stayed the rest of the day and she forgot her work. They wandered together over the campus and she told him about the buildings and pointed out her window. She took him into the chemistry laboratory, empty by the end of the day, and explained to him what she was trying to do, and he listened, straining to understand the union of the elements.

'I sure do wish I had education,' he said with such longing that she could not bear his deprivation.

'Clem, why can't you give up the store and go to college? Lots of fellows work their way through, or very nearly.'

He shook his head. 'I can't afford to do it. I'm too far on my way. Besides, I haven't time for all of it. I just want to learn what I need—this chemistry stuff, for instance. I have an idea I could discover a whole lot of new foods. Has anybody gone at it that way?'

'Not that I know of,' she said.

They took the eight o'clock train to town and had a sandwich together at a cheap restaurant. The night was warm and the darkness was not deep when they were finished. They walked up and down the platform together, hand in hand, dreading to part, now that they had met.

'When shall we meet again?' she asked.

'I don't know,' he said. 'I ought to ask your father, I guess. Isn't that the right thing?'

'I wish nobody needed to know,' she cried with passion. 'I wish you and I could go off together and nobody ever know.'

'I guess that wouldn't be just the right thing,' he said in a reasonable voice. 'I'd feel a whole lot better if I wrote to your father telling about all this. Maybe I ought to tell William.'

'No!' Henrietta cried. She scuffed the edge of her shoe along the black cindered ground. 'I want it all to myself—until we really are married.'

'Won't you tell William?' Clem looked grave.

'No,' Henrietta said in the same passionate voice. 'At least we don't have to tell William.'

'He'll have to know sooner or later,' Clem said.

'Let him find out!' she cried.

The train came racketing in, drowning their voices, and they kissed again quickly, mindful of people about them though they were all strangers, and then Clem swung himself up the steps and she stood with her hands in the pockets of her green coat, watching until the train was gone.

V

'THERE'S a letter from your mother,' Candace said to William. She never opened letters addressed to him after she discovered during her honeymoon that he did not like it. She wondered sometimes if she were stupid because she could never foresee what he would like and what he would not. But once she knew she never forgot.

It was December and they were in the town house. Next week she must gather herself together for Christmas. She clung to these last days of the year, spending the midday hours in a large glass-enclosed porch. She was pregnant with her second child, and next summer there would be another baby.

Just now, Willie, William's namesake, was nearly two years old. She had been married more than five years. She lay on a long and comfortable chair, feeling a little exhausted, perhaps from her horseback ride in the Park. She had not told William that the doctor had forbidden riding because she did not intend to obey such orders. William, had he known, would have insisted upon obedience.

He sat down beside a small metal table and tore open the envelope thick with Chinese stamps. Two letters fell out, one with his father's writing and the other from his mother. He chose his mother's first, for she gave him the most news about what was happening in Peking. She gave the incidents and his father provided the commentary. William was profoundly interested in what was taking place there, for he believed that it was a preliminary pattern of what must happen all over Asia, a surging rise of the common people he feared and distrusted. The mob upon the Peking street had become a memory stamped upon his brain. The one power that could control such madness was in the unconquerable Empress. He remembered the brave old face, impatient and arrogant, bent above him when he was a little boy. He remembered the times he had climbed Coal Hill to look down upon the roofs of her palaces. Having now seen many mansions, he realized that the Old Empress had a magnificence that no mere millionaire could buy. Her palaces were forbidden to all men but no one could forbid an American boy to climb a hill and look down upon her roofs of porcelain blue and gold and upon her marble pillars, and anyone who passed could stare at her closed gates of enamelled vermilion.

Early in July his mother had written of a garden party to be given in September in the Summer Palace and to which all diplomats and their friends had been invited. Now he read that it would never take place. The Old Empress had fallen ill on a bright day in the early autumn, his mother wrote. The young Emperor, sitting at his desk, was disturbed by a eunuch running in and crying out, 'The Old Buddha is dead!' Without one word, without waiting one instant, the young Emperor began to write upon the sheet of paper he had been preparing for the brushing of a poem. Instead of the poem he wrote an order for the death of that statesman who had betrayed him to the Old Empress ten years earlier, when he had dreamed of making his country new again. Before he could seal the paper, the eunuch came running in to cry still more loudly, 'The Old Buddha lives again!' She had rallied to live weeks longer.

William kept silent, for Candace could not know what the Old Empress meant to him. He read on. She had rallied more than once after that, determined to outlive the younger Emperor whom she so distrusted for his eagerness to change old ways for new. He, too, was ill, and she lived and lived again when she heard he was not dead. When she heard that at last he was gone, she gave a great gusty sigh and was willing to die.

'I of scanty merit,' the haughty old woman wrote in her last message to her people. 'I have carried on the government, ever toiling night and day. I have directed the metropolitan and provincial leaders and the military commanders, striving earnestly to secure peace. I have employed the virtuous in office and I have hearkened to the admonitions of my advisers. I have relieved the people in flood and famine. By the grace of Heaven I have suppressed all rebellions and out of danger I have brought back peace.'

William smiled grimly. Brave Old Empress, brave until the end! She had not died until she had seen that weakling dead, a degenerate youth, a puppet in the hands of revolutionists, who would have unleashed all the madness of the people.

Candace watched him but he did not know it. She could never read his face but she saw the passing smile and wanted to know its cause. 'What is it, William? Has something happened?'

'Something is always happening,' William replied. He curved his lips downwards very slightly. He was reading his father's letter, a short one, ending as usual with a bit from the Chinese classics. 'We are upon the threshold of wonderful events, now that the cruel old woman is gone,' his father wrote. 'As Mencius said four hundred years before Christ, "The people are the foundation of the State; the national altars are second in importance; the monarch is the least important of them all." My son, I wish your life could have been spent here in China. It is the centre of the coming world, though few know it.'

William smiled again at this, a different smile. He did not for one moment believe that China was the centre of the world and he did not agree with Mencius.

Candace, watching his face, felt one of her waves of recklessness creep upon her. Why was she afraid of William? She had not been afraid of him before she was married and she could think of no single reason, certainly no incident, to explain why she should now feel that he might be cruel. Jeremy was partly responsible. Jeremy was drinking too much. She had tried to say something to her father about it but he refused to believe it. His religion was a cushion against everything that he did not like and he took refuge in it without shame. There was no use in talking to her mother and she was afraid to tell William. He was hard enough upon Jeremy in the office—hard upon Seth, too. Seth was the chief copy editor. Jeremy was managing editor and stood between Seth and William. William insisted on seeing all the copy and Seth had to make it follow the policy William outlined for his staff upon every event as it came about in the world.

'We don't have to think,' Jeremy had said with his too sprightly humour. 'It's wonderful not to have to think, Candy. It leaves you so much time.'

Seth was not so gay. He refused to talk about William and with Candace he was exceedingly formal. She had to ask Jeremy what was the matter with Seth.

'An independent mind,' Jeremy said with his changeless merriment. 'It's one mind too many. We don't need it. We have William's.'

No one could contradict William. The fantastic success of his newspapers was the final answer to any disagreement with his decisions. In five years the one newspaper he had begun in New York had grown into four, the others published in Chicago, St. Louis, and San Francisco. With a wily combination of pictures, cartoons, and text, William had devised something that had become indispensable to millions of people he never saw. His papers were small enough to handle easily on the subways and while men were eating their lunches at crowded drug-store counters. He gave them exactly what they wanted: financial and business news in a brief space, with a short half-column of prediction and advice; news in carefully chosen pictures of tense drama, the photographs cropped to show nothing but concentrated action; news in capsules of simply written, carefully shaped text, suited to millions of people who read with difficulty and thought very little, and who craved constant diversions because of their inner emptiness. William was too clever to preach. What he wanted could be done by his choice of what news to tell and how it was told. Elimination was half the secret of his power, and headlines were the rest of it. Head-lines alone could tell people how to think.

Jeremy, Martin Rosvaine, and Seth James met sometimes to talk of the papers and of William. They were awed by his genius while they grew more and more afraid of him.

'In another ten years William will be telling the world what to think and nobody will know it,' Martin said. 'Of course

Aunt Rosamond simply loves it. She won't let him pay her back her hundred thousand.'

Aunt Rosamond, as soon as she heard that Roger Cameron had given William a hundred thousand dollars, had insisted on matching it. William had returned Roger's money but it was true that Aunt Rosamond refused any such return.

'The interest is my annuity, William, dear boy,' Aunt Rosamond cackled in her hoarse old voice. She was almost blind but now and again she insisted upon a visit from William, and he treated her half affectionately. There was something he liked in the rude, ruthless, selfish old woman who enjoyed his success and laughed at his newspapers.

'Wonderful trash,' she called them when they were alone, and gave him a dig in the ribs with her sharp elbow.

Upon the three young men, however, William's monstrous and increasing success was beginning to have effect. Martin had attacks of conscience, irritated by Aunt Rosamond's greed, Seth threatened rebellion against William's interference with copy, and Jeremy had begun to drink. The long indecision about Ruth, the months when they were half engaged, the months when he felt he did not want to marry anybody, other months when it was Ruth he did not want, had become years. Through it all her unchanging patience, her unfailing sweetness and faithful love had never let him go. In the end Ruth had won.

A month ago Candace thought Jeremy had softened and become more like the boy she had always known, a moody boy, gay with a gaiety she disliked, but capable at times of thoughtful gravity, hours when he could talk with her, moments out of which he sometimes brought a handful of verses to be cherished. He had not written poetry for years, but now perhaps he would again and she hoped he would, for it was good for him to write poetry. Something in him was crystallized and so became permanent.

She thought she understood the change in him when he told her that he had made up his mind to marry Ruth. He had really fallen in love with Ruth at last, she believed, though Jeremy gave as his reason when he told her so that Ruth was the opposite to William and therefore he could not help loving her.

'But you did like William in college,' Candace said.

'I got to depend on him,' Jeremy said. 'I couldn't have passed my exams without him. I have the same feeling now.'

'You don't have to work at all,' Candace said. 'You and Ruth could live somewhere quite happily. Father wouldn't mind!'

He looked at her with bewildered eyes. 'I don't know why I can't do that,' he said.

Only then did she really begin to think about Ruth. 'Jeremy, I haven't said I'm glad. But I think I am. Will William like it?'

'Of course he won't,' Jeremy said. 'Even Ruth thinks that.'

'Oh, why not?'

'He has an instinct to deny everybody except himself. He likes to feel he has no flesh and blood of his own. He'd like to have a myth about him that he was born without parents—pure son of God.'

Candace was shocked. 'That's a mean thing to say when I'm going to have a baby.'

'Oh, the baby will certainly be another son of God,' Jeremy had said too flippantly. He had been lying on his back on the grass, his body limp, his voice lazy, staring at patches of sky between the leaves of the maples. Candace had not answered him.

'William,' she now said, 'I want to tell you something.'

William folded the letters from China. 'Well?'

'Jeremy and Ruth are engaged at last,' she said baldly. 'I'm glad. It's been on and off for years—he couldn't make up his mind.' She turned her head to look at William and saw a bluish flush upon his face.

'When did this take place?' he asked.

'About a month ago.'

'And you have known all this time?'

'Not quite all.'

204

She waited for his anger but it did not fall. The bluish flush died away and he was more ashen than ever.

'Don't you think it's rather nice?' she asked.

He got up, his letters in his hand. 'I don't think one way or the other about it,' he said. 'It seems to me a matter of no importance at all.'

'Then you won't mind her being married here?'

'I suppose not.'

'I'd like to make it a pretty wedding—soon, before I get too clumsy. They don't want to wait.'

'Do as you please,' William said. He hesitated a moment and then went on rather abruptly. 'These letters give me an idea for an editorial I'd like to write for tomorrow. I hope you won't mind if I don't show up for dinner.'

'I'll miss you,' she said with her coaxing smile.

'I'm sorry,' he said rather formally. He bent over her, however, and kissed her hair before he went his way. She watched him as he walked and seeing his bent head, his hands holding the letters clasped behind his back, she thought suddenly that he looked like a priest. That, perhaps, was what William should have been.

Ruth was married on New Year's Eve and Henrietta was her maid of honour. Upon this Ruth had insisted, and Candace had chosen the wedding garments. Ruth of course must wear white satin, but Candace designed for Henrietta a thick, clinging silk of daffodil yellow to be worn with a wide green sash. Henrietta's darkness was made to glow. She did not protest. Holding within her breast the ineffable secret of Clem, she allowed herself to be dressed for the first time in her life with purpose for beauty.

She was twice in William's house, and the first time was after the fitting of her dress, when Candace brought both young women home for luncheon. William was not there, but Jeremy was. He had left the office brazenly early, without telling anybody.

'What is the use of being William's brother-in-law if I have to be afraid of him?' he inquired of them. 'He can't fire me.'

'Oh, Jeremy,' Ruth cried, softly shocked.

'Jeremy is not to be taken seriously since he grew up,' Candace told Henrietta. 'He used to be quite serious when he was a little boy.'

They were at the long table in the big dining-room, and the mahogany shone through Italian lace. They sat two by two, Henrietta beside Candace, and the ends of the table were empty, though the butler had set William's place. His place was always set, whether he came or not.

'When I was a little boy I was serious because I thought I was going to die,' Jeremy said, tilting his wine glass as closely as he could without spilling the red wine. 'Now I know I have to live. One has to be gay when one cannot escape life. Eh, Ruthie?'

'I don't know what you're talking about,' Ruth cried happily.

The wedding was beautiful. William gave Ruth away since their father was in Peking, and against his dignity her white softness was the contrast of a rose against rock. The wedding was in William's house, although Ruth had wanted a church wedding, and had thought that it would be in St. John's where William and Candace went regularly on Sunday mornings. So it had been planned. But William, at Christmas-tide, had come into some strange conflict with the rector, which he had never explained, and had withdrawn his membership. He went to church no more and it would have been too conspicuous to have allowed the wedding to take place somewhere else. It was only a small wedding. Ruth had never come out, and she knew few people. There was no reason, William told Candace, why his friends, or hers either, should be invited to come to see a young woman married of whose existence they had only accidentally heard.

The large drawing-room made a pleasant place. The florist set up an altar at one end and Ruth's college preacher came to marry them. William was kindly even to Henrietta, and to his grandparents he was almost gentle. They had aged very much. Henrietta matched him in being kind, and thought of Clem and still could not bring herself to speak his name.

None of them were staying after the wedding. They went with Jeremy and Ruth to the dock and saw them aboard a ship for France. William was not with them. A call from his office had compelled him away. Then, with her daffodil dress packed carefully in her suit-case, Henrietta went home with her grandparents.

That night she told them about Clem. They sat together in the large and now rather shabby living-room, and she tried to make them see why she must marry Clem.

'He is the only person in the world who knows everything about me,' she told them.

They listened simply, knowing somehow that there was very much that they did not know. China was a land they could not imagine and it seemed to them monstrous and inexplicable.

'You won't be going back to China, I hope,' her grandmother murmured.

'I don't know what Clem will do,' Henrietta said. 'He is always thinking about the world. If he goes of course I will, too.'

The old couple had had a hard day and they were not interested in the world. Mr. Vandervent yawned and touched the bell. When Millie, who always sat up until the family was in bed, came he asked for milk.

'Make it hot, Millie, and put a little sherry wine in it.'

'I will, Mr. Vandervent,' she answered.

A few minutes later, drowsily drinking his sherried milk, he nodded his head to Henrietta. 'I suppose it is only what we must expect,' he said vaguely. They went upstairs to bed without asking her anything more and she sat down at her desk to write Clem a long letter.

'Clem, I want to be married now. I don't want to go on with my doctorate. . . .'

After her graduation from college she had decided to go on with her doctorate in chemistry with the hope that she could be useful to Clem. This was after something he had said one day.

'I do wish I could have studied chemistry, hon,' he had said. 'Take soy-beans, for instance. Remember how the

Chinese eat bean curd? You reckon you know enough to help me, hon?'

'I'd have to study some more,' she said.

She was still a little hurt because he had cried out eagerly, 'Do you reckon you could, hon?' But she would not let herself be hurt with Clem. She knew his greatness. He could not put himself first.

After she had finished college, *summa cum laude*, an honour of which she scorned to tell William and which Clem could not fully comprehend, and which seemed only to surprise her parents, she had entered Columbia for more work in chemistry. Now, half-way through, suddenly she could not go on.

She gave her wild arguments to Clem, that nobody loved her and that she was too lonely to live. Even at college she had been lonely because, not having lived in America, she could not talk with other girls. She wanted to be with Clem, and him alone, and never leave him.

Clem sent back words grave and wise about finishing her education and not regretting things later, and about not being able to forgive himself if afterwards she were sorry. When he had a torrent of letters from her all saying the same thing over and over again, he knew that it was true that she could die of her loneliness, because it was like his, a spiritual hunger that sent out seeking roots to find an earth its own. It was time for them to come together.

He went to her one day in June and made himself known to her grandparents to satisfy his own conscience, since he could not speak face to face with her father nor would Henrietta allow him to tell William of their love. The old couple were bewildered and anxious to do no wrong, but when Clem talked to them a while they were glad to think that there was nothing they could do. The young people had made up their minds.

'You may write to Father and Mother and tell them you cannot do anything about us,' Henrietta said.

Her grandfather sighed. 'We won't write, Henrietta. We'll leave it to you.'

'It's up to you young people,' her grandmother murmured. 'We've done our best.'

Henrietta was moved to kiss them both for the first time in her life. She was a new creature now that she had made Clem understand that it was right for them to be married at once. She was almost gay. No wedding, she said, for whom had they to invite?

As soon as Clem had the licence, she and Clem and the grandparents went one evening to the parsonage of the Presbyterian church near by and there they were married. She wore her yellow dress, and Clem bought her some shell-pink roses to hold. He had bought, too, a wide, old-fashioned gold wedding ring, the only ring she had ever possessed. When Clem put it on her finger she knew it would be there forever, enclosing dust when she was dead.

They went back to the house soberly to eat of a cake Millie had made and drink a toast in burgundy wine from a bottle her grandfather opened. Then she changed into her dark blue silk suit, the only new garment she had bought, and she had a strange uncertain feeling that though her grandparents yearned over her, they were glad to see her go, glad to get youth out of their ageing house. They were tired and they wanted to sleep.

VI

HENRIETTA sat sewing in the small living-room of her home. She was not good at sewing. Her fingers were clumsy and the thread knotted often, but it did not occur to her to give up merely because she was not adept and so she sewed steadily on, glancing only occasionally through the window by which she sat. The scene was simple enough, a street of cheap houses much like this one that she and Clem had rented next to the store. Whatever grace the street had came from two rows of maple trees which were now beginning to show the hues of autumn. It was late afternoon and under the trees children were playing in the leaves, running hither and thither, apparently unwatched unless a quarrel brought a mother to the door.

'You, Dottie! Stop kicking your little brother!'

'But I wanna!'

'I don't care what you want. Stop it, I say!'

She wondered if Clem wanted children. They had never talked of children, each for some unspoken reason. She was not sure whether she even wanted children. She had never got used to living in America and she would not know how to bring up a child. In China there had been the amahs. Here she would have to wash all the child's things, and tend it herself when it cried. Besides, Clem was enough. He was a dozen men in one, with all the great schemes in his head. It would be as much as she could do to see that he lived to carry them through.

That he would succeed she did not doubt. From the moment she had seen him in the dingy college sitting-room she had believed in him. Trust was the foundation of her love. She could not love anyone unless she trusted and for that reason she really loved no one except Clem and her father.

As long as she lived she would not forgive William because he was angry when he found that she had married Clem. She had written to Ruth, after all, and at first Ruth had not dared to tell William the whole truth. She had let William think the marriage had not yet taken place and he tried to stop it, thinking it still only an engagement. He had actually cabled to Peking to his mother. When she opened the cable from her mother forbidding her too late to marry Clem, she had known it was William's doing.

'That ignorant fellow!' William had called Clem, and Ruth had told her.

Even Ruth was sorry. 'I wish you'd told us, Henrietta. It wasn't kind. He isn't suitable for you. You won't be able to bring him to William's house.'

'I shall never want to go to William's house.' That was what she had answered. She would never be afraid of William, however many newspapers he had. Clem was so innocent, so good. He did not like her to say anything against William.

'He's your brother, hon—it would be nice if you could be friends.' That was all Clem said.

When she told him how William felt about their marriage, Clem only looked solemn. 'He don't understand, hon. People are apt to make mistakes when they don't understand.' She could not persuade him to anger.

She had written to her parents herself, a vehement letter declaring her independence and Clem's goodness, and her father had replied, mildly astonished at the fuss. 'I don't see why you should not marry Clem Miller. I should be sorry to see you in the circumstances of his father, but nowadays nobody lives by faith alone.'

Her mother had been surprisingly amiable, sending as a wedding present a table-cloth of grass linen embroidered by the Chinese convent nuns. Henrietta guessed shrewdly that her mother did not really care whom she married.

As for Clem, he wistfully admired William's success.

'If William could get interested in my food idea, now, how we could go! He could set people thinking and then things would begin to happen.'

'He doesn't want them to think,' Henrietta said quickly.

'Oh now, now!' Clem said.

The clock struck six and up and down the street the supper bells rang. She rose to look at the roast and potatoes in the oven and to cut bread and set out milk. Clem would be home soon and he would want to eat and get back to the store. She moved slowly, with a heavy grace of which she was unconscious. Her immobile face, grave under the braids of her dark hair, seldom changed its expression. Now that she was with Clem her eyes were finer than ever, large and deep-set, under her clear brows; yet at times they held a look of inner bewilderment as though she were uncertain of something, herself perhaps, or perhaps the world. It was no small bewilderment thus revealed but one as vague and large as her mind, as though she did not know what to think of human existence.

The door in the narrow hall opened sharply and then shut, and the atmosphere of the house changed. Clem had come in.

'Hon, you there?' It was his greeting although he knew she was always there.

'I'm here,' she replied. Her voice was big and deep.

He came to the kitchen, his light step quick-moving. Their eyes met, she standing by the stove with a pot holder in her hand, and he crossing to the sink to wash. He washed as he did everything, with nervous speed and thoroughness, and he dried his face and hair and hands on a brown huck towel that hung on the wall. Then he came to her and kissed her cheek. He was not quite as tall as she was.

'Food ready?'

'I am just dishing up.'

He never spoke of a meal but always of food. He sat down to the roast she set before him and began to carve it neatly and with the same speed with which he did all else. Two slices cut thin he arranged on a plate for her, put a browned potato beside them, and handed the plate to her. Then he cut his own slice, smaller and even thinner.

'Can't you eat a little more, Clem?' Henrietta asked.

'Don't dare tonight, hon. I have a man waiting for me over there.'

'You didn't want to bring him home?'

'No. I was afraid we'd talk business all through our food

and my stomach would turn on me again. I want a little peace, just with you.'

She sat in silence, helping him to raw tomatoes and then to lima beans. Then she helped herself. Neither spoke while they ate. She was used to this and liked it because she knew that in her silence he found rest. They were in communion, sitting here alone at their table. When he was rested he would begin to talk. He ate too fast but she did not remind him of it. She knew him better than she knew herself. He was made of taut wire and quicksilver and electricity. Whatever he did she must not lay one featherweight of reproach upon him. Sometimes she tortured herself with the fear that he would die young, worn out before his time by the enormous scheme he had undertaken, but she knew that she could not prevent anything. He must go his own way because for him there was no other, and she must follow.

In this country which was her own, she still continued to feel a stranger and her only security was Clem. Everything else here was different from Peking and her childhood and she would not have known how to live without him. When sometimes in the night she tried to tell him this he listened until she had finished. Then he always said the same thing. 'Folks are the same anywhere, you'll find, hon.'

But they were not. Nobody in America was like the Chinese she had known in Peking. She could not talk to anybody in New Point about—well, life! They talked here about things, and she cared nothing about things. 'All under Heaven . . .' that was the way old Mrs. Huang used to begin conversation when she went over to the Huang hutung.

She looked at Clem and smiled. 'Do you remember how the Chinese loved to begin by saying, "All under Heaven"?'

'And go on to talk about everything under heaven!'

'Yes—you remember, too.'

'I wish I didn't have to hurry, hon, but I do.'

'I know, I don't know why I thought of that.'

They were silent again while he cleaned his plate and she pondered the ways of men and the things for which they sacrificed themselves. William, sitting in his splendid offices in New York, was a slave to a scheme as much as Clem was, and yet how differently and with what opposite purpose! She could not have devoted herself to Clem had he wanted to be rich for power. He did not think of money except as something to further his purpose, a purpose so enormous that she would have been afraid to tell anyone what it was, lest they think him mad. But she knew he was not mad.

Clem put down his knife and fork. 'Well, what's for dessert?'

'Stewed apples. I would have made a pie but you said last time——'

'Pie won't leave me alone after I've eaten it. I can't be bothered with something rarin' in my stomach when I've got work to do.'

She rose, changed the plates, and brought the fruit. He ate it in a few bites, got up and threw himself in a deep rocking-chair, and closed his eyes. For ten minutes he would sleep.

She sat motionless, not moving to clear the table or take up her sewing. She had learned to sit thus that his sleep might not be disturbed by any sound. His hearing was so sharp that the slightest movement or whisper could wake him. But she did not mind sitting and watching him while he slept. They were so close, so nearly one, that his sleep seemed to rest her, too. Only her mind wandered, vaguely awake.

He opened his eyes as suddenly as he had closed them, and getting up he came back to his seat at the table facing her.

'Hon, I feel I'm wasting you.'

She could not answer this, not knowing what he meant.

'Here I have married me a fine wife, college educated, and all she does is to cook my meals and darn my socks!'

'Isn't that what wives are supposed to do?'

'Not mine.'

He looked at her fondly and she flushed. She had learned now that she would never hear the words of love that women crave from men. Clem did not know them. She doubted if he had ever read a book wherein they were contained. But she did not miss them for she had never had them, either. She knew very well that Clem was the only person who had ever

214

loved her, and of his love she was sure, not by words but by his very presence whenever he came near. The transparency of his being was such that love shone through him like light. It shone upon her now as he sat looking at her, half-smiling. She saw memory in his eyes.

'Remember that brown Chinese bread we used to have in Peking, hon? The kind they baked on the inside of the charcoal ovens, slapped against the side, and sprinkled with sesame seeds?'

'Yes, I remember . . . the flat ones. . . .'

'Yes.'

'What about it, Clem?'

'I don't know. I get a hankering sometimes to taste it again. What say we go back, hon?'

'To China, Clem?'

'Just for a look round. I might forget what used to be if I saw what Peking is like now.'

He looked white and tired and her heart felt faint. Why did she always have that premonition, undefined, unreasonable, that she was stronger than he, more indestructible, more lasting? No flame like his burned within her, and she was not consumed.

'It would be good to go back, Clem.'

'Think so, hon? Well, we'll see.'

He got up with his usual alertness and the premonition was gone. There was no reason to think—anything! But when he was gone she sat thinking and idle. Yes, she remembered the loaves of sesame bread hot from the oven of the old one-eyed vender. She had often slipped through the unguarded back gate and, creeping beside the wall of the mission compound, she had waited, hidden by a clump of dwarf bamboo at the end of the wall. She could hear even now the vender's high call as he came down the street, always at the same hour, that hungry mid-morning hour on Saturday when she and Ruth were supposed to be doing their lessons for Monday. He always looked behind the bamboos for her and grinned when he saw her, his jaws altogether toothless.

'Hot ones,' she always said.

215

'Do I not know?' he retorted, and reaching down into the little earthen oven he peeled the bread cakes, two of them, from the sides. His hands were always filthy. Flour and dough blackened by smoke clung in their cracks and his nails were black claws, but she would not think of that in her hunger for the bread. She paid him two pennies and ran back into the compound, the cakes under her jumper. Ruth would not eat them because his hands were dirty and so she ate them herself, the flavour delicious, the sesame seeds nut-like in their delicacy. Clem had eaten that bread, too, but William never had. Like Ruth, William would have thought of the man's dirty hands, but she and Clem thought of the bread, hot from the coals. It was good bread.

She rose and began to clear the table. What Clem was doing was as simple as what the old vender did. Two cakes of bread, for a penny apiece; the old vender made it and went about selling it. If it was good enough people bought it, that was all. Not only bread, either! If anything was good enough and cheap enough, people wanted it. That was all. What Clem was doing was simple and tremendous, so simple that people did not think he was doing anything, and so tremendous they would not have believed it had they known. Only when they saw the finished thing, the bread, the meat, the food, standing there ready to be bought, cheap and good, would they believe. And believing they still would not understand.

Sometimes at night Clem wanted to read the Bible. They did not go to church and neither of them said their prayers unless they felt like it. But sometimes he wanted to read aloud to her. The night before, when they were in bed, he had lighted the lamp and taken up the small old Bible he kept on the shelf under the bed-side table. He turned to the place where Jesus had taken the loaves and fishes and had fed everybody that was hungry, and he read it slowly, almost as if to himself, while she listened. When he had read of the baskets of crumbs that were filled he closed the book and lay back on the pillow, his hands behind his head, his eyes fixed on the ceiling.

'That's what I aim to do,' he had said. 'In my own way, of course. But I like to read once in a while of how somebody else did it. We have the same idea—feed the hungry. I've got to find some way of making food cheaper, hon. I wish I could make it free. There ought to be a way for a starving man to get food without paying for it. There must be a way.'

When the table was cleared, the dishes washed, she sat down again to her sewing. The afternoon sun shone down on the quiet street. It was as peaceful and permanent a scene as a woman could look upon, and millions of women looked out upon just such quiet streets in small towns all over America. They would expect to spend their lives there, rearing their children, caring for their grandchildren. But Henrietta, lifting her eyes, knew that for her the street was only a moment's scene. Clem wanted her to go with him, and there was no end to a road once he had set his feet upon it.

Clem was master now in the store. He had bought out Mr. Janison after he and Henrietta were married, and Bump, too, was a full partner. Clem was immensely proud of Bump and, since he was a college graduate, Clem treated him with something like reverence. It was a miracle to Clem to see that the lost child had become a serious, spectacled young man, honest and painfully hard working—though unfortunately without a sense of humour. Bump listened to everything Clem said, and to his nonsense as well as to his commands, to his dreams as well as to his calculations, he gave the same intense attention. He gave his advice when Clem asked for it, which was often, and tried not to be hurt when Clem did not take it. Clem was an individual of deepest dye, and in his way a selfishly unselfish man. He paid no heed whatever to any schemes for the benefit of mankind except his own. He was convinced more than ever that any government would fail unless people were first given a steady diet of full meals, but given this diet almost any government would do, and he preached this as a gospel.

With Bump at his side, always with a pad and pencil, Clem toured the country in one of the earliest of the Ford cars. In the villages and out-of-the-way places, wherever crops rotted because the railways could not serve the farmers, he found ways of conveying the foods by hack, by wagon, and as time went on by truck to railways or to markets. His markets he established anywhere there were people and food near enough to be brought together. Travellers came upon huge, hideously cheap structures in the midst of the tents of migrant workers as well as in the slums of great cities. Some of the structures were permanent, some were immense corrugated iron shacks, made to be taken away when people moved on.

In spite of himself, Clem was beginning to make money. He looked at Bump with a lifted right brow one day and threw half a dozen cheques at him across the big pine table in the back room of the store, where he made his head office.

'More stuff for the bank, Bump. I'll have to begin thinking of ways to spend it. All I need ahead is enough to start the next market, but it keeps rolling in. Guess I'll have to begin on the rest of the world.'

In this instant an old smouldering homesickness sprang into flame. With money piling up he could go to China at last. He had no wish to stay there. He wanted merely to go back to walk again the dusty streets, to enter again Mr. Fong's house, and to see for himself the graves of his parents and sisters. For Yusan, reviving his English, had written to him long ago that Mr. Fong had gone secretly for the dead bodies and had buried them outside the city in his own family cemetery upon one of the western hills. Upon two heavy Chinese coffins, in each of which was a child with a parent, Mr. Fong had sealed the lids, had lied to the guards at the city gate, and pretending that the dead were his brother and his wife, stricken together of a contagious fever, he had put the wounded bodies into the earth. Could Clem see for himself not only the graves of his dead, but also the faces of the living people friendly again and cheerful as he remembered them, then some secret load of which he never allowed himself to think might roll away. He would be homesick no more for any other country. But he could not go without Henrietta. He could hop into his Ford, rebuilt to his order so that it would survive equally well the hill roads in West Virginia and the sands in Nebraska, and he could leave her for weeks, so long as they were on the same soil. But he could not contemplate the ocean between them.

One day last November he had seen an item in the country newspaper, the only newspaper he read. There was a big head-line, and it was not even on the front page. Nevertheless it was a piece of news whose importance no one but himself in the town, perhaps no one but himself in the state and perhaps in the nation could understand. The Empress of China was dead. This in itself was enough to change the atmosphere of his living memory.

Clem read and sat down on a keg and read again. So she was dead, that gorgeous and evil woman, whose legend he had heard in the city over which she had brooded, a monstrous, gaudy bird of prey! When he thought of her gone, of Peking freed of her presence, of the palaces empty, bonds fell from his heart. His parents, his little sisters, were avenged. He need not think of them any more. The past was ended for him.

Now, with these cheques before him, it suddenly came to him that it was time to go to China.

'Bump!' he cried. 'Take over, will you? I'm going home.'

Bump nodded, and the young clerks glared at Clem. But he saw nothing. He walked home with his brisk half-trot and opened the front door and shouted.

'Hon, I guess we're going to China now!' From far off, somewhere in the back-yard where she was taking dry fresh clothes from the line, came Henrietta's voice.

'All right, Clem!'

Swaying in a temperamental train northwards from Nanking, Henrietta gave herself up to nostalgia. In their small compartment Clem gazed, ruminating, from the dirty windows. It was comforting to see good green fields of cabbage and young winter wheat. The Chinese knew how to feed themselves. His stomach, always ready for protest, was soothed and he turned to Henrietta.

'You know, hon?'

'What should I know?' A flicker upon her grave lips was her smile for him.

'When I get to Peking I am going to hunt up one of those

old Mohammedan restaurants and get me a good meal of broiled mutton. I have a hunch it would set well with me.'

'If you think so then it will,' she replied.

They had received no mail for weeks, but she had supposed that at this time of year her parents were in Peking, and soon she would meet them. How she would behave depended upon how they received Clem. Her father, she knew, would be amiable, his nature and his religion alike compelling him to this, but her mother she could not predict. To prepare them she had telegraphed from the bleak hotel in Shanghai. To this telegram she had no answer while they waited for hotel laundry to be done. Twenty-four hours was enough for laundry, but a zealous washerman starched Clem's collars beyond endurance for his thin neck, and the starch had to be washed out again. The laundryman declared himself unable to cope with collars that had no starch, and Henrietta had borrowed a charcoal iron from a room boy and ironed for a day while Clem roamed the streets of the Chinese city. They left the next day without waiting for the telegram. Her father might be on one of his preaching trips, her mother perhaps visiting in Tientsin while he was gone.

At Nanking, however, a telegram reached her, forwarded from the hotel and provoking in its economy: DR. AND MRS. LANE LEFT FOR UNITED STATES.

'But why?' she asked Clem.

'We'd better go on to Peking and find out,' he said. 'We've been travelling too fast for letters, hon.'

So they sat in the compartment and watched the landscape turn from rolling hills to the flat grey fields of the north. Clem was unusually silent and she knew that he was facing his own memories at last. They were tender towards each other, thoughtful about small comforts, and now and again at some well-remembered sight and sound, a chubby child barefoot in the path, the clear sad note of a blind man's small brass gong, they looked at each other and smiled without speaking. She did not ask Clem what his thoughts were, shrinking from intrusion even of love upon that gravity.

The country grew poorer as they went north and villagers,

despoiled by bandits of their homes, came to the train platform to beg. They stood in huddles, holding up their hands like cracked bowls, wailing aloud the disasters that had fallen upon them. A few small coins fell out of the windows of second- and third-class compartments and once she put out her hands filled with small bills and saw the unbelieving joy upon the faces of the people.

'American—American!' they shrieked after her beseechingly.

'I'm glad you did that, hon,' Clem said.

'It's no use, of course,' she said and got up and went to the club car because she could not sit still. There, his back to the window and the ruined village and the beggars, a young Chinese in a long gown of bright blue brocaded silk was looking at a copy of one of William's newspapers. She wondered how he had got the paper, but would not ask. Doubtless some American traveller had left it at a hotel, and it had been picked up eagerly, as all American papers were. She sat down near him and after a few minutes he pointed to the photographs.

'Is this your country?'

'Yes,' she said. 'It is the land of my ancestors.'

'How is it that you speak Chinese?'

'I lived here as a child.'

'And you come back, when you could stay in your own land?'

'Not everything there is as you see.'

'But this is true?'

He kept his eyes upon pictures of rich interiors of millionaires' houses, upon huge motor-cars and vast granaries and machinery which he could not comprehend.

'Such things can be found,' she admitted.

She wanted to explain to him how anything was true in America, all that he saw and all that was not there for him to see. But she knew it was no use beginning, for he would only believe what he saw, and then she was really convinced that William had done this with purpose, that there would never be anything in the pages of William's papers except what he wanted people to read, the pictures he wanted them to see. And so, no one would ever really know America, and to her the best of America was not there, for the best was not in the riches and the splendour, in the filled granaries and the machines.

She got up because she did not want to talk to the young man any more and went back to the little compartment. Clem sat asleep, his head bobbing on his thin neck. A frightening tenderness filled her heart. He was too good to live, a saint and a child. Then she comforted herself. Surely his was the goodness of millions of ordinary American men, whether rich or poor, and Clem was not really a rich man, because he did not know how to enjoy riches, except to use them for his dreams of feeding people. He liked his plain old brass bed at home, a thing of creaking joints and sagging wire mattress, and he still thought a rocking-chair was the most comfortable seat man could devise. He was narrow and limited and in some ways very ignorant, but all the beauty of America was in him, because he talked to everybody exactly the same way and it did not occur to him to measure one man against another or even against himself.

She sat down beside him. Softly she put her arm around him and drew his head down to rest upon her shoulder and he did not wake.

In Peking Clem continued silent. Against his will the horror of old memories fell upon him. Here he had been an outcast child respected neither by Americans nor Chinese, because of his father's faith and poverty. By accident the hotel where he and Henrietta lodged was upon the very street where he had fought the baker's son and where William had descended from his mother's private rickshaw. He pointed out the spot to Henrietta ten minutes after they had entered the room and for the first time he told her the story. Listening, she discerned by the intuition which worked only towards Clem, that the old pain still lingered.

'William was a hateful boy,' she declared with fierceness.

Clem shook his head at this. He was repelled by judgements. 'I was a pitiful specimen, I guess,' he dismissed himself. 'We'd better go and find out about your folks, hon.'

.So they left the hotel and walked down the broad street, followed by clamouring rickshaw men who felt themselves defrauded of their right to earn a living when two foreigners walked.

'I'd forgotten how poor the people are. I guess I never knew before, being so poor myself.'

'Here is the back gate of the compound,' Henrietta said. 'I used to creep out here to buy steamed meat rolls and sesame bread.'

They entered the small gate and walked to the front of the square brick mission house.

'I was here once,' Clem said. 'It all looks smaller.'

The house was locked, but a gate-man ran towards them.

'Where is Lao Li?' Henrietta asked.

The gate-man stared at her. 'He has gone back to his village. How did you know him?'

'I grew up here,' Henrietta said. 'I am the Lane elder daughter. Where are my parents?'

The gate-man grinned and bowed. 'They have gone to their own country, Elder Sister. Your honoured father grew thin and ill. He goes to find your elder brother, who is now a big rich man in America.'

'Can it be?' Henrietta asked of Clem.

'Could be, hon—want to go right home?'

She pondered and spoke after a moment. 'No—we're here. Haven't I forsaken them to cleave to you, Clem? I really have. Besides, Mother would go straight to William, not to me.'

Clem received this without reply, and they went away again. The quiet compound, budding with spring, was like an island enclosed and forgotten in the midst of the city. The only sign of life was two women and a little boy at the far end of the lawn, digging clover and shepherd's-purse to add to their meal that night.

'It all seems dead,' Henrietta said.

'It is dead, hon,' Clem replied. 'In its way all that old life is dead, but the ones who live it don't know it—not even your father, I guess. What say we find the Fongs?'

Mr. Fong had prospered during the years of civil war. Ignoring the political manœuvres of military men and passing by in silence the rantings of students upon the streets, he had begun to stock his bookshop with other things people wanted to buy, needles and threads, brightly coloured woollen yarns, clocks and dishes, machine-knitted vests and socks, leather shoes and winter gloves, pocket-books and fountain-pens and tennis shoes, pencils and rubber hot-water bottles. Most of his goods came from Japan and he was uneasy about this, for young students who were also zealous patriots often ransacked shops, heaped the goods in bonfires, and pasted labels on the shop windows announcing that so and so was a traitor and a Japan lover. Mr. Fong made two cautious trips a year to Japan to buy goods, and he had consulted with the Japanese businessmen with whom he did such profitable trade, and thereafter his goods were marked 'Made in U.S.A.' A small shipping town in Japan was named Usa for this convenience. Mr. Fong had then continued to prosper without sense of sin, for he considered all warfare nonsense and beneath the notice of sensible businessmen. He had peace of mind in other ways, for his family shared his health and prosperity and his eldest son had continued to improve the English which Clem had long ago begun to teach him. Yusan was now a tall youth, already married to a young woman his parents had chosen for him, and she had immediately become pregnant.

On a certain clear cool day in early spring Mr. Fong felt that life would be entirely good if politicians and soldiers and students were cast into the sea. His content was increased by the pleasant smell of hot sugar and lard that Mrs. Fong was mixing together in preparation for some cakes, helped by his eldest daughter, who was already betrothed to a young man whose father was a grain dealer. Mr. Fong's two younger sons, Yuming and Yuwen, were playing with jackstones in the court, for the holiday of the Crack of Spring had begun.

Upon this pleasant household Clem and Henrietta arrived. The door was opened by Yuwen, who had been born after Clem went away. Nevertheless the American was a legend in the Fong family and Yuwen recognized him with alacrity and

224

smiles. He left the door ajar and ran back to tell his father that Mr. Mei had come back. Mr. Fong dropped his pipe and shouted for Yusan, who was in his own part of the house and made haste to the gate.

With hands outstretched he greeted Clem. 'You have come back—you have come back!' he spluttered. 'Is this your lady? Come in—come in—so you have come back!'

'I have come back,' Clem said.

Thus Clem with Henrietta at his side entered again this fragment of the old world of his childhood and smelled again the familiar smells of a Chinese household, a mingling of sweetmeats and incense and candles of cowfat. There was even the old faint undertone of urine, which told him that Mr. Fong had not become more modern during the years and that he still stepped just outside his door when it was necessary. Smell of whitewash from the walls, smell of old wood from the rafters, and the damp smell of wet flagstones in the court were all the same. The pomegranate tree was bigger, and the goldfish in the square pool, roused by the sun, were huge and round.

Clem gazed down into the shallow pool. 'Same fish?'

'The same,' Mr. Fong said. 'Here everything is the same.'

A scream made them turn. Mrs. Fong rushed out of the open doors of the central living-room.

'You are come—you are come!'

She took Clem's hand in both of hers. 'He is like my son,' she told Henrietta. Her round face was a net of smiling wrinkles.

'You must take her for your daughter-in-law,' Clem said. 'Her father is Lane Teacher.'

'A good man, a good man!' Mr. Fong cried.

Yusan came out next and he and Clem shook hands in the foreign fashion, and then Yusan put his hand over Clem's. 'We have often asked the gods to bring you back to us.' To Henrietta he said with great courtesy, 'My inner one asks you to go to her. She is very big just now with our first child, and does not like to come out before men she has not seen before.'

'Come with me,' Mrs. Fong said, and Henrietta stepped over the high wooden threshold.

'We will sit in the sun,' Mr. Fong said to Clem. 'I do not need to be polite with you. Yuming, Yuwen—do not stand there staring. Go and fetch tea and food.'

The three men sat down upon porcelain stools set in the court and Mr. Fong surveyed with love this one returned. 'You are too thin,' he told Clem. 'You must eat more.'

'Elder Brother, I have a weak stomach,' Clem replied.

'Then you are too agitated about something,' Mr. Fong said. 'Tell me what it is. You must not agitate yourself.'

Thus invited Clem began talking, as he always did sooner or later, about his hope of selling cheap food even here in China.

Mr. Fong and Yusan listened. Yusan never spoke before his father did, and Mr. Fong said, 'What you have undertaken is far beyond the power of one man. It is no wonder that you have a weak stomach and that you are too thin. A wise man measures his single ability and does not go beyond it. What you are doing is more than a king can do, and certainly more than the Old Empress ever did. As for these new men we have now, they do not think of such a thing as feeding the people.'

'Are they worse rulers than the Old One?' Clem asked.

Mr. Fong looked in all four directions and up at the empty sky. Then he drew his seat near to Clem's and breathed these words into his ear.

'In the old days we had only certain rulers. There was the Old Buddha and in each province the viceroy and then the local magistrate. These all took their share. But now little rulers run everywhere over the land. It is this little man and that little man, all saying they come from the new government and all wanting cash. We are worse off than before.'

The two younger boys came out with an old woman-servant bringing some of the new cakes and tea.

'Eat,' Mr. Fong said. 'Here your mind may be at peace and your stomach will say nothing.'

Not in years had Clem eaten a rich sweetmeat, but he was

suddenly hungry for these cakes that he remembered from his childhood. He took one and ate it slowly, sipping hot tea between each bite.

'When one eats lard and sugar,' Mr. Fong said, 'hot tea should surround the food. . . . Thus also one drinks wine with crabs.'

Clem said, 'Strange that I do feel peace here as I have felt it nowhere else. In spite of the wars and the new rulers, I feel peace here in your house.' His Chinese lay ready on his tongue. He spoke it with all the old fluency and ease. His thoughts flowed into soft rich vowel sounds in the rising and falling tones.

'We are at peace here,' Mr. Fong agreed. 'The outside disturbance has nothing to do with our peace within. Stay here with us, live here, and we will make you well.'

In a corner Yuming and Yuwen were eating cakes heartily in front of a fat Pekingese dog, who snuffled through his nose and blinked his marble-round eyes at the hot delicious fragrance. It did not occur to either boy to share his cake with the dog. To give a beast food made for human beings would have been a folly, and the Fongs did not commit follies. A hard, age-old wisdom informed them all. Clem sat watching, relaxed, though he was not less aware of all that waited upon his conscience. Peace was sweet, and sweet it was to find nothing changed. Of all places in the world, here was no change.

In the small square central room of the three rooms which Mr. Fong had allotted for his son and his son's wife, Henrietta sat between Mrs. Fong and Jade Flower, who was Yusan's wife. Each held one of her hands and stroked it gently, gazing at her and asking small intimate questions.

'How is it you have no child?' Mrs. Fong asked.

'I have never conceived,' Henrietta replied. She had been afraid at first that she could no longer speak Chinese, but it was there, waiting the sight of a Chinese face. Something warmly delicate, the old natural human understanding she remembered so well and had missed so much was between her and these two.

Mrs. Fong exclaimed in pity. 'Now what will you do for your him?' 'Him' was husband. Mrs. Fong was too well-bred to use the word.

'What can I do?' Henrietta asked.

Mrs. Fong drew nearer. 'You must mend your strength. You are both so thin. Stay with us and I will feed you plenty of red sugar and blood pudding. That is very good for young women who do not conceive quickly. When you have been with us a month, I will guarantee that you will conceive. My son's wife was less than that.'

'Fourteen days,' Jade Flower said in a pretty little voice, and giggled.

Mrs. Fong frowned at her, then smiled and concerned herself again with Henrietta.

'Have you been married more than a year?'

'Much more,' Henrietta said.

Mrs. Fong looked alarmed. 'You should not have waited so long. You should have come to us before. Do they not understand what to do in your country?'

'Perhaps they are not so anxious for children,' Henrietta replied. She could not explain to this woman, who was all mother, that Clem was somehow her child as well as her husband, and that she did not greatly care if there were no children, because she did not need to divide herself. Mrs. Fong would not have understood. Was it not for the man's sake that a wife bore children?

'It may be better to take a second wife for him and let her bear the children for both of you,' Mrs. Fong said.

'This is not allowed in our country,' Henrietta said.

Mrs. Fong opened her eyes. 'What other way is there for childless wives?'

'They remain childless,' Henrietta said.

Jade Flower gave a soft scream. 'But what does he say?'

'He is good to me,' Henrietta said.

'He must be very good,' Mrs. Fong agreed. She stroked Henrietta's hand again. 'Nevertheless, it is not wise to count on too much goodness from men. Little Sister, you shall drink red sugar in hot water and I will kill one of our geese and make a blood pudding.' She looked at Henrietta. 'Can you, for the sake of a child, drink the blood fresh and hot?'

'I cannot,' Henrietta said quickly.

'That is what I did,' Jade Flower urged. 'I drank it one day and soon I had happiness in me.'

Mrs. Fong frowned at her daughter-in-law and smiled at Henrietta. 'We must not compel,' she advised. 'Not all women are alike. Some women cannot drink blood, not even to have a child. If they drink it, they vomit it up. I will make it into a pudding. Two or three puddings, one every day. Then we will see—we will see——' and she stroked Henrietta's hand.

'You trouble yourself without avail,' Mr. Fong said to Clem. They had been several days in Peking, living in the home of the Fong family. Clem's digestion ran smoothly and he was more quiet in mind than he had been for years.

'How do I trouble myself?' he asked.

They sat in the big family room, a comfortable, shabby, not-too-clean place, where the dogs wandered in and out and the cats sprawled in the warmest spot of sunshine, and neighbour children came to stare at the Americans, while Mrs. Fong bustled everywhere. Henrietta was unravelling an old sweater to knit a new jacket and cap for the Fong grandchild to be born now at any hour.

Mr. Fong cleared his throat and spat into a piece of brown paper which he then threw under the table. 'You think that you, one man, can feed the whole world. This is a dangerous dream. It only gives you the stomach trouble of which you have told me. Nothing is more dangerous than for one man to think he can do the work of all men.'

Clem's skin prickled at this criticism. He was secretly proud of his dream, which he had done so much to fulfil. At heart a truly modest man, he had nevertheless the modest man's pride in his modesty in the face of achievement.

Mr. Fong, wrapped in an ancient black silk robe long since washed brown and ragged at the edges, perfectly understood

229

what Clem was feeling. He looked at him over his brass spectacles and said, emphasizing his words with his forefinger. 'It is presumptuous for man to consider himself as a god. The head raised too high even in good will be struck off too soon. Each should tend only his own. Beyond there is no responsibility.'

He picked up a cat that happened to be lying by his chair and held it comfortably about its belly. 'This creature is blind. I do not feed any of the cats, not even this one. They are here to catch mice. But the other cats bring at least one mouse each day to this blind cat.'

The aged cat, outraged by his grasp, now scratched him with both hind and forelegs and yowled. Immediately three cats came into the room and looked pleadingly at Mr. Fong, who dropped the cat and wiped his bleeding hand on his gown.

'Please continue to teach my husband,' Henrietta said. 'I want him to live a long life.'

Mr. Fong inclined his head. He was so much older than Clem that he knew he could say anything to him. Meanwhile nothing Clem said impressed him. Yusan listened with deference, since in this case he was the younger man, but he had no wish to take the part which Clem wanted to put upon him.

'I shall certainly see that my own family is fed, and such others as are dependent upon us. It would be foolish to go further.' This was Yusan's conclusion. He went about these days from shop to house in perpetual readiness to hear a small loud cry from the three rooms which were his home under this roof, and he was impervious, in his generation, to the cries of others.

Clem, walking with Henrietta one afternoon upon the city wall, a vantage which gave them a wide view over the roofs of houses and the green trees of the courtyards, paused to gaze down into the vast square of the city. The palace roofs were brilliant under the sun of autumn and the temple roofs were royal blue. 'I guess Yusan doesn't get my ideas,' he said sadly enough to arrest Henrietta's wandering attention.

'Oh, well,' she replied for comfort, 'there aren't any very hungry people around. Maybe that's why. Even the beggars are fat.'

She loved Clem with the entire force of her nature, but she had never shared his sense of mission. For that, too, she must perhaps thank this city where she had spent her childhood and where she had learned early that women were of little value. It was a lesson to be learned soon, for it needed to be lifelong. Nothing in America had taught her more or differently. She was useful to Clem, and as long as he needed her, her life had meaning.

'I wish I could see Sun Yat-sen,' Clem said suddenly. 'I believe he'd understand what I'm talking about.'

'Who knows where he is?' Henrietta asked.

Clem paused for thought. 'I believe Yusan knows.'

'Then ask him,' Henrietta suggested.

Instead Clem decided to ask Mr. Fong. He did not believe that there were secrets between this father and son.

Mr. Fong received the question with calm.

'The time is not ripe for Sun Yat-sen's return,' he said.

'Where is he, then?' Clem demanded.

'Perhaps in Europe, perhaps in Malaya,' Mr. Fong said. 'He is gathering his powers.'

'At least he is not in China?'

'Certainly he is not in China,' Mr. Fong said firmly.

Clem said no more. The atmosphere in Peking was one of waiting, neither anxious nor tense. Empire had gone, in all but name, and the people did not know what came next. But they were at peace. They had never been dependent upon rulers and governments. Within themselves they had the knowledge of self-discipline. Fathers commanded sons, and sons did not rebel. All was in order, and would remain in order so long as the relationship held between the generations. Meanwhile the people lived and enjoyed their life.

Clem's early mood of unusual relaxation changed to restlessness. The peace of the Fong household began to weigh on him. The grandchild was born, fortunately a son, and Yusan was immediately absorbed in fatherhood. Old Mr. Fong relapsed into being a contented grandfather. Although Clem and his wife were welcome to stay the rest of their lives, they were becoming merely members of the family.

The end of the visit came on the day when Mr. Fong and Yusan hired four rickshaws and took Clem and Henrietta outside the city walls to the graves upon the hills. The visit had been many times postponed, Mr. Fong saying that Clem must not be disturbed by sorrow until his digestion was sound. Suddenly he had decided upon the day, and Yusan had so told Clem on the night before.

'Elder Brother, my father has prepared the visit to your family tombs. Tomorrow, if you are willing?'

'I am ready,' Clem said.

So they had set out, and an hour's ride had brought them before two tall, peaked graves. Clem stood with bowed head while Mr. Fong and Yusan thrust sticks of incense into the ground and lit them and Henrietta picked wild flowers and laid them upon the weedy sod. There was no other prayer. Clem took Henrietta's hand and they stood together for a few minutes, he remembering with sad gravity what was long gone, and she comforting him.

When the moments were over they got into their rickshaws again, and when Clem got back he went aside with Mr. Fong and tried to tell him his gratitude.

'You have kept the graves of my parents as though they were your own family,' Clem said.

'Are not all under Heaven one family?' Mr. Fong replied.

Nevertheless he perceived thereafter Clem's restlessness. One day he invited Clem to come into his private office, a small square room behind the shop, with enclosed shelves upon which were the old account books of five hundred years of Fong shopkeepers.

Mr. Fong closed the door carefully and motioned Clem to a seat. Then he opened a drawer of his desk and took out a slip of paper upon which an address was brushed in Chinese characters.

'Go to this place,' Mr. Fong said. "You will find the one you seek. Give him my name to send you in, and if he asks for

232

further proof, describe this room. He has sat upon that very chair where you sit.'

Clem looked at the paper. It bore an address in San Francisco.

'You had better go at once,' Mr. Fong said. 'He comes back soon. Something will happen this very month here in this city. Whether it fails or succeeds he will come back. If it is successful he will take power. If it fails, he must come to comfort his followers.'

Clem got up. 'Thank you, Elder Brother,' he said to Mr. Fong. 'I hope I can repay you for your faith. I hope he'll listen to me.'

The next day he left Peking, Henrietta with him, but not yet understanding why he must go away so quickly.

'I'll tell you, hon,' Clem said. 'I'll tell you as soon as I have time.'

There was time only when Clem was imprisoned by the sea. In Shanghai he spent money like the rich man he was that he might get berths upon an Empress ship leaving the dawn after they had arrived. He could haggle over the price of an overcoat and he had never worn a custom-made suit in his life, but when it was a matter of getting what he wanted, money was only made to be used. They caught the ship, and Clem, studying time-tables, planned the swiftest route from Vancouver to San Francisco. The English ship was still the most swift.

'One of these days we'll fly, hon,' Clem said to Henrietta. 'Before I die, that will surely be.'

'We'll fly in heaven, I suppose,' Henrietta said now with her small smile.

'Long before that,' Clem said. 'It'll be a sorry thing for many if they have to wait for heaven!'

At last, almost reluctantly, on the second day out, he told Henrietta why it was he wanted to see that man, Sun Yat-sen.

'He's going to get China, see, hon? I can feel it in my bones. The people there are just waiting for somebody to save them, and he has risen out of nowhere, the way saviour men always

233

do. They come up out of the earth, see? They get an idea, a big idea—just one is enough. He's got the idea of giving the Chinese people their own government. Well, he'll do it if he can get them to believe in him. People got to have faith, hon. He's got to have faith, too. Everybody who does anything has got to have faith in a big idea. So I'm going to him, and I'm going to say, look, if you give the people food, they'll believe in you. Now how are you going to give your people food? Some men do it one way, some another, but nobody ever got people to follow him without giving them food. People have got to be fed. Remember Jesus and the loaves and fishes.'

He was standing against the rail, his back to the sea, and Henrietta was lying on the long chair he had lugged here by a lifeboat on the highest deck, away from everybody as she liked to be. By squinting a little she gazed at his face, and imagined that the bright sea shone through his eye sockets, so blue were his eyes this day. The colour of his eyes was a barometer of the measure of his hope. When he was on the crest of a new hope, his eyes were sea blue, and when he was cast down, as sometimes he was, they were almost grey.

'He'll listen to you,' Henrietta said. 'I'm sure he will listen to you.'

The train from Vancouver reached San Francisco just after sunset. Clem deserted Henrietta at the station.

'Hon, you can get yourself to the hotel, can't you? Hop into a hack with our stuff. I guess the Cliff House is all right. Wait there for me—don't go out walking by yourself or anything!'

It was Clem's fantasy that Henrietta must not walk out alone after dark lest she be molested.

'You'd better tell me where you are going,' Henrietta said. 'If you don't come back I'll know where to look for you.'

'I'll get back all right,' Clem said. 'Chinese all know me, I guess.'

He hurried off, too busy to do what she asked, jumped into a horse-cab, and gave directions. Then he sat, taut, leaning dangerously forward while the cabman drove him over the rough streets. He sought the Chinese rebel in one of the miserable iron shacks which had sprung up in the ruins of old Chinatown after the great fire. The old dark beautiful city within a city, small and close, set like a gem within San Francisco—the haunted narrow streets that were the centre of Chinese life transplanted and nourished by generations of homesick Chinese—had been wiped out. Those living creatures who remained alive had made such shelters as they could, and they walked the streets, still dazed and lost. There was no beauty springing new from ashes.

Clem, however, did not include beauty within the necessities. Oblivious to ugliness, he dismissed the cab and walked briskly through the dim streets to the address he had memorized, so often had he read it. Even the smell of old Chinatown was gone, that mingling of herbs and wine, that scent of sandalwood and incense, that sad sweetness of opium, and the lusty reek of roasting pork and garlic and noodles frying in sesame oil. The sound of temple bells was gone, and the venders were no more. The clash of cymbals from the theatre was silenced and the theatre itself was still in ruins. Instead the night air was weighted still with the acrid smell of ash and seaweed and charcoal smoke from the braziers of families cooking in the open.

On the old Street of Gamblers, its iron gates a ruin of twisted rust, Clem found the place he sought. The door was locked, a flimsy partition of wood, and he knocked upon it. It was not opened at once and he heard the sound of voices within.

'Open the door!' a strong voice said. 'Of whom am I afraid?'

Then it was opened, and a cautious yellow face peered into the twilight.

'What ting you want?' the face asked.

'I am looking for the Elder Brother,' Clem said in Chinese.

Clem held up his left hand and on the palm he traced with the forefinger of his right hand the ideograph of Sun.

'Come in,' the face said. The door opened widely enough to let Clem in. The shack was one room, partitioned by a curtain, and it could be seen that it belonged to a laundryman. The face belonged to the laundryman, and he went back to the table piled with the clothes he was ironing, paying no further heed to Clem.

Two men sat at a small table scarcely larger than a stool. One was Sun Yat-sen, the other was the cramped, humped figure of an American.

Clem spoke to Sun. 'I am sent here by Mr. Fong, the bookseller on Hatamen Street, in Peking.'

'I know him,' Sun replied in a quiet voice.

'I have come with an idea which may be useful to you,' Clem said.

'I have no seat to offer you,' Sun replied. 'Pray take mine.'

He rose, but Clem refused. The laundryman came forward then with a third stool, and Clem sat down. Sun did not introduce the American.

'Proceed, if you please,' he said in his strangely quiet voice. 'I am to set sail shortly for my own country, and these last days, perhaps hours, are valuable to me.'

'Has the news been good or bad?' Clem asked.

'It is bad,' Sun said. 'I am used to bad news. But I must get home.'

The hunchback interrupted him with a high, sharp, positive voice. 'The news will always be bad unless you have an army. No revolution has ever succeeded until there was an army.'

'Perhaps,' Sun Yat-sen said, without change in voice or face.

'I haven't come to talk about an army,' Clem said. He felt uncomfortable in the presence of the white-faced hunchback. He hated intrigue, and he did not believe revolutions were necessary. People fought when they got hungry. When they starved they were desperate. But after it was over everything depended again on whether the new rulers fed them. If not, it all began over again.

'I want to talk to you about food,' Clem said abruptly. 'I want to tell you what I believe. People will never be permanently at peace unless the means of getting food is made regular and guaranteed. Now I have worked out a plan.'

He leaned forward, and began to speak in Chinese. Thus he shut out the hunchback. He had a feeling that the hunchback was an enemy. That small bitter white face, tortured with a

236

lifetime of pain and misfortune, spoke cruelty and violence. But if he had thought by speaking in Chinese to drive the man away, he failed. The hunchback waited motionless, his eyes veiled as though he were asleep. The laundryman stopped ironing and listened to Clem's quick, persuading words.

'True, true,' he muttered, to no one.

Clem's eyes were fixed upon the face of the revolutionist. He studied the high forehead, the proud mouth, the wide nostrils, the broad and powerful skull. He could not tell whether or not he was impressing his own faith upon this man.

Sun Yat-sen was a good listener. He did not interrupt. When Clem had made plain his desire to organize in China a means of food distribution that would guarantee the contentment of the people, Sun Yat-sen shook his head.

'I have only so much money. I can choose between an army which will fight the enemies of the people and set up a righteous government for the people by the people and of the people, or I can, as you suggest, merely feed the people.'

'Your government will not stand if the people are not fed,' Clem said.

Sun Yat-sen smiled his famous winning smile. 'I have no government yet. First must come first, my friend.'

'Only if the people have food will they believe in you,' Clem said. 'When they believe in you, you can set up what government you choose.'

'It depends on one's point of view,' Sun Yat-sen said suddenly in English. 'If I set up a government then I shall be able to feed the people.'

The hunchback came to life. He opened his narrow and snake-like eyes.

'Exactly,' he said. 'Force comes first.'

Clem got to his feet. 'It is a misfortune that I didn't find you alone,' he said to Sun Yat-sen. 'I guess I have failed. But you will fail, too. Your government will fail, and somebody else will come in and the way they will get in is just by promising the people food. Maybe they won't even have to deliver. Maybe by that time the people will be so hungry that just a promise will be enough.'

Sun Yat-sen did not answer for a moment. When he did speak, it was to say with the utmost courtesy as he rose to his feet:

'I thank you, sir, for seeking me out. Thank you for caring for my people. I am touched, if not convinced.'

His English was admirable, the accent faintly Oxford. It was far better, indeed, than Clem's American speech, tinged with the flatness of Ohio plains.

'Good night,' Clem said. 'I wish you luck, anyway, and I hope you won't forget what I've said, even if you don't agree with me, because I know I'm right.'

VII

CANDACE felt that William was annoyed. He stooped to kiss her as usual, but she was sensitive to his mood after these years of marriage, and she saw a wintry stillness gathered about his heavy brows and firm mouth. When he spoke his voice was formal.

'I am sorry to be late.'

'Are you late?' She yawned nicely behind her hand. 'Then I'm late, too. I was tired when I came home from the matinée.'

'Was the play good?'

'You wouldn't think so.'

She rose from the chaise-longue where she had been drowsing and looked from the window. Far below the vast park lay in shadows, pricked with lights. 'I do hope the children are home. Nannie keeps them out too late. She is a fiend for fresh air.'

'There was a strong draught along the hall from the nursery door, and so I suppose they are home,' William replied.

'Why do you think her first impulse upon entering a room is to open the windows?'

She asked the useless question while she was pulling on the satin slippers she had kicked off when she threw herself down. William seated himself in a chair and took his characteristic pose, his small dark hands gripped together, his legs, long and thin, crossed. Whatever the fashions for men, he wore his favourite grey, dark with a faint pinstripe, and his tie was dark blue. He did not answer his wife. This, too, was usual. Candace asked many questions she did not expect to have answered. They were the queries of her idle mind. He had once given them thought until he discovered them meaningless.

She straightened her skirt and sauntering to her dressing-table she picked up a brush and began smoothing out her short curls. Something was wrong but if she waited William would tell her. It might be anything, perhaps that he did not like the odour of food floating upstairs from the basement kitchen. The maids left the doors open in spite of her orders. Perhaps it was only while watching her as she brushed her hair he was reminded that she had decided to have her hair cut against his wishes.

'I had a letter from my father today,' William said abruptly.

'I thought something was wrong,' she said, not turning round, but seeing him very well in the mirror. His face, always ashen, was no more so than usual. Something in his Chinese childhood, a doctor had said, perhaps the dysentery when he was four, had left his intestines filled with bacteria now harmless but more numerous than they should be.

'They have decided to take their furlough, after all,' he said.

She went on brushing her hair, watching his face. 'That's good news, isn't it? I have never seen your father, and the boys have never seen even your mother.'

He frowned and the thick dark brows which always gave his face such sombreness seemed to shadow and hide his deep-set eyes. 'It is a bad time for me, nevertheless. I'd just decided to launch the new paper at once instead of waiting until spring.'

She whirled round. 'Oh, William, you aren't going to start something more!'

'Why not?'

'But we don't see anything of you as it is!'

'I shan't need to work as long hours as I did with the others. I've made my place.'

'But why, when we're making money? You sacrifice yourself and us for nothing, darling!'

She let the brush fall to the floor, and flew to his side and dropped on her knees, leaning her elbows on his lap and beseeching him. 'I have always to take the boys everywhere without you. All last summer at the seashore you only came down for week-ends, and scarcely that! It isn't right, William, now when they're beyond being babies. I didn't say anything when you were getting started, but today, just when I was thinking we might go to the theatre sometimes together!'

He was entirely conscious of her beautiful face so near his, and he would have given much to be able to yield himself to her, but he could not. Some inner resistance kept him even from her. He did not know what it was, but he felt it like an iron band round his heart. He could not give himself up to anyone, not even to his sons. He longed to play on the floor, to roll on the carpet as Jeremy did with his little daughters, but he could not. He was most at ease when he sat behind his great desk in the office giving orders to the men whom he employed.

'I went to the theatre with you only last week,' he reminded her.

'But that was an opening night, and you know what people go to that for—to see and be seen. I want us just to go sometimes all by ourselves, and only for the play.'

He did not enjoy the theatre, but he had never told her so. He could never forget that it was only a play. No stage excitement could reach him when he was fed daily by the excitement of his own life, his secret power which he felt growing beneath the power of the printed words he set upon his pages. He alone chose those words. What he did not want people to know he did not allow to be printed. They learned only what he selected. Sometimes, meditating upon his responsibility, he felt himself chosen and destined for some power over men which he had not yet reached. He had been reared in Calvinism and predestination, but in his rebellion against his childhood he had rejected all that his father taught him. He had become almost an atheist while he was in college. Now he was made religious by his own extraordinary success. In the few years since he had put out the first of his newspapers, their sales had soared into millions. Yet he was not satisfied. Even now, travelling upon a train, he could feel vaguely hurt that on every other seat there should be lying the crumpled sheets of a paper thrown away. People ought to keep what he had so carefully made. Then his mood changed to pride. There were two of his papers to one of any other. Such colossal success meant something. There was a God, after all—and predestination.

'What are you thinking about?' Candace asked.

The question slipped from her tongue, and she wanted it

back instantly but it was too late. William disliked to be asked what he was thinking about. It was an intrusion and she knew now that he guarded himself even from her. It had taken her time to learn this and meantime she had wept a good deal alone. Tears, she had now learned, only irritated him. She shed no more of them.

'No—don't answer me,' she said, and impulsively she put her crossed fingers on his lips.

He took her hands rather gently, however, and did answer her. 'I was thinking, Candy, that it is a great responsibility for one man to know that he feeds the minds—and the souls —of three million people.'

'Three million?'

'That is the number of our readers today. Rawlston gave me the last figures just before I came home. A year from now he says it will be twice that number. I suppose I am worth more than a million dollars now.'

She was used to her father's joking, 'A millionaire? Nothing to it. Just keep ridin' high and never look down.'

'You've made a great success, William.' She was not at all sure that this was the right thing to say, and with his next words she knew it was not.

'I'm not thinking only in terms of personal success. It is easy to be successful here in America. Anyone with brains can make money.'

'But you do like money, William.' Her sense of being wrong compelled her to justify what she had said. Besides, it was true. In his own way William valued money far more than she did or ever could.

'It is only common sense to have money.' His voice was dry, his eyes severe and grey. 'Without it one is hamstrung. There is no freedom without money.'

She remembered something she had heard her father once say. 'A man needs enough room to swing a cat in.' Room, that was what money gave. A big house to live in, months in which to idle beside the sea, to live winter in summer and summer in winter, to buy without asking the price.

'Yet you don't seem to enjoy life very much, William,' she

242

said rather painfully. She had a profound capacity for enjoyment without a sense of guilt. Her father had frankly enjoyed getting rich and he distrusted all charities. She teased him sometimes by saying that he had become a Christian Scientist so that he could ignore the sufferings of others.

He had grinned and refused to be teased. 'Maybe you're right, Daughter. Who knows why we do anything?'

Then he had turned grim. 'If I see somebody starving, with my own eyes, I'll feed 'em. I won't pay out good cash for what I don't see. Ten to one they're lazy. If they hustled like I did. . . .'

Even going to church, while a social duty, had nothing to do with giving his money to strangers. Roger Cameron had cultivated no conscience in his children, and Candace had grown up believing that pleasure was her normal occupation, once the dinner was planned and the children cared for. But no pleasure she devised could coax William from himself, or whatever it was that he dwelled upon in his soul. A ball which she planned as happily as a child might plan a birthday party fretted him with detail. A dish badly served spoiled his dinner. A servant who was not well trained—but of servants she would not think. He demanded of those in his service a degree of obedience and respect and outward decorum which had made her wretched until her father had found her crying one day. He had a way of coming to see her alone when he knew William was at his office. He took a cab and came all the way from Wall Street to arrive at three o'clock in the afternoon or at eleven o'clock in the morning.

On one such a visit he said, after he had inquired as to the cause of the tears his shrewd eyes had seen in spite of powder and even a dash of rouge, 'You can't find Americans who'll give William the service he wants. We don't respect ourselves enough yet. We've always got to be showing that we're independent and don't have to obey anybody. Besides, we're too honest. When we hate anybody we act ugly. You hire your house full of English, Candy—they can act nice while they're stirrin' up poison for you. An English servant can polish your shoes as though he loved it. Of course he don't.'

So she had filled the house with English servants, and a butler and a housekeeper kept their eyes upon William, the master.

'I don't know that life is merely to be enjoyed,' William now said.

She was still crouching beside him. Idly she had taken one of his hands and playing with the fingers she noticed the strange stiffness of his muscles.

'What's life for?' she asked, not expecting an answer. 'I don't know; I don't suppose anyone does, exactly. We're here, that's all.'

'It is for something more than amusement.' He disliked her playing with his hand, and he drew it away, ostensibly to light a cigarette.

She felt his dislike and got to her feet gracefully, took his head between her hands, and kissed his forehead.

'Poor darling, you're so serious.'

'I don't need your pity.'

'Oh, no, William, I didn't mean that. Only, I enjoy life so much.'

She drew back and met the hurt look she feared. Why could she never learn how easily wounded he was? She cried out. 'How silly we are to keep talking about nothing when you haven't even told me your real news! When are your father and mother coming?'

He was relieved to be able to withdraw from her. 'I had a cable this afternoon. They sailed the thirteenth on an Empress ship.'

'Then in a fortnight——'

'More or less. Just when I shall be busiest.'

'Never mind, I'll look after them. Dad has time, too, now he's retired enough to stop away from the office if he likes. And there's Jeremy and Ruth——'

'I shall need Jeremy.'

Of the young men with whom he had begun the paper only Jeremy was left. One by one the others had deserted him. Martin Rosvaine had gone into the production of motion pictures and Blayne into the State Department with aspirations for an ambassadorship. He had not missed these two, but he had been sorry when Seth James quarrelled with him, for he valued Seth's brilliant and effervescent mind, the ideas which poured forth like sparks from a rocket. Most of them were useless, but he watched the scintillating performance because there were always one or even two or three ideas upon which he seized. They had made a good pair, for Seth's weakness was his inability to discriminate between good ideas and foolish ones, and the paper would have been bankrupt had he been given authority. For that reason, William told himself, he had been compelled to keep control in his own hands even to the extent of buying up stock. Jeremy, of course, had never been a threat. He worked when he wished, and William had learned to hire an understudy for him. But even yet he missed Seth, who had left him in anger and still refused to communicate with him.

The quarrel had been over a small matter, a difference of opinion so common to them that William had not troubled even to be polite. He had merely thrown abrupt words over his shoulder one night when they were all working long past midnight. Seth had said something about a story of some long-orphaned children in a foster home on a Pennsylvania farm. The farmer had lost his temper with a boy—he was still a boy, though a man in years—and the boy in terror and self-defence had rushed forward with a pitchfork, which had pierced the farmer's leg. The wound was slight but the farmer had hacked the boy with an axe with which he was chopping wood and the boy had bled to death within an hour. There had been scandal enough so that Seth had gone impetuously to the scene himself to check the copy he was reading, and had come back flaming with anger at the conditions he found in the farm-house: two half-starved grown girls, both mentally retarded, and a fat cruel old woman, and the boy hastily buried without anyone coming to investigate. The farmer lay in bed and babbled about self-protection. Seth had routed out police and they in turn had produced a thin frightened woman who claimed that she was only an employee of the organization that had placed the children and that she did not know whether there were

245

any relatives. In the end the local publicity had spread to reach Ohio, whereupon Clem Miller of all people had come to Pennsylvania to see what was going on. He had taken the two girls away with him and had told the police that the place was not fit for any children, big or little.

To Seth Clem had said with furious zeal, 'I hope you'll tell William to make a real spread of this. Everybody in America ought to know about it. It's a strange and pitiful thing—this was my grandfather's place. He hung himself in that barn because he was too soft-hearted to get a neighbour off a farm—mortgage was called in. I came here myself when I was a kid, not knowing. These people were here already. I ran away—wanted all the kids to come with me, but only one would come.'

'It's nothing but a local mess and of no significance,' William had said upon getting Clem's message.

'But the boy's death is significant,' Seth had insisted. 'The very fact that orphaned children could be farmed out like that to such people, and no one care——'

'Well, no one does care,' William had retorted.

Seth's answer had taken a long moment in coming and William, his mind upon his editorial, had not turned around. It came at last.

'You don't care, that's a fact,' Seth had said in a still voice. 'You don't care about anybody, damn you!'

He stalked to the door. 'I'm not coming back here.'

'Don't be foolish,' William said.

He had been very angry, nevertheless, when Seth walked out of the office. During the sleepless night in which he told Candace nothing except that the bread sauce on the pheasant he had eaten for dinner had not agreed with him, he made up his mind that when Seth came back in the morning he would ignore the whole matter. Otherwise he would have to fire him. But Seth did not come back. William had never heard from him since, but so far as he knew he was doing nothing of any use. He had backed two or three quixotic magazines, none of which were succeeding. Fortunately for Seth his father, old Mackenzie James, and Aunt Rosamond, too, had left him

246

plenty of money. When William thought of their quarrel, as he often did, he was still convinced that he was right. A local murder in itself was not important. But William could never forget a wound and Seth had wounded him deeply. This was important.

He felt himself misunderstood; of all his men he thought that Seth had understood him best. For William did not think only of himself. All that he did, his monstrous effort, his tireless work, was, he believed, to make people know the truth. Why else did he scan every photograph that was to be printed, why read and read again the galley proofs except that he might make sure that the people were given truth and nothing but the truth? He had tried to say something like this to Seth one day and Seth had laughed.

'Truth is too big a word for one man to use,' Seth had declared. 'For decency's sake, let's say truth as one man sees it.'

To this William had not replied. It was not truth as he or anyone else saw it. Surely truth was an absolute. It was an ideal, it was what was right, and right was another absolute. Facts had little to do with either. Facts, William often declared to his young sub-editors, were only trees in a forest, useless until they were put to use, bewildering until they were chosen, cut down, and organized. The policy was to establish what was right, as a man might build his house.

'Our materials are facts,' William often said to his staff, looking from one tense young face to the other. The men admired him for his success, swift and immense. He was upheld by their admiration and only Seth had insisted on seeing the confusion behind their eyes. 'When we know what we want to prove, we go out and find our facts. They are always there,' William said.

After Seth had deserted him, for to William it could be called nothing but desertion, he had only Jeremy of the old gang. The rest of his huge staff was made up of many young men, whose names he was careful to remember if they were executives. To the others he paid no heed. They came and went and he judged them by the pictures they sent in and the

247

copy they wrote. His young sub-editors made up the paper, but he himself was the editor-in-chief, and mornings were hideous if he did not approve what they had done. For he must approve. No one went home unless he did—no one except Jeremy, whom he could not control. Jeremy alone at midnight put his hat on the side of his head and took up his walking-stick. He would always be a little lame, and he made the most of his limp when he went into William's office.

'Good night, William, I've had enough for today.'

William never answered. Had Jeremy not been the son of Roger Cameron he would have thrown him out and closed the door.

'Ruth and I will take care of your parents,' Candace was saying. 'They'll stay here, I suppose?'

'I suppose so,' William replied. He rose. 'I shall have to get back to the office tonight, Candace. We'd better have dinner at once.'

Left alone after dinner, Candace put the two boys to bed, annoying the nurse Nannie by this unwanted help. The house was so silent afterwards that she went to her own room and turned on all the rose-shaded lights and lay down to read, and then could not read. Instead she thought about William, whom she loved in spite of her frequent disappointment in their life together. She was not a stupid woman, although her education had been foolish, as she now knew. A finishing school and some desultory travel were all she had accomplished before her wedding day, and since then her life had been shaped around William's driving absorption in the news-papers. She could not understand this absorption. Her father had worked, too, but only when it was necessary. Other people worked for him and he fired them when they did not do what he told them. A few hours in his offices sufficed to bring the money rolling in from hundreds of stores all over the country. It would have been so pleasant if William had been willing to go into the Cameron Stores, but this he had refused to do. She did not know what he really wanted. When they were married she supposed he wanted only to be rich, for of course only rich men were successful. Yet he could have been rich almost at once had he taken the partnership her father had later offered him.

Thus she discovered that he wanted something beyond money. Yet what more was there than a handsome and comfortable home, a wife such as she tried to be and really was, wasn't she, and dear, healthy boys? One day, soon after they were married, in those days when she still thought that she could help him, she had said she thought his picture papers were childish and he had replied coldly that most people were childish and his discovery of this fact had given him the first idea for his papers.

'I like people and you hate them,' she had then declared in one of her flashes.

'I neither like them nor hate them,' he had replied.

Yet she believed that he loved her, and she knew she loved him. Why, she did not fully know. Who could explain a reason for love? Seth James had once wanted her to marry him. Since they were children he had talked about it, and Seth was good to the soul of him, kind and honest—yet she could not love him.

Surely it was strange not to know William better after years of marriage. She knew every detail of his body, his head, nobly shaped, but the eyes remote and deep under the too heavy brows; a handsome nose William had, and a fine mouth except that it was hard. His figure was superb, broad-shouldered, lean, tall, but when he was naked she looked away because he was hairy. Black hair covered his breast, his arms, his shoulders and legs. She disliked the look of his hands, though she loved him. Yet how little love revealed! What went on in his mind? They were often silent for hours together. What did he long for above all? It was not herself, nor even the two boys, though he had been pleased that his children were boys. He did not care for girls, and this she had not understood until one day Ruth had told her that in Peking the Chinese always felt sorry for a man when his child was born a girl. It was a sign of something unsuccessful in his house. No matter how many sons a Chinese had he always wanted more.

'But William isn't Chinese,' she had told Ruth, making a wry face.

Ruth had given her pretty laugh. Then she had shaken her head rather soberly. 'He's not really American, though, Candy.'

What was really American? Jeremy was American, and Ruth had adapted herself to him, copying even his speech. They were quite happy since they had the two girls. Ruth had been absurdly grateful when Jeremy seemed really to prefer girls. She loved Jeremy with her whole tidy little being and had no thought for anyone else, except William. William she was proud of and afraid of, and the only quarrel she had with Jeremy was when she asked him not to make William angry. Jeremy, of course, was afraid of nothing, not even of William.

Yet William loved his country. He was capable of sudden long speeches about America. Once at an office banquet to celebrate his first million readers, William had talked almost an hour and everybody listened as though hypnotized, even Candace herself. The big hotel dining-room was still and suddenly she began to smell the flowers, the lilies and roses, on the tables, although she had not noticed their fragrance before. Words had poured out of William as though he had kept them pent in him. She heard the echoes of them yet.

'It is the hour of American destiny.

——We have been sowing and now we are about to reap. I see the harvest in terms of the whole world.

——The world will listen to our voices, speaking truth.

——We are young but we have learned in our youth to control the forces of water and air—the forces which are locked into ore and coal.

——Old countries are dying and passing away. England is weak with age, an ancient empire, her rulers grown tired. France is sunk in dreams and Italy slumbers. But we of America, we are awake. The name America will be heard among every people. It is our time, our hour. It is we who will write the history of the centuries to come. . . .'

Candace had listened, alarmed and half ashamed and yet fascinated. This was William, her husband!

That night in the silence of their own house she had been unusually silent. He had seemed exhausted, his face pallid as water under a grey sky, and he did not speak to her.

'You were very eloquent tonight, William,' she had said at last, because something was necessary to be spoken between them. 'I suppose your preacher father is somewhere in you, after all.'

'I wasn't preaching,' he had said harshly. 'I was telling the truth.'

At this moment the telephone rang upon the small rosewood table beside her bed and, lifting the receiver, she heard her father's nasal voice.

'William?'

'William is at the office, Father,' she told him. 'There's only me at home.'

He hesitated. 'You in bed, Candy?'

'Not really. I'm just upstairs because I don't like being downstairs alone.'

'Maybe I'll come around. Your mother's got a sick headache and she's gone to sleep.'

'Do, Father. I'll come down and be waiting.'

Such visits at night were not unusual. Her father liked to walk in darkness when the city streets were empty, and once or twice a month he rang the doorbell and when the door was opened stood peering doubtfully into the hall. 'William here?'

It was always his first question, though why Candace did not know, for sometimes he came in whether William were home or not, to stay a moment or an hour. He had a delicacy which told him, his foot upon the threshold, whether his visit was opportune.

Tonight she was more than usually pleased, for she was in a mood to talk and there was no one with whom she could talk more easily than with her father. Her mother was well enough when it came to the matter of servants and children

251

but tonight she wanted to talk about something more, although she did not know exactly what.

When the door-bell rang she hastened downstairs to open the door herself, for the maids were asleep. Her father stood upon the big door-mat, looking grey and cold and yet somehow cheerful, the tip of his long nose red and his eyes small and keen.

'This is nice,' he said as she took off his overcoat. 'I feel in the need of a little light conversation. It looks like rain and my knees are stiff.'

'You shouldn't be walking on such a night,' she scolded with love.

'I shan't yield my life to my knees,' he said.

The fire was red coals in the living-room grate and he took the tongs from her. He was skilful at fires, manipulating the live coals under the fresh fuel and coaxing a flame from the least of materials. It was one of his pet economies, left over from the days when as a child he had picked up coal from the railway yards in a Pennsylvania mining town.

When the fire was blazing he sat down, rubbing his hands clean on his white silk handkerchief. 'Well, how's tricks?'

'Oh, we're all well,' she replied. 'Willie is on the honour roll at school. William was quite pleased. The real news is that William's parents are coming from China.'

'I thought they'd decided to stay another year.'

'So did I.'

'It's the old lady, I imagine,' he said thoughtfully and gazed into the fire. 'I suppose William's glad?'

Candace laughed. 'He seems rather annoyed.'

Roger Cameron liked to hear his daughter laugh. He looked up and smiled. It was a pleasant moment, the big room shadowed in corners and lit here by the fire and the lamp. She looked pretty in a rose-coloured wool dressing-gown, pretty and maybe happy, too. For a while after her marriage he had wondered if she was happy and then had decided she could be, mainly because she had a fine digestion and no ambitions. He had taken care in her education that she should not be placed in the atmosphere of ambitious women. There were such women in the Stores, and none of them, he believed, were happy. His secretary, Minnie Forbes, whom he had employed since she was twenty-one, was devoured with dry unhappiness, perhaps because Minnie would have been shocked to know that she was in love with her employer. Roger knew very well that she was and was grateful for her ignorance. He himself loved his wife in a mild satisfactory way, and had no desire to love anyone else. The brief months when as a young man he had been passionately in love with her he remembered as extremely uncomfortable, for he could not keep his mind on his business. He had been relieved when he discovered that she was not the extraordinary creature his fancy had led him to imagine her, and then he had settled down to the homely and unromantic married love which he had enjoyed now throughout forty peaceful years. He and his wife were deeply attached, but she did not regret his business trips, and he enjoyed them with the single-minded pursuit of more business.

'William never did quite know what to do with his family,' he now said.

'Are they queer, Father?' Candace's blue eyes were always frank. 'I can't seem to remember even his mother very well.'

'I suppose anybody that goes off to foreign countries is queer in a way,' he replied. 'Ordinary folks stay at home. Still, they are always taking up collections in churches and all that. William's father is no more than a preacher who goes beyond what's considered his average duty. "Go ye into the world", and so on. But nobody much takes it seriously, except a few. They're always good men, of course.'

'And the women?'

'I don't believe Mrs. Lane would have gone on her own hook. I suppose she went because he did. Not too much sympathy between them, as I remember.'

He did not want to tell his daughter that he remembered Mrs. Lane as a pushing sort of woman. Maybe she wasn't. People often became pushing when they were with a rich man. He had got used to it. Anyway, it was all in the family now.

'Jeremy's little Mollie is a cute trick,' he said, smiling.

'She is,' Candace agreed. 'Ruth tells me she talks all the time. When she comes here she is shy and won't say a word.'

'She talks to me if I'm by myself. It's wonderful to watch the first opening of a child's mind.'

'Ruth and I are going to have to look after Mother and Father Lane. William is working on a new paper.'

'What's he want with more work?' Roger took out his pipe. He had not begun smoking a pipe until recently and he still felt strange with the toy. But he had wanted something to occupy his hands.

'The Duke of Gloucester knits,' he said, perceiving a gleam now in his daughter's candid blue eyes. 'That's all very well for an Englishman. We American men aren't up to it yet. I don't really like this smoking, but it takes time to fill the pipe and light it and it goes out a good deal. It's all occupation.'

'What's the matter with you American men?' Candace asked, her eyes bright, her mouth demure.

'An Englishman is never afraid of being laughed at,' Roger replied. 'He just thinks the other fellow is a fool. But Americans still can't risk anybody laughing at them. I can't, myself. Tough as I am I couldn't knit, even if I wanted to. I don't want to, though.'

'You don't want to smoke either,' she mocked.

He grinned at her sheepishly and went on with his manœuvres while she watched, still ready to laugh. 'I guess I like to play with fire,' he said when at last he was puffing smoke, his eyes watering. 'What I like best is getting it ready and striking the match.'

'Oh, you.' She yawned softly. 'No, I'm not sleepy. I keep worrying about what I'll do with William's parents. Why don't you help me? Suppose they want to stay here in the house all winter?'

'Let them do what they want and you go your ways,' he replied. 'Be nice to them and leave them free. That's what most old folks want. Don't worry yourself.'

'Didn't you ever worry about anything?'

'Sure I did. When I was young I worried my stomach into a clothes-wringer. One day a doctor said I'd be dead in a year.

I made up my mind I wouldn't. But I had to quit worryin' my stomach. Lucky the Stores were on their feet. That was the time I knew Jeremy never would take over. Well, I didn't need him, as it turned out, or anybody. It's a great thing to be able to manage your own business. I kind of hoped once that William would come in, but it's just as well. William is cut out for what he's doing.'

'What do you think William really wants, Father?'

So seldom did she ask a serious question that he looked rather startled and put his pipe on the table to have it out of the way.

'What do you mean, Candy?'

'Well, we have lots of money.'

'It's wonderful what he's done.'

'But he doesn't enjoy it. Even when we have a dinner party it seems he can't enjoy it. It has to be more than a party, somehow. And there is no use taking a vacation. When we went to France last summer, he spent the whole time arranging for a European edition. I went around by myself until in Paris I met some of the girls I'd known in school.'

'William's ambitious,' Roger said reluctantly.

'For what, Father?'

'I don't believe he knows,' Roger said. 'Maybe that's what bothers him. He don't know what to do with himself.'

There was something so astute in this that Candace laid it aside for further thought.

'I wish I could teach him how to play games and enjoy horseback riding.'

'He rides well enough.'

'He does everything well, and doesn't care for any of it. I love him and I don't understand him.'

There was a hint of fear in her voice; only a hint, but he did not want to hear it. He was getting too old for sorrow. He could not even read a sad book any more. When it began to get sad he shut it up. He had seen too much trouble that he could not help, or maybe he did not want to help.

'You don't have to understand people,' he said in his driest tones. 'There's so much talk about understanding this

255

and that nowadays. Most of the time nobody understands anything. If you love him, you don't need to bother about understanding, I reckon. Just take him as he acts.'

He began to feel restless as he always did when he smelled trouble. He had a wonderful sense of smell for trouble, and when he caught that acrid stench, however faint, he went somewhere else. So now, though he loved his daughter, he rose and put his cold pipe into his pocket.

'I guess I'll be getting along home.' He bent over her and kissed her hair. 'Don't you worry, my girl. Just treat the old folks nice and let them do what they want.'

'Good night, Father, and thank you.'

He ambled out of the room and she sat a few minutes alone. She was shrewd in her naïve way and she knew his wilful avoidance of trouble. But she was enough like him to sympathize with it. What he had said was comforting. It was easiest, after all, not to worry about understanding people, and surely easy just to love them, whatever they did, so long as they were not cruel in one's presence. And William was never cruel to her or to the children. He had never whipped the boys, however impatient he became. Jeremy, in a flurry of wrath, could upturn the fluffy skirts of a small girl over his knee and give her a couple of paddles and then, his anger vented, turn her upright again and kiss her soundly. William did not kiss his sons, either. He never touched them.

Ah well, she was glad she loved him. Love, her father had said, was enough.

The moment William looked at his father as he came off the train, he knew that here was an old man come home to die. The sight and the knowledge stunned him. As always when he was moved he felt speechless. Ruth stood beside him and on the other side were Candace and Jeremy together. They had not brought the children because of the crowd and the late hour. The lights of the station fell upon his father's white face and gaunt frame. He had grown a beard, but even its whiteness did not make the white face less pale. His mother was stouter and older, as strong as ever. It was she who saw them first and she who greeted them. He felt her firm kiss on his cheek.

'Well, William!'

'Yes, Mother.'

But he kept looking at his father. This old, old man, this delicate ghost, the dark eyes living and burning and the pale lips folded quietly together in the white beard! He took his father's hand and felt it crumple into a few bones in his palm.

'Father——' he cried, and put his arms around his father's shoulders. He turned to Jeremy. 'You take care of them, Jeremy—the women and the—the baggage. I'm going to get my father out of this.'

'But he's ever so much better,' his mother cried.

'He doesn't look better to me,' William said. His lips felt stiff and he wanted to cry. He pulled his father away, his arm still about the thin old body. 'Come along, Father. The car is here.' Why hadn't his mother told him?

The chauffeur was standing at the open door of the car. William helped his father in and wrapped the rug warmly about his knees. 'Drive straight home, Harvey,' he called through the speaking-tube.

The heavy car swayed slowly into the traffic. William sat looking at his father. 'How do you really feel?'

Dr. Lane smiled and looked no less ghostly. 'You didn't think I would look the same after all the years?'

It was the first time he had spoken and his voice was soft and high, almost like a child's.

'But are you well?' Now that William was alone with his father he could control his unexpected tenderness.

'Not quite,' his father said.

He looked so patient, so pure, that William felt he saw him for the first time. To his own surprise he wanted to take his father's hand and hold it, but he felt ashamed and did not.

'Have you seen the doctor?' He spoke again with his usual abruptness.

'Yes, that is why we left Peking so suddenly. He thought I

257

should be examined here.' Dr. Lane's smile was tinged with unfailing sweetness.

'What did he say it was?'

'It seems I have had sprue for a long time without quite knowing it. It destroys the red corpuscles, I believe.' Dr. Lane spoke without interest in his corpuscles.

William heard and made up his mind quickly. He would get the best man in the world on tropical diseases—send to London for him if necessary. He felt an imperious anger harden his heart. 'I should have thought mother would have noticed.'

'One doesn't notice, I suppose, living in the same house for so many years,' his father replied. 'I didn't notice even myself. Tired, of course, but I thought I was just getting old.'

'You are going to rest now,' William commanded.

'That will be nice,' his father replied. His voice became fainter and fainter until with these words it was only a whisper. William took up the speaking-tube. 'Drive as fast as you can. My father is very tired.'

The car speeded under them smoothly. Dr. Lane leaned his head back against the upholstered seat and closed his eyes and seemed to sleep. William watching him in profound anxiety. He would get his own doctor tonight immediately after they reached home; he would be afraid to sleep unless somehow his father was fortified.

When the car drew up at the door he got out first and with the tenderness so strange to himself he helped his father up the steps and into the hall. The butler was waiting and took their hats and coats. At the foot of the great stairway he saw his father stand back and look up as though at a mountain he could not climb.

'I will carry you up,' William muttered.

'Oh, no!' Dr. Lane gasped. 'I shall be quite able in a moment.'

William did not hear him. In a daze of love such as he had never felt for any human creature, he lifted his father into his arms and, horrified at the lightness of the frame he held, he mounted the stairs. The old man, feeling his son's arms about him, gave himself up with a sigh and closed his eyes.

What befell William in the weeks that followed he was never able himself to understand. Its effects did not appear fully for many years. He seemed to be alone in the world with his father, and yet the dying saint was someone far beyond being only his father. For the time during which this presence was in his house William scarcely left his father's room. He discerned with new perception that this spirit, preparing for departure, was ill at ease except alone and he was therefore brutal with his mother. He said to Candace and Ruth, 'Mother must not come near him. It is your business to see that she is taken out of the house on any pretext you can think of.'

He bullied the American doctors cruelly, declaring them incompetent. He himself cabled to the great English specialist in tropical diseases, Sir Henry Lampheer, demanding his instant attendance. Under the roaring waves of the Atlantic Ocean this communication went on, hour after hour.

Sir Henry's reply to William's command was British and stubborn. HAVE CONSULTED WITH YOUR DR. BARTRAM. OBVIOUS MY SERVICES TOO LATE. STARVATION RESULT OF DESTROYED TISSUE. INJECTIONS MAY PROLONG LIFE.

William was imperious with the Englishman. SET YOUR OWN PRICE.

Sir Henry lost patience and his haughty irritation carried clear beneath the raging Atlantic tides. NO PRICE POSSIBLE FOR FOLLY OF LEAVING IMPORTANT PATIENTS HERE. ADVISE DEPENDING UPON YOUR OWN PHYSICIANS.

YOU PROPOSE TO LET MY FATHER DIE?

GOD DECREES, Sir Henry cabled, refusing blame. YOUR FATHER AN OLD MAN CRIPPLED BY FATAL DISEASE.

MY FATHER COMES OF LONG-LIVED FAMILY, ALSO GREAT RESISTANCE OF SPIRIT, William retorted.

To this affirmation Sir Henry replied coldly, DIAGNOSIS CLEAR. INJECTIONS EMETINE, BLAND DIET, MILK, BANANAS, POSSIBLY STRAWBERRIES CERTAINLY LIVER ESSENCE, ABSOLUTE REST, CONSULT BARTRAM.

The cables ticked themselves into hundreds of dollars, and after their futility William felt all the old rage of his boyhood mount into his blood. The damned superiority of the Englishman, the calm determination not to yield, the rigid heartless courtesy—he knew it all in Chefoo when the British Consul-General's son was at the top of the top form.

Blind with fury, William shut off the Atlantic Ocean and the British Isles and all the rest of the world. He was in his office, having left his father for an hour with two trained nurses, and Ruth to see that the fools did not neglect him. Now he called in his chief editor, keeping his finger on the electric button until Brownell came in on the run, his eyes terrified.

'Hold up the new dummy,' William ordered. 'My father is very ill. I can't get Lampheer to come over, he's determined to let my father die—just another American, I suppose —typically British! I don't know when I shall be back. I shall have to leave you in charge. If it's absolutely essential call me, but if it's not essential, I'll fire you.'

'I'll do my best, Mr. Lane.'

'Very well.'

William was putting on his overcoat and hat. Brownell sprang to his aid.

'Here, let me help.'

'Get back to your job,' William ordered, and hastened from the room.

Yet he knew Sir Henry was right. That was the worst of all, next to the fact of death itself. Now day by day he sat beside his father's bed, silent in the silence of his house, having ordered the nurses to stay in his dressing-room unless they were needed and forbidding any others except Dr. Bartram. Sir Henry would have been foolish to come and yet he ought to have set a price. Every man had his price and William could have paid it. His father was a man of importance, the father of William Lane, a rising power in America. It was an insult he would not forgive, and he added it to the mountain of insults he had taken in his boyhood. Sitting beside his dying father he brooded upon the mountain and how he would level it, by what means and with what purpose. Those tiny islands, clutching at half the world, those arrogant men sitting in their dinner jackets at solitary tables in jungles, served by millions of dark men—it was monstrous. His country, his beautiful youthful America, despised and laughed at, even as he himself had been laughed at by stupid English boys who could not spell? In those days he had been ashamed of his father because he was only a missionary, but now that missionary was the father of William Lane. The missionary was lifted up out of his humility and poverty. He had become the father of a man whose first million was doubling itself.

Tears stung William's eyes. Money could not delay by one hour the death of his father, even his. He leaned towards the bed and took his father's hand in his own. The hands were not alike. He had his small dark hands from his mother. His father's were big and bony, and now how thin and helpless.

'Father——' he whispered. For a moment he thought him dead.

But Dr. Lane was not dead. He turned his head slowly, the same nobly shaped head that he had given to his son when he begot him.

'Yes, William?' The voice was faint but clear.

'You know I am doing everything I can?'

'Yes, my son. . . . It is quite all right. . . . I must die, you know.'

'I can't let you die.'

'That is very good of you, William. . . . I appreciate it. . . . To want me to live——'

'Because I need you, Father.'

The words broke from him and the moment he had spoken them he knew them true. He had never really talked with his father and now it seemed to him that to his father alone could he speak of himself and the immense restlessness that filled him day and night. Now that he had set up this vast successful machine that brought money rolling in whether he was there or not, then what next? Now that he had power, millions of people his, too, looking at the pictures he chose, reading the words he wrote or permitted to be written, what next?

'Father, if you leave me—if you really think——'

'I know. . . . God has told me.'

'Then tell me before you go—what am I to do?'

'Do?'

'With myself.'

He saw his father's dark eyes open wide with final energy. 'William, you must listen to your own conscience. . . . It is the voice of God . . . in your breast. "Remember now thy Creator in the days of thy youth." All that you have—all your great gifts, my son . . . dedicate them to God. Oh God—I thank thee—thou hast—brought me to my son in time——'

The faint voice died away and the old man fell into sudden sleep as he did after the least exertion. He did not speak again.

William sat beside him through the hours. The nurses came and went, doing their duty. The doctor came, spoke a few words. 'It can't last, Mr. Lane. Any moment, I am afraid.'

William did not reply. That night, twenty minutes after midnight, his father without waking ceased to breathe.

Clem had plunged himself again into his own country. He had failed in China but he was not discouraged. Such was his faith in that which he believed. He had said very little to Henrietta about the brief visit to the shack in San Francisco, but she comprehended the refusal and perceived that as usual Clem had only been strengthened by it.

'Some day they'll see I'm right, hon,' he told her. 'They' were the powers, those who did not believe in his faith, the greedy, the selfish, the politicians, the small-minded. He did not hate, neither did he despise. Instead he was possessed by vast patience, a mighty omniscience. He could wait.

Meanwhile he worked. He decided to open his largest and cheapest market in Dayton. Each of his markets had its own peculiar name. This one he called 'People's Choice'.

'I don't want a chain name,' Clem said when Bump spoke of the advantages of a chain of markets all called by the same name. 'I want people to think the markets are theirs. Each one must be different, suited to a town and its folks.'

People's Choice was his first city market and he built it outside the city where land was cheap, at the end of a trolley line.

On the opening day Henrietta had come to help. Clem had lured thousands of people by his announcement of free foods on this first day. By ten o'clock the trolley-cars were crowded beyond control and well-fed people were struggling to reach counters where loaves of bread, pounds of cake, and baskets of fruit were waiting to be given away. The day was clear and cool and through the great glass windows the sun poured over stacked counters and heaped bins. Clem had devised an effect at once modern and old-fashioned. Apples were piled upon the floor in corners, and bananas hung from the ceiling.

'Help yourselves, folks,' Clem shouted cheerfully. 'Take a pumpkin home and make yourselves a pie. Here's old-fashioned molasses—dip it up, folks! It's bottling that makes it come high—five cents a dipper, folks! I bought it in N'Orleans for you—by the barrel, folks—and plenty. Here's bread—take a loaf, and here's butter from Wisconsin—straight from the farmers, and that's why I can afford to give it away today. Tomorrow you'll pay less for it than you pay in any store in the city. If anybody is hungry he can have a loaf free. Give and it shall be given unto you. Don't take it if you're not hungry, but if you're hungry and can't pay for it, we'll always give it to you. No caviare here, folks, no fancy notions, just plain food straight from the people who raise it.'

In and out among the surging, staring people he wove his way, alert, smiling, his sandy head held high, his small blue eyes snapping and twinkling and seeing everything at once. He wore overalls of denim like his clerks, or 'hands' as he called them, and his hands were men from anywhere, two Chinese boys who were working their way through college, a Negro he had seen in Louisiana and liked, Swedish farm-boys from Minnesota. He had picked his men and trained them himself, saying that clerks from other stores were no good to him.

His business was unorthodox and filled with risk, and when a man became fearful because of small children and a nervous wife, he let him go and found the boys, the young who dared to be reckless. He would sent Bump overnight to California or Florida to buy up carloads of cheap oranges, to West

263

Virginia to sweep up a harvest of turnips that were overloading the market, to Massachusetts to bid for a haul of fish that threatened to bring down the price on New York markets. Wherever there was unwanted food, food about to be thrown away, as Maine farmers were about to throw away half their crop of potatoes last summer, Clem or Bump was there. Clem trusted no others to buy for him, since in the narrow margin of buying and selling lay his profits and in his profits was his ability to expand his markets and his faith. His heritage from his father was an invincible belief in goodness, not in the goodness of God to which his father had so persistently trusted, but in the goodness of man. Clem believed more profoundly than ever that with his stomach full, any man preferred to be good. Therefore the task of the righteous, of whom Clem considered himself one, was to see that everybody had food.

In his hours of dreaming, for he did no work on Sunday and his markets were rigidly locked on that day, he gave himself up to still more huge fantasies about feeding all the hungry in the world. There in his ugly little house in New Point, Ohio, where he lived in complete happiness with Henrietta, he saw the people in China and India someday crowding to his markets. His failure with Sun Yat-sen in San Francisco, his conviction of future success made his dreams the richer and more real.

He recalled the long journey he had made on foot from Peking to the sea. The old agony of the moment when he saw his parents and sisters murdered had softened and dimmed. Instead he remembered the winding cobbled roads of the country that tied the villages together, the dusty foot-paths on either side of the cobbles, the fields green with new wheat in spring, with the tall sorghum corn in summer. Someday in those Chinese villages and market towns his foods would stand displayed.

People's Choice promised, even this first day, to be instantly successful and Clem saw himself growing still richer. According to any rules he should not be getting so rich. He had no desire to be a millionaire like William, and he was almost ashamed of his mounting bank accounts. But he never gave money away. Some deep prejudice against organized charity, against packaged religions and vague idealism, made him keep his hands in his pockets. He gave to any man or woman or child who wore a ragged coat or who needed a doctor, and a few words scribbled on a torn scrap of paper or an old envelope provided food from his nearest market for anyone, from a hungry college student to a passing drunk or a springtime tramp. But he gave no large cheques to soliciting treasurers and college presidents, and the churches, even in his home town, had come to look for no more from him than ten dollars dropped into the collection box at Christmas.

Bump, that cautious and careful young man, mindful of his college degree in economics and business management, warned him that sooner or later the organized food interests would attack him.

'You can't go on underselling them without their trying to get your hide,' Bump warned. His relationship to Clem remained nebulous, profound though unexpressed. Clem was too young to be his foster-father and he had never offered to be his brother. Bump was shrewd and he recognized in Clem a genius inexplicable. It was comprised of a daring that was absurd, a *naïveté* that was laughable, an ignorance that was almost illiterate, and out of daring, *naïveté*, and ignorance Clem succeeded in all he did. He had found a formula so simple that only a man as simple as himself could have proved it valid.

He declared it to gaping, staring thousands at noon this day of the opening of his new market. Six trumpeters, hired for the occasion, blew a frightful blast as the hour struck noon. The crowd, transfixed, paused to turn their heads towards the source of noise, and there in the centre of the glittering brass, set upon a sort of balcony of boards rigged with ropes, they saw Clem in his overalls, with a megaphone.

'Folks!' he shouted. 'This is more than just a market. It is a sign of what I believe in, a manifestation of my faith. "Faith is the evidence of things hoped for," the Bible says, and "the evidence of things unseen." Well, my hope is to see no more hunger, anywhere in the world. Food is the most important thing in the world. Food is one of a trinity with air and water. If I were President of the United States, which otherwise I am glad I am not, I would make bread and meat, milk and eggs, fruit and vegetables free to everybody. Then we would have no more war. It would be cheaper to feed people free like that than it would be to have a war, like what may come out of Asia some day if somebody don't do something, because the people are starving.'

The people stood motionless, listening and wondering if he were mad. He took a deep breath and began again.

'Now don't get me wrong. I don't believe in charity, nor do we have to have the government doing this kind of thing. I'm not president, don't expect to be, don't want to be. But I'm doing what I can here, and you see it, don't you? If it's good, if it helps you, then all I ask is for you to believe in the idea. Thank you, folks—that's all. And let me tell you that you'll find free box lunches packed and ready for you down at the south end of the market. Ice-cream is free for everybody, so's milk and soda pop. Have a good time, folks!'

He was in a frenzy of happiness. To the people who milled around him during the afternoon he talked in a stream of advice, explanation, and remonstrance. 'What you'll find here is not all foods, but just the essential foods and all cheap. I buy surpluses and that means whatever is in season and therefore cheapest. For instance, last winter when the big cold in the West was freezing cattle solid, I bought 'em that way and sold beef cheap. Price of meat came down right away. The beef was good, too. Freezing made it tender.

'Now here in this market, you won't find cucumbers in January. But you'll find mountains of them in summer when you want to be making your pickles. And I provide recipes, too. Where do I get them? From people like you. When you make something good write in and tell me about it. Look at that pile of leaflets there—take some—take a lot and give 'em to your friends. They'll tell you what to do with cucumbers when they're cheap and how to make jelly out of apple peelings and what not to throw into your garbage pails. Buy cheap, and don't waste. We could feed the world on what we throw away—yep, that's true, too. Nobody needs to starve—not anywhere in the world!'

People listened and laughed. 'You sound like a preacher!'

Clem grinned his dry sandy grin. 'Maybe I am—a new gospel I preach unto you. Nobody needs to be hungry.'

It was in the midst of such harangue in the late afternoon that he saw Henrietta standing in the far corner, very quiet in her dark blue suit and hat, and holding in her hands a yellow slip of paper. He was used to telegrams from his scouts scattered over the country, announcing a glut of oranges in the south-west or corn in Indiana or truck-garden stuff in New Jersey. Such telegrams had to be heeded immediately and so he suddenly stopped talking and wove his way through the crowds, pushing them gently with his sharp elbows.

Face to face with Henrietta, he reached for the telegram which she gave him and then he saw that it was not what he thought.

The telegram was signed by Mrs. Lane. YOUR DEAR FATHER PASSED ON LAST NIGHT. FUNERAL WILL BE THURSDAY. PROSTRATED WITH GRIEF. WILLIAM WONDERFUL. LOVE MOTHER. Instantly Clem forgot the crowds and the great success of his day. There was no spot in the huge cheap building where he could draw his beloved aside into privacy. Glass and brick pillars gave only the illusion of shelter. But he made of himself a shelter for the tears now rising slowly to her eyes.

'Hon, you go to the hotel right away. I'll send Wong with you. He has his little tin lizzie here. He'll put you on the train for New York. If you need anything in clothes, you can buy it there—a black dress or so. I'll be there tomorrow. I hate to have you alone tonight without me, but you'll not blame me for that.'

'I wish I could have seen him just once,' Henrietta murmured, wiping her eyes behind the shelter of his shoulders. She was taller than he and yet just now he managed to stand a little above her upon a collapsed cardboard box. 'I ought to have made William tell me. Ruth ought to have written—no, it was my own fault.'

For she had been cool to her parents when they got home

because they had gone to William and had not thought of coming to her. No one had told her how ill her father was. Even the letters from her mother had not said he might die. She might have known when she had no letter from him, except that he seldom wrote to his daughters, and always to William. And Ruth would never face the worst.

'It's a shame,' Clem muttered. 'It does seem as though your folks could have sent word.'

'I may not see him even now,' she went on. 'It would be just like William to go straight on with everything, as though no one else existed.'

'You go along quick,' he advised.

Stepping back he motioned to Wong, one of the Chinese students. He was a tall slender fellow from a town near Peking.

Clem said in Chinese, too low for anyone to hear or wonder at the strange tongue. 'Wong, you take Mrs. Miller please to the hotel to get her bag and then to the railway station and buy her a Pullman ticket to New York on the first train. Her honoured father has just died.'

Wong had heard of the venerable Dr. Lane, the mildest of missionaries, and he clucked his tongue against the roof of his mouth. 'The day of a father's death is worse than any yet known in a person's life,' he said gently.

He slipped off his white coat and changed to the one he wore outside the market. In half an hour Henrietta was on the way to the station in his old Ford car. Driving nimbly between the trolley-cars and the traffic, Wong tried in his courteous fashion to comfort Henrietta by all that he had heard about Dr. Lane.

'We heard even in our town that it was your honoured Old One who did not fear to approach that Devil Female King, the Empress, and tell her that she did ill to favour the Boxers. Again we heard, I from my father, since I was then very young, that when she came back again to the city, pretending that no evil had been done, your honoured Old One would not follow the other foreigners to her feasts. He held himself aloof. Your Old One loved the people and not the rulers.'

268

'I have not seen my father for all these years,' Henrietta said. 'Now I shall never see him again.'

'It was for our sakes that he cut himself off even from his own country,' Wong said in a heart-broken voice.

At the station he bought her tickets and a small basket of fruit. When he had seen her into her seat, had adjusted the window shade, had said good-bye, he went outside on the platform and there he stood, his hat held against his breast until the train pulled out.

Henrietta had never been in William's new home. Since she had sent no telegram to announce her coming, she took a cab and arrived at the door of the handsome house of grey stone, which stood between two smaller ones on upper Fifth Avenue. She rang the bell and the door was opened by an English manservant.

'I am Mr. Lane's elder sister,' she said in her somewhat cold voice.

The man looked surprised and she saw that he had not known of her existence.

'Please come in, Madame.'

He ushered her into a large room and disappeared, his footsteps silenced by thick carpets. Henrietta sat down in a deep chair covered with coral-coloured velvet. The room astonished her. Grey, coral, smoke-blue were mingled in velvet hangings and carpets. It was a room too soft, too rich, too opulently beautiful. Candace had thus surrounded the heavy furniture William had bought and which she disliked. In the centre of the room upon a round mahogany table stood a vast Chinese bowl of silver-grey pottery, crackled with deeper grey veins. It was full of pale yellow roses. This then was the way William lived. He must be monstrously rich. Or perhaps it was only the way Candace lived, and perhaps it was she who was too rich.

Henrietta reflected upon William as she had remembered him in Peking. The memory was not dimmed by the image of what he now was. A sulky, dark-browed boy, who snarled when she spoke to him! Why had he been always unhappy?

At school in Chefoo he had seldom spoken to her, even when they passed in the corridors. If her mother sent a message to them both in a letter to her, she had to send it to him in a note by a Chinese servant. Ruth had been too young to go away to school and so she had never seen the worst of William, for if he was unpleasant at home he was unbearable at school.

Henrietta had a vague understanding of him, nevertheless, as she sat thoughtfully by the window of this room. William could not endure to be outdone by anyone, but at school no American could be as the English were and there William felt himself unjustly surpassed. Moreover she herself surpassed him in their studies, and she had gone to some pains as she had grown older to hide from him the marks which made him hate her, too. And why should this only brother of hers suffer so much when, had he been content with himself, he might have been very happy? A handsome boy he had been, and his mind, developing more slowly than hers, was a good and even brilliant mind, likely now to have gone far ahead of hers. His intolerable, bitter, burning pride had poisoned him to the soul, a pride begun by their foolish old Chinese amah, who because he was a boy among girls, had loved him best and praised him most and made them all worship him as the young prince of the family—a pride fostered, certainly, by being an American among Chinese. But here in America itself there were no princes.

The door opened and Candace came in, trailing the lace ruffles of her *négligé*. It was almost noon and she had not yet dressed herself for the day. But so immaculate, so exquisite was she in her rose and lace, her fair hair so curled and smoothed and waved, that Henrietta felt dingy after her night on the train.

Candace held out her hands and her rings glittered. 'Not to tell us that you were coming, you naughty thing!'

She had grown soft and was prettier than ever, slender but rounded and feminine and too tender in voice and eyes.

'I thought you would expect me to come at once,' Henrietta said. She submitted to a scented embrace and sat down again.

270

Candace sighed. The tears came to her violet eyes. 'William is not to be consoled. He sits there beside his father day and night. He will neither eat nor rest. Your mother is sleeping. She is very tired. Ruth has gone home for a bit to be with her children. There is nothing to do here but wait.'

'Clem will be here tomorrow,' Henrietta said.

'How good of him to get away,' Candace said.

'It is not good of him,' Henrietta replied. 'He does it for me.'

She found herself with nothing to say and so she sat for a moment in silence while Candace twisted the rings on her fingers. Then Henrietta made up her mind. She did not intend to be cowed by this house or by any of William's belongings or indeed by William himself.

'I would like to go to my father, please, Candace. I have not seen him at all, you know.'

Candace looked distressed. Her mouth, soft and full and red, looked suddenly childish and she bit her lower lip. 'I don't know if William will——'

'William knows me,' Henrietta said. 'He will not blame you.'

She rose and Candace, as though she submitted by habit, rose too, and in silent doubtfulness she led Henrietta across the hall through another large room—a music room, Henrietta saw, since it contained a grand piano and a gramophone set into a carved cabinet, and then across a hall which ended in a conservatory, and at last to heavy closed doors of polished oak. Here Candace paused and then she slid the doors a small distance apart. Over her shoulder Henrietta looked into an immense library, in the centre of which stood a bier. There William sat. He had drawn a leather arm-chair close enough to see his father's face. A tall pot of lilies stood at the foot of the bier. Upon this scene the sunshine of the morning streamed through high southern windows.

Henrietta gently put Candace aside and entered the room. 'William, I have come.'

William looked at her startled. Then he rose. 'You came early, Henrietta.' His voice, deep and always harsh, was composed.

'I came as soon as I had Mother's telegram.'

Candace had closed the doors and gone away and they were alone. She went to the bier and looked down upon her father's face. It was as white as an image of snow. The long thin hands folded upon the breast were of the same deadly whiteness.

'I am glad you have not sent him away,' Henrietta said.

'Whatever had to be done was done here.'

'He is desperately thin.'

'He was ill for two years,' William said. 'Of course Mother did not realize it, nor did he complain. His intestines were eaten away by the wretched disease. There was no hope.'

Neither of them wept, and neither expected weeping of the other.

'I am glad he did not die over there,' William said.

'Perhaps he would rather have died there. He loved the Chinese so much,' Henrietta said.

'He wasted his life upon them,' said William.

He spoke without emotion, yet she felt his absolute grief. He revealed himself in this grief as she had never seen him, a gaunt lonely man, still young, and his pride was bitter in his face, in his haughty bearing, in the abrupt movements of his hands.

'It is a comfort to you that he came here to die.' This she added in sudden pity for him.

'It is more than a comfort,' he replied. 'It was his last mission.'

She turned her gaze then from the calm dead face to look at William and perceived in his stone-grey eyes a look so profoundly strange, for that was the word which came to her mind, that she was for the first time in her life half frightened of him.

William had no impulse to tell her of those last words which his father had spoken. For him they had indeed taken on the importance of prophecy. His father, he had learned from his mother, had a premonition of approaching death during the last year in Peking. He had long refused to come back to

272

America because, he said simply, he wanted to die in China and be buried there. Yet when he felt death imminent he changed his mind. 'I must see William,' he had told her one night when he woke as he often did long before dawn. 'I must see my son. I want to talk with him. I have things to tell him.'

Here his mother had paused to wipe her eyes and also to ask him in curiosity, 'What things did he tell you, William?'

He could not share even with her the solemnity of those last words his father had been able to speak. They were few, far fewer than he had meant to speak, William felt sure, had he not been so ill in the last weeks before the end. And yet in few words all was said. He understood that his father had come thousands of miles by land and sea to speak them to his dear and only son, and so he forgave his father everything, all the shame of being his son, the disgrace of the lowliness of being the son of a poor man and a missionary. By his love for his son and by his death his father had lifted himself up into sainthood. There was symbolism here which in its way was as great as that of the Cross. He was his father's only begotten son, whom his father so loved. . . .

'William, are you sure you feel well?'

Henrietta's anxious voice flung ice upon his burning heart.

His old irritation flared at her. 'Of course I am well! Naturally I am tired. I don't expect to rest until after the funeral tomorrow. I think you ought to go and see Mother.'

'Candace said she was sleeping.'

'Then it is time she woke.'

He took her elbow and led her out of the room. In the hall he pressed a button and the man appeared again. 'Take my sister upstairs to my mother's room,' William ordered.

'Yes, sir. This way if you please, Madame.'

The sliding doors closed behind Henrietta and she was compelled to follow the man, her footsteps sinking again into heavy carpets across the hall and up the stairs and down another hall to one of a half-dozen closed doors. Here the man knocked. She heard her mother's voice. 'Who is it?'

'Thank you,' Henrietta said, dismissing the man with a nod. She opened the door. There sat her mother at a small desk, fully dressed, her steel-grey hair swept up into a thick knot on top of her head. She was writing and she lifted her pen and turned her head.

'Henrietta, my dear!' She rose, majestic, and held out her arms. 'My dear daughter!'

Henrietta allowed herself to be enveloped and she kissed her mother's dry cheek. She saw in the first glance that although her mother had aged or weathered into a dry ruddiness in the years since they had last met, she was not changed. Neither life nor death could change her. There was nothing new here. Her mother planned what to do, how to behave, what to say. Henrietta withdrew herself and sat down and took off her hat and coat.

'Mother, it was so strange to find you and Father gone away when we got to Peking.'

'You should have told us you were coming,' Mrs. Lane said, 'then you needn't have come all that way.'

Henrietta refrained from mentioning Clem, his reasons for wanting to go to China, the suddenness of their departure.

'Please, Mother, tell me everything.'

Her mother could tell only so much as she could comprehend of what had gone on.

'Everything got harder in Peking,' her mother began. 'It wasn't in the least as it had been in the dear old days. You remember, Henrietta, how easy everything used to be? When you were a child, I was received most courteously wherever I went, merely because I was a foreigner. That was after the Boxer Rebellion, of course. Peking was heavenly then. I got to be fond of the Old Empress, really fond! I went with Mrs. Conger sometimes to call and Her Majesty used to have one of her ladies explain to me, so that I could tell Mrs. Conger who spoke no Chinese at all, how sorry she was for all that had happened, and how she understood that we were all there for the good of China. Then she would reach out her hand and stroke mine. She had the most beautiful old hand—so delicate, covered with rings, and then the long enamelled

274

nail protectors. It was really wonderful to see her. I don't think most people understood her. I used to tell your father so, but he would never trust her, no matter what I said.'

'When did Father fall ill!' Henrietta asked.

'It began soon after that upstart Sun Yat-sen stirred up the people. Your father was so worried. I told him that nothing would be made better by his worrying, but you know he never listened to me. In his way he was frightfully stubborn. And things began to get so hard. After the Empress died the wonderful courtesy just ended—like that! Even the people on the streets began to be rough to us. They didn't seem to want us in Peking. Your father was stoned one Sunday night on his way to chapel.'

'Stoned—for what?' Henrietta asked.

'For nothing—just because he was a foreigner. Then it got better again. Oh dear, you've been away so long! It's difficult to explain. But it has been one thing after another, a revolution about something all the time, and when I told your father he was looking thin he always said he couldn't leave.'

'And when he did leave he wanted to go to William.'

'He got the idea suddenly that William needed him. I remember he said a queer thing when we were standing on the deck as the steamer pulled away from Shanghai. He was staring at the shore and then he said, "But what shall it profit a man if he gain the whole world and lose his own son"?'

Henrietta did not answer. She did not listen any more to her mother's prattling voice. A strange thing for her father to say, and what did it mean?

Henrietta went herself to the station to meet Clem. With his usual skill, perfected by constant travel, he managed to catch a train at the last moment possible in time to get to the funeral. Had there been half an hour's delay it would have been too late. But Henrietta had now come to believe that there would never be such delay upon any train which Clem chose to take. Luck was the aura in which he lived.

Thus she stood waiting on the platform while the train drew in, accurate to the second. Clem was always the first passenger to get out. She saw him swing himself down, shake his head at a porter and come hurrying towards her, carrying his small bag. William's chauffeur stepped forward to take it but Clem resisted.

'I'm used to carrying my own suit-case, thanks.'

He threw the man a brief bright abstract smile, then forgot him. 'Henrietta, gosh—it's good to see you! How are you, hon?'

'Come on, Clem. We haven't a moment.'

'Funeral isn't till four, is it? Lots of time.'

This Henrietta would not allow. 'Come on, do. Everybody's waiting.'

'Everybody's early then.' But he humoured her, seeing that her eyes were washed with weeping.

They got into the big heavy car which William had imported from England. Clem lifted his sandy eyebrows and said nothing, but Henrietta understood his reproach.

'Never mind, he always hates England and yet he worships everything English.'

'I don't mind. Anything to tell me, hon?'

'Not now, Clem. Afterwards.'

They drove in silence through the bright New York streets. He saw her dressed for the first time in black. She looked handsome but he had better sense than to tell her so now. He wanted to share her sorrow but he could not. When he thought of Dr. Lane's death he saw with dreadful renewal the sight of his own father lying with his head half severed from his neck, in the midst of the other dead. He wanted to talk quickly about something else, tell her how triumphant the market opening in Dayton had really been, and yet he knew that he should not speak of that, either, here or now. To escape the inescapable memory he stared out into the streets, trying to catch from the passing windows ideas for advertising, for displays, for announcements, and while he did so he felt guilty because he dared not think of Henrietta's grief. She could not comprehend, perhaps, though he had told her everything, how memory could pervade his whole life if he gave it the least chance at him. He crowded it out by his constant activity, by his incessant planning and incredible accomplishment.

'You are never still,' she said with sudden and extraordinary impatience.

He looked at her, astonished.

'Oh, Clem!' She seized his hand in both of hers.

He saw tears brimming again into her eyes. 'I know, Henrietta. I don't know why I can't sit still.'

She was broken by his humility. 'Don't mind me. I can't tell you why I feel so mixed up.'

'That's all right.'

He made a superhuman effort then and did sit still, forcing his hand that held hers to be still, keeping his feet from twitching or shuffling, refusing to recognize the itch of his nose, his cheek, the nervous ache of arm or leg, the innumerable minute demands of his tense frame.

She was grateful and in silence they sat while the car swept them up to the huge church on Fifth Avenue where William had commanded that his father's body be laid. Here she and Clem got out and mounted the marble steps. In the lobby they were met by an attendant of some sort, who guided them in silence to an area of pews tied in with black ribbon, where the family was assembled. To her surprise she saw even Roger Cameron and his wife, Roger lean and aged and looking as permanent as a mummy. Her seat and Clem's had been kept beside William. She sat down.

Clem looked across Henrietta into William's eyes, grey under the heavy brows. He felt a shock in his breast. The tall grim boy he had seen on the Peking street had grown into a tall grim man. In the one glance and the brief nod Clem saw the long square face, the pallid skin, the deep-set eyes and black brows, and the strained handsome mouth. Then he sat down, forgetting the dead. William was unhappy! The sorrow of the last few weeks could not have worked quickly enough to carve his face into such lines. But why should William be unhappy as well as sorrowful? Unhappiness was something deep, permeating the very sinews of a man's soul.

'The Lord giveth and the Lord taketh away.' The rich

and polished voice of the robed minister rolled from the chancel. Clem breathed hard and tried not to shift his feet. The flowers were too fragrant, the church too warm. Upon the bier he saw a white-faced statue, handsomely clothed and surrounded with flowers so skilfully that they made a background for him. This statue did not look in the least like Dr. Lane, whom he remembered as a quiet melancholy saint, always withdrawn though kind. This dead man looked proud and even haughty. His features were too clear, the eyebrows touched with black, the lips with a pale red, the nose perperfected, the sleeping eyelids outlined. The head had immense and marble dignity. As he remembered, Dr. Lane had walked with a slight stoop, a humble pose of the head, and his features though good were blurred with the thoughtful doubt of a man who always saw the other side of everything.

William, he supposed, had ordered all to be of the best, and so they had made the best of Dr. Lane. Clem disliked what he saw and feeling the impulse to move now become uncontrollable he stealthily shifted his feet, scratched his wrists and palms, and even rubbed his nose with his forefinger while a woman with a loud clear soprano sang a hymn, 'For All the Saints Who from Their Labours Rest.' Henrietta pressed his arm with her shoulder and he became quiet again.

The minister got up and began a eulogy of Dr. Lane, whom he had never known, and Clem listened. All the facts were right, he supposed—Dr. Lane, the father of William Lane, one of America's great figures, was born of a distinguished and scholarly family. Although his family had not entirely approved his becoming a missionary he had persisted in his noble determination, in which he was joined by a fine young woman of equally good family. It was not usual that two young people of such position gave up all to follow after Christ in a heathen country. There Dr. Lane's efforts had seen singularly blessed. He had become important not only in the mission field but in his interpretation of the Chinese mind during the political crisis of recent years.

'The fellow isn't saying the really important things,' Clem told himself. It was strange that William had not pointed out to the minister that his father understood the Chinese and appreciated them and that he had not always wanted to convert them. That was why they had liked him. William should have told the small good things his father did, how he always put his hand into his pocket when he saw a beggar. . . .

Dr. Lane, now, would have understood how he himself felt about getting food to people, quick and cheap. He would have enjoyed telling him about his markets and how he planned to find something that could be done anywhere in the world. He could have told all that to Dr. Lane, things he had not even told Henrietta, though she always stood by him whether she believed he could do it or not. But Dr. Lane would have believed it, maybe.

Clem stole a glance at William's profile. They were standing up. The funeral was almost over. Maybe he would be able to talk with William tomorrow when this was past. There was the grave yet.

Around the open grave he stood among this family he did not know, yet to which he belonged because he and Henrietta belonged together. He saw them all, Jeremy and Ruth and the girls—cute little things, dressed in white instead of black, little white fur hats and coats. He had never seen Jeremy or Ruth or Mrs. Lane. They were the sort of people he did not know.

While the minister spoke his solemn rich words and crumbled earth upon the coffin, Clem stood looking brightly abstracted, entirely unconscious, while his mind glanced at the various miracles of his life, first of which was that Henrietta had wanted to marry him. Seeing this family, he could not understand it, though he was not humble, either. The miracle was that, having been born among these people, she should have had the wit to see what he was and what he could do before he had done it.

He looked at her as she stood, her black-gloved hands clasped, her strong profile bent, her eyes upon the ground. He loved her mightily, he loved her the way he loved his work, the way he loved his dream. It was one of the big things. But she was whole and entire without him. He did not think of her as a part of himself because he thought nothing of himself. He did not know how he looked or what sort of a man he was. He was as fleshless as a grasshopper.

He was glad that Henrietta had never spoken to him of having children. He had seen too many children starving to death. The villages on that long and lonely march from Peking to the sea had been busy with children, dirty, laughing, hungry—so many children in the world, anyway. When he thought of children he always thought of his sisters as he had last seen them and his mind swerved away from that again. He had to be free to accomplish the thing for which he was born and children ought to be kept at home, treasures in a box. If his sisters had been kept at home they would have been alive today. He did not ever want children.

Tim and Jen and Mamie! When he had hurried back to the farm after reading the ghastly story that held the head-lines for a day, Tim was dead and buried. Pop Berger was in bed sick and he cried whenever anyone spoke to him. A police guard sat by the bed and there were reporters everywhere. Mom Berger kept the girls in the kitchen with her and the doors shut. There had been a square-set newspaper fellow there whose name was Seth James. He had gone away after he heard Clem was going to take the two girls to Ohio.

'You're the only decent person I've seen,' the fellow had said and had shaken Clem's hand up and down hard half a dozen times.

Clem had not known what to do with Mamie and Jen. They had cried when he took them away. But Henrietta had been nice to them and after a while they learned to wait on people in the store. Then, after they had fattened up a bit and got better looking, they had both married farm-boys. Mamie had died when her baby was born but Jen, who he had always supposed could not live long, was growing stout and talkative. Food had done it, of course—plenty of good food.

He came to himself suddenly when Henrietta put her hand on his arm. The funeral was over and he was ashamed that he had not kept his mind on it. He turned, obedient to her touch, and joined the solemn family procession back to the funeral cars.

The procession stopped at William's house and the family descended and entered the huge front door, held open by the footman, who wore a proper look of gloom. Roger Cameron and his wife had gone home, their car swerving past the ones that stopped. When Candace had begged her father to come in and stay the evening with her he had refused. 'I swore ten years ago I would never go to another funeral before my own, and it was only because your mother forced me that I have come today. You'll have to get through the rest of the day the best you can, Daughter.'

Candace went upstairs and changed her black garments for a soft white gown whose collar she tied with a black ribbon. Then she hurried downstairs to see if the tea which William had ordered to be ready was set upon the table. It was more than a usual tea. Henrietta and Clem were taking an early train and Jeremy and Ruth must go home to their children. There was ham and sliced cold chicken upon the buffet and she knew that the cook had beaten up a custard dessert. By her command there were no flowers on the table. She had seen so many flowers this day that she did not want any more. Red roses perhaps next week! The dreadful thing was that she had felt no sorrow; a mild sadness, of course, such as death always persuades, but not sorrow. It was impossible to grieve for an old man to whom she had scarcely spoken, a sweet old man, she saw, even through his illness. But what troubled her was that she had not been able to share William's sorrow. He treasured it, he kept it to himself, he endured with such nobleness that she felt repelled and then was angry with herself. She dreaded tomorrow when nobody would be here—except, of course, his mother. For the first time she felt glad that his mother was going to spend the winter with them. Perhaps together they could understand William better and make him happy.

At this moment while she moved about the dining-room, Henrietta's husband came to the door and looked in. He made her think of a bird, slender, bright-faced, boyish, making so many little quick unconscious movements. He was completely different from Henrietta and yet there was something between

281

them. She did not see why William had been angry when Henrietta married Clem.

'Come in, Clem,' she said sweetly.

He came in, his hands in his pockets jingling something, keys, coins—no, a small bottle of pills which he now brought out. 'Can I find some water somewhere? All this has brought on my nervous indigestion.'

She lifted a cut-glass carafe from the sideboard and he whistled softly when he took it. 'Solid, isn't it?'

'A wedding present. If you saw the amount of cut glass I have packed away, beside all this!'

'Swell wedding, must have been. But then, William would have that. Did he ever tell you we met once?'

'No, did you?'

He rolled pills into the palm of his hand, threw them in his mouth, gulped them, and washed them down with water he poured into a goblet on the table. 'Maybe he has forgotten, but I never have. A Chinese boy and I were kind of dancing round each other ready to let out our fists when William came by and stopped us.'

'Did he know you?'

Clem grinned mischievously and she saw freckles under his pale skin. 'No—but he knew who I was.'

'What do you mean?'

'I came from the wrong side of the tracks, see?'

'There were no tracks in Peking, were there?'

'Oh, yes, there were. The Lanes were aristocrats compared to us. Dr. Lane got a salary every month. They lived in a compound. My father hadn't any salary. He was low enough to live on faith alone.'

They spoke in half whispers, almost guiltily, enjoying the respite from gloom. He had a sense of humour, Candace saw. And Clem saw a pleasant pretty woman, an honest woman at that, not too smart maybe, certainly not grand like his Henrietta, but nice to talk to, especially after a funeral.

'Christians are like other people. What'll I call you—Mrs. William?'

'Oh, call me Candy.'

'Candy, eh? Nice name for you. My father was ignorant, Candy, just plain uneducated like I am. There's a difference, though. I wanted an education and he didn't believe it was right. He thought God would provide everything—even food, you know. Dr. Lane knew better. He was real well educated. Of course my father was only a farm-boy.'

Candace stared at him, not comprehending in spite of what she heard. He tried further.

'All the well-heeled missionaries who didn't have to trust God looked down on us, naturally. I guess my poor old dad was a sort of beggar sometimes. When he saw us hungry and no food in sight he used to push God a little.'

'How?'

Clem's face turned red and the freckles disappeared. 'He went to the other missionaries—or even to the Chinese—and told them we had nothing to eat.' He tried to laugh. 'Kind of tattle-tale on God, I guess! Anyway, I don't like to think of it.'

'I'm sure William has forgotten all of that,' Candace said, on a rush of pity and vague affection for this too honest man.

'Maybe,' Clem said. He looked sober and began jingling his pockets again.

Something haunted his restless blue eyes and Candace went on pitying him. 'You're very happy with Henrietta, aren't you? She adores you, I think. When she talks about you she looks as though she were thinking of her child as well as her husband.'

'There is nobody in the whole world like Henrietta,' Clem said. The red had left his face as quickly as it had come and the freckles were back. 'I don't know what I'd do if I didn't have her. She's my life's foundation. I'll build all sorts of superstructures, maybe, in what I'm trying to do about food, but she keeps me steady. And here's the thing—she never discourages me.'

'Wonderful! And what are you trying to do about food, Clem?'

'Oh—just feed the world.'

'Hush!'

She put a hand, pretty and ringed, upon Clem's arm. They

listened and she took it away again. William entered the room, and she turned to him.

'Clem and I are here waiting, William. Everything is ready.'

'I don't know where everyone is,' William said.

He sat down in a great Jacobean chair that stood beside the long windows opening to a wide terrace. He still wore his black suit and above the dead hue of the broadcloth his face was whiter than ever, his brows more intense.

'Clem was talking about feeding the world.'

William glanced from under his eyebrows, and Clem suddenly heard the jingling in his own pockets and took his hands out of them.

'You are in the food business, aren't you?' William asked without interest.

'Yes,' Clem replied. 'I've just opened a big new market at Dayton, Ohio.'

'What has that to do with the world?'

'Just a beginning,' Clem said without humility. He was surprised to find that he rather enjoyed talking with William. There was an edge to it. Walking briskly across the floor he took the other Jacobean chair on the opposite side of the window and turning sidewise began to talk with sudden fluency.

'I began in the simplest sort of way—with a grocery store, in fact, in a small town, New Point, Ohio. It's still the home base. I have no family, you know—Boxer Rebellion put an end to that.'

'My father told me,' William said.

'Yes, well, we don't have to remember the past. But the way we had to live when I was a kid I suppose made me awful interested in food. Can't eat much myself—I have nervous indigestion. All that wonderful stuff on the table there—I won't hardly touch it. A cup of tea maybe and a little chicken. Bread poisons me, though I make the finest bread. Say, William, do you remember Chinese bread?'

'My mother never let us eat Chinese things.'

'Well, we were thankful for that bread at our house. It was a lot easier to take than starvation. I learned what good bread was. I might send you a few loaves of my product.'

284

William was too shocked to thank him. 'Is your business successful?' he asked coldly. The fellow looked like a country storekeeper.

'I undersell every staple,' Clem said with pride. 'I watch the surplus everywhere in the country. Got twenty men doing just that. Some day I'll be watching world surpluses. Then I'll be doing what I mean to do.'

'You actually plan to establish a world food monopoly?' William for the first time in days looked interested.

'Hell, no!' Clem said cheerfully. 'I'm not interested in monopolies. I'm interested in getting people fed. If they can't pay for it I give it to them.'

'You mean you *give* food to people?' William's voice was unbelieving.

"Why not, if they're hungry?"

'But you can't stay in business that way.'

Clem wriggled in the huge chair, scratched one cheek and then the other with one hand, and then pulled the short hair over his right ear and rubbed both knees. 'I don't know why,' he said humbly, 'but I'm a millionaire already—or almost.'

Candace, seated upon one of the gilt dining chairs, suddenly began to laugh, and William turned upon her.

'Why do you laugh, Candace?'

She buried her face in her hands and shook her head, still laughing. What had made her laugh was the look on William's face, but she could not tell him. 'It's so funny,' she gasped, her face still in her hands. 'It's so funny to get rich giving food away.'

'Nonsense,' William said. 'Of course he doesn't give it all away.'

'But to give any of it away,' she murmured. She found her handkerchief and wiped her eyes. Then she caught Clem grinning at her wryly.

'It is funny,' he agreed. 'It's darned funny. I can't explain it. There's some sort of magic hidden in the golden rule—I can't explain it any other way.'

Upon this conversation, which had become entirely repulsive to William, Mrs. Lane now entered, followed by Jeremy

285

and Ruth. Behind them came Henrietta with her hat on, ready for the train. William rose. 'Let us take our places,' he said quietly. 'Mother, please sit at my right. Ruth at my left, Jeremy at Candace's right, and Henrietta next. Your place, Clem.'

When they were all seated William lifted his head and fixed his eyes on a point above Candace's head at the end of the long lace-spread table. She saw that there was something he wanted to say to them.

'It has not been our habit in this house to have grace before meals. Perhaps we have grown careless. But from this day on, in memory of my father, I will say grace at meals in my house.'

His eyes fell and for an instant Candace's caught them. He saw love and pity rush into tears and he bent his head to avoid the sight.

'Dear William,' his mother whispered, and put out her hand to him. But he did not pause to look at Candace or touch his mother's hand. He bent his head and began to pray in a tense, low voice:

'Our Father, for the food that thou hast given us, receive our thanks. Bless this food to our use and us to Thy Kingdom, Amen.'

It was the grace that his father had used throughout the years of his missionary life.

VIII

CLEM bided his time. His faith, fulfilling itself by his steady success, was only embattled when he met with opposition. He was amazed when he discovered those who would have laughed at him had he failed, but who were angered by him when he did not fail, and who attacked him finally for undermining their own markets. These were the consolidated groceries and food companies, the chain stores which were beginning to form a net over the whole country. They declared that they, too, were selling to the people cheap and good food, and they began their warfare by insidious advertising against Clem's wares, saying that cheap surplus foods were not guaranteed foods and carried in them the germs of disease and decay. Buy only our packaged foods, they screamed, buy foods only with our seal upon them.

'We must get some big lawyers,' Bump told Clem. During the war he had served as a food expert, and had won a medal for saving the nation millions of dollars in food, buying where experience with Clem had taught him to buy and buying, too, with Clem's help. Somewhat reluctantly, when the war was over, he had married a German girl, Frieda Altmann, with whom he had fallen in love while he was overseas, and they now had two fat children who looked, he often felt, entirely German. Nevertheless his Frieda was good and a fine cook and she adored Clem, whom she considered a god, and she was humble before Henrietta, whom she loved with enthusiasm. But Frieda did all things with enthusiasm.

Clem had only to be driven into a corner to become cool and aggressive. He hired two clever lawyers, Beltham and Black of Dayton, and entered into the private war which was to last as long as he lived.

For Clem himself the First World War had been an atavism which could not be understood. Europe he knew little and his inclination was to think of it as a small and diverting piece of

287

ground which included England. He had run over there, as he put it, the summer before the war, Henrietta, of course, going with him. He still refused to allow an ocean between them. A few weeks in England had sufficed.

'Can't tell these people anything,' he said to Henrietta. 'They think I have only one idea. Well, that's all I need. If an idea is big enough a man don't need but one.'

He surveyed the tidy farms and smooth green hills of England with something like cynicism. 'I seem to see India behind all this,' he said. 'I see Egypt and the Middle East. Some time we got to go and take a look at India, hon, and see the green hills there and the fat people. All these beef roasts and steaks and legs of mutton!'

In Europe he looked for hunger and found little. Instead he found prudence and habitual scarcity. The French threw nothing away and this he approved. A fish head belonged on the dish and not in the garbage can.

'There is no sweeter meat than the cheeks of a carp,' Mrs. Fong used to tell him in Peking and he had never forgotten.

The farms in Denmark were Clem's delight. He visited them without introduction, appearing at a barn door while Henrietta lingered in the road outside. Sometimes he called her, sometimes he did not. One morning he beckoned to her fiercely.

'Come here, hon—this fellow has an idea!'

She looked into the wide barn door and there in the shadowy depths she saw the Danish farmer painting the walls. Pots of paints, green and sky blue, stood on the floor of beaten earth, and with a large brush, not of a house-painter but of an artist, the farmer was painting the walls with scenes of green meadows and running water under blue skies.

When he saw their admiration and surprise, he grinned and spoke to them with a few words of the English he had learned in folk school.

'For winter,' he explained. 'Make cows happy. Grass nice, thinking summer.'

'Ain't that smart?' Clem asked, turning to Henrietta. 'He knows the cows get bored in the winter locked up in the barn, and so he wants to make them happy. Good fellow!' He clapped the thick-bodied farmer on the back. 'Nice idea! Bet they give more milk, too.'

They began a conversation of gestures and a dozen or so words. Clem picked up languages quickly and he carried small pocket dictionaries everywhere. From the Dane he learned that it was hard to export as much butter as they had to England, because English farmers had their own butter. Yet Denmark needed more coal, English coal, which was going instead to Italy to buy fresh fruit. If the new refrigerator cars really began to run in large numbers, then Denmark would have even less coal.

Clem became concerned in the perennial question of distribution.

The monstrous folly of starvation anywhere in the world impressed him day and night. Food was abundant upon the land and in the sea. However many people were born and lived, there was more food than they could possibly eat. In America he saw apples rotting in orchards; corn used for fuel; granaries filled with wheat so that public money must buy still more granaries; eggs spoiling for lack of consumers; potatoes fed to beasts; fish made into fertilizers. Denmark had only butter to sell, but Americans had too much butter and would not buy. Argentine beef sold for pennies a pound because there was too much meat. The same story was everywhere in the world of starving people and rotting plenty.

'There has got to be some sort of over-all,' Clem said thoughtfully. 'Not government, either—but what?' He had absorbed from the Chinese a deep distrust of government. Men in power, he had once declared, became more than men. They fancied themselves gods. Henrietta had laughed when he said this. She did not often laugh, and when she did he always wanted to know why. 'Sometimes you act a little like God, yourself,' she had replied.

He was inexplicably hurt. 'No—no—don't say that, hon! Maybe like a father. Only like a father, though.'

She was learning to sheathe her bluntness because she did not always know what could hurt him. He went about so shining in his hopefulness, so childlike in his goodness, so impregnable in his devotion, that it seemed nothing could hurt him. Then she found that she alone could do the damage. Opposition from others, their laughter, their disbelief, he could and did ignore or accept as persecution by evil. But she whom he loved, who loved him, could pierce his bright armour and bring tears to his eyes. The first time she saw the tears she had wept with shame, had sworn to herself that she would never laugh at him, never caution him, never show doubt—nay, more, she would never feel doubt. The one sin she could commit, she told herself, was to hurt Clem.

The years had passed and still they had no children and still she did not mind. Clem filled every need of her being, and she devoted herself to him, taking over almost without his knowing it all the things which he hated to do; the meticulous detail of business, the bills, the arrangements for shipping, the delivery of car-loads of foods, the refrigeration and preservation and then disposals. More and more she and Bump conferred on the carrying out of Clem's decisions, daring and bold as they were, sometimes involving the loss of thousands of dollars as well as the possibilities of profits as great. Neither of them questioned what Clem decided to do. It remained for them merely to discover how to do it.

During the war, however, he had made a decision of his own so peculiar, so unlike him, that for a while Henrietta wondered what change had come in him that she did not understand. He had begun in recent years to read faithfully William's newspapers. What he thought of them he never said, but his intense look, his frequent silences when he had studied a tabloid carefully, made Henrietta long to put a question to him. But she did not. He had never allowed her to complain to him fully about William.

'He's your brother, hon,' Clem had said. 'He's part of your family. A family is a great thing to have. China would have died and disappeared long ago if it hadn't been for the way families stick together over there.'

'I hope you won't try to make me stick to mine,' Henrietta had retorted.

In one of William's papers, more and more filled with

pictures, Clem had discovered during the war a feature about Chinese coolies digging trenches in France. He found it one Sunday when he was at home, and sitting on the small of his back in a large arm-chair, his feet propped on the rungs of another chair in front of him, he had stared at the bewildered faces of Chinese farmers in France, staring back at him from the pages.

'I bet they don't have a notion of why they're there or why they're digging those trenches,' he told Henrietta.

It was a peaceful morning in America, and town-folk walked quietly past the house with their children on their way to church. Henrietta looked at Clem. She knew him so well, so familiar was every line of that thin square face and every note of his brisk hurried speech, that she divined at once that in his musing tone and his meditative eye a plan was beginning to shape. She waited while she polished the silver, a task which she usually planned for this time when Clem was at home. She sat at the dining-room table covered with newspapers upon which the silver was spread.

'I bet those Chinese were just carted over there like cattle,' Clem mused. After a few minutes more he got up.

Henrietta followed him with her watchful look. 'Can I get you something, Clem?'

He was hunting for paper and pen. 'I want to write to Yusan. What are those Chinese farmers doing over there in France? I bet somebody's up to something.'

She rose and found paper and pen, an envelope and the proper stamps, and when he had scrawled one of his brief letters, she sealed it and put it aside to mail in the morning.

This was the beginning, as she knew it would be. The end was several months later when Clem and Yusan met in Paris. Clem, leaving her in charge, for Bump was now in the war himself, put the ocean between them for the first time.

'I'll only be gone a couple of weeks, hon,' he said. Agony was plain on his face. 'I don't know why I'm doing this, but somehow I have to. . . .'

'That's all right, Clem,' she said. It was not all right, it was far from all right, and she felt the physical tearing of her heart out of her flesh as she stood on the pier and watched him go away, his face whiter, his figure smaller as the ship moved towards the sea.

And Clem, his eyes fixed upon her who made his whole home, cried out against his own folly. Had Bump been at home he would have brought her along, but without Bump only Henrietta could hold together in his absence the vast structure of his markets. What drove him to France he scarcely knew except that when he hesitated the faces of the bewildered Chinese were there before him. He saw them in their villages, in their own fields, in the streets of the cities into which they flooded in times of famine and starvation. How could they understand France? He would get Yusan started and then he would come home again to Henrietta, maybe run over again a couple of times to see how they were making out, but taking her with him next time, for sure.

In Paris he met Yusan, who wore a new suit of Western clothes. At first Clem scarcely recognized him in the crowd of Frenchmen, except that they were all talking and Yusan was standing immobile, silent, watchful, and therefore as conspicuous as a statue of gold. Clem caught his hand and forgot for a moment even Henrietta.

'Yusan!'

'Elder Brother!'

They broke into Chinese simultaneously and the French men and women stared and cried out to heaven in admiration at such fluency, nothing of which was comprehensible to them. Clem liked the French people and bustled his way among them with the same assurance he had at home in America or in China. They had the same mixture of naturalness, simplicity, shrewdness, humour, childishness, and sophistication that made Americans and Chinese alike, too, and he had pondered this until he remembered that all children and old people are alike, the one because they are young and the other because they are old, the young knowing nothing and accepting everything, and the old knowing everything and therefore accepting anything as possible.

Yusan, following Clem's directions, had come over with a

shipload of the coolies, as they were called. He had volunteered as an interpreter for them, and had been accepted. Now at last his English, learned so early and of late years revived and maintained because of Clem, was of the utmost use. He had his men already established in barracks near the front, where new trenches must continually be dug. At night they lay down to the sound of the booming cannon, and sometimes the Chinese in the farthest sectors were killed, even as the French, the English, and the Americans were killed. But the Chinese had no inkling of why they were there or why they were killed. They had been lured by the promise of pay for their families at home and a little for themselves, and they were here.

Clem left Paris the same day with Yusan, travelling by train and by military truck. He had his own pass, stamped and signed in Washington before he left, and he was sent through without delay, Yusan at his side. The days on the ship had filled Clem to bursting with plans and ideas and he paused only briefly to ask about Yusan's family.

'All well,' Yusan said. 'Two more grandsons I have given my parents or they would not have let me come, except that you asked it.'

'What about Sun Yat-sen?' Clem asked.

Yusan shook his head. 'One reason I was glad to come with you, Elder Brother, is that everything is altogether confused. Sun Yat-sen has not tied our country together. He was too much in Japan, and Japan wants to eat us alive. Now this has become clear to all in the Twenty-one Demands. It is true that Sun has left Japan, but he does not know what to do next. First we are a republic and then we are not a republic. He has destroyed the old government but he does not know how to make a new one.'

Clem remembered that dark night in the tin hut in San Francisco and now described it to Yusan. 'I told him he ought to get down to the people. I told him if he didn't get the people fed and looked after, he would surely fail.'

'He will always be a hero, Elder Brother,' Yusan said. 'We will not forget that he freed us from the Manchu yoke. But he

293

has not led us onwards from there. He wants obedience and when we hesitate, he says we are like a tray of sand. Elder Brother, you know we Chinese always work together. But we do not believe all wisdom is in one man.'

'Well,' Clem said briskly, dismissing the revolutionist. 'I guess he has to learn in his own way. Now, Yusan, here's my idea——'

He caught a certain quizzical look in Yusan's dark and narrow eyes and he grinned. 'Don't you get me mixed up with Sun! I'll give you my ideas but I don't insist on anything. You do what you like with them. My ideas are a gift. Take them or leave them.'

'Elder Brother, I accept the gift,' Yusan said.

Neither of them looked out of the window at the lovely French landscapes that fled past one after the other. Night fell and they approached the war sector and they did not see that beauty had ended and the barrenness of death was about them. From the train they got into a truck and drove through the night over roads once smooth and now rutted with shell holes. This in turn gave way to rough bare ground and so they came to their destination. Clem walked into a barrack filled with homesick Chinese men, not one of whom could read or write or even speak with the people around him. In the dim light they lay on army cots and listened to one man who played a wailing village tune upon a two-stringed violin he had brought from home.

'Brothers!' Yusan cried above the music. 'Here is the Elder Brother of whom I have told you!'

They got up from their cots, the fiddler stopped his wail, and the lantern lights were turned up. Clem saw himself surrounded by the familiar faces, the brown, good faces, the honest eyes, of Chinese villagers. He felt again the old love, paternal perhaps, but grateful and rich with faith. These were the good, these were the simple, these were the plain of the earth. He began to speak to them:

'Brothers, when I heard you were here, I feared lest you might be suffering, and so I have come to see if your life is good and what can be done to help you if it is not good.'

294

'He left his home,' Yusan put in. 'He came a long way over the sea and he can be trusted. I have known him since my childhood.'

The men were silent, their hungry eyes fixed upon Clem.

'Are you well fed?' Clem asked.

The men looked at one of their number, a young strong fellow with a square fresh face. He spoke for them:

'We are well fed but with foreign food. We are treated kindly enough. Our sorrow is that we cannot write to our families or read what they have written to us. We can neither read nor write.'

'The letters can be read to you,' Clem said. 'Letters can also be written for you.'

The young man looked at his fellows and began again. 'Why we are here we do not know. Is our country also at war?'

'In a way, yes,' Clem replied. 'That is, China has declared war against the Germans.'

'We do not know the Germans,' the young man said. 'Which men are they?'

Clem felt his old sickness of the heart. 'None of us know our enemies. I also do not know a single German. Let us not think of them. Let us only think of ways to make your life better.'

For how could he or anyone explain to these men why there was a war and why they had left their homes and families and come here to dig trenches for white men to hide themselves in while they killed other white men? Who could explain such things to anyone? The world was full of discontent and because people were hungry and afraid they followed one little leader and another, hoping somewhere to find plenty, and peace for themselves and their children, even as these men had been willing to come so far, not because they believed in what they did, but that their families at home might receive each month some money wherewith to buy food.

Clem spent most of that night talking with the men, asking them questions, too, and writing down their answers. He spent the next days with Yusan planning, and a full month he spent getting what he needed to fulfil those plans from officers who considered him mad. But Clem was used now to men who thought him mad and he paid no heed to what they thought of him, spending his energy instead on getting them to do what he needed to have done until in sheer angry impatience they yielded and cursed him and wanted him gone.

By the end of the month he had helped Yusan to set up a school where the men could learn to read and write, if they wished, and he set up an office, with two Chinese from Paris, to read the men's letters from home and write in reply. He set up also a small shop, to be supplied regularly from Paris with Chinese foods and sweets and tea. Once a week he planned a night of amusement, a place where the Chinese could hear their own music, could eat their own sweetmeats and drink tea together, and see Chinese plays and Western pictures. He hired a Chinese cook who was given a licence to vend his own wares and make his living thereby. He established Yusan in all this, and in his first moment of leisure he discovered that he was homesick for Henrietta and could no longer endure his absence from her, although he had scarcely thought of her for the whole month, even as he had not once thought of himself.

He bade Yusan good-bye then, took a ship for home, and reached his house on a Saturday afternoon, so white and spent that Henrietta cried out at the sight of him as he entered the picket gate.

She was at home, as she was now as much as she could be, for she expected Clem at any moment, though he had not said he was coming. Her own longing for him reached across the sea and yearned for him with such intensity that she could divine, or she felt she could, the time when he would be coming.

'Oh, Clem!' she cried at the front door.

'Hon——'

They fell into each other's arms. He felt her sturdy body and she was frightened at the thinness of his shoulder-blades under her embrace.

'You've worked yourself to skin and bones!' she cried with terrified love.

296

'I'll be all right after a few days at home. My stomach went back on me a couple of weeks ago.'

They parted, their hands still clinging, and she led him in, made him sit down, and restrained herself from fussing over him, which he could not endure.

'I'll make you a cup of tea. Can you eat an egg?'

'I could eat a beefsteak, now,' Clem said. He looked around the shabby room fondly. 'I guess I was crazy to go away, hon. Now that I'm back it seems crazy. But I had to go, and I'm not sorry. How's tricks?'

'Don't talk about tricks!' Henrietta retorted. 'You rest yourself, Clem, do you hear me?'

'Why, hon, you aren't mad at me, are you?' His face was amazed. She had never been cross with him before.

To his further amazement now she began to weep! Standing there by the kitchen door, she took up the edge of her apron and wiped her eyes. 'Of course I'm not mad,' she sobbed. 'I'm just scared, that's all! Clem, if anything happened to you—if you should die—I wouldn't know what to do. Being without you just these weeks—I'm all upset——'

'Great guns,' Clem muttered. He got up and went to her and put his arms around her again. 'I'm not going to die, hon. I wouldn't think of such a thing.'

She put her head on his shoulder and he stood quietly supporting her, loving her and not telling her how he really felt. He was not going to die, but he felt tired to the bone. The sight and the memory of those dark honest bewildered faces in France never left him for a moment. Nor were they all. In the fields of France there were such faces, and the same faces were here in the fields of Ohio, upon the streets of villages and in the slums of cities, not all honest and many far from good, and yet with the same confusion and bewilderment. And most dreadful of all, they were upon the fields of battle, and they lay dead in the mud of death. No, he must not die, but he was tired enough to die. Nobody knew what he was trying to say; not even those whom he wanted to save could understand.

But he must not give up, for all that. He must take up again where he left off.

297

This meant, as he discovered in the years that followed the war, an organizing of his markets and facing limitations and legalities which irked and distracted his free-thinking mind. The war fought for freedom brought with victory a loss of freedom for everyone, and there were times when Clem felt this loss descend most heavily upon himself. He was used to visiting another country as men visit a neighbouring county, careless of all save his purpose in going. Now there was no more of this carelessness. Passports and visas made him groan, and even Bump could not assuage his irritation either by speed or by early preparation. Clem felt it an infringement upon his rights that he could not decide suddenly to go to India by the middle of next week or drop in on Siam and see how the rice crop was going.

His first visit to India grew out of a brief meeting, quite accidental, with a young Hindu in London during the war. They had met in the Tube, and had sat side by side for a few minutes. Clem had begun instantly to talk and then, forgetting his own destination, had got off with the young Hindu and had gone with him to his rooms in lodgings near the Tube station. Ram Goshal had at first been astounded by this slender, sand-coloured American and then had succumbed to Clem's frightful charm. Clem discovered that Ram Goshal, although the son of a wealthy Indian, had given up society life to work for Gandhi, whom he had met a few years before when Gandhi, that rising star, had gone to London from South Africa with an Indian deputation. Ram Goshal had come back with Gandhi to London at the beginning of the war and at a meeting of Indians, Gandhi insisted that it would not be honourable in the time of England's trial and trouble to press their own claims for freedom. Self-denial at such an hour, he said, would be dignified and right and gain more in the end because it was right.

Ram Goshal, reared in sensitive tradition, had been won anew by the largeness of Gandhi's mind. He had declared himself his convert, though troubled by his father's wealth, which was in great modern industries in India, of which Gandhi did not approve.

'God forbid,' Gandhi had said, 'that India should ever take to industrialism after the manner of the West. The economic imperialism of a single tiny island kingdom is today keeping the world in chains. If an entire nation of three hundred million people took to similar economic exploitation it would strip the world bare like locusts.'

Clem could not, however, agree entirely with what Gandhi said, as Ram Goshal had quoted it.

'You can't get rid of something just by stopping it,' Clem had told the young Indian. 'Industrialism is here to stay. We've got to learn how to use it. We can't go back to the first century because we don't like this one.'

Ram Goshal had begged Clem to go to India. 'You will understand India,' he declared, his eyes dark, huge, and liquid with admiration. 'You are like us, you are a practical mystic.' Then those profound eyes, haunted with the endless history of his people, glinted with humour as he gazed upon Clem. 'You remember what Lord Rosebery said about Cromwell?'

'I am not an educated man,' Clem said humble before this young scholar of the East.

'He said that Cromwell was a practical mystic, the most formidable and terrible of all combinations. That is you, too —therefore I do beseech you to stop in my country and look with your own eyes upon my starving people.'

Clem could refuse neither such warmth, such eloquence, nor the brown beauty of the young Indian's face and he promised to go as soon as possible after the war.

He decided suddenly one January day that he would take a few months off from the constant persecutions of his rivals, the chain groceries, being moved to this by a letter from Ram Goshal, now in India. Gandhi was then in the full tide of the non-co-operation movement and Ram Goshal was in some trouble. His father disagreed with Gandhi, and, had Ram Goshal not been his only son, would certainly have disinherited him.

Clem read this letter thoughtfully and handed it to Henrietta.

'Hon, I feel I better go over and see for myself whether the

299

British intend to do any better about feeding the people of India. If they don't, I guess Gandhi is right. But I want to be sure about the British.'

'Of course, Clem,' Henrietta said. She suspected that Clem, whether consciously or not she did not know, was thus postponing a decision which Bump and the two young lawyers were pressing upon him. That Clem might defeat the purpose of the organized groceries to put him out of business, they declared, he must organize himself into Consolidated Markets, Inc. Clem, in spite of the three young men, still refused. He wanted most of his markets movable, his clerks ready to go wherever surplus foods were stagnant. Vast buildings and established staffs did not interest him. He did not want a name. His business was simply to gather food together and get it to people in need. When the need was over, the supply would cease.

While Henrietta thus suspected Clem she saw him look at her with sudden love.

'What is it, Clem?'

'Hon, the two words you said. . . .'

'Yes, Clem?'

'You said, "of course." That's what you always say to my notions—— Wonderful wife!'

So rarely did he speak words of love that tears gathered under her eyelids. 'I mean it, dear.'

'I know it.' He bent and kissed the thick coil of hair on top of her head, and so began the journey to India.

In Bombay they went straight to Ram Goshal's house, a gorgeous palace outside the city beyond the Towers of Silence. Ram Goshal's father was fat, quarrelsome, clever, and he gave Clem no chance to talk, and perforce Clem listened.

'I do not oppose freedom, you understand, Mr. Miller. You Americans, I understand, love freedom very much. But the British have not oppressed me. I tell my son it is entirely because of the British that we are so prosperous. Gandhi is not so prosperous with them, but we are not Gandhi. There is no reason why we should fight his battles.'

Ram Goshal, too filial to argue against his father, sat

miserable in silence, taking his opportunity at night to keep Clem wakeful for hours. This combined with Indian food cut the visit short. All the courteous welcome and the eagerness of father and son to win America to their side could not mitigate the indigestibility of Indian food. Clem's delicate stomach rebelled at curry and pepper and fried breads. In England he had rejected great roasts and thick beefsteaks, boiled cabbage and white potatoes, and now in India he rejected coco-nut meats and sweets, peas overcooked and pepper-hot and every variety of food too highly seasoned.

Indian food cast his frame into rebellion and Henrietta took him to an English hotel, where he fasted for three days and then took to tea and soft-boiled eggs, while Ram Goshal stayed by him to see him well again.

Clem smiled his white and childlike smile. 'I'm a fine one to be telling people about food, Ram Goshal. I have to live on pap.'

'You are like Gandhi,' Ram Goshal said. 'You use your body merely as a frail shelter, a house by the wayside, something that barely serves while your spirit lives and does its work.'

Clem was too American for this Indian ardour. 'I hope I am a man of common sense,' he said briefly. 'Certainly I'm sorry about my weak stomach.'

As soon as he was well he wanted to leave Bombay, and saying farewell to Ram Goshal, he wandered about the country for weeks with Henrietta to see how the people fared. It was impossible to travel alone, and they were forced to hire a bearer, a servant to look after them, a dark Moslem named Wadi, who encouraged them to look at Moslems and avoid Hindus until Clem discovered what was happening. Thereafter to a pouting Wadi he decreed the day's journey, poring over books and maps the night before. There was no sightseeing. Clem wanted to go to villages, to see what people had in their cooking-pots and what they grew in their fields. He grew more and more depressed at what he found. After they left the coastal plains there was nothing, it seemed, but endless deserts.

'The land is poor, hon,' Clem said. 'I don't know what these books are talking about when they say the people are poor but the land is rich. I don't see any rich land.'

He turned northwards at last to New Delhi, strengthened by rising anger and determined to cope with the rulers of empire in their lair. The stony hills outside the window of the train, the sparse brush, the dry soil, the pale spots of cultivation increased his wrath, until when he reached the monumental capital of empire, he was, he said, 'fit to be tied.'

Yet in justice he was compelled to admit that empire alone was not to blame for half-starved people and skeleton cattle. Whoever ruled India, still the sun shone down in sultry fury upon the blackened earth. It was winter in Ohio, a season which there meant snow upon level plains and rounded hills, and in New York meant lights shining from icy windows and snow crusted upon sidewalks and trampled into streets, and red-cheeked women at crowded theatre doors. In India it meant the slow mounting of a torrid heat, so dry that the earth lay empty beneath it. Over the sick surface thin animals wandered dreaming of grass, and thin human bodies waited, feeble hands busy at pottery wheels, the dry earth stirred into clay with a bowlful of water to make more empty bowls, plenty of bowls that could be broken after they had been touched by the lips of the unclean.

'A few wells here and there,' Clem said to Henrietta, his skin as dry as any Indian's, 'and this desert might be planted to grain.'

But wells were not dug and who could blame men that they did not dig wells when the sun burning upon a dead leaf turned it crisp, charred at the edges and wrinkled as a dead baby's hand?

In the capital Clem, a pure flame of zeal, marched into the marble halls of empire and demanded to see the Viceroy. An American millionaire may see even the King and so he was received, making his way unmoved between rows of turbaned underlings. A mischievous old face, Indian, shrewd and obsequious, peered from under a multi-coloured pile of taffeta.

302

'I am Sir Girga—honoured, sir, to conduct you to His Excellency the Viceroy.'

The mischievous old face, set upon a waspish body and a pair of tottering legs, guided him into a vast hall where The Presence sat, and there brought him before a cold English face made courteous by splendour.

Clem, knowing no better, sat down on a convenient chair surrounded by space and then began to tell the ruler how subjects could and should be fed.

'Irrigation is the first thing,' he said in his dry nasal American voice. He was unexpectedly hot and he wished he could take off his coat, but he went on. 'The water table in India is high, I notice. Twenty feet and there is plenty of water—sometimes even ten or twelve. By my calculations, which I have taken carefully over sample regions, India could feed itself easily and even export food.'

The Viceroy, immaculate in white tusser silk tailored in London, stared down on him as upon a worm. 'You do not understand our problems,' he said in a smooth deep Oxford accent. 'More food would simply mean more people. They breed, Mr.——' he paused to look at a card which Sir Girga obligingly held out for him to see—'Miller.'

'You mean it is the policy of your government to keep people hungry?' Clem inquired.

'We must take things as we find them,' the Viceroy replied.

In England, Clem reflected, this might have been a nice sort of fellow. His face was not cruel, only empty. Everything had to be emptied out of a man's heart if he sat long in this vacuum. Clem looked around the enormous hall, embellished with gold in many varieties of decoration.

'I see your point,' he said after a long while. And then, after another while he said abruptly. 'I don't agree with it, though.'

'Really!' There was a hint of sarcasm but Clem never noticed sarcasm. He went on.

'We've never tried feeding the world. Ever seen how much meat comes from a sow? She farrows big litters until you don't know what to do with all the pork. Of course in America we throw away mountains of good food, besides eating too much. You English eat too much, too, in my opinion—all that meat!'

The face continued empty and looking at it Clem said, 'I will grant America is the most guilty of all countries, so far as waste goes.'

'Undoubtedly you know,' the Face said.

Clem said good-bye after a half-hour of this. He then walked behind the trotting Sir Girga who saw him through the forest of lackeys to the front gate, beyond which an absurd Indian vehicle called a tonga awaited him, to the derision of the lordly Indian door-men.

He went back to the hotel where in one of the rows of white-washed rooms Henrietta sat in her petticoat and corset cover, fanning herself. 'We'll just mosey along to Java before we go home,' he told her. 'It's about as I thought. They aren't interested in feeding people.'

In Java he was stirred to enthusiasm by the sight of land so rich that while one field was planted with rice seedlings, another was being harvested. Men carried bundles of rice over their shoulders, the heads so heavy that they fell in a thick, even fringe of gold. The Dutch were more than polite to an American millionaire and he was shown everywhere, presumably, and everywhere he saw, or was shown, a contented and well-fed people. It was only accidentally that he found out that there was an independence party. One night when he was walking alone, as no foreigner should do in a well-arranged empire, a note was thrust into his hand and when he got back to the hotel and a lamp he found that it was a scrawl in English which said that he ought to examine the jails. This of course he was not allowed to do.

It was a good experience for Clem. He was thoughtful for some days on the voyage home and Henrietta waited for what he was thinking. As usual it came out in a few words one night when they were pacing the deck.

'We've still got freedom in America, hon,' he said. 'I'm going home and look the whole situation over again and see if Bump and those lawyer fellows are right. If I have to organize

I will, but I want to organize so that I'm not hamstrung by laws and red tape. I'll organize for more freedom, see?'

'I believe that is Bump's idea,' Henrietta said.

Clem would not accept this. 'Yeah, but his idea of a man's independence and my idea are not the same. He's like those lawyer fellows—he wants laws as clubs, see? Clubs to make the other fellow do what you want! But my idea is to use laws to keep my freedom to do what I want. I don't want to interfere with the other fellow, or drive him out of business.'

There was a difference, as Henrietta could see, a vast and fundamental difference. Clem was non-competitive in a competitive world. It was strange enough to think that it had taken India to show Clem the value of law in his own country, but so it had done, and when they reached home Clem plunged into. this new phase of his existence. Beltham and Black summoned to their aid an elder firm of lawyers as consultants, and Bump frankly sided with the four lawyers. Against them all Clem sat embattled day after day across the old pine table that still served him as his desk.

'What you want is impossible, Clem!' Bump cried at last. He was tired out. The lawyers were irritable at their client's obstinacy. Those were the days, too, when Frieda was expecting her third child and she was homesick for Germany, so that Bump had no peace at home, either.

Clem lifted his head, looked at them all. He was dead white and thin to his bones, but his eyes were electric blue.

'Impossible?' His voice was high and taut as a violin string. 'Why, Bump, don't you know me after all these years? You can't say that word to me!'

IX

IN the rich years that followed the First World War William profited exceedingly. His tabloids were the most popular newspapers in the country and he had several foreign editions. The old offices were long since deserted and he owned a monumental building on the East River.

He was still not satisfied. He wanted his country to be the greatest country in the world, not only in words and imagination and national pride, but in hard fact. He saw American ships on all seas, and American newspapers, his papers, in all countries, American names on business streets, and above all American churches and schools everywhere. America was his country, and he would make her great.

This was the motor behind the scheduled energy of his life. He gave huge sums to American foreign missions, always in memory of his father. He established a college in China, known as the Lane Memorial University, although he steadfastly refused to meet face to face the missionaries whose salaries he paid. He had set up an organization to do that, the Lane Foundation. He had never gone back to China, although sometimes he dreamed of Peking at night when he was especially tired, foolish dreams of little hutungs, quiet between enclosing walls, wisps of music winding from a lute, sunshine hot on a dusty sleeping street. Memories he had thought forgotten crept out at night from his mind exhausted by the day. He ignored them.

These were the times in America when anything could be done. Yet he was not doing all he dreamed of doing. The common people, as he called them, meaning those ordinary folk who come and go on the streets on foot, by bus and street-car, those who crawl under the earth in subways and live on farms and in small towns and mediocre cities, all these who bought his newspapers as surely as they bought their daily loaf of bread at the corner grocery, they were not of enough importance to govern, even by their yea or nay, the possible secret country which he now perceived lay behind the façade of present America. He had thought, when he was in college dreaming of vast newspaper tentacles, that if he had the common people under his influence he could guide the country. He never used the word 'control' and indeed he honestly abhorred it. But guidance was a good word, the guidance of God, which after his father's death he himself continually sought as power and money accrued. Common people were weak and apathetic. They listened to anybody. Now that radio networks were beginning to tie the country together, his newspapers could no longer exclude. This troubled him mightily. Print had its rival. He considered making his newspapers almost entirely pictorial, so that reading was unnecessary, and then rejected the idea. Pictures could not keep common people from listening to the radio, which also required no reading. He must secure ear as well as eye and he began to plan the purchase of key networks.

In all this Candace was of no use to him. She had grown indifferent to the frightful responsibilities he undertook as his duty and she had even quarrelled one day with his mother. He had never been able to discover either from her or his mother what had taken place, except that he had been the subject of their difference. Candace had simply laughed when he pressed her for detail.

'Your mother has lived too long in Peking.' It was all she would tell him.

His mother went a little further. 'I hate to say it, William, but Candace doesn't appreciate you as a wife should. Whether she understands the wonderful work you are doing is quite beside the point. I didn't always understand your dear father either, and certainly I could not always sympathize with his ideas or even with all that he did, but I always appreciated *him*.'

Candace had grown strange and reckless in these years after the war, likely on any Sunday morning to announce that she was going to the beach with the boys instead of sending them to Sunday School. That William himself did not go to church had nothing to do with his sons, who, he felt, should be taught some sort of religion. Indeed, he himself, since his father's death, had felt the need to find God anew, but he could not return to the pusillanimities of his former rector. He sought a firmer faith, a stronger church, and there were times when he thought of Catholicism. This, however, had nothing to do with Candace and the two boys. The seashore place was another recklessness of hers, although he had quite willingly bought the mile of private ocean front in Maine. She had declared that she wanted only a shack, to which he had simply said there was a right way to do a thing, and comfort he must have, even though in summer he could only be there a day or two a week. He had hired a young architect who designed an extraordinary house on top of a grey cliff, and a sliding staircase, like an escalator, which let them down to the sea and to a huge *cabana*. Altogether it was effective and he was proud of it.

He had to acknowledge to himself now that Candace had never meant very much to him, and it had been years since he needed anything of Roger Cameron. When Mrs. Cameron died last year old Roger told William that he wanted to sell his shares in the newspapers.

'The dividends are going up,' William said.

'That's why I want to sell,' Roger had replied.

This made no sense but William did not reply because he was vaguely wounded. His pride rose and he sent a memorandum to the business manager that he wanted all shares in the corporation bought up so that he might be sole owner. When the reports came in he saw the name of Seth James. Seth was now backing a new daily paper that William saw at once was doomed to die. Seth should have known better, he had told himself, as with complacency he studied the first issues. 'The paper with a purpose,' Seth had foolishly announced. Of course people would not buy it. People did not want to be taught. They wanted to be amused. William himself was never amused. It was Jeremy's task to find among thousands of photographs for his tabloids, pictures sorted by twelve girls under twenty years of age, those scenes which would make people laugh. Horror was as good as laughter and horror William himself could judge. A murder skilfully portrayed, a strangled woman, a dying child, a family weeping after the father was crushed under a truck, a maniac escaped, an aeroplane that crashed into a small home on Long Island, these were all pleasing to people.

Yet such was William's conscience since his father's death that he allowed no issue of a paper to be sent to the people without its quota of religion. He truly believed in God. His own being, ordered by purpose, convinced him of the existence of God and his tabloids carried photographs of churches and ministers, priests and nuns. William was not narrow. People worshipped God in many ways, though he rejected any form not Christian. He had disagreed with Estey, his new assistant editor, over a photograph of the Panchen Lama—news, yes, but not religion. People the next week saw the benign face of the Lama appearing side by side with the President's wife in her Easter frock.

On a day in early October he sat thinking of these things in his immense office on the top floor of his own building. The office opened into a handsome apartment where he could sleep on the nights when he had to work late. Casper Wilde, the young English modernist, had designed it for him. William had wanted it done by a Swedish architect, but when he examined the designs laid before him he had been forced to see that there was nothing to equal English modern in its conservative and heavy soundness. It was exasperating but true. In spite of the World War there was as yet no crack in the armour of the British Empire. His reporters, stationed permanently in India as in almost every other country, informed him of bitter disappointment among Indians after the war.

'Educated Indian opinion complains that Britain shows no signs of fulfilling war-time promises for independence, made to leading Indian politicos. Rumours are that in the next war Indians will seize the opportunity for rebellion.'

This perhaps was a crack in the imperial armour, but no more. William had no sympathy with independence for India.

His imagination, anchored by the mob in the Peking street, saw in India those faces darkened by the Indian sun and multiplied by swarming millions. If and when the crack became disaster for the British Empire, his own country must be ready to assume control.

America was young. When this crazy period of post-war play was over, Americans would see their destiny and grow up. In his editorials he skilfully reminded them now and again of that destiny. He roused their pride by pictures of the greatest factories in the world, the largest airships, the fastest trains. It troubled him that the American army and navy were not more impressive. When the navy decided upon manœuvres anywhere in the world he sent a flock of photographers with them. Bright sea and flying flags and ranks of men in white duck made wonderful pictures.

The people were still in a playful mood. On this bright autumn afternoon even he was not inclined to be critical. Times were good and people had money to throw away. He himself would play if he could, but he did not find the usual diversions amusing or playful. At Chefoo he had learned to play a brilliant game of tennis, cruel in cuts and slashes, all but dishonest and certainly ruthless, but he seldom played. There was no incentive for he had no competitors. The careless padding about the courts with Candace at Crest House, his home on Long Island Sound, or on week-ends facing Jeremy who refused to be any man's enemy even at sport, could not divert his mind. He liked an enemy and with an enemy in tennis he came nearer to amusement, enjoyment, relaxation, perhaps, than at any other sport, when occasionally he found an opponent equal to him.

He sat rigidly in front of his huge circular desk, his hands clenched in fists upon its blonde surface, thinking. He had everything in his life except human companionship. He was remote from every human creature, even from Candace and his sons, and certainly from his mother and sisters. He had no one near him, neither man nor woman. Jeremy had long ago taken his position as a jeering light-minded brother-in-law who knew he could not be fired because it would make an office scandal. Yet Jeremy had a flair which gave the papers the humour that no one could supply. William because he did not know how, and the staff because they were afraid of him. Jeremy could have been his friend, William sometimes thought with a certain wistfulness, but he did not want to be. Perhaps he could not understand or value the purpose for which William lived. The Camerons were all light-minded. Old Roger nowadays was as gay as an ancient grasshopper and Candace had grown benign and careless of her figure. She laughed at everything Jeremy said when the families were together and even Ruth could not make her mindful of what was dignity. William knew that Ruth was his life-long possession, but he wondered sometimes in the gloom in which he lived whether, were he permanently out of earshot, she too would laugh. He had, in short, no one of his own. His sons did not interest him. He was as lonely as a king.

Nevertheless, like a king, he reflected, he could not put out his hand to anyone without it being misunderstood. The gesture of ordinary friendship was impossible for him. If he put out his hand it must be for a purpose that was not yet clear to him. He doubted very much whether there was a woman in the world who could give him real companionship. Only his loneliness was plain to him, and profound.

In this state of mind he left his office rather early and entered his waiting car. The chauffeur was surprised and pleased to see him. Doubtless the man had a family and thought of getting home early. William did not ask, however. He merely gave his abrupt nod and said, 'Direct to Crest Hill.' He wanted to go home and survey his house and his wife. There was no reason why, having achieved everything else, he should not have personal satisfaction. It seemed a small thing, but without it on this opulent autumn afternoon nothing he had was all it should be.

At Crest Hill Candace had spent a beautiful, idle day. It was what she called a day of grace, of which there were too few in every season. Thus although leaves had fallen and the first frosts had killed the flower borders, although her furs had been brought from storage, yet the day was as warm as June's best and she had done nothing at all. The outdoor swimming-pool had been emptied and cleaned for winter, but she had ordered it filled again and had spent the morning in and out of the pool quite by herself and happy. She missed the boys but they had been going away to school for years and William she had learned not to miss, wherever he was. The huge house was unusually beautiful, the doors and windows open and the bowls on the table were full of late roses. Her rose gardens were sheltered by the greenhouses and escaped the early frosts. She was the most idle of women and enjoyed her idleness. A moment at the telephone could summon to her any of a hundred or so friends, men and women who were eager to share her genius for enjoyment, but she seldom summoned them. She liked best to be with Ruth and Jeremy and their little girls, and she disliked actively, out of all the world, only William's mother. For her own father she had a delicate affection so appreciative that she welcomed his coming to her but she made no demands upon him. She made no demands upon anyone, being content in herself. Marriage with William had not given her high romance, but then she did not want such romance. She would have had to live up to it.

She was not prepared therefore for William's too early arrival. At five o'clock, she told herself, she would leave the sun-soaked court surrounding the swimming-pool and she would go upstairs, dry her hair, and put on a thin soft dress of some sort over her slip. Never willingly did she wear girdle or corset or any of the garments that women used to restrain themselves. What she would have done had she been fat she never stopped to ask herself, since she was not really fat. Old Roger's leanness had so blessed his daughter that even carelessness had made her only gently plump.

At five o'clock William entered the wide hall of his house and inquired of the man who took his hat and stick where Mrs. Lane might be found.

'Madame is in the court, sir,' the man replied.

William walked down the hall which bisected the huge house and stood between the open double doors. Candace

312

was climbing out of the pool. Her blonde skin, sunburned to a soft pale gold, was pretty enough in contrast to the green bathing-suit she wore. Her long fair hair was wet and hanging down her back. She was a pleasant sight for any husband, and William felt vaguely angry that a woman who looked as Candace did should not provide for him the companionship which he needed. What, for example, could they do together now? She played a lazy game of tennis and she could not keep her mind on bridge. She enjoyed horseback riding and rode well, but there was no companionship in that pastime. He preferred to ride alone in the morning before breakfast.

'Why, William,' Candace called. 'Has something happened?'

'Certainly not,' he replied. 'Why should you think so?'

'You're home so early.'

'It was hot in town.'

'Come into the pool.'

'No, thank you.'

William did not enjoy swimming, either in the pool or the sea. He swam well, for he had been taught to do so at the English school. His hatred of the water went back to the day when a firm young English swimming master had thrown him into the Chinese sea, out of his depth, to compel him to swim for his life.

'Then I'll get out,' Candace said, and began to wring the water out of her hair.

'Don't trouble yourself,' William said. 'I'll go upstairs and change.'

'Will you come back?'

'If you wish.'

'Of course I do.'

She dived into the pool again and he went upstairs slowly to his own rooms. His valet had foreseen his need and had put out for him a suit of cool tusser silk that had been packed away and now brought out once more for the unseasonable heat. William showered and shaved himself, for hot weather always made his black beard grow too fast. Then he dressed and went downstairs again, wishing restlessly that he could think of

313

something he could enjoy. Candace was still in the pool, but a servant had brought tall glasses of some drink and set them on a table under an umbrella.

He sighed and stretched himself in a comfortable chair. Candace saw him and swam slowly to the end of the pool and got out. She wrung her hair again, wound it on her head and wrapped a huge English bath-towel about herself. William found no towels in America big enough for him, neither did he like coloured towels. Miss Smith the eleventh had once ordered six dozen enormous English bath-towels from London and had sent them to Ireland to be monogrammed. Only Candace had other towels than these. In her own bathroom shelves she kept towels of peach and jade green. In public, however—that is, before William—she enveloped herself in one of the six dozen.

'I'll just slip on something and be back,' she told him. He looked unusually handsome at this moment and impulsively she bent to kiss him. His dark hair was thinning slightly on top of his head, a spot she did not often see.

'William, you are getting bald!'

It was a wifely remark but the wrong one, she saw, the moment it was spoken. He did not reply; his eyebrows drew down and his mouth tightened.

'Not that it shows,' she said hastily.

'It must show or you would not have seen it,' William retorted.

'Oh well,' she said, laughed, and went on.

Upon him the careless remark fell like an arrow dropped from the sky. He was reminded that he was middle-aged. If he was ever to get anything out of life he must do it now. Decision accumulated in him. He recognized the process. A trickle, a slow stream, a monstrous river of feeling suddenly broke into inevitable sudden decision.

He would divorce Candace if necessary in order to get companionship before he died. He would find somewhere in the world the woman he needed.

Lying in the warm declining sun he felt the deep and habitual tension suddenly relax. He had made a decision which though massive was right and therefore irrevocable. All his large decisions had come suddenly after long periods of indecisive restlessness. When he saw what he must do it was like coming out of a tunnel into the light. He closed his eyes and sipped his iced drink. He was not a simple physical creature such as he believed most American men were. He was not interested in dirty schoolboyish talk, and jokes about sex bored him. Something in his birth and childhood, the deep maturity of the Chinese, perhaps, or the intolerable wisdom of England, had aged even his youth.

When the thought of England came to him, he felt a strange nostalgia. He did not want to go back to China, but to go to England might give him the rest that he needed. Alone in England even for a few weeks, as silent as he wished, with nothing planned and yet ready for anything that might occur to him, he could cure himself, or be cured, of his spiritual restlessness. The peace that passeth understanding, of which his father spoke so often, might yet be his.

But he must be alone. Merely to be alone, he now felt, would bring him some of the peace. He thought of his office and the quiet apartment opening into it, and was eager to be there where he need not speak to Candace or see her. He got up and went into the house and met her coming downstairs, in a floating chiffon dress of apple green.

'I shall have to go back to town,' he said abruptly.

'Oh—I am sorry for that.'

She spoke sincerely but without petulance. After these years she was accustomed to William's sudden decisions. She would wait until he was gone and then she would call up Jeremy. If he and Ruth were at home she would drive over to their house and dine with them. William's mother was there, but on this heavenly evening she could bear that. Jeremy's house stood near the water, its lawn sloping down to the Sound, and the moon would be beautiful upon the waves.

'Shall you be late, William?'

'I don't know. Don't sit up for me, of course.'

'If I am not here, I'll be at Jeremy's. Don't sit up for me, either.'

She put her hands on his shoulders and pressed herself against him. He kissed her cheek but did not respond to the pressure. Ah well, her father had said loving was enough! She made it do.

William could have explained to no one his impulse towards England at this hour of his life. He had been often to England in recent years, but only for short times and for business. Now he wanted an indefinite time which might be short or long. He told himself that this depended upon how he felt. Actually he knew that he was going on a search, a romantic search, absurd if it were spoken and therefore it could not be spoken. His real life had always been secret. Now he felt the need to confide. Vague need, vague longing, the middle-aged desire to live before he died, the thirst to learn how to enjoy before he lost the power, these were his private reasons, not to be shared.

He stayed in London for some days, ostensibly to attend a few business conferences. He toyed with the idea of setting up an entirely English office for the publication of a purely English tabloid and to discuss this he met Lord Northcliffe for a week-end, and acknowledged frankly his debt to the master journalist.

'I saw one of your papers in the reading-room at Harvard, my lord, and began that very day to plan my life around a newspaper like it.'

'Really,' the stubby lord said without surprise. 'We've a bit in common, you and I, haven't we? Success from the middle classes, eh? Your father was something odd, as I remember—so was mine.'

William preferred not to answer this. He remembered that this baronet had once put on his head a hat worn by Napoleon and had said without vanity, 'It fits me, by Jove!' Since then he had spent some of his swift wealth upon such fantasies as arctic exploration, had forced upon his quiet countrymen noisy motor-cars, had given prizes for aeroplane models and attempts at flying, and now clamoured for fellow patriots to prepare themselves against the dangers of a rising Germany.

There was something about this plebeian lord which repelled

William. They parted without being friends, the Englishman feeling with amazement that William was what he had never seen before, an American snob, and William feeling that England was better than this Englishman thought she was and that he was somehow unworthy. If he had met Alfred Harmsworth as a schoolboy he would have fought him and easily licked him. He sat, later that week, for an evening under the scintillations of an ageing Herbert Wells, refusing, however, to join in the absurd games devised for his amusement. He remained saturnine even before the brisk sallies and the ceaseless flow of his host's fixed though fluid opinions.

After three or four weeks of being a quiet guest, unobtrusively American in English country houses, William met a young man to whom he was exceedingly attracted. He could not account for the singular strength of this attraction until he discerned in the young man a faint resemblance to the hero of his youth in the Chefoo school, the son of the British ambassador. This young man's name was Michael Culver-Hulme, a name ancient enough in English history and with many branches. In the stillness of a Sunday afternoon before tea at Blakesbury House, where William had been invited by Lord Saynes, who had heard of his wealth and power, he met Michael.

Culver-Hulme, a distant cousin of Saynes, had asked frankly for the chance to meet the American whom everybody had heard about and almost no-one had seen. Lord Saynes had laughed.

'What do you want to meet the chap for?' he had inquired of Michael.

Michael had replied, 'I've a fancy to see him, that's all. My uncle went to school with him—my mother's brother. He's told me rather grim tales. He's quite proud now of having gone to school with him, though in the old days they all made fun of him. It seems he used to stalk about the school grounds rather like a silent and haughty young Hamlet.'

On this Sunday afternoon, beneath a sky of milky November blue, the Englishman saw William leaning lonely against a stone wall, gazing across the lawns to the valley beyond. He went to him with the bold and entirely natural charm which was both assured and youthful.

'I say, sir, I hope you don't mind if I butt in?'

'Not at all,' William said. He smiled slightly. 'Our World War seems to have left its effect at least upon the English language.'

'Not so much as your wonderful papers, sir. I wonder if you know how much they're admired? I've heard that Northcliffe himself has taken a point or two.'

William felt the soft warmth of young flattery steal about his heart. He was flattered often enough, but this English flattery was sweet, and he did not discard it with his usual cynicism.

'I wonder if you could by any chance have had a relative once at an English school in China? I don't believe in coincidence. But you look alike.'

'Not coincidence, sir. Many of our family have been in China or India. It's a family tradition. It was my uncle, I think. He's often spoken of you and been quite proud about it.'

Ancient wounds began to heal in William's heart, but he maintained his dignity and only slightly smiled. 'I remember him as an autocratic young man, quite beyond noticing a mere American.'

'He knows better than that now, sir.'

Michael waited and when nothing more followed, he began again with imperturbable chatty briskness. 'I wish you'd come and have a week with us, Mr. Lane. My father and mother would be enormously pleased, and I'd be honoured.'

'I'm here on a holiday,' William replied. 'That perhaps will excuse my ready acceptance of a kindly invitation. I should like to come and call upon your father, if I may. If you are there, it is all the better.'

'Then will you consider it an invitation, sir? If so, you'll have a note from my father. What week, sir?'

'Week after next?'

'Splendid! Shall you be in England for Christmas?'

'No, I must be home before then. My sons will be coming home from college.'

'Splendid! Where are you stopping?'

'I am at the Savoy.'

'Good! Then you'll hear from us. Hulme Castle, near Kerrington Downs.'

'Thank you.'

The two words were so spoken that they seemed dismissal but Michael refused to accept them. He divined in the American a diffidence so combined with pride that it had become arrogance, a knowledge of superiority augmented by the fear of an incomprehensible inferiority. This American had all the kingdoms of the earth, a handsome body, a shrewd mind, wealth that had become a fable about which people guessed and gossiped on two sides of the ocean, and from all this a power was emerging which Michael knew was viewed with gravity even in the Foreign Office.

An immense curiosity sprang up in his somewhat light and inquisitive mind, and he imagined himself talking William over with his sister, Emory.

'He's not a proper American at all. With just a little changing, he could make a fair stab at being an Englishman, if he wanted to. And the odd thing is that he would and he wouldn't want to——'

To bring his mind back from such words, he began to describe to William the recent hunting he had shared with his uncle in Scotland. Then a bell rang suddenly from the house and broke across Michael's endeavours to amuse.

'That's tea, I'm afraid,' he said cheerfully, and thankful to be relieved of the conversation, he was liberal enough to wonder if William felt a like relief and thought that he possibly did.

Hulme Castle, William discovered, was one of the relics of the time of William the Conqueror and since it was near Hulme Forest, it had often been the hunting box of kings. In the fifteenth century it fell into disrepair, its last use being to shelter a mistress of the then ruling king. In the early sixteenth century it was given to a newly created earl, who rebuilt the castle but not the keep, rebuilt also the Great Hall, and

319

discovered among old ruins a chest left by King Edward III. In the seventeenth century King James visited the castle while hunting and in the eighteenth century the then existing earl finished the rebuilding of the whole castle, remodelling the kitchens entirely and adding a handsome picture gallery. No building had been done since. The present occupants were the Earl, his wife, his son Michael, and his daughter Emory. On the third Sunday of every month the castle was open to the public except for the rooms occupied by the family.

So much William discovered from a small book he found in the British Museum. He had taken time to find out all he could about Hulme Castle. It was a small estate but an ancient one.

From the main highway through the Downs William, seated in the heavy motor-car he had bought for his stay in England, saw Hulme Castle on a low and pleasant hill. Twin towers of Norman architecture guarded the entrance through which, on a soft grey English day, he approached his destination. The chauffeur pulled a huge knocker and the door was opened by a man in some sort of informal livery.

'Hulme Castle?' the chauffeur inquired, knowing well enough that it was.

'Hulme Castle,' the manservant replied.

William got out, properly dignified, and mounted the shallow stone steps.

The manservant took his things. 'Mr. Lane?'

'Yes.'

'Come in, please, sir. We were expecting you. I will show you your room, sir. This way, please, sir.'

A huge table stood in the middle of the entrance hall and behind it double stairs wound upwards to right and left. Upstairs William went down a long and wide hall into a large room, quite modern in its decoration. A small coal fire burned in a polished grate under a carved mantelpiece, upon which the only ornament was a silver bowl of ash-pink roses.

'Tea is being served in the Panel Room, sir, to the left at the bottom of the stair,' the man said and disappeared.

William went to the wide leaded window. The sill was deep

in the thick stone wall and he looked down over the tops of oaks still green. The hill declined sharply beneath this western wall and on the horizon the sun was setting, pink among the grey clouds. The castle was filled with silence and with peace, and he saw no human being. A feeling of rest and remoteness stole upon him and he sighed.

He stepped into the same stillness a few moments later when, having washed his hands and face, he went downstairs. The door of the Panel Room was open and he heard someone playing the piano. Of music he knew nothing and he had not missed it, but he was intelligent enough to know that the person now playing was a musician. He crossed the hall, entered the door, and saw something that he might have imagined. A long, beautifully shaped room, panelled in oak, spread before him. At the far end was a large fire-place, and above it the coat of arms of Hulme. Before the fire a tea table was set and an old man, the Earl himself doubtless, sat in an easy chair of faded red leather. Across the fire-place sat Lady Hulme, unmistakable, tall, thin, weathered, and wearing an old tweed suit. She was knitting something brown. Michael leaned against the mantel, his hands in his pockets, gazing at the fire, and at the piano sat a woman in a long crimson dress.

She lifted her head and smiled, a gesture of invitation, while she went on playing softly and firmly the closing chords. The Earl saw him and then Michael, and with the same smile and gesture they waited, Michael half-way across the room, the Earl standing. Lady Hulme lifted her large pale blue eyes, dropped them again, and continued knitting.

At the piano the last chord sounded deeply. Michael leaped forward and wrenched William's hand.

'How awfully good of you to come! This is my father—and my mother.'

William touched the Earl's dry old hand and received a nod from Lady Hulme.

'Very good of you,' the Earl murmured. 'It's a long way from London, I'm afraid. We're very quiet.'

'I like quiet,' William said.

He turned, still delaying, still dreading.

321

'This is my sister Emory,' Michael said simply.

William took a long cool hand into his own. 'I'm afraid I interrupted the music.'

'We were only waiting for you,' she replied.

'Emory, pour tea,' Lady Hulme commanded. 'I've dropped a stitch.'

She moved to obey, and for one instant William looked down into eyes dark and clear, set in a pale and beautiful face. He saw her mouth, the lips tender and delicate, quiver and smile half unwillingly, or so he imagined. She was tall and so thin that she might have been ill except for the look of clear health in her eyes and her pale skin.

'Do sit down,' she said in her sweet English voice, and seated herself by the tea table. 'I'm filled with curiosity about you. I've never met an American.'

'I am not typical, I am afraid,' William replied, and tried not to stare at her hands as they moved above the cups. They were exquisite hands, and there was something about them so familiar that he frowned unconsciously to remember. Then memory came back to him. He had seen hands like these long ago, when as a little boy with his mother, he had looked at the hands of the Old Empress in Peking, the same thin smooth hands!

'Come along, Emory,' Lady Hulme said in her husky voice, still knitting briskly. She paused, however, to pull a bell rope with vigour as William sat down, and the manservant came in with a plate of hot scones on a silver tray.

'Hallo, Simpkins,' Michael said. 'How is it you're passing the tea today?'

'Matthews has mumps,' Lady Hulme said. 'It's absurd, really, but he caught them from the new housemaid, I believe.'

'He did, my lady,' Simpkins said very gently.

Lady Hulme turned to William. 'I hear you have pots of money. Here's your tea.'

'Don't heed my mother,' Michael said rather quickly. 'She likes to think she's daring. Why do you say such a thing, Mother?'

'Why not?' Lady Hulme retorted. Her face remained

322

expressionless, whatever she said, the large eyes like pale lamps in her face that was reddened by sun and wind. 'I can't think of anything nicer than having pots of money. One needn't be ashamed of it. I wish your father had it.'

William took his tea and helped himself to thin bread and butter and a hot scone. Some pleasant-looking cake waited upon a small, three-tiered table, but he knew, from school memory, that it would not be passed to him until he had eaten his bread and butter and scone. Sweets came last or not at all.

No one noticed his silence. Lord Hulme was eating with enjoyment, and drinking his tea from a large breakfast cup.

'I hope you weren't sea-sick,' Lady Hulme said.

'Thanks, no,' William replied.

'It's so beastly when one is,' Lady Hulme observed. 'Of course American men are not so heartless as Englishmen. Malcolm always has believed that I am sea-sick purposely.'

'You are, my dear,' the Earl said.

'There, you see,' Lady Hulme said. 'We went to Sicily for our honeymoon thirty-five years ago and I got ill in the little boat that took us across the channel and had nowhere to lay my head. He wouldn't let me put it upon his knee.'

'Oh, come now,' the Earl retorted. 'As I remember, I hadn't the chance to walk about—your head was always on my knee.'

They wrangled amiably, worrying the old subject between them, and Emory sat watching them with amused and lovely eyes, glancing now and again at William. She did not interrupt and at last Lady Hulme was weary.

'More tea all round,' she announced.

The Earl, revived by tea and argument, turned to William, 'I see those papers of yours sometimes. What sort reads them, shopgirls and so on, I suppose!'

Michael sprang into the arena. 'Everybody reads them, Father.'

'Really? Mostly pictures, though, aren't they?'

William took the Englishman into his confidence. 'Our people don't read very much. One has to use pictures to convey one's meaning.'

323

'Ah, then you have a purpose?' Lord Hastings said rather quickly.

'Doesn't everyone have a purpose?' William replied. 'The power potentiality of several million people is a responsibility. One cannot simply ignore it.'

'Ah,' the Earl said. He tipped his cup, emptied it, wiped his moustache with his lace tea napkin, rolled it up, and put it in the cup. Then he got up. 'I suppose you'd like a walk? Michael and I always get one in before dinner.'

The early twilight was not far off and William would have preferred to stay in the great fire-lit room with the beautiful woman who sat in such silent repose, but some compulsive hand from the past reached out and he rose. After tea at school the headmaster ordered a walk for everyone. Not to want fresh air was a sign of laziness, weakness, coddling one's self, all English sins.

'Those boots right for mud?' Michael was looking down at William's well-polished country oxfords.

'Quite all right,' William said.

They tramped out into the shadowy fragrance, Michael respectfully in the rear. The Earl lit a short and ancient pipe, refusing William's aid. 'Thanks, no—I've got long matches —have 'em made to order. They've a chemical in the tip that keep them from blowing out in a wind.'

After this a long silence fell as the three men walked through country lanes. William knew the English silence and he determined that he would not break it. Let these Englishmen know that he could endure the severest test! The Earl turned away from the drive and across a sloping lawn to a meadow. At a gate in a white fence he paused again to fill his pipe.

'I've never been to America. Michael is always wanting to go. But since he's the only son, I've forbidden it—for the present.'

Michael laughed. 'I have to marry and present him with an heir before he'll let me go anywhere.'

'That is the way the Chinese feel, too,' William said. 'But I hope you will visit us some day.'

'Where do you live?' the Earl inquired.

'I have a house in New York and another in the country.' William's voice was as detached and tranquil as any Englishman's.

'You do yourselves very well, you Americans!'

'Not better than you English!'

'Ah, but it's taken us thousands of years.'

'We had a bigger bit of land to begin with.'

The Earl knocked the ash from his pipe and opened the gate. A hen pheasant started out of the grass and he watched her scuttling flight. 'What fools we were to go after India instead of keeping America!' He was filling his pipe again. 'Think of what the Empire would be if we'd really fought you rebels in 1776 instead of hankering after the flesh-pots of that sun-blasted continent! It would have been to your advantage as well as ours. We'd have been invincible today against Germany or Russia if we'd been one country.'

'We, on the other hand, might have been merely a second Canada,' William said. 'Perhaps we needed independence to develop.'

'Nonsense,' the Earl retorted. 'It's stock that counts. The people of India have no stamina—always burning with some sort of fever of the spirit. It's the unhealthy climate.'

'I can't imagine ourselves part of an empire,' William said.

'Not now, of course,' the Earl conceded. He stole a sharp shrewd darting glance at William. 'Certainly not when you're dreaming of your own empire.'

'I doubt we want an empire,' William replied.

Nevertheless the idea played about his mind as they walked across the meadow. Empires had their day, and the ancient British Empire was dying as surely as the sun was setting across the wooded hill opposite the brook. He saw the sunset bright in the still-flowing waters.

'Do you fish in the brook?' he asked Michael.

'Nothing much there,' Michael replied. 'A trout now and then.'

'The boys in the village catch everything. They've got very lax about poaching,' the Earl said rather angrily.

They reached the brook after another silence and stood

325

gazing into its shallow clarity. There were minnows in plenty darting about under the surface, snatching at the last chance for food. The Earl stirred them with his walking-stick. 'There're always minnows, somehow.'

He said it in a musing voice but William saw no significance in the words and did not answer.

'Millions of minnows,' Michael said.

The Earl was looking across the brook as though he pondered the other side and then changed his mind. 'We'd better go back, I dare say. The evening is turning chill.'

They climbed the hill again, this time in silence that none broke. When they entered the great square hall of the castle, Simpkins met them and took their hats and sticks. The Earl yawned.

'We'll meet again at dinner—in an hour.' He walked away with his heavy step, and William stood uncertainly.

Michael, so fresh and friendly, now seemed uncertain too. 'I hope you won't mind my parents, sir. I always forget how they are until I'm home again. Will you come in by the fire or go upstairs?'

'I shall enjoy you all,' William said with unusual grace. He looked into the great room behind the hall and saw it empty. Lady Emory had gone. 'And I think I shall go upstairs until dinner.'

After that day William made no pretence to himself. For the first time in his life he had fallen desperately in love.

His eyes, covert but acute, had searched every woman whom he had met and others whom he had not met. Their eyes in turn had gazed upon him with courtesy and with indifference. The young had looked upon him as old and forbidding, and from those who were not young he had averted his own eyes. English women did not age with grace or beauty. He found them garrulous or caustic, and from sharpness he shrank by instinct. He wanted intelligence but not sarcastic wit which he was not skilled enough to master, and therefore despised. If he disapproved he said so plainly and finally. Sarcasm, he said often, was the exhibitionism of a showy but weak ego, the displeasure of a coward, and the natural refuge of those who had only their tongues for weapons.

All that he had ever dreamed of England and what England had meant to him, all that he had never acknowledged even to himself, now centred in a woman whom he did not ask himself if he understood, for he knew she understood him. He was able to talk at last and to tell her all that he had never told anyone. She listened, her eyes thoughtful and kind. Kindness was her genius. It shone not only upon him but upon everyone who was near her. Her father and brother basked in it, accepted it, took it for granted, imposed upon her, William decided, during the week of days that followed one after the other. Guests came and went and drew from her kindness what they needed. She was busy continually and yet she had time for him, lending him her whole attention in the hours they were together.

He supposed she was not young—that is, she was certainly not a young girl. She was perhaps thirty. He could not understand how it was that he had found her unmarried and one day told her so in words that he feared were crude. She hesitated, then said with scarcely a change in her look or in that sweet, deep voice:

'I suffered the same fate that so many Englishwomen did. My fiancé was killed during the war. He was Cecil Randford, son of the Earl of Randford. We had grown up together.'

William heard the name with pangs of jealousy which he tried to hide. 'Forgive me,' he muttered.

'I do,' she replied simply.

By the third day he wished that he dared to ask her to call him by his Christian name. Lady Emory had a sort of intimacy which Mr. Lane did not have. If he had been Sir William! But he was not. He fretted himself about his courtship. There was so little time. He wanted to get it over, to have her love him quickly, to take her home with him soon and begin their life together. When he went back at Christmas he wanted to get through the hateful business of telling Candace and his sons, and of consulting with his lawyers and his public-relations men as to how divorce and remarriage might be accomplished swiftly and privately. He ground his teeth when he thought of the pleasure that common people took in these matters, which should be as private as a man's own thoughts.

Meantime it was impossible to talk to the Earl or to Lady Hulme, he discovered. He did not exist for them, and yet they were aware that in his way he was important because he was rich. Nor was he at ease with them even though his week was swiftly passing. This castle, this English family, he approached with a diffidence that he would not recognize, although he had long since reached a height in his own country that made a secretary's telephone call enough to open even the door of the White House—not the big front door into which sightseers and patriotic Americans swarmed but the side door where a huge brass key is kept turned. He reminded himself that the Earl of Hulme was not the King of England, that there were many peers of whom he was only one.

The first sight of the castle by daylight had been comforting. It would take a great deal of money to modernize it. For fifty bedrooms there were only five baths, inconvenient, and of plumbing so ancient that tanks of water hung above the toilet seats, and water for the enormous tub was warmed by gas heaters that threatened to asphyxiate bathers unless carefully tended. William was surprised to have a manservant remain in the room, his back carefully turned, when he took his bath the first night, because the heater had looked for the last few months as though it might explode if overworked, and Americans, as everyone knew, insisted on having their tubs full.

'It was much easier, sir, in the old days when we fetched in tin baths,' the man had said, not looking round.

'Why don't you get some American plumbers?' William asked, submerged in soap-suds. The water was beautifully soft.

'They could never understand the system, sir,' the man said. 'Let me know when you've quite done, sir. I'll turn it off and get quite out of your way.'

He did so a few minutes later, and William, wrapped in a bath sheet, had returned to his own room down a hall an eighth of a mile long.

Here in his vast room he felt the silence centuries deep about him. It made him think of Peking and temples and palaces and the Old Empress again. It was the atmosphere he loved, and he would have given his soul to have been born to it, for it was something which could not be imitated or made. To belong in it, to know the certainty of place, would have given him peace. Yet he was ashamed to acknowledge his own longing. Before these English he must be his best, an American, rich, powerful, able to hold his own, a republican among aristocrats. He looked at himself in the long gilt-framed mirror and chose a sombre tie.

Lady Emory had neither wish for love nor expectation of it. Her self-control was absolute and by now had penetrated every fibre of her being. She had been reared in self-control and believed that decency depended upon it. Only with Cecil, whom she had trusted entirely, had she felt she did not need to think of herself, and so she had loved him with warmth and reality, if not with heartiness. Nevertheless she was glad now that she had not married him, since he would have been killed, anyway, and not having married him, she had learned to be glad that she had not slept with him that last night before he joined his regiment. They had discussed the last night frankly, as they discussed everything, their vocabulary being the same and their thoughts and ideas identical. It was not a question of sin or decency or of personal morality, since they were irrevocably in love. It was the far more important matter of an heir. Unlikely as it was that there could be any issue after a first and single union it was still possible that she might have a child, the heir of Randford.

'I shouldn't like him born anyhow, you know, darling,' Cecil had said.

'We should have married,' she had murmured.

'I hate these hurried, patched-up weddings,' he had persisted. 'I want to marry you in state, my darling. The Earls of Randford have always married their wives in the little abbey, and the tenants would hardly forgive me, you know, if I scamped it.'

'What if——' she had not been able to finish.

'No ifs,' he had said gaily. He was **a god,** young and blond, defying death.

So they had denied themselves for the sake of the child, who was never to be born, though they could not know it, and she had not allowed herself to regret her acquiescence. Cecil had felt his duty to his race, and though he loved her and she had never doubted his love, he drew her into his duty. This she had understood, for she had been reared within it, too. A noblewoman, however loved and cherished for her own sake, was none the less dedicated to the sacred future. She would not have been happy, either, had she forgotten that. Their love was purified by their faith in themselves and their kind, their belief that they were more than simple human beings.

Now that Cecil was dead she was released from that duty. There was nothing sacred in her being anything except herself. She knew no other heir of England whom she wanted to marry, or who wanted to marry her, and had there been such a one, it was doubtful whether the high sense of obligation would have been enough. With Cecil she could consecrate herself, but without him, and therefore without love, even duty was not enough for her. There was no reason why she should consider it necessary merely to produce an heir for an ancient house. She was quite free.

Such freedom led to the immense restlessness which her self-control concealed beneath a cloak of consideration and kindness, these being also essentials of habitual good breeding. Only Michael divined that beneath the cloak so gracefully worn she was trembling with discontent.

'You need to get away,' he had told her. 'You are jumpy.'

'I am not jumpy,' she had replied with unusual brusqueness.

'Don't pretend,' Michael had said. 'You ought to marry. Cecil has been dead for years.'

'I don't see anyone to marry,' she had retorted.

'I'll look about,' he had promised in a lordly way.

To which she had merely said, as she used to say to him when he was a little boy, 'Don't be silly.'

Nevertheless he had come back from London some months later with the preposterous declaration that he had found a chap, an American, who might be amusing for her to marry. Such conversation of course was not carried on before their parents. Even so, she had been irritated by it. 'I can't imagine any marriage amusing,' she had told him. They were outdoors in the yew garden, and she was on her knees by the Italian fountain, cleaning away fallen leaves. Michael stood watching her, not offering to help. He did not like to dirty his hands.

'This chap isn't amusing, exactly,' he said. 'He's rather terrifying actually—immensely tall and thin, greenish-grey eyes under black brows, and that sort of thing. He looks immensely unhappy, I must say, the way Americans do if they are not the giggling kind. He's searching, if I'm not mistaken.'

'Searching?' She had looked up.

'He's rich as mud,' Michael said. 'It can't be that. I can't make him out, except that there's power in him.'

'What power?'

'I don't know—energy, smothered under something, impatience held down, enemy of everybody! He's not friendly, doesn't put out his hand when he sees you. I've invited him down—you'll see.'

She had been attracted to William Lane the moment she had looked up from the piano and had seen him standing there. She had gone on playing so that she could look at him without speaking. He was not youthful, and above all things now youth wearied her. For the first time in these ten years she had found herself conscious of being a woman, not young but still beautiful and wanting so to be thought.

She had seen very soon that William thought her beautiful not merely for herself, but for what she was over and beyond. He valued her for what she had inherited, but which was nevertheless a part of her, and it pleased her to have it so. He could not, she believed, have fallen in love merely with beauty. A chorus girl whom a king might love would have repelled him.

Pondering upon this, asking herself why it was that kings and peers throughout the history of England could so joyously lie upon hay and straw with milkmaids and gipsies who could not be queens, she penetrated the secret of William's soul. He wanted a queen that he might be king. His kingdom he had made, a modern kingdom, money and power in absolute combination now as always, and over it he reigned ably enough. But the secret longing was in his soul unrevealed, and perhaps unknown even to himself. If she accepted him, he would be assured. He would have evidence of what had been unseen, he would become in substance that which he had hoped he was.

At thirty, she reflected, as the days of that week passed, a woman accepts quickly or she rejects. He was in the decade beyond her and was, moreover, a man accustomed to quick decisions. He let her know within a few days that his was made. When he left Hulme Castle at the end of the week he managed to say good-bye alone with her, and she helped him to arrange it so.

'May I come back in a fortnight?' he asked.

'We shall be happy to see you,' she had replied, purposely conventional.

'It will be a long fortnight for me, Lady Emory.'

She had only smiled at this, and she looked down and saw his hand clasping hers. A strange small hand he had, curiously hairy!

'Come,' she said to herself in silence, 'let's not think of such things as that!'

To discipline herself, she let him hold her hand a second longer.

When William came back after a fortnight he found Lady Emory so composed, as she led him on the second evening to a part of the castle still unknown to him, that he wondered if she had divined his thoughts. He was surprised to feel his heart begin to beat more quickly than he had ever felt it before.

'You haven't seen the gallery, I think.' She opened a panelled door, and he saw a space, seemingly endless, hung with paintings. 'Let's walk right away down to the end. The view is the loveliest picture of all.'

He followed her a long way to the great windows from ceiling to floor at the end of the gallery, and when she sat down on a yellow satin sofa he took his seat there, too, but not near her.

She looked at him, her dark eyes quietly waiting, and he saw with some shock that she was used to men falling suddenly in love with her, that she was prepared, and then he dreaded so soon to put her to the test of proposal.

'Did you know I grew up as a boy in China?' he asked her abruptly.

'Yes. But what makes you think of it now?' Lady Emory asked.

'Something about this castle, the silence here, and the moon shining as it used to on a palace in Peking.'

'The moon was late tonight.'

'Do you take an interest in the comings and the goings of the moon?' He accompanied this unusual triviality with an effort at a smile.

'No, except that from a window in my room it rather forces itself upon me.'

He did not reply to this, and after a while she said, 'Tell me something about your childhood in China. I've never been anywhere except in Europe.'

'I don't want to think of my childhood,' he said with the strange sort of abruptness which she was beginning to realize did not mean irritation.

'Was it unhappy?' she persisted.

'No, just useless to me.'

'Useless?'

'Yes. I was the son of a missionary. You don't think there could be any advantage to me to have missionary parents, do you? I kept it a secret all the time I was at college. It was a fearful disadvantage to me even in the English prep school I went to in China.' He wanted her to know the worst about him, and he pressed the point. 'To be the son of a missionary made my class-mates think I must be queer. As a matter of fact, my father was rather remarkable. I didn't discover it, though, until he came home to die in my house.'

'Tell me about him.' Her voice led him on.

'Some time, Lady Emory. I don't want to talk about him now.'

'Wait,' Lady Emory said. Her brown eyes widened a little

333

and her soft voice took a slight imperious edge. 'I wonder if I know what you want to talk about to me. If I do, I beg you to remember that we scarcely know each other.'

'You may not know me but I know you,' William replied. Passion seized him with a violence monstrous even to himself. He did not want to wait one moment to take this beautiful Englishwoman into his arms. He wanted her now; he wanted it settled.

Lady Emory looked frightened. 'How can you know me?'

'I've always known England,' William said. 'I've always loved England, against my will, I confess, but there it is. Now I've found you and you are the personification of all that I have loved.'

'Michael said you were married——'

'That has nothing to do with you or me.'

'No.' Her word was a breath, a sigh, and he let it be acceptance. He took one step and she rose at his approach, and he drew her into his arms. Sweet and fearful was this exultation, his soaring pride in what he had, this arrogance of love! He was speechless, his face in the darkness of her hair, and he did not notice her silence or the still motionlessness with which she stood.

She was shocked to discover that the conviction in which she had sheathed herself since last she stood in Cecil's arms was entirely false. She did not feel repelled at all by another man's body pressed against her own. She had supposed it would be intolerable, eternally abhorrent, and it was not. It was even pleasant and comforting, as it would be pleasant and comforting to live in riches and plenty, no more a burden to her parents because she did not marry, no more a charity for Michael when his inheritance came to him. England was old and tired, and somehow with her dead lover it had died for her. America was young and strong, a rising empire, and to go there now, to leave England and take her own unspent womanhood with her, would be the nearest happiness that she could know. And this American, she perceived, contrary to what she had always heard about Americans, was neither stupid nor boyish.

334

'You can't love me—as quickly as I have loved you—I don't expect it——' William was stammering these broken sentences.

She was an honest woman, though beautiful, and what she now knew she would do, she wanted done with all her heart.

She stepped back, but only a little, and she let him hold her hands. 'I suppose it is too soon,' she said frankly. 'But I don't think it is at all impossible—William!'

July in Ohio could be as hot as in India. Henrietta felt the heat. She had spent the last month with Clem in Mexico, where he had gone to confer with the Food Minister who wanted American wheat. Washington had been apathetic, and he had called on Clem, who, after listening carefully, had insisted on seeing Mexico for himself, so that he would know just how much the people needed wheat. He had not noticed the hot weather. His blood ran cool and he was thinner than ever. Mexican food was poison to him, the tamales hot as Indian food and even the vegetables full of red peppers, the spinach boiled to the colour and taste of dead grass. He doggedly ate the native foods here as elsewhere, however, because he wanted to know what the people lived on, and afterwards was tortured with the dyspepsia that got worse as he grew older. He had promised to get the wheat somehow, and they had come home.

Their house now as they opened the front door was hot and dusty and the air was stale.

'You get your dress off, hon,' Clem said to Henrietta. 'Go upstairs and put on a wrapper and relax. I'll open the windows.'

Henrietta obeyed without answer. She had begun to gain weight and it was a relief to get out of her corset. She went upstairs into the large bathroom which Clem had fitted up himself and modelled after the ones in India. She stood in the big zinc-lined tray and filled a jar with water from the tap; then with a dipper she poured it over herself Indian fashion. The house was full of things that Clem had admired in other countries. He liked chopsticks, for instance, better than knives

335

and forks. They were cleaner, he said. The water was luke-warm, but even so, cooler than she was. She towelled herself and then put on the *négligé* that Clem always called a wrapper. She did not mind. It was comfortable to live with a man who did not know what she wore.

She went downstairs to unpack the groceries they had bought for supper. Clem had taken off his coat and sat in his white shirt-sleeves at the dining-table, figuring on a sheet of paper. His shoulder-blades were sharp and the back of his neck was hollowed. He had lost weight in the Mexico heat. She did not speak aloud her worry. Nothing annoyed him more than to hear her worry about his being thin.

She sat down in a large wicker chair, tore open the envelope which was postmarked New York City, and began to read to herself. The first paragraph revealed catastrophe. Her mother wrote:

'I am glad your poor father has passed on. He could never have endured what is about to happen to our family. I have wept and prayed to no avail. William is adamant. He is beyond my reach. I remember when he was a small infant upon my bosom. I know he is my son, but I cannot recognize him. What have we done to deserve this?'

Thus far Henrietta went without comment to Clem. Then she saw the next sentence and a smothered cry escaped her.

'What is it?' Clem asked.

He turned from his figures. It was not like Henrietta to cry out about anything. Now her large grey eyes were wide, staring at the sheet she held. They were the colour of William's eyes but not like them in their depths.

'William is going to divorce Candace!' She breathed the words with the utmost horror, and he received them with horror as they looked at each other.

'What's Candace done?' he asked sternly.

Henrietta returned to the letter. 'She can't have done anything,' she murmured. Her eyes swept down the page. 'Mama doesn't say—yes, she does. She says Candace is just

336

what she always was—there's no excuse for William—he doesn't even make an excuse—you know how he is. He always does what he is going to do and never says why. Mama says it's just an infatuation. It's an Englishwoman he met. on his trip.'

Henrietta would have cried had she tears, but she had none. Against William her heart hardened, and she crushed the letter in her hand and threw it into the woven wicker waste-paper basket. She had never loved Candace, but now she almost loved her. Long ago she had left her father's profound faith, but she had a sort of religion, fed by Clem's unselfishness and devotion to his single cause. The Camerons were good people, in their way as good as her father had been, and all the old decencies remained. A man did not divorce his wife without cause, and the best of men did not divorce their wives for any cause. William had left the ranks of the good.

'I don't ever want to see William again,' she declared with passion. Clem rose from his chair and came over and knelt beside her. She put her head down and upon his narrow, bony shoulders. His thin arms went round her.

'There, there,' he muttered.

'Oh, Clem,' she sighed, half heart-broken. 'I am glad you are good. It's your goodness that I trust.'

He pondered this, patting her back in a rhythm. 'Maybe we need some sort of religion, hon,' he said at last. 'We grew up with God, you know. We. haven't deserted Him exactly; we just haven't known how to fit Him in.'

'You don't need anything; you're just naturally good.'

'I might be on the wrong track, always thinking about food. Man does not live by bread alone.'

She pressed his head against her cheek. 'Don't be different, Clem!' Then after a minute, 'Poor Candace! I must write her a letter.'

She got up and sat down where Clem had sat, and saw upon the pages of yellow paper he used for his endless figuring the words: 'Average yield per acre (Mexico)' followed by lines of calculations of Mexico's millions of people. She tore off a yellow sheet, too tired to look for better writing paper.

337

'Dear Candace,

'We are just home from Mexico. I found Mother's letter here. I cannot say a word of comfort to you. I am ashamed that William is my brother. None of us have ever understood him. Mother is glad my father is dead and I think I am too, unless Father could have kept William from being so wicked.

'There is nothing I can do, I guess. It's too late. I don't pray as I used to but if I did, I would go down on my knees. Perhaps I should even yet. I feel closer to you than I ever have. And there are the two boys—how they must despise their father! It is all wicked and you have never deserved anything like this. I cannot imagine what reason he gives. You are so pretty and so good tempered. I hope William suffers for this.'

Candace read the letter in her old room at her father's house. She smiled rather sadly, thinking that she had never known Henrietta until now, when the bond between them was broken. She glanced at the small silver clock on the dressing-table. She was no longer William's wife. The decree was to be granted at noon, and it was now six minutes beyond. She had been acutely aware of the time as it had passed and then had forgotten it for a few minutes and in that little space of time it was over. She let the letter drop on the floor and leaned her head back against the back of the chair and closed her eyes.

She had protested nothing. That was her pride. Jeremy had flung himself out of William's offices for ever, he said, but when she saw Ruth she had made him go back. Ruth had no defence for William—she was too gentle and good for that. But she did not blame him, for to her alone William had explained himself, and she had tried to explain him also to Jeremy and to Candace. 'He's always been different from everybody,' Ruth said in her earnest, sweet little voice. 'He's been so lonely all his life. I sometimes think if Father hadn't died. . . . Father understood William, but he had to wait for him to grow up. I remember Father saying that once.'

'It's his own fault if he is lonely,' Jeremy had retorted. 'He holds himself above everybody. Yes, he does, Ruth. He lords it over us all.'

'I know it seems that way, Jeremy, but really inside he's quite lost.'

Jeremy had snorted and Ruth nodded her head up and down very positively. 'Yes, William is lost. He needs something he hasn't got. None of us can give it to him.'

Upon this Candace had spoken. 'If Emory can give it to him, then I shall be glad.'

'Oh, Candy, you're so generous,' Ruth had cried, the tears streaming from her soft blue eyes.

But still she had defended William in her heart, and Candace saw it, and because Jeremy loved his wife he, too, would allow William his way. She had no knight, unless her old father came forward. But he evaded life nowadays, indeed not from lack of love, so much as from too much love. So sensitive had he grown as age came upon him, so excessively tender, so wishful that human beings should all be happy, that when they were not he could not bear to be near them. So because she loved him, Candace had shielded her heart from her father and affected to be gay about William's new love, and she insisted that of course he must marry Emory, and she even pretended that she and Emory could and would meet and be friends, while in her heart she knew that this could never be.

With her sons, she was cavalier. Will and Jerry, though tall young men, still cared more for football than for anything else on earth. 'We mustn't blame your father,' she had said to them brightly. 'The truth is, our marriage never quite came off, if you know what I mean. Why should you know? It's like a flower that doesn't quite bloom. Still, I've had you two and that is a great deal to get out of one marriage.' She had looked from one solemn young face to the other.

'Are you going to marry again?' It was Will's question. She met his young grey eyes and shook her head, still playfully. This was her protection now and for ever, not to care too much, not to mind. She thought of fallen leaves floating upon

339

the surface of the swimming-pool, of leaves drifting down from the trees, of a bird resting upon the waves of atmosphere, of flower petals dropping upon the grass. Her father was right. Escape life, perhaps, but certainly escape pain! The blow had been dealt.

Jerry, the younger, had spoken with sudden rage. 'Why don't you go and see that woman and tell her she has no right to——'

'Shut up,' Will said for her. 'You don't understand. You're only a kid.'

Neither son had spoken one word of their father. He was immovable, unchangeable; none could reach him. Whatever he did was done. He was absolute.


William had needed none of them, not his mother, not Ruth. No one existed for him except himself, his monolithic being, his single burning purpose, more consuming than any he had ever known. He was ruthless in his office, angry with all delay, intolerably demanding upon his lawyers.

He had tried to compel Candace to go to Reno so that in six weeks he might be free. She had refused, and old Roger Cameron had demanded an appointment. William had refused that. He gave orders that he would not speak with anyone on the telephone. He lived entirely in his apartment at the office and made no communication with his sons. After he was married to Emory he would let them see for themselves why he married her.

When he discovered that Candace was not going to Reno, he went himself. He endured weeks of loneliness without Emory, days when he called her by telephone that he might hear her voice and assure himself that she still lived, that she had not changed her mind, that she had no thought of delaying their marriage. His decree granted, he left by the next train and, speeding to England upon the fastest ship, he went straight to Hulme Castle.

She was there waiting for him, the wedding day set two days hence, and when he had her in his arms, he let down his heart. He put his face into the soft dark hair.

'Oh, my love——' They were words he had never used to Candace.

'You look fearfully tired, William.'

'I shan't be tired any more, Emory.'

She did not reply to this, and he stood for a moment letting his weariness drain away in the silence.

'Two days from now we'll be married.'

'Two days,' she echoed.

'I wish it were now.'

To this, too, she made no reply.

They were married in the room where they had first met. She did not want to be married in Hulme Abbey, where, had Cecil lived, the ceremony would have taken place. Her parents had agreed, and so an altar had been set up in the drawing-room. No one was there beyond her family and the vicar and his wife and a few people whom William had never seen before. 'A quick, quiet wedding,' he told her, and she obeyed.

UPON a gay and prosperous people the thunder clouds of the Great Depression now crashed down their destruction. In the late summer, Clem had felt something was wrong. He could not define, even to Henrietta, his uneasiness, beginning at first as a personal discontent in his own mind, though he tried to do so one Sunday, the last in August. She was aware of his eternal searching for causes and, by her listening silences and her careful questions, helped him to see more clearly the vague shapes he perceived in the future.

Long ago Henrietta had come to understand that in Clem there was something of the seer, if not of the prophet. His instinct for humanity was so delicate, his perception of mankind so ready, that without magic and entirely reasonably he was able to forecast the possible in terms amazingly definite. Had he lived in ancient times, she sometimes mused, had he been born in those early ages when people explained the inexplicable, the mystic man, by saying he had been fathered by a god or had seen gods upon the mountains or in the flames of a burning bush, struck perhaps by lightning, they would have cried out that Clem was a prophet sent to them by God and they would have listened to him. And, were they frightened enough, they might have heeded him in time to avert disaster.

Now Clem and Henrietta, seated in rocking-chairs upon their own narrow front porch, looked to the passer-by no different from any other middle-aged couple upon the street of an ordinary Ohio town. He talked and she listened and questioned. He was in his shirt-sleeves and an old pair of grey trousers, and she saw that the collar of his blue shirt was torn. She resolved to throw it away secretly when he took it off that night. Clem was miserly about his clothes and declared them good enough to wear long after they had reached the point of dusters and mops.

'I can't just tell you in so many words how I feel about things,' Clem said. 'It's like sitting out on the grass on a nice bright day and then suddenly knowing that the earth is shaking under you—not much, but just a little. Or it's like being in the woods, maybe, and wondering if you don't smell smoke somewhere.'

'If you were in the woods and smelled smoke,' Henrietta said, 'you'd find out first which way the wind was blowing and look in that direction, wouldn't you?'

Clem flashed her an appreciative look. 'I've thought of that. I can't tell which way the wind is blowing—not yet. Crops were good enough this year, at least taking the country as a whole. Maybe things are all right. Maybe it's nothing but my own queasy stomach. I oughtn't to have eaten those corn dodgers last night.'

'I'll never have them again,' Henrietta said.

Clem went on after a few seconds of rocking. 'The trouble is that the way things are now in the world, we're all tied together in one way or another. There might be an earthquake somewhere else which would upset us, too.'

She did not reply to this. The evening was pleasant though hot, and children in bathing-suits were playing with hoses, spraying each other and shrieking with laughter. Clem, deeply troubled by thoughts which were now roaming the world, saw nothing.

'The news from abroad is not bad, though, Clem,' she reminded him. 'Yusan says the new government in China is bringing order and getting rid of the warlords, at least, and pushing Japan off. And Goshal says that Gandhi has made a sort of interlude in India.'

Clem got up. He walked across the porch, took out his pen-knife, and began to cut a few dead twigs from a huge wisteria vine that Henrietta had planted the first spring she came to New Point. Now, a thick and serpentine trunk, it crawled to the roof and clung about the chimney for support.

'Goshal is a Brahmin no matter what I try to tell him,' Clem said. 'What you call interlude, hon, is only a truce. Gandhi has got the British to compromise for a while for just

343

one reason, and Goshal can't see it. The price of food has gone down so much that millions of peasants are going to starve, hon, if something isn't done quick.'

'City people will have more to eat if food is cheap,' Henrietta said.

'Most people don't live in cities,' Clem said. 'That's not the point though, and I am surprised at you, hon. If the peasants and farmers starve it doesn't help the factory workers in the long run. Gandhi is right when he says everything has to be done for the interests of the peasants. They're basic everywhere in the world.'

Henrietta felt clarification begin in the waters of Clem's soul. He was clipping one twig after another and they fell upon the wooden floor of the porch with soft dry snips of sound.

Clem went on, almost to himself. 'And I don't know what to think about things in China. A new government? Well, any government, I guess, is a good thing after all these years of fighting and goings on. I don't blame Yusan for being glad about that. But I wrote him yesterday and told him that if this Chiang Kai-shek didn't get down to earth with all his plans and study what the people need, it will be the same story. You don't have to be an Old Empress to make the same mistakes.'

Henrietta was rocking back and forth silently, her following thoughts circling the globe.

'I don't know,' Clem muttered. 'How can I know? I don't believe Japan is going to let things lay the way they are. They've been afraid for centuries, those people! They've got themselves all stewed up—can't blame them, though—the way different nations have gone over and sliced off big hunks for themselves. "We're next", that's what the Japanese have been thinking for a mighty long time, hon! "If we don't get going and carve ourselves out something big, we're next." That's what they think. Maybe they're right, who knows? Only thing I know, hon, is that the earth is shaking right here under my feet. I don't like the looks of things.'

He lifted his head and looked away over the house-tops and beyond the trees. 'Talk about smoke—the wind is from Europe, I reckon.'

344

The cyclone struck in October. Bred in the storms of the world, it had gathered its furious circular force in the angry hunger of the peoples of Europe, and then reaching its sharp funnel across the Atlantic Ocean it struck in Wall Street, in the heart of New York, in the most concentrated part of America.

Clem, on that first fatal morning, reached out of the front door to get the morning paper, half his face lathered with shaving soap. He saw the head-lines as black as a funeral announcement and many times as large upon the front page, and knew that what he had feared had come. He wiped his cheek on the sleeve of his pyjamas and sat down in the kitchen to read. Henrietta was making coffee. When she saw his face she set a cup before him and went out into the hall, got his overcoat, and wrapped it about him. Over his shoulders she saw the frightful announcement, CRASH IN WALL STREET SHAKES THE NATION!

'Tell Bump to get down here as fast as he can,' Clem ordered. 'You and me and him have got to get right to work, hon.'

She obeyed him instantly as she would have obeyed the captain of an overloaded and sinking ship. There was no time to waste.

Clem dressed and ate a hasty breakfast, and being immediately beset by the demons of indigestion, he was swallowing pepsin tablets when Bump came into the house. Henrietta had cleared the dining-room table of dishes and cloth, and Clem spread out the big sheets of white wrapping paper upon which he always did his large-scale figuring.

'Sit down,' he told Bump. 'We're going to have the worst depression in the history of the world. We got to get ready to feed people the way we've never done before. I'm going to open restaurants, Bump. It won't be enough now to sell people food cheap. We got to be ready to give it away, cooked and ready to swallow, so that people won't starve to death right here in our own land.'

He outlined in rapid broken sentences what he believed was sure to happen and Bump listened, cautious and reluctant and yet knowing from past experience how often Clem was right.

'We can hardly feed the whole nation, Clem,' he said at last.

Clem was immediately impatient. 'I'm not talking about the nation. I'm talking about hungry people. I want to set up restaurants in the big cities as quick as we can. Our markets will supply our own restaurants. Whoever can pay will pay, of course. At first most people can pay and will want to. But I am thinking of January and February, maybe even this winter, and I'm thinking of next winter and maybe the winter after. That's when things will get bad.'

It was impossible to get so huge a plan going as quickly as Clem thought it should and could. But it was done or began to be done within a time that was miraculous. Clem bought a small aeroplane which Henrietta, much against her secret inclination, learned to fly lest Clem insist on doing so, and he, as she well knew, was not to be trusted with machinery. He expected divine miracles from engines made by man, and while she had submitted for years to his mistreatment of automobiles, his wrenchings and poundings of parts he did not understand, the frightful speed at which he drove when he was in a hurry, she could not contemplate such manœuvres in the air.

She made a good pilot, to her own surprise, for she was an earth-bound creature and hated suspension. Clem as usual was surprised at nothing she did, insisting upon her ability to do everything. At as low a height as she dared to maintain, they flew from city to city, her only apparent cowardice being that when they went to the coast to set up Clem's restaurants in San Francisco and Los Angeles, she avoided the Rocky Mountains, and flew far south in order to escape them. Pilot and attendant, she followed Clem while, with his superb and reckless disregard of all business principles, he established during that first winter six restaurants across the country on the same magnitude as the markets. For these restaurants he hired Chinese managers.

'Only Chinese know how to make the best dishes of the cheapest food,' he explained to Henrietta. 'They've been doing that for thousands of years.'

Knowing the importance of the spirit, he summoned his new

staff to a conference in Chicago, where he put them up at a comfortable hotel while he talked to them about starvation, and how to prevent it. He worked out one hundred menus, dependent upon raw materials of the markets, and laid down the rule which should have ruined him and which instead led him eventually to new heights of prosperity.

'Any time anybody wants a free meal in any of our restaurants they can have it,' he said firmly. 'Of course they can't order strawberries and cream, but they can have meat stew and all the bread they want, and they can have baked apples or prunes for dessert. Nobody will know whether they pay for it or not. They'll get a check same as everybody else, and they'll go up to the cashier and just tell her quiet-like if they haven't any money.'

'How many times can one man eat free?' Mr. Lim of San Francisco inquired.

'We don't ask that,' Clem said. 'We don't ask anything, see? If anybody's hungry, he eats. At the same time, we'll serve other foods, cooked so good that people who have got money will pay for it. And our restaurants will look nice, too, so that people will want to come there. They won't seem like hand-out places.'

The Chinese exchanged grins. Their salaries were secure, and so they were highly diverted by this mad American. Since he had appealed to their honour they were prepared to respond with their most ingenious economies and seasonings. He in turn accepted their promises with complete faith.

'We can do such things as you talk,' Mr. Kwok of New York Chinatown now said. 'Only thinking, however, is that we better hire our own cooks and waiters, each of us somebody he knows good.'

'Sure,' Clem agreed. 'That's all up to you. I hold you responsible, each for your own place.'

'Must be order, you see.' This was Mr. Pan of Chicago. 'I know Americans think all equal, but Chinese know better. For making something go, especially cheap and good, one man is top and everybody else in steps below, each man top to next man and next-to-top man is reporting to very top man.

347

Each man is servant and at the same time boss, except bottom man, who is anxious for rising and does his best.'

'Sure,' Clem said. 'You put it neat.'

With the simplest of casual organization, Clem arranged his markets and restaurants in an endless chain of co-operation. He did not expect perfection and did not get it. Nepotism in two of the restaurants was a drain on profits until he discovered it and fired the two managers and hired new ones. With the old managers went the entire staffs and with the new ones came new and chastened ones. The other four managers approved the changes and worked with the greater integrity and zeal. Clem's *Brother Man Restaurants* without advertising lost no money the first year and saved thousands of people from hunger so quietly that the public knew nothing about it. Three per cent of the people who ate free meals could have paid and did not. This was balanced by sums from people who could and did pay extra because they liked the food. Clem was brazen about accepting such extra pay. On the bottom of the menu cards in large bold letters he printed this legend:

OUR PRICES ARE TOO LOW FOR PROFITS. IF YOU HAVE GOT MORE THAN YOUR MONEY'S WORTH FROM SOME DISH YOU HAVE ESPECIALLY ENJOYED, PLEASE PAY WHAT YOU THINK IT IS WORTH. THIS MONEY WILL GO TO FEED THE HUNGRY.

A surprising number of people paid extra, but Clem was not surprised. His faith in humanity increased as he grew older and made it unnecessary, he declared, for any further faith.

'The way I look at it is this, hon,' he said to Henrietta on one of their long flights across the plains of the West. 'Everybody needs faith. Some people find it in God or in heaven or something way off. Take me, though, I get inspiration out of my faith in people here and now.'

In the middle of the next winter, however, Clem found himself puzzled. He was feeding people on a huge scale, not only through his markets but through his restaurants, and he saw that it was not enough. He turned his eyes away from the bread-lines and knew that at last he had met a task that was beyond him.

The effect of this discovery upon him frightened Henrietta. She saw his first excitement and exuberance, his immense rise of energy, his self-confidence, and even his faith pass into an intense and grim determination as the hordes of the hungry increased over the nation. They gathered in the cities, for country people can hide themselves snugly into their farms and eat the food they produce and stop buying. Furniture and machinery which they had been tempted to buy on instalments they relinquished, wary of their savings. They had lived without radios and without cars and washing-machines and they could again. They withdrew into the past and lived as their grandparents had done and did not starve. They could still sleep in ancient beds and use old tables and sit on ladder-back chairs.

It was the cities that frightened Clem. Even in the cities where he had his restaurants, the bread-lines began to stretch for blocks. When he found a family with seven children starving in New York he came back to Henrietta in the small room at a cheap hotel, which was his usual stopping-place.

'I wouldn't have thought it could be, hon,' he said mournfully. 'Maybe in China or India, but here? Hon, how am I going to get the government to understand that people have got to be fed? A war will come out of this, hon. People won't know why there's a war and they'll think it's because of a whole lot of other things, but the bottom reason is because people can't buy food because they don't have the money to buy it with. That makes men fight.'

'Clem, you look sick!' Henrietta said. 'I'm going to get you a doctor.'

'I am sick,' Clem said. 'But it's a sickness no doctor can cure. I'll be sick as long as things go on like this.'

At noon he refused to eat and Henrietta went downstairs to eat alone, ashamed of her steady appetite. If Clem could only separate his soul from his body! But he could not and his body shared the tortures of his harassed soul. He blamed himself for things being what they were, and this Henrietta would have thought absurd except she had seen in her own father when she was a child the same suffering for the sins of others.

'Did we do our duty as Christians'—she remembered her father saying that year when they had left China, that fearful year when Clem had been left alone in Peking—'the world in a generation would be changed.'

Clem was like that, too. He wanted the world changed quickly because he saw it could be changed and he fretted himself almost to death because other people did not see what he did. Troubled and sad, she ate her robust meal, chewing each mouthful carefully because she believed Fletcher was right about that. She had got interested in Fletcherism because of Clem's indigestion, and especially because he was always in such a hurry that he swallowed his food whole.

When she went upstairs again he was lying on the bed, flat on his back, and she thought he was asleep. She tiptoed in and stood looking down at him. His hands were clasped behind his head, and his eyes were closed. Then she saw his lashes quiver.

'That you, hon? I've been lying here thinking. I believe I've got an idea.'

'Oh, Clem, I hoped you were asleep! If you won't eat——'

'I will eat, but you know how I am. If I eat when I'm thinking something out the food just lays on my stomach. Hon, I am going to see your brother William.'

She sat down heavily in the soiled arm-chair. 'Clem, it won't do a bit of good.'

'It might, hon. He's got a new wife.'

'Nobody could have been nicer than Candace.'

'Maybe so. She was mighty nice. But if William loves this woman, maybe it has done something to him. Maybe it's stirred his heart.'

'I hope you don't want me to go with you.'

'I was kind of hoping you would.'

'Clem—it won't help! He's invincible now. Everywhere we go people are reading his nasty little newspapers.'

'He must feel something for people, hon.'

'No, he doesn't. He hates people. He despises them or he wouldn't make such newspapers for them. I know why he does it, too. He feeds them the worst stuff so as to keep them down. It's like feeding the Chinese opium—or giving whisky to the Indians. People learn to like it, and because they like it they will follow the person that gives it to them.'

Clem, always generous, shook his head at this picture of William. 'I kind of think I'll go right away and see for myself, hon.'

Henrietta's anger rose in spite of love. 'Very well,' she declared. 'Go if you must. But I will not go with you.'

He sighed and got off the bed. He put on his coat and smoothed his hair with his hand. Then he bent to kiss her tenderly.

'You don't feel mad with me, do you?'

'Oh, no, Clem, except——'

'Except what?' He paused and looked down upon her, his eyes bright blue in his white face and his lips pursed quizzically.

'Clem, you're too good, that's all. You won't believe that anybody isn't good.'

'That's my faith, I guess.'

He turned at the door, looked as if he were about to say something more, kept silent instead, and went his way.

Lady Emory was alone for luncheon. She was, of course, Mrs. William Lane, and by now she was well used to it in all external ways. She was beginning to feel that the huge comfortable house in uptown New York was her own, and in certain ways that Hulme Castle could never be. From earliest memory she had known that while Hulme Castle was her shelter, it was not her home. William had divined this very soon after their marriage and had offered to put at her disposal as much money as needed to repair the castle and put in bathrooms.

'It will make you feel more free to go there and stay as long as you like, now that you are my wife,' he had said quite gracefully.

Her father had refused the gift, however. He saw no need for more bathrooms since he himself still used a tin tub brought into his room in the mornings and set before the fire.

'I believe William would like to come here and stay

sometimes, Father,' she had replied to this prejudice. 'He would feel less like a guest if he had some part in the castle.'

She said this quite as gracefully as William had, but her father had only grumbled and it had taken Michael to persuade him to let William repair at least the west wing as a place where Emory and her husband might stay when they came to England. Lady Hulme had early discerned in William a rather touching desire to own some part of Hulme Castle, and so she had been grateful to Michael who, after all, was the one most to be considered, since he was the future heir.

As for America, as far as Emory had seen it, it was amazing. The people were very friendly, perhaps too friendly. She had been invited to a great many dinner parties and everybody had persisted in calling her Lady Emory, and this made her feel at home. William, too, called her Lady Emory in the house to the servants. Naturally when he introduced her it was as his wife, Mrs. Lane. She felt in spite of his real love for her that she did not know him as well as she hoped she would one day. He had a strange and almost forbidding dignity which she did not dislike, although she saw that it cut him off from ordinary people and even from her, sometimes. She was used to that. In his way her father had a dignity, too. He would have been outraged by familiarity from his inferiors.

Moreover, there was something about this dignity of William's which ennobled her and their life. She was proud of his straight, handsome body and was well aware of their regal appearance together.

He never talked to her of his first wife. In marriage he and she were utterly alone, and for this she was grateful. Instead, he told her much about his boyhood in Peking, and she who had never thought of China as a place existent upon this earth, now perceptively saw him there, a tall solitary boy, august in his place as the only son of the family, hungry for communication when there could be none, alien from his parents and sisters as he was from the Chinese he knew, who apparently were all servants.

'Did you not know any Chinese boys?' she asked.

'They were not allowed in the compound,' he replied. 'My

352

mother did not like them to hang about. Even my father's study had a separate entrance so that when the Chinese came to see him they need not enter the hall.'

'Did you try to know anybody secretly?' she asked.

'It would not have occurred to me,' he replied sincerely.

Then bit by bit there came out the remembered fragments of his life in the Chefoo school and here she perceived he had been shaped. She saw the proud boy slighted and condemned by the careless lordly English boys she knew so well, for Cecil had been such a boy. Unconsciously William revealed to her his wounds never healed.

It was not all bitterness. He could speak sometimes of wide Peking streets and of the beauty of the porcelain roofs on the palaces of the dying empire. He told her one meditative evening how his mother had taken him to see the Empress when he was a small boy. 'I bowed before her, but I didn't kneel because I was an American. The Chinese had to kneel and keep their heads on the floor. I remember her thin hands —yours remind me of them. They were narrow and pale and very beautiful. But the palms were stained red and the long nails shielded in gold gem-studded protectors. I looked at her face—a most powerful face.'

'Did she speak to you?'

'I don't remember that. The people called her the Old Buddha. They were afraid of her, and so they admired her. People have to have someone like her. I was sorry when she died and that revolutionary fellow, Sun Yat-sen, took over. People can't respect a common fellow like that—someone just like themselves. Maybe this new man, Chiang Kai-shek, will be better. He is a soldier, used to command. There is no democratic nonsense about him.'

Emory listened, knowing that he was telling her things he had never told anyone, things that he had forgotten and now drew up out of the wells of his being. At the bottom of everything there was always a permanent complaint against his parents because they had robbed him of his birthright of pride. It had been impossible to explain to them why he was ashamed, and he was the more ashamed because he had the agony of

353

wanting to be proud of his father, and then the humbling realization of knowing that there was something of his father in himself in spite of this hatred, and that he could not simply enjoy all that he had, his money and his great houses and the freedom that success should have bought him, because he could never be free. God haunted him.

This was the bitterness and the trouble and the terror that she found in William's soul. It made her thoughtful indeed. His conscience was the fox in his vitals.

Upon such musing alone and by the fire in the drawing-room of her American home she took her usual afternoon tea on the cold January day. It was not often that she was alone but she had felt tired, the intense activity of this new world city being something to which she was not used. She had been invited to a cocktail party given for that playwright now most successful upon Broadway, Seth James, and when she telephoned to William that she would not go he had replied that he himself must go, since Seth had been a former employee with whom he had disagreed, and if he did not go, it might appear that he held a grudge.

'Do go, by all means,' Emory had said at once.

She found it comfortable to be alone for an hour. It seemed difficult to be alone in America, although in Hulme Castle it had been the most natural state. Now, after she had eaten some small watercress sandwiches and drunk two cups of English tea, she went to the piano William had had made to order especially for her touch and sitting down before it she played for perhaps half an hour, transporting herself as she did so to some vague and distant place that was not America and yet not quite England. She had no wish to return to Hulme Castle, and she was quite happy here in this house, as happy as she thought she could be in mortal life. Cecil had left her entirely now, even her dreams, and she seldom thought of him.

In the midst of her music the door opened and she heard the slight cough with which the second man announced his deprecatory presence.

'Well, Henry?' she called, softening her melody without stopping it.

354

'Please, madame, Mr. Lane's brother-in-law is here.'

'Mr. Jeremy Cameron?'

She had met Jeremy and William's rather sweet sister Ruth. She had found it difficult to get on with Ruth's soft effervescence, but Jeremy she thought charming, although it was unfortunate that he was also the brother of William's first wife.

'I do hope you won't mind it that I am Candace's brother,' Jeremy had said directly when they were first alone. 'I assure you that Candace entirely understands about things. She wouldn't mind meeting you, as a matter of fact—she's a warmhearted sort of creature.'

'I don't mind in the least your being her brother,' Emory had replied.

'It's not Mr. Jeremy, please, madame,' Henry now said. 'It's the other brother-in-law—a Mr. Miller, I believe.'

'Oh——' Lady Emory rose from the piano. She knew about Henrietta who, William said, had married a strange sort of man named Clem, who had made an odd success in food monopolies. While she stood in the middle of the floor somewhat uncertain as to how she would receive Clem or whether she should receive him at all, he was at the door looking altogether shadowy, with his sandy grey hair blown about.

'Do come in,' she said.

She was struck by his excessive thinness and the startling blue of his eyes.

'You look cold!' she said with her involuntary kindness. 'I think you should have some hot tea.'

To Henry, still hovering in the doorway, she said with distinctness, 'Please fetch a pot of hot tea, Henry.'

'Yes, madame.' Henry's voice breathed doubt as he disappeared.

Clem saw a woman, a lady, who was all gentleness and kindness. It was true that he felt ill for a moment when he first came in. He had eaten nothing since morning.

'I guess I am a little hungry,' he said, and tried to smile.

She had him in a comfortable chair instantly and put a hassock under his feet. The fire burned pleasantly and the vast room was quiet about him. Everything was comforting and warm, and he sighed away his haste and intensity. In his taut body one muscle and another relaxed. The man came back with hot tea and she poured him a cup.

'Bring him a soft-boiled egg,' she told the man.

'I can't eat eggs,' Clem protested.

'Indeed you can,' she replied with firmness. 'You want an egg—you are so pale.'

'No milk in my tea, please,' Clem said.

While he waited he drank two cups of the delicious hot tea and ate one of the hot biscuits she called scones, and when the egg came it was two, served in a covered cup. There were triangles of toast with it and he ate and felt renewed to the soul.

'Wonderful what food can do,' he said and smiled at her and she smiled back.

'I don't know what to call you,' he said next.

'Emory, of course. You're Clem, I know.'

'Aren't you a lady or something?'

'In a way. Never mind that, though, now that I'm an American.'

Clem folded a small lace-edged napkin with care and put it on the tray.

'I see you believe in feeding folks and that's what I came to see William about. Maybe he's told you about me?'

'I believe he said you deal in foods?'

'I like to put it that I deal with people and getting them fed.'

He leaned forward, looking extraordinarily restored and reminding her somehow of the young men in London who were always talking in Hyde Park. She had never stopped to listen to any of them but often they had the same sandy look and shining, too blue eyes. While she sat gazing at him and thinking this, Clem was fluent in preaching his own gospel to this kindly, attentive woman. He had all but forgotten that she took Candace's place and that he ought not to like her so much, but he did like her. Candace had been kind, too, but it was with a child's kindness and he had never been sure she understood him. But this woman did understand and she was not at all a child. There was even something sad about her dark eyes.

356

'You see what I mean?' he paused to ask.

'I do see, indeed,' she replied. 'I think it is a wonderful idea, only of course you are far ahead of your times. That's the tragedy of great primary ideas. You won't live to see it believed or practised that people have the right to food as they have the right to water and air. The holy trinity of human life!'

He could not bear to have her merely understand him or even believe in him. When one believed, one must act.

He put forth his effort again. 'We've got to get people to see this, though. That is what I came to William for. He has such power over people.'

Emory looked at him with new and sudden interest. 'Has he really?'

He was entirely sensitive to this interest and anxious to make the most of it. 'I can't tell you how great his power is. His newspapers go into every little town and household—little easy papers that everybody can read. And then there's the pictures. If people don't want to read they can look at the pictures. I read them, too, and look at all the pictures. The queer thing to me is that you don't learn anything, though—Miss—Lady——'

'Just Emory,' she reminded him.

He could not quite manage it. 'I mean that it's all amusing and nice but you don't learn anything from it. You don't learn why it is that the people in Asia want a better life and you don't learn why it is that things don't look so good even with the new government in China.'

At the thought of China Clem fell into thought. 'I don't know——' he murmured. 'I can't tell. I don't think things are going right over there. Maybe I'll run over as soon as I see this depression through.' He lifted his head. 'What I wanted to talk to William about—if he could get converted, so to speak, to this idea of feeding people. It won't be charity. It won't cost us money.'

He began to explain the golden rule of his restaurants and somewhere in the midst of it they looked up and saw William at the door, upon his face surprise and disgust.

357

'Come along in, William,' Emory said at once. 'I am listening to the most fascinating man. It's Clem.'

Thus she conveyed to William that he was to take from his face that look calculated to wound, and that he must come in and sit down and be kind to Clem, because she wished it. Their eyes met for a brief full second and William yielded. He yielded to Emory as he had never yielded to anyone.

'How do you do,' he said to Clem.

'Fine,' Clem said. 'How's yourself?'

William did not answer. He sat down and took from Emory's hand a cup of tea.

'I really came to see you,' Clem said looking at him. 'But I have surely enjoyed talking to your good wife here. She has treated me well—fed me up and all. I didn't eat lunch today.'

William did not show interest.

'Will you have a sandwich or a scone?' Emory murmured.

'Neither, thank you,' William said.

Clem felt the atmosphere of the room change and he made haste to say what he had come for. Probably they wanted to be alone and anyway he had been here long enough.

'I don't want to waste your time, William, but I do want to give you an idea. Or set it before you, anyway. I read your editorials every day and I see that you put in one idea every day, I guess an idea of your own. I can't agree with most of them but that's neither here nor there. It's a free country. But I notice that people take your ideas pretty nearly whole- sale. I move around a lot through the country and I hear men say things that I can see come right out of your mouth, so to speak. I can see you understand how most people are. They don't know much and they talk a lot and naturally they have to have something to say and so they say what they hear some- body else say or what they read in the newspaper. I admire the way you can lay down something in a short plain way.'

'Thank you,' William said without gratitude.

Clem never noticed irony and he accepted the words as they stood. 'That's all right. Now here's my idea. How about getting it across that we ought to give away our surpluses to the people who don't have food? I mean these men in the bread-lines, and selling apples on the street, and the families hungry at home. It won't cost a thing.'

'What surpluses?' William asked in a cold voice.

'Our surpluses,' Clem repeated stoutly. 'Even now we have surpluses, while the people are starving because they can't buy food. It's money that's short, not food.'

William set down his cup. 'What you propose would upset our whole system of government were it carried to its logical conclusion. If people have no money they can't buy. Your idea is to disregard money and give them food free. Who is to pay the men who produce the food?'

'But producers are not getting anything, anyway!' Clem cried. 'The food is rotting and they are short, too.'

'It is better to let the food rot than it is to undermine our whole economic system,' William said firmly.

Clem gave him a wild look. 'All right, William, pay the producers, then! Let them be paid out of tax money.'

'You mean the government ought to feed the people?' William was shocked to the soul. 'That's the welfare state!'

'Oh, God!' Clem shouted. 'Listen to the man! It's the people I'm thinking of—the starving people, William! What's a nation if it's not the people? What's business if there's nobody to buy? What's government if the citizens die?'

'This is quite ridiculous,' William said to Emory. He rose, towering over Clem, who rose to meet him. 'We will never agree,' William said formally. 'I must conduct my publications as I see fit. Believe me, I am sorry to see anyone hungry, but I feel that those who are hungry have some reason to be. Ours is a land of opportunity. My own life proves it. No one helped me to success. What I have done others can do. This is my faith as an American.'

For a moment Emory, watching the two embattled men, thought that Clem would spring at William. He gathered himself together, his fists clenched, his eyes lightning blue, electric with wrath. He glared at William for a long second and suddenly the wrath went out of him.

'You don't know what you do.' The words came out of

Clem like a sigh of death. He turned and went away as though he had been made deaf and struck blind.

When he was gone William sat down again. 'Pour me another cup of tea, please, Emory.' He tried to make his voice usual.

'Of course, William. But is it hot enough?' She felt the pot.

'It is all right, I am sure.'

He waited until he had tasted the tea. 'You see, Emory, how impossible the fellow is.'

'I don't understand your American system yet, I'm afraid, William. Are there actually people starving?'

'Some people, of course, need food,' William said in a reasonable voice. 'Charities, however, are alert. There is free food; the very thing he talks about is being done. I have given a great deal of money myself this winter to charity, in your name and mine together.'

He paused, but she did not thank him and he went on. 'Who are these charity cases but the ones they have always been? They are the unskilled, the uneducated, the lazy, the drifters, the hangers-on, all the marginal people that are to be found in any modern industrial nation. In the ancient agricultural civilization of old China they were taken care of by the immense family system. Industry, of course, changes all that.'

'Shouldn't there be some other means found to take the place of the family?'

'There are means,' William said with an edge of impatience. 'Believe me when I say that nobody needs to starve here in America if he works. Even if he doesn't want to work he need not starve. There are charities everywhere.'

'I see,' Emory said, her voice so soft that it was almost a whisper.

They did not speak for a few minutes, and when William put out his hand to her she took it and held it in both her own. It was the best hour of the day, this quiet one between tea and dinner. If they had guests they were friends and if they had no guests it was like this, William always tender towards her.

She knew he loved her most truly. Indeed she knew he loved no one else. In some way she could not herself understand she had unsealed his heart which without her had been like a tomb. She was awed by this love for she had never known her power before. Cecil had loved her but she had perhaps loved him more than he did her. She had belonged to him but somehow William belonged to her. She was afraid, sometimes, for could not such possession place too great a demand upon her? She was not quite free any more because his love encompassed her about.

'I am ashamed that my sister's husband should have forced his way into this room and destroyed your peace,' William said.

'Oh, no,' she said. 'It was very interesting. As a matter of fact——' but she left her sentence there and he did not ask for its end. Instead he got up and bent down to kiss her. She rather enjoyed his kiss and she leaned back her head to receive it.

'I want to keep you happy,' William said in a voice stifled by love. 'I don't want you troubled.'

'Thank you, dear,' she said. 'I am not troubled.'

He went away and she heard him mount the stairs to his rooms. He would bathe and change and come down again soon looking rested and handsome, the gentleman that he was of wealth and increasing leisure. He did not need to work as once he did, he had told her only yesterday. They might go to Italy this winter, stopping at Hulme Castle, of course.

She sat for a moment thinking of this and of Clem. Then with a sudden decisive movement she touched the bell. There was really nothing she could do about Clem. She had chosen William and her world was William's world.

The door opened. 'Take away the tea things, please, Henry,' she said in her silvery English voice. 'I am going upstairs and if any one telephones I am not to be disturbed.'

'Yes, madame,' Henry said.

From William's house Clem went downtown. He wanted comfort and reassurance. Henrietta could always give him comfort and encouragement but no one, not even she, could understand that now at this moment he needed the reassurance of fact. He must learn by actual test whether what he was doing was more than he feared it was, a drop in the vast bucket of human hunger. He avoided the hotel and taking a bus he swung downtown to Mott Street where his largest restaurant stood. It was a dingy-looking place now but there was no need to have it otherwise. People had already learned that they could get free food there, too many people. He saw many men and some women with children standing in a ragged shivering line waiting in the wintry twilight and he pulled up his collar and stood at the end. In a few seconds there were twenty more behind him.

They moved step by step with intolerable slowness. He must speak to Kwok about this. People must be served more quickly on such bitter nights. Speed was essential. They must hire more waiters, hire as many people as necessary.

He got in at last and took his place at a table already crowded. A waiter swabbed it off and did not recognize his guest.

'Whatcha want to eat?' he asked, still swabbing.

Clem murmured the basic meal. He waited again, glancing here and there, seeing everything. The room was far too crowded but it was warm and reasonably clean. It was big but not nearly big enough. He must see if he could rent the upper floor. In spite of the crowd the place was silent, or almost silent. People were crouched over the tables, eating. Only a few were talking, or laughing and briefly gay.

His plate of food came and he ate it. The food was good enough, filling and hot. The waiter kept looking at him and Clem saw him stop a moment later at the cashier's window. He ate as much as he could and then leaned to the man next him at the long table, a young unshaven man who had cleaned his plate.

'Want this?' Clem muttered.

The sunken young eyes lit in the famished face. 'Don't you want it?'

'I can't finish it——'

362

'Sure.'

The waiter was watching again but Clem got up and went to the cashier's window with his check. He leaned towards the grating and said in a low voice, 'I'm sorry I can't pay anything.'

The sharp-faced Chinese girl behind the thin iron bars replied at once and her voice and accent were entirely American. 'Oh yes, you can. You aren't hungry—not with that suit of clothes!'

'My only decent clothes,' Clem muttered.

'Pawn them,' she said briskly. 'Everybody's doing that so's to pay for their meals.'

He turned in sudden fury and walked across the restaurant, pushing his way through the waiters. He went straight to Mr. Kwok's small office and found him there in his shirt-sleeves, the oily sweat pouring down his face.

'Mr. Miller——' Mr. Kwok sprang to his feet. He pointed to his own chair. 'Sit down, please.'

Clem was still furious. 'No, I won't sit down. Look here, I came in tonight to see how things were going on. I told the cashier I couldn't pay just to try out the system. That damned girl at the window told me to go pawn my clothes!'

Mr. Kwok sweated more heavily. 'Please, Mr. Miller, not so mad! You don't unnerstan'. We going broke this way— too many people eating every day. In China you know how people starving don't expect eating every day only maybe one time, two time, three time in a week. Here Americans expecting eating every day even they can't pay. Nobody can do so, Mr. Miller, not even such a big heart like yours. It can't be starving people eat like not starving. It don't make sense, Mr. Miller. At first yes, very sensible, because most people pay, but now too many people don't pay and still eating like before. What the hell! It's depression.'

The wrath went out of Clem. What the Chinese said was true. Too many people now couldn't pay. The job was beyond him, beyond anybody. Too many people, too many starving people.

'I guess you're right,' he said after a long pause.

363

He looked so pale when he got up, he swayed so strangely on his feet that Mr. Kwok was frightened and put out his hands and caught Clem by the elbows. 'Please, Mr. Miller, are you something wrong?'

Clem steadied himself. 'No, I'm all right. I just got to think of something else, that's all. Good night, Mr. Kwok.'

He wrenched himself away from the kind supporting hands and went out of the door into the street. His idea wasn't working. Nothing was working. People were pawning their clothes in this bitter weather. They were being asked to pawn their clothes, pawn everything they could, doubtless. The waiters had been told to look and see what people wore. He remembered the hungry boy who had seized his plate and eaten the left-overs like a dog. That was what it had come to here in his own country. Someday people would be eating grass and roots and leaves here as they did in China.

'I got to get down to Washington,' he muttered into the cold darkness. 'I gotta get down there one more time and tell them. . . .'

He found his way to the hotel where Henrietta waited for him, alarmed at his long absence.

'Clem——' she began, but he cut her off short.

'Get our things together, hon. We're taking the next train to Washington. I'm going to get to that fellow in the White House if I have to bust my way in.'

He did not get in, of course. She knew he could not. She waited outside in the lobby and read a pamphlet on a table full of pamphlets and magazines that had been sent for the President to read. He had no time to read them and they had been put here to help the people who waited to while away the time. In a pamphlet of five pages, in words as dry as dust, in sentences as terse as exclamations, but passionless, she read the whole simple truth. For twenty-nine months American business had been shrinking. Industrial production was fifty per cent of what it had been three years ago. The deflation in all prices was thirty-five per cent. Profits were down seventy-five per cent. Nineteen railways during the last year had gone bankrupt. Farm prices had shrunk forty-nine per cent so far and were still going down. But—and here she saw how everlastingly right Clem was—there was more food than ever! Farmers had grown ten per cent more food in this year of starvation than they had grown three years ago in a time of plenty.

'Oh, Clem,' Henrietta whispered to her own heart. 'How often you tell them and they will not listen! O Jerusalem, Jerusalem, how often. . . .'

She put the pamphlet back on the table and sat with her hands folded in her lap and her head bowed so that her hat hid the tears that kept welling into her eyes. It was for Clem she wept, for Clem in whom nobody believed except herself, and who was she except nobody? William had hurt him dreadfully but she did not know how because Clem would not tell her what had happened. He had spoken scarcely a word all the way down on the train. She had tried to make him sleep, even if they were only in a day coach—he wouldn't spend the money for berths—but though he leaned back and shut his eyes she knew he was not sleeping.

He came into the waiting-room suddenly and she saw at once that he had failed. She got up and they went out of the building side by side. She took his hand but it was limp, and she let it go again.

'Did you see the President?' she asked when they were on the street. The sun was bright and cold and pigeons were walking around looking for food, but no one was there to feed them.

'No,' Clem said. 'He was too busy. I talked to somebody or other, though, enough to know there was no use staying around.'

'Oh, Clem, why?'

'Why? Because they've got an idea of their own. Want to know what it is? Well, I'll tell you. They've got the idea of telling the farmers to stop raising so much food. That's their idea. Wonderful, ain't it, with the country full of starvation?'

He turned on her and gave a bark of laughter so fierce that people stared, but he did not see their stares. He was loping

365

along as though he were in a race and she could scarcely keep up with him.

'Where are we going now, Clem?' she asked.

'We're going home to Ohio. I gotta sweat it out,' he said.

The nation righted itself in the next two years, slowly like a ship coming out of a storm. William wrote a clear and well-reasoned editorial for his chain of newspapers and pointed out to his millions of readers that the reforms were not begun by Franklin D. Roosevelt, the new President, but by Herbert Hoover who should have been re-elected in sheer justice that he might finish that which he had begun. It was already obvious, William went on, that the new inhabitant of the White House would run the nation into unheard-of national debt.

What William saw now in the White House was not the mature and incomparable man, toughened by crippling experience. He saw a youth he remembered in college, gay and wilful and debonair, born as naturally as Emory to a castle and unearned wealth but, unlike her, not controlled by any relationship to himself. Roosevelt, secure from the first moment of his birth, was uncontrollable and therefore terrifying, and William conveyed these fears in his usual editorial style, oversimple and dogmatically brief. To his surprise, he experienced his first rebellion. Millions of frightened people reading his editorials felt an inexplicable fury and newspaper sales dropped so sharply that the business office felt compelled to bring it to William's notice. He replied by a memorandum saying that he was sailing for England and Europe, especially Germany where he wanted to see for himself what was happening, and they could do as they liked while he was gone.

Emory received the news of the journey with her usual calm. They had not gone to England or Italy the year before, and she felt a change now would be pleasant. Alone with William she might discover what it was that kept him perpetually dissatisfied, not with her, but with the very stuff of life itself. She never mentioned to him her discernment of his discontent, for by now she knew it was spiritual and that he was only beginning to perceive this for himself. She refused again a

366

thought which came to trouble her. Did William feel a lack in her own love for him? Was there such a lack? She made no answer. He had so much. He had all the money he had ever imagined he would have, and the most successful chain of popular newspapers. He was already planning the next presidential candidate, for this man in the White House could not possibly survive a first term. That he hungered for something he did not have, something more than woman could give, was now plain, perhaps even to William himself.

Or did his spirit seek after his father? One day on their voyage, William said, 'I often think about my father. I wish you had known him, Emory. You would have understood each other. He was a great man, never discovered.'

'I wish I might have known him, dear,' she observed. They were in their deck-chairs after breakfast and the sun was brilliant upon a hard blue sea.

'I wonder . . . I often wonder. . . .' William mused somewhat heavily.

Emory delayed opening her novel. 'About what, William?'

'Whether he would approve what I do—what I am!'

Approval. That was the word, the key! She saw it at once and grasped it. William needed the approval of someone he felt was his spiritual superior. For she knew that he was a man of strongly spiritual nature, a religious man without a religion. Emory herself was not spiritual, not religious at any rate, and she could not help him. She did not carry the conversation beyond her usual mild comment.

'I feel sure he would approve you, William, but I wish he were here to tell you so.'

Within herself, after that conversation, she began the active search for the religion that William needed. It must be one strong enough for him, organized and ancient, not Buddhism, which was too gentle, not Hinduism, which was too merciful, not Taoism, which was too gay, imbued as it was with human independence even of God, and Confucianism was dead. She knew something of all religions, for after Cecil's death she had searched the scriptures of many and in the end had grown indifferent to all. Instead of religion she had developed a deep native patience, and detached by early shock, nothing now could disturb the calm which had grown like a protective shell, lovely as mother-of-pearl, over her own soul. She wished indeed that she could have known his father, for in that dead father, she felt sure at last, was the key to this living husband of hers. His mother, she had soon found, had been merely the vessel of creation.

Emory rather liked the vessel, nevertheless. She comprehended early with her subtle humour that there was not an ounce of the spiritual in her mother-in-law's bustling body. Mrs. Lane used God for her own purposes, which were always literal and material, revelling in William's success, in his wealth, in new relation to an English Earl. Soon after William's marriage she had announced that she was going to England and that she would enjoy a visit at Hulme Castle. Emory had written to her own mother with entire frankness, saying that her mother-in-law would be the easiest of guests and not in the least like William. 'Old Mrs. Lane is always ready to worship,' Emory wrote, and drew a small cat face grinning upon the wide margin of the heavy hand-made paper that bore her name but also the Hulme coat of arms.

She had seen Mrs. Lane off and upon the deck of the great ship had given her a huge corsage of purple orchids which would last the voyage, a package of religious novels, and a box of French chocolates. 'Food for body and soul,' she had said with private cynicism. Mrs. Lane, who had a strong digestion and liked sweets, did not comprehend cynicism. She had thanked her new daughter-in-law with the special warmth she had for the well born. She stood at the hand-rail of the upper deck, wrapped in a fur coat and a tightly veiled hat, and waved vigorously.

At first the divorce had seemed horrible to her, until she discovered how thoroughly she approved of Emory and her English relations. She made compromise. It was not as if William needed the Cameron money any more. Emory was really much better suited to him in his present position than Candace was. Men did outgrow women. There was no use pretending, although, thank God, her own husband had

368

never outgrown her. Such remarks she had poured into Ruth's ears, and Ruth always listened.

This mother, Emory had soon perceived, was of no real use to William, and at first she thought that any connexion between William and his mother must have ended with the physical cutting of the umbilical cord. Later she had seen that she had been wrong. Mrs. Lane had created a division in William. To her he owed respect for wealth, for castles, for birth, for——

At this point Emory checked herself. She was being nasty, for did she not enjoy William's wealth? Worse than that she was being unjust to him, whose soul hungered after higher things than those which he had. She wanted William to be really happy and not in the way that America meant happiness, which was something too fervid and occasional. She wanted William to be satisfied in ways that she knew he was not. She wanted his restless ambition stilled, and the vague wounds of his life healed. Some of them she had been able to heal merely by being what she was, English and his wife.

Hulme Castle was unusually beautiful on the afternoon when they were driven up the long winding road from the downs. The winter had been mild, the chauffeur said, explaining the amount of greenery about the old towers and walls.

Her parents were in the long drawing-room, though it was not yet noon, and she was touched to think they were waiting for her, putting aside their usual morning pursuits.

'My dears——' she said, bending to kiss them.

William was quietly formal and nothing much was said. Her parents did not feel at ease with him, nor, as she saw, quite at ease even with her. Then Michael came in dressed in his riding things and ease flowed into the room with him.

'I say, you two—you haven't been shown up to your part of the castle yet?'

'You told us not,' Lady Hulme reminded him.

'No. Come along. I wanted to show it to you,' Michael said.

They followed him, laughing at his impatience, and then Emory saw that even William, so scant in his praise of anyone, was touched by what Michael had done. He had really made a small private castle of one wing. It had its separate entrance, its own kitchen, and four baths.

'I shall be able to rest here, Emory,' William said so gravely that she perceived he needed rest.

'Come along, William,' Michael said when they had seen everything. 'We'd better leave Emory for a bit with her mother. I have to ride to the next town to see about getting a tractor. I thought we'd get our luncheon there, perhaps. You could advise me—it's an American machine.'

Emory laughed. 'You're not very subtle, Michael, but then you never were.' They laughed with her and went off, nevertheless, and she lunched with her parents.

The castle, she discovered, was in a strange state of flux. Her father, deeply angry over the increase in death duties, was threatening to move into the gatehouse with her mother and a couple of servants and let Michael take the castle and assume title so far as was possible. She listened to this talk at the immense dining table, her father at one end, her mother at the other, and she in between as she used to be.

'It's hard on a man not being able to finish his days in his proper place,' the Earl said.

He fell into silence over his roast beef and pork, a silence which his wife could not allow for long.

'What are you thinking of, Malcolm, pray tell?' Lady Hulme asked. She did not drink port for it made small red veins come out on her nose.

'Do you remember, my dear, that old chap we dug up in the church when we put in the hot-water pipes?' the Earl asked with entire irrelevance.

'Father, what makes you think of him now?' Emory asked.

'He'd been lying there a hundred and fifty years, you know, and his bones were as good as anything, white as chalk, but holding together, you know,' the Earl replied.

Lady Hulme was diverted by the memory. She remembered perfectly clearly the June morning years ago when the men

370

came to say that they had struck a coffin in Hulme Abbey and both of them had gone over to look at it. The coffin was only wood and was quite gone really except for bits of metal, but there in the dust lay the most beautiful silvery skeleton. Luckily it was not a Hulme ancestor but some physician who had served the family and had been given the honour of burial in the abbey.

'You don't think that he took drugs or something that kept his bones hard?' she now asked.

'Might have,' the Earl conceded. 'Still, perhaps it was only the dryness of the abbey, eh? Maybe the hundreds of sermons the vicars preached, eh?'

He choked on his own humour and exploded into frightful coughing. Lady Hulme waited. He choked rather easily nowadays, especially on port. When he subsided, red-eyed and gasping, she felt it wise to change the subject, lest he be tempted to another joke.

Before she could speak Emory lifted her head.

'Hark—— Isn't that the horses?' They listened.

'Yes,' she exclaimed. 'It's William.'

She got up with her stealing grace and went out, and Lady Hulme said aloud what she had been thinking.

'Do you like Emory's husband—really, I mean?'

'How could anybody like him?' the Earl replied in a voice restored to common sense. 'There is something feverish in him.'

'I thought he seemed as cool as anything today.'

'He is the sort that burns inside, you know, my dear, like that what's-his-name from India that we dined with once at Randford. I don't know how the Earl felt but I know I was jolly glad to be away after dinner.'

'What's-his-name' was a small dark man named Mohandas Gandhi. He had come over to England for conferences and he had refused to wear proper clothes or eat proper food. The Government had been compelled to recognize him, nevertheless, and there was a frightful picture of him taken with the King and wearing almost nothing—just the bed sheet or whatever it was that he wrapped about his nakedness. It did

371

seem that when a man came to a civilized country he might behave better. When the Earl of Hulme had muttered as much behind his moustache to the Earl of Randford, his host had smiled and murmured in reply:

'You are simple, my dear fellow. Gandhi is too clever for you. His hold on the masses of India is immense just because he won't wear anything but the sheet. That's what the peasants wear and they like to think that one of them wears a sheet right in the presence of you and me and even the King. It makes them trust him. If he put on striped trousers and a morning coat, they'd think he had betrayed them.'

The Earl of Hulme had been stupefied by such independence and now felt that if something had been done about it then India would not be dreaming today of getting away from the Empire. What would happen to the world if men were allowed to come into the presence of their betters dressed like goat-herds? Upon that day he had stared a good deal at the small man whose perpetual smile was as cool as a breeze, and after an hour of this persistent gaze he had discerned beneath the coolness what he called the fever. He recognized it because he had seen it elsewhere. There had been a curate in his youth who had burned to improve the lot of the tenants, and he had seen the old Earl, his father, fly into fury.

'Read your Bible, sir!' the old nobleman had thundered at the tall, hungry-eyed curate. 'Does it or does it not say that I am to put my tenants into palaces?'

'It says the strong must bear the burdens of the weak', the foolhardy man had replied.

That was the curate's end. He had killed himself as nicely as though a rope had been put about his neck. He had left in disgrace and was never heard of again. But young Malcolm, watching, had felt the fever burning inside that lean frame. On the last day, when he thought the curate had gone, he found himself face to face with him in the park. The chap had walked about to find him.

'Malcolm——' That was what the man had actually dared to call him. 'Malcolm, you are young and perhaps you will listen to me.'

'I don't understand,' he had stammered, angry and taken aback at such daring.

'Don't try to understand now,' the curate had urged. The fever was plain enough then. You could see the flames leaping up beside him somewhere and shining through his pale eyes. 'Just remember this—unless the hungry are fed, you will be driven away from all this. It is coming, mind you—you've got to save yourself. I warn you, hear the voice of God!'

He had wheeled without answer and left the curate standing there and he had not once looked back.

'Nonsense,' Lady Hulme now said. 'William is a very handsome man. I don't see the least resemblance to any Hindu, not to speak of that odd man.'

She broke off, noticing how brightly the sun shone through the bottle of port. Suddenly she felt that it was a pity not to taste so beautiful a liquid. If her nose grew red it would not matter—poor Malcolm had long since ceased to notice how she looked. She poured herself a glass of the rich port, very slowly, the sun filtering through the crimson wine.

. . . Outside in the soft English sunshine Emory was listening to the last fragments of a conversation which had been of more than American tractors.

'I can't tell yet whether it's good or bad,' Michael said. 'I can only say that there's something new happening in Germany and Italy. New, or maybe something very old, I can't tell which. If it goes well it'll be a new age for Europe and therefore the world. I don't think things will go well.'

'You don't believe that democracy will work in Europe, do you?' William asked.

'Of course not,' Michael said impatiently. 'But it's these chaps—Hitler, you know, and Mussolini. They've no breeding. Get a common man at the top and ten to one he can't keep his senses about him.'

Emory cried out, wary of a certain reserve in William's look, 'Oh, Michael, how silly of you. As if we weren't all common at bottom! Who was the first Earl of Hulme, pray? A constable of Hulme Castle, that's all, and a traitor against his King, at that.'

373

Michael was stubborn. 'That's just what I said. He couldn't keep his senses. He got thinking he was greater than the King.'

'What happened to him?' William asked with restrained curiosity.

'The Queen Mother got her back up,' Michael said. 'There was a long siege and our arrogant ancestor was starved into obedience.' He lifted his whip. 'You'll see the marks of the battle there, though it was more than five hundred years ago.'

Upon the thick stone walls were ancient scars and William gazed at them. 'A very good argument against everybody's having enough food,' he said thoughtfully. 'Food is a weapon. The best, perhaps, in the world!'

The day ended peacefully as usual; but William was restless during the night and rose early. He wanted, he explained to Emory, to go to Germany and see for himself. To Germany then they went.

In Berlin William had suddenly decided that he wanted Emory to see Peking. He had met Hitler and had been reassured. Out of post-war confusion and the follies of the Weimar government, Hitler was building the faith of the German people in themselves and their destiny. The whole country was waking out of despair and discouragement. Trains were clean and on time, and Berlin itself was encouraging.

'There was nothing to worry about here,' William said in some surprise. 'I don't know what Michael was talking about.'

After his talk with Hitler he was even more pleased. 'The man is a born leader,' he told Emory, 'a Carlylean figure.' It was then that William decided to go to China, telling Emory that he felt that he could never explain himself to her altogether unless she saw the city of his childhood. They boarded a great Dutch plane that carried them to India and Singapore and from there they flew to China. Of India Emory saw nothing and did not ask to see anything. Cecil's family had been dependent upon India and her curiosity had died with him.

They spent nearly two weeks in Peking. They wandered about among the palaces, now open to tourists, and William searched the painted halls, the carved pavilions, for the throne room where as a child his mother had led him before the Empress.

'William, after all this time, can you remember?' Emory asked, unbelieving.

'I remember the Empress as though she had set a seal upon me,' William replied.

He found the room at last and the very throne, but in what dust and decay!

'This is the place,' William said.

They stood together in silence and looked about them. The doors were barred no more and pigeons had dirtied the smooth tiled floors. The gold upon the throne had been scraped off by petty thieves and even the lazy guard who lounged in the courtyard offered them a sacred yellow tile from the roof for a Chinese dollar. William shook his head.

'I wonder,' Emory said in a low voice, 'if one day Buckingham Palace will be like this?'

'I cannot imagine it,' William replied, and as though he could not bear the sight before them, he turned abruptly from the throne. 'Let us go. We have seen it.'

'Perhaps it would have been better not to have seen it,' she suggested. 'It might have been better to remember it as it was.'

To this William did not reply.

There was something of the same decay in the compound where he had been born and which had been his home. It was not empty. A thin little missionary was there, a pallid man who came to the door of the mission house, a shadow of a man, William thought with contempt, a feeble small fellow to take his father's place! The little man looked at them with bewildered and spectacled eyes.

'This was Dr. Lane's house, I believe,' William said, and did not tell him who he was.

'That was a long time ago,' the mild man said.

'May we look over the house?' Emory asked. 'We knew Dr. and Mrs. Lane.'

'I suppose so—my wife isn't in just now—she's gone to the Bible women's meeting.'

'Never mind,' William said suddenly. 'I have no desire to see the house.'

They left at once and William, she divined, was thinking of his father. He thought a great deal of his father in those days in Peking—sometimes with the old bitterness but more often with a longing wonder at the happiness in which his father seemed to live.

'My father was anchored in his faith,' William said. 'I have often envied him his ability to believe.'

Emory said at this moment what she had been thinking about for a long time. 'I do think, William, that you ought to see a priest. A Catholic, if possible.'

He turned upon her his dark look. 'Why?' But she fancied he was not surprised.

She responded with her gaze of clear kindness. 'I cannot give you peace,' she said. 'If peace is what you need——'

He denied this abruptly. 'I don't need peace.'

'Whatever it is you need,' she amended.

He did not reply to this but she did not forget his silence. They left Peking soon after that day, and in a few weeks were in New York and William plunged into feverish work.

Left to herself, Emory went out more than she had before. Even she was getting restless. The world was so strange, so full of horrible possibilities!

At a cocktail party one day many months later Emory observed an unusual figure, and seeing it was reminded of the unforgotten conversation in Peking. A tall cassocked priest stood near the door. He had an angular worn face and quietly gazing at him as she drank tea instead of cocktails she saw his hands, worn and rough, tightly clasped before him. His hair was a dark auburn and his skin was florid. As though he felt her eyes, he looked at her. His eyes were very blue. She turned her head and at the same moment she felt hands upon her shoulders. Looking up then she saw Jeremy Cameron, and she smiled at him. 'Jeremy, you wretch, you and Ruth haven't come near us since we came home!'

'Ruth is still at the seaside with the children. She'll be back

Monday. Here's someone who wants to meet you. Emory, this is Father Malone—my sister-in-law, Father, Lady Emory Hulme or Mrs. William Lane, as you please.'

Jeremy had been drinking, she saw. The dark pupils of his eyes were huge and set in reddened whites and his thin smooth cheeks were flushed.

She turned to smile at Father Malone. He stooped over her hand. 'It is your husband I really want to meet and this explains my presence at an occasion so strange to me,' he said in a rugged voice. 'I've just come from China, where I believe he was born.'

'Oh, I'm glad.' Genuine gladness indeed was in her voice. 'Why not come home with me now? We can talk a little while before my husband comes in. He'll be late. We were in China, ourselves.'

'I heard,' Father Malone said simply.

Jeremy rocked back and forth on his heels. 'William was looking at Father Malone's pictures today—wonderful pictures—people starving to death, somewhere in China of course—babies like dead mice, their arms and legs—wonderful. He hadn't time to meet Father Malone himself and turned him over to me. He wants the pictures, though.'

'Famine,' the priest said simply. 'That's why I am here. I am sent to collect funds.'

His dark eyes were magnetic. Emory found herself looking at him and then not looking away quickly enough. He did not mind how long she gazed at him, and there was no personal response from him to a beautiful woman.

'Do let's go.' She got up impulsively.

The controlled grace of her movements was self-conscious and yet none the less graceful. They left in a few minutes, the priest a handsome yet ascetic shadow behind her, and in the comfortable sound-proof car, riding through the evening traffic in perfect quiet, she put her questions. Father Malone answered them with simplicity and frankness, or so she thought. Yes, he had been many years in China, not in Peking, or the big cities, but in his own mission in a country region. He was a country priest and had been twenty years there

377

'You must have been very young when you first went.'

Yes, he had been young, only a little more than twenty-five. He had gone to help an older priest, who had died after a few years, of cholera, and then he had carried on

'Do you feel your work is successful?'

'I do not think of success.' The sombre voice, expressive of any emotion one might choose to imagine, made music of every word. 'In the long process of the Church one man's work is only a link in the chain of eternity.'

'I do believe,' she said, with purposeful frankness, 'that you have been sent to me at this particular moment. I will not pretend that I am a religious woman for by looking at me you will see that I am not. But I love my husband and he needs something I cannot give him. He is a naturally religious man, and he does not know it. He has grown rich so fast. You know his father was a missionary.'

'I do know,' Father Malone said. 'That is why I have come to him first—that and his great wealth.'

'His father was a Protestant, of course,' Emory went on. 'I never knew him, but he has left an indelible impression upon William's soul. William, being a very clever man, can scarcely accept the sort of religion that his father had. He will need something much more subtle, if I may say so.'

'The Church has everything for all souls,' Father Malone said. His voice, so full of confidence, his mild and handsome profile gazing ahead into the turmoil of the crowded streets, renewed Emory's admiration without in the least moving her heart. But then, her heart knew no hungers.

The heavy car drew up at the house and the chauffeur sprang out and opened the door of the car. They mounted the marble steps. The evening air was sweet and cold, and the lights of the city were twinkling. At the top of the steps Emory touched the bell and upon impulse that seemed sudden she looked up at the tall priest.

'I'm very happy. I want my husband to be happy too.'

'Why not?' Father Malone replied. He smiled down upon her, celibate and ascetic though he was, and by that smile he made himself her ally.

378

William, coming in later than he had said he would, paused as Henry took his things. He heard a man's voice.

'Who is here?' he demanded.

'A friend of madame's, sir. He's a priest, sir. She brought him home with her. He's to stay for dinner, sir.'

Henry disappeared and William went quietly up the stairs. And why a priest? He was fearfully tired and wanted to be alone. The old sense of emptiness was creeping back into him again though he had been married so few years. He avoided knowing it. If Emory could not fill the emptiness then nowhere on earth could he find peace. He refused thought and began instead to worry about lesser matters. Jeremy, for example, getting drunk and coming into the office to announce loudly his disgust with his job and with everything and that he wouldn't resign and wanted to be fired! He would have to talk with Ruth as soon as she came back. She ought not to linger on at the seaside, leaving Jeremy at loose ends.

He shrugged his shoulders abruptly. Why should he, in his position, be troubled about anyone? The familiar hard surface crept over his mind and spirit and he proceeded to bathe and dress in his usual evening garments, laid out for him by his valet. He was hungry. The day at the office had been long and the proofs of his editorial more than usually full of mistakes. He would have to find another editor. It seemed stupid that his young men could not adjust themselves to his demands. He kept them young, letting them go soon after thirty-five, because youth was essential to the style he had developed.

His mind, ranging among faces and men, lingered upon Seth James. He had not seen Seth for a long time, but he had kept within his knowledge all that Seth had done since the success of his play on Broadway. Seth had started another magazine which had failed. William's private scouts told him that Seth had lost more than a million dollars on it. Perhaps it was time to bring him back—if he wanted him. But could Seth be convinced? He might talk to Emory about it, get her, perhaps, to go after Seth. She had a sort of integrity which he could neither fathom nor reach.

He had not told her that a few days ago he had met Candace

379

upon the street, and had hesitated, not knowing whether to speak or not. She had decided the matter quickly by putting out her gloved hand.

'William, surely you won't just pass without speaking?'

He took her hand, felt embarrassed, tried to smile. 'I wasn't sure you'd want to.'

'There is no reason why I wouldn't want to speak to you, William.'

'How is your father?'

'Just letting himself get old—sleeping a good deal, a saintly stillness over him, all the time.'

'I hope he doesn't dislike me?'

'He doesn't dislike anybody.'

They stood between two passing streams of people and he was afraid one of the damned gossip columnists might see them together and put out a story in a newspaper or on the air. This was intolerable and so he had lifted his hat abruptly and left her. There was no reason to tell Emory. The meeting meant nothing.

When he was dressed the emptiness came over him again. It was more than emptiness. He felt a strange and puzzling gnawing of the heart which he could not explain. What was he doing that he should ask himself how much money he had. There was more than he could possibly spend with his decent and frugal tastes. His houses were finished and beautiful and to Emory he gave an income extravagantly large. Candace, too, he had not stinted and his sons both had had allowances beyond their needs. His yearly gift to his father's mission was a solid foundation upon which others built. For his mother he had arranged an annuity of ten thousand a/year. He had done everything he ought to do.

He should perhaps have entered politics long ago, instead of building his newspapers. This thought, disturbing him very much, caused him to sit down in his leather easy chair and close his eyes. His small hairy hands gripped the carved ends of the hand-rests. He should not have been content with the power of shaping the minds of people by choosing what pictures they should see, what news they should read, what ideas, in short, should be offered to their minds. This was only passive government. There was nothing stable in America. This country which William longed to love and did love with fear and anger and contempt, had no bedrock of class, no governing element such as England had. Wealth was the only vantage. William despised charm and knew that he had none of it. And yet without it, he knew, he could never have won, not in America, not in this, his own country. Think of that fellow in the White House! He gave up the notion of politics and opened his eyes. He could not descend to the sordid race. Besides, what if he had been defeated? Folly, folly! He was pre-eminent as he was and without a rival in sight. What more did he want than he had? He wanted to be satisfied with himself and he was not.

A tap at his door made him get up and go to the window. 'Come in!'

'Madame asks if you are ready, sir,' Henry said behind his back.

'I am coming down at once.'

He passed the man and went down the wide curving stairs, comforted for the moment as he often was by the vista of his home, the huge beautiful rooms spreading from the great entrance hall. He ought indeed to be satisfied with himself. Roger Cameron had been satisfied with half of this. Scrambling up that cliff, those years ago, he had not dreamed of such a vista, all his own.

He crossed the hall and went into the drawing-room at the right. A tall figure rose at his entrance and stood with clasped hands. Emory spoke from a low rose-red velvet chair.

'William, this is Father Malone. He was in your office today with some pictures and Jeremy brought him along to the cocktail party, and I brought him home to you.'

The strong hands unclasped and the priest put out the right one, not speaking. William felt it powerfully about his own much smaller hand, and quickly withdrew it.

'I am sorry I was busy when you were announced in the office today,' he said, looking away. He took a glass of sherry from a silver tray presented now by the butler.

Father Malone sat down. A perfect quiet pervaded his being and from this quiet he looked at William so steadily that William felt himself compelled to respond, and turning he looked down into the profoundly dark and deep-set eyes.

'The reason I brought him home,' Emory went on, 'is because Father Malone comes from some place quite near Peking and I thought you would enjoy one another.'

William sat down. 'Indeed?'

'Your father was a missionary?'

'Yes.'

'I, too, am a missionary,' Father Malone said after a moment. 'I have been recalled for a time to collect famine funds. I brought with me the pictures which you saw today. I hoped that you would want to print them for I am told your publications reach millions of Americans, and they might be moved to send me money for food.'

'Thousands of pictures come to me every week,' William said. 'I may not be able to use many of yours. Besides, we have our own photographers who know exactly what I want.'

'You do not feel moved to present the appeal for the starving?' The priest's deep voice was calm and inquiring.

'I hesitate to embark upon relief work,' William replied. 'One doubts the basic efficacy of it in a country so vast as China. Famine is endemic there, as I remember.'

'You feel no duty towards those people?'

William looked at him again unwillingly. 'Only in memory of my father.'

'You deny the memory,' Father Malone said. So positive was his voice that William was instantly angry.

'Dinner is served,' the butler announced at the door.

They rose, Emory first in her rose and grey taffeta, and behind her Father Malone, stark and severe in his black garments, and William a little distance behind him. The priest's words had fallen upon his angry heart like a sword.

'You have been stifling your soul,' Father Malone said to William Lane. He was very tired. The special mission which he had assumed as he came to know William was nearly completed. It had not been easy, far more difficult indeed than feeding the starving children and praying for the ignorant peasants who were his flock in China. The Church there was gracious to the ignorant. It did not expect a peasant to understand the mysteries. To come to Mass, to wear an amulet, to know the name of the Virgin and one or two saints was as much as he insisted upon in his village. Even confession he did not press, for how could an old man or even a young woman confess when they did not know sin? The knowledge of sin was for their children, the second generation, and in that knowledge it was his duty to instruct them. By the fifth generation he expected a priest. The Church was infinitely patient.

'You have denied your Lord,' he said.

He had tarried for days in this vast and wicked city, for so he had felt he should do. Yet when he found that the wife of this rich and powerful man believed that her husband sought God, he had felt unable to undertake so vast a responsibility alone. He had gone immediately to his local superior, Monsignor John Lockhart, to ask for direction.

John Lockhart was an Englishman, a priest of high intellect and conviction, who might have become a Cardinal of the Church had he been ambitious. But he did not wish to enter into the higher arenas, where, he thought, though without disloyalty, the air was not so pure as it might have been. Princes of the Church were subject, perhaps, to some of the temptations of earthly kings. This did not keep him from believing that the Church was the best means yet devised and developed for the guidance and control of weak and faulty human nature. He listened carefully to the shabby priest from China, who sat on the edge of his chair and talked diffidently about William Lane.

'A man stubborn in his own pride,' Monsignor Lockhart said after listening. 'Nevertheless he has seen religious righteousness in his father and he cannot forget it. He was reared with a conscience. He has repudiated it until now. As you have told me, you have had only to look at his face to see it tortures him.'

'Does he know it?' Father Malone asked.

'No, and it is your duty to make it known to him,' Monsignor replied.

Father Malone did not answer this. He continued to sit on the edge of his chair, his hands clasped in front of him in his habitual manner. He knew what he was, a missionary priest, a hewer of wood and a drawer of water in the palaces of the Church.

'In famine times I know that many souls are driven to the Church,' Monsignor continued. 'It is our duty to feed body and soul. But sometimes there is one man who can at a certain moment be worth more to the Church than ten thousand others, and William Lane is one of them. He is very powerful and he does not know what to do with his power. He seeks to direct but he himself needs direction. In his discontent he has married again, but he cannot be satisfied with women. His hunger is of the soul.'

Father Malone had listened, and had prayed, when he was alone again, that he might see clearly what he ought to do. He did not presume to approach God directly with his own words, but while his lips murmured the beautiful Latin syllables his heart poured into them his own desire to draw to God this singular and powerful man  The task was not easy and he knew, in his humility, that he could not complete it. It would be necessary for some higher priest, some more astute mind, to fulfil the mission, perhaps the Monsignor himself. There were distances in William Lane that a common priest like himself could not reach, and depths from which he shrank.

'You have told me more than once that I have denied my Lord,' William now said with some impatience. 'I am not aware that I have done so.'

Father Malone was alarmed at the fierceness of William's eyes, at the vehemence in his voice. He had lived long among a gentle people and he missed them. His soul loathed the flesh-pots among which he sojourned. At Monsignor's command he had continued to accept William's hospitality and he had a room and a bath here in this velvet-lined house. The bed was

384

soft and he could not sleep upon it, and at night he had at first laid himself upon the floor and even the floor was too soft with carpet and undercarpet. Then he found that the bathroom floor was of marble and upon that surface he laid himself and found it warmed with inner pipes. He longed for his earthen-floored cell and for the icy mornings of a northern Chinese winter and a bowl of millet gruel. The flash of silver and the smoke of hot meats upon the lace-covered table in this house filled him with a sense of sin. How could he speak of God here? And the woman, telling him again and again how much he did for her husband and all the time she herself took not one word of what he said to herself!

He went increasingly often to Monsignor for counsel and he had said on his last visit, only two days ago, 'Would it not be well to separate the man from the luxury which surrounds him? How can we find his soul when it is sunk in the flesh-pots?'

Monsignor had looked at him out of deep, shrewd eyes. 'In what sense separate?' he inquired.

'William Lane is at heart an ascetic,' Father Malone replied. 'He possesses much, but he eats little and his ways are frugal. He does not drink much wine, he does not often smoke tobacco. We could make a priest out of him could we get him alone into the wilderness. If I took him back to my village, I could even entice him to love the people, which is the beginning of righteousness.'

'To what end?' his superior inquired.

Father Malone was astonished. 'To the end that his soul may be saved!'

Monsignor got up and walked about his library. It was a noble room, and the mahogany book-shelves reached from floor to ceiling. He had the finest religious library in America and was among its most learned prelates, in spite of his lack of religious ambitions.

'You go beyond your duty,' he said sharply. 'I have told you only to awaken his soul.'

'I have done so,' Father Malone replied. He was almost as uneasy here as he was in William's house. It was not for him

385

to question the ways of his superiors. The Holy Father himself lived in a great palace which was one of the wonders of the world. God used riches as well as poverty for His own glory, he reminded himself.

'Continue then until you receive my next instruction,' Monsignor said.

So Father Malone had gone back to the rich house again. At this moment, however, when he sat alone with William in the silent opulent room, remote from any life he knew, he felt that the end of his work had surely come and that he must beg his superior to release him. He knew that William did deny his Lord, for he felt denial everywhere in this house, in William and in his wife and in the very existence of this place and in all it contained. But he could not explain how he felt this or why. Monsignor had not approved his speaking of poverty. Had he not received this disapproval he would have said earnestly to William, 'You must give up all this and follow Christ.' But he did not dare to say this. He felt puzzled and tired and in spite of constant refusal he knew that he had eaten too much and too richly. Sitting in a high-back Jacobean chair which he chose because it alone had a hard wooden seat, he twisted his work-worn hands.

'It is time for me to leave you,' he said to William. 'I have been detained by God to remind you of your father and of the land where you were born and to guide you to think of these things. Beyond that I am not able to go. I must commend you to Monsignor Lockhart, who is a wiser man in the Church than I am. I have no great learning. My books are fewer than a hundred. He has thousands of books upon his shelves and in many languages. He is continually in communication with those who know the Holy Father, whose face I shall never see.'

William did not deny this. He had indeed been stirred to the bottom of his soul by Malone. He envied the priest his unmoving faith, his confidence in prayer, his conviction of duty, the same faith, confidence, and conviction which his own father had possessed. But William was not able to proceed beyond the impulse of envy and of longing. His spiritual hunger had been increased and not satisfied. His loneliness was more and not less.

'Perhaps you are right,' he said. 'Yet I am very grateful for what you have done.'

'It is not I but God working through me.'

'Then I thank God. Perhaps, in spite of not seeing it yet, my feet have, nevertheless, been set upon a path.'

'Monsignor Lockhart will lead you the rest of the way,' Father Malone replied.

Upon this they parted. In a short time Father Malone had packed his Chinese bag of split and woven rattan, and he refused the offer of William's car. 'I must report to my superior,' he said, 'and it is only a short distance upon this same Avenue. Let me walk. It will make me feel I am on my way home.'

William was perceptive enough to know what he meant and he let him go.

When Emory came home in the late afternoon she missed at once the third presence in the house. She had been on an ordinary errand to have her hair dressed, and when Henry opened the door to her he told her that the master had not returned to his office. She found William in the rather small room which they used as a sitting-room when they were alone. He was stretched upon a reclining chair, gazing into the coals of a dying fire. He had not put on the lights, and there was a strange atmosphere of life and death in the room. She touched the switch by the door and the wall lights flamed.

'William, are you ill?' she exclaimed.

'No,' he replied. 'I have been thinking all afternoon. Father Malone has gone.'

'Gone?'

'He says he wants me to go directly now to Monsignor Lockhart. He thinks it is time.'

She came to him and knelt at his side and put her hand on his that were folded across his body. 'William, please do only what you wish!' she now said.

He moved his hands from under hers rather sharply. 'No one can make me do otherwise!'

'But be sure that you know if they try.'

'You don't flatter me, Emory. I am usually considered astute enough.'

He was determined to be hurt and she refused to hurt him. 'I'm being stupid.' She got up and then sat down in a chair opposite him. 'It's hot in here. Shan't I open the window?' The house with its central heating was always too hot for her English blood.

'I am not hot.'

I suppose it's because I have just come in from outside.'

She sat still for a few minutes, and then stealing a look at William she grew alarmed at the whiteness of his face. She got up again and went to him and curled on the floor beside him. She took his hand and leaned her cheek against it and made to him a complaint she had never made before.

'You haven't loved me all the time Father Malone's been here.' She put the palm of his hand against her soft red mouth.

Among the American women she was learning to know, there was shrewd interchange at once cynical and enjoyed by them. 'You don't know your man until you've slept with him,' was the common creed. They were all healthy handsome women, to whom chastity was not a jewel without price. Yet not one of them would have entertained the possibility of a lover, for their husbands were richer than potential lovers and men of position which they did not care to threaten. The difference between men, they frankly acknowledged, lay in their bank accounts rather than in their persons. They considered themselves exceedingly fortunate women and so they intended to live virtuously. But Emory was virtuous by nature.

She felt the palm under her lips tighten. It was impossible for William to speak of love. She crushed her mouth against his palm, tasting its flavour of soap and salt. If within a moment he did not respond she would laugh at herself and tease him for being so earnest about everything. 'Don't be so serious, darling—let's go drown ourselves somewhere! Nobody will notice the difference and it would be fun. Something we've never done before!'

But tonight she would not need such nonsense. She recognized the familiar signs, the tightening of nerve and muscle, the response to his strangely awkward, rather short fingers. He sat up suddenly and drew her against him and she held her breath. He was always abrupt and unsharing but she was used to that now. He had to dominate her and though she had resisted this at first, now she no longer did so. Sex for a woman was nothing. It expressed no part of her being. It was an act of play, of symbolic yielding, a pleasant gesture, pleasing to receive and to give, a thing to forget, the preliminary to a possible experience of motherhood with which the man had little to do. She had decided against motherhood when she saw Will and Jerry. Candace had given William his sons and she divined that more sons would be meaningless for him and for her. With Cecil's death had gone any need for a son of her own. She divined also that William could care nothing for daughters.

'Lock the door,' William commanded her. . . . She had a healthy body and she did not shrink from whatever William demanded. She accepted sex in exactly the same way that she enjoyed a cup of tea or a meal. There was nothing mysterious about it or even very interesting. What was interesting was William. She got to know him better in this brief occasional half-hour than she could in a month of living. There was something cruel about him—no, not actually cruel, but he needed frightfully to be sure that he was right. Somewhere along the way of his childhood and his youth he had been so wounded in his self-love that now he knew best, he always knew best. And yet his self-confidence, his wilfulness, his determination to make others obey him was not solid to the bottom of him. Sometimes when she had obeyed him utterly his command broke. He could not go on. He was not sure of himself. But why not? Who threatened him now?

So it happened tonight. In this quiet hour between day and night, when the servants were busy in the remote regions of the house, they had the complete privacy he demanded. Father Malone was gone. It could not have happened had he been in the house. And still William could not succeed. The fiasco came as it had sometimes before, though not always. Then why tonight?

She waited a moment to make sure that it was to be so, and then it was so. He lay back exhausted without fulfilment. She buried her head against him, and began stroking his hand gently. It was listless and he did not speak a word. He never did.

This went on for what seemed an endless time. The room grew darker. Somewhere, at last, far off, the gong rang warning that dinner was only half an hour off. She let his hand fall and felt a wave of relief. Better luck perhaps, next time!

'I think Father Malone was right,' she said in her ordinary voice. 'I do think you ought to go and see Monsignor Lockhart.'

XI

WHEN the Second World War broke out Clem made up his mind to ignore it. 'Let her blaze,' he told Henrietta in cosmic anger. 'It's all got beyond me.'

'Aren't you going to close the restaurants now?' Henrietta had asked when people were working again on war jobs.

'I've been thinking about that,' Clem said. 'I don't want to be in the restaurant business. I guess I'll let the fellows have them. They can set up for themselves somewhere or they can stay where they are. They've got to promise me, though, that they'll keep giving free meals when necessary.'

'Since they've made money, I imagine they won't mind that,' Henrietta said. Chinese could always take care of themselves with ancestral prudence.

By that time the government had ordered surpluses given outright to hungry people. Nobody knew how much of this giving away was the fruit of a certain day when Clem at last sat with that fabulous man in the White House who could not stand up unless somebody helped him. Clem got on well with him. He tried to remember that the man behind the big desk covered with small objects was the President of the United States, but most of the time he forgot it. They talked all over the world. The man behind the desk showed extraordinary knowledge and also profound ignorance, and he did not care who knew it. Clem tried to tell him about China and then gave up. There was too much the man did not know. He knew as little about India, and believed that the only problem there was too many people, and Clem laboured earnestly to make him see this was not true. India could produce plenty of food for many more people.

'China, for instance, is nearly self-supporting in food,' Clem said. 'She doesn't import anything hardly. She grows immense amounts of food.'

'Seems to me I've heard of starving Chinese all my life,' said the man with the big smile.

'That's because they need railways and truck highways,' Clem said. 'They can't move surpluses. They starve in spots. It's the world situation in a big nutshell. Before you can have a steady peace, you've got to be able to move surpluses.'

The war had broken out in China and in Europe and it meant that in China at least there would be fewer new highways than ever. Still the big man did not care much about China. That was to come later. Clem went away attracted and confounded. The big man didn't see the world as round. For him it was flat. He couldn't imagine the underneath. The whole world would have to blaze with war before the big man understood that the world was one big round globe.

It had never been easy for Clem to write letters but when he got home to Henrietta he began the series of letters which were his effort to educate the man who didn't know the world was round. Sometimes these letters were long but usually they were not. The big man never answered them or acknowledged them himself, but Clem hoped that he read them. In them he tried to put down all he knew, including excerpts from the letters which Yusan wrote him.

'Of course we ought to help lick the Japs in China now,' Clem wrote, 'but that is just the first step. As far as that goes the war really began when we let them have Manchuria. The next real job will come after the war when Chiang Kai-shek will have to hold his people together. It is easier for a soldier to keep on fighting than it is to get down to the necessary peace. It will be the Communists next, for sure, and that's what we have got to reckon with. My advice now is to give some little hint of friendship for the people of India so as to begin to win friendship from Asia. I know you don't want to get Winston worked up, but you could just say a word or two in the direction of India in your next fireside chat and this would please Indians by the million as well as Chinese. If you would say you believe in the freedom of peoples but say it now, within this week, which is a time of crisis we don't know anything about over here, it would mean everything. Next month would be too late. They are all waiting.'

Clem had bought his first radio especially to hear the President, but he did not say one word about India or the freedom of the peoples in his next fireside talk. The famous voice came richly over the wires. 'My friends . . .' but it didn't reach as far as China or India or Indonesia. Clem listened to the last rousing words and shut off the radio and was gloomy for so long that Henrietta was worried. She and Clem were no longer young and she wished that he could stop his world-worrying. Other people would have to take over and if they didn't, it could not be helped. Clem's stomach had been better after the depression but this Second World War was making it worse again.

When she said something like this to Clem he would not listen to her. 'I'm used to my stomach by now, hon. It hasn't won out on me yet.'

'You haven't won out either, Clem,' she said sharply. 'It's a continual struggle and you know it.'

He grinned at her, although there was nothing cheerful to grin about. Pearl Harbour had done him as much damage internally as it had done the Hawaiian Islands and he did not dare to tell Henrietta that all his old symptoms had returned, and that he was afraid to eat.

When America had finally swung into war he offered himself as a super-cook and was actually put in charge of the mess halls and kitchens of barracks near Dayton. While the war went on and he still continued his long-distance education of the White House, conducted without any response whatever, Clem made some thousands of American boys happy by excellent food and pleasant dining halls where they were allowed to smoke and where cages of singing canaries brightened up their meals. Outside the dining-room Clem made the administration furious by the economics he suggested and even put into force so that his regiments, as he called them, became notorious or longed for, depending upon whether a man was brass or buttons.

Clem himself considered it piddling. He was marking time

until the end of the war when he intended to marshal all his theories into one vast gospel and present them to the White House and then to the nations. He had long ago forgotten William's rebuff and he remembered now only the grace and kindness of William's wife, and he dreamed secretly without telling Henrietta that after the war was over he would go back to William, not this time to advocate a theory but with a formula in his hand, a formula for a food so cheap that until the world got its distribution fixed up, people could still be kept from starving.

He set up a small laboratory in the basement of the house and with Henrietta to help him with her knowledge of chemistry refurbished and brought up to date with some new books, he began to work with the best soy-beans he could get, the beans that Chinese farmers grew for their own food. Clem planted these seeds and tended them like hot-house asparagus, and as the war continued his harvests grew until he had enough soy-bean meal to make real experiments possible. He and Henrietta ate one formula after another, and studied seasoning and spoilage.

'We ought to have a real food chemist,' Henrietta told him on one of these days. 'I don't know how to get the taste you want, Clem. I don't even know what it is.'

'It's kind of like those meat rolls I used to eat at the Fongs',' Clem said dreamily.

'But you were a half-starved boy then and anything would have been wonderful,' Henrietta suggested.

'Yes, but I never forget.'

Clem never forgot anything. He did not forget how it had felt to be a half-starved boy and his unforgetting mind made him know how people anywhere felt and what they wanted. The man in the White House could have got from Clem an accurate temperature of most of the world's peoples in the crowded countries of Asia, but he did not know it, or even that he needed to know it. Meantime Clem had isolated himself from the war and was living ahead in the years after, when the new world would begin.

'War's nothing but an epidemic,' he told Henrietta. 'If

you don't prevent it in time it comes and then you have to go through with it. I'm glad we have no children, hon.'

'We might have had a girl,' Henrietta said with a wry smile.

'No, I'm glad we haven't. She'd have been in love with a boy.'

The long process whereby William Lane decided to become a Catholic was one of combined logic and faith. His conscience, always his most fretful member, had become irritated beyond endurance by the monstrosity of his success, which was now uncontrollable. He needed to do nothing except to read his newspapers critically and then keep or discharge his editors. From somewhere in his ancestry, distilled through generations of New England lawyers, preachers, and reformers, he had received the gift of the critical mind attuned to his times. Long ago he had become as independent as a feudal baron. His chain of newspapers rested upon the solid properties of his own printing presses, and these in turn were set upon the sure output of his paper mills, which in finality rested upon the firm foundations of timbered land, stretching in miles across spaces of the north, in Canada as well as in the United States. He was impervious to the dangers and restrictions possible even to him, as the war blazed separately first in Asia and then in Europe. A pity about Hitler! Had he been well advised, Hitler could have been a saviour against Communism, the final enemy.

Upon this frightful morning after the attack on Pearl Harbour, when his valet drew the window curtains, William was weighed down by the necessity of making up his mind quickly upon a new policy for his staff. People must know immediately where he stood.

As usual when he felt confusion he decided to talk with Monsignor and he telephoned before he got up.

'Yes, William?' Monsignor said over the telephone. After two years or so, they had come to this intimacy. 'How can I help you?'

'I feel confused,' William replied. 'This war is bringing

many problems. I must decide some of them today. I should like to talk with you this morning before I go to my office.'

'I am at your disposal,' the priest replied.

So William went immediately after he had eaten. Emory always breakfasted in her room, and he saw no one except servants whom he did not count. The morning sun shone down upon the magnificent granite Cathedral near the priest's private home. Both stood in the upper part of the city against a background of skyscrapers, and their solidity was reassuring. Even bombs could scarcely prevail against the ageing grey structure of the Cathedral, as formidable as the medieval castle. He rang the bell at a Gothic doorway and was immediately admitted by a young priest who led him in silence over thick velvet carpets spread upon stone floors. There was not one moment of waiting. It was an atmosphere far more courteous than that of the White House, where last week William had gone to call upon the President, repressing his personal dislike to do his patriotic duty, and had been kept waiting for nearly a quarter of an hour. In the end Roosevelt, though jovial, had not seemed grateful for William's offer of help.

Monsignor's library was a beautiful room. The crimson of the carpets was repeated in the velvet hangings at the Gothic windows, and mahogany bookcases reached to the arched ceilings. The air was warm and slightly fragrant. There was a great deal of gold decoration centring in a massive crucifix that hung in a long alcove, but carried out also in wide gold satin bookmarks, in the frames of two or three fine paintings.

Monsignor Lockhart was a handsome man, erect and dignified. His features were clear and he had fine, deep-set eyes of a clear hard blue.

'Sit down, William,' he said.

William sat down in a cushioned Gothic chair and began to consider his worries. There was nothing wrong in his daily life. He had no sins. He was entirely faithful to his wife and she to him. He knew that Emory, although she was a beautiful woman, was also fastidious, and he trusted her entirely and had never regretted his marriage. In her way she was his equal. There was no man in America above him in influence and few as rich. Had he been English he would of course have had a title. In that case he would have been poorer than he was, and Emory would not have enjoyed poverty. She had the finest jewels of any woman he knew. Emory in soft black chiffon, high at the neck and long sleeved, wearing her diamonds, was all he conceived of as beauty in woman. She had become a Catholic with him, and she liked wearing black chiffon and diamonds. With her dove-grey frocks she wore pearls.

No, his worries were entirely a matter of his responsibilities to the world, to the millions of people who looked at the pictures he alone chose and who read what he allowed to be printed. He wanted God's guidance for this enormous responsibility, and for the stewardship, too, of his vast wealth. He did not want to give his money to any cause or organizations which would not submit to his direction. Unless he directed, he could not be sure of the right use of his support. He never gave money to a person.

He made known his wish to do right, never stronger than now, in view of the mounting war, and Monsignor listened thoughtfully, his hands folded. They were much alike, these two men, and they knew it. Towards human beings they were almost equally paternal. Priest and man, they had already what this world could give.

'I grieve for the peoples,' Monsignor Lockhart said. 'In a war it is the innocent who suffer. The Church must assuage. You, William, must assuage. There will be much sorrow and death. You and I know how to find a comfort more profound, but the people are children and they must be comforted as children. God uses mysterious ways. Riches as well as poverty may serve Him. Continue as you have been doing, William. Do not try to take the people into high and difficult places, where they become afraid. Show them family life, show them love and kindness still alive, the ever protecting power of religion. The Church is eternal, surviving all wars, all catastrophes. Indeed, for us, God uses even wars and catastrophes. When men are afraid and distressed they come

397

to the Church for shelter. So it will be again as it has always been.'

There was an atmosphere of calm reassurance in all the priest said and did. William, listening to that voice, so richly humane, so profoundly dominant, was aware of comfort stealing upon his own soul. It was good to be told that he must do only what he had been doing, good to remember that he was part of the vast historic body of the Church, which continuing through the ages, must continue as long as man lived upon this earth. The order, the structure, the cell-to-cell relationships of the Church comforted him. Outside all was disorder and upheaval but within the Church each had his place and knew it.

The two men were in strange communion. Around them was the deep rich silence of this house, devoted, in its beauty, to God. Although the morning was cold, in the vast velvety room the atmosphere was tempered with warmth and the proper degree of humidity for the leather-bound volumes. Between the two men the fire burned. Under the high-carved mantelpiece the flames quivered intense and blue above a bed of hard coal. Each man admired the other, each knew that his heart was set upon the same goal, each felt the keen thrusting of the other's thought.

Between the two men was the still deeper bond of secret knowledge of each other. Though they spoke with reverence of the Church, each knew that the Church was a net as wide as the world, gathering into itself all men. It was the means of divine order, the opposite of man's chaos.

William sat in long silence. With the priest he felt no need of constant speech. The huge room was restful to him.

'This room is beautiful,' he said at last. 'I have often tried to analyse its effect upon me. I believe that order expresses the secret. Everything has its place and is in its place.'

'Order is the secret of the universe,' the priest replied. 'Only within order can men function.'

An hour later William went away. The wisdom he craved, the guidance he sought, the confirmation of himself and his own will, the approval of what he wanted to do, all these he had found as he always did. He felt strong and dominating and sure of himself. The ancient foundations held. The Church was founded upon a Rock.

He entered his office shortly before noon and the current Miss Smith waited in electric nervousness for the buzz upon her desk that was his summons. When she entered his office he was already sitting behind his semicircular desk and she approached him, trying to smile. It would have been easier if her office had opened to the side of the desk so that she might sit down quickly with her pencil and pad. But there was only one door into the vast imposing room and whoever entered must make the long approach to the spare stern figure sitting behind the semicircle. She reached it at last and drew out her hidden stool and sat down.

'Take a memorandum,' William said. His voice was not in the least haughty and he would have been surprised to know that Miss Smith was afraid of him and often had a fit of crying after she left him.

'Memorandum to the editors,' William said. 'Begin! "I have decided to support the British Empire. For the coming struggle, we must stand with England on the side of order in the world. Further details will follow within the next twenty-four hours." That's all, Miss Smith. I do not wish to be interrupted until I call you.'

He spent the rest of the day alone and in profound thought, writing slowly upon large sheets of heavy white paper. When he had finished his meditation his blueprints were clear. He had mapped out his plans for the next two years. At the end of two years the war should be won or at least victory plain. He felt strong and clear in mind, his pulse was firm, his heart at peace. An impulse of thankfulness welled up in him, and he bowed his head in one of his brief but frequent prayers. He had learned from Monsignor to find in solitary prayer a solace and a release.

He had a flash of intuition now while his head was bent upon his folded hands and his eyes closed. Across the world Chiang Kai-shek also prayed. William had chosen only last week a feature about China's strong man, and among the pictures was one of him at prayer. The Old Tiger, the Chinese called him, and it was a noble name. All strong men prayed. He could go to see the Old Tiger. A vague home-sickness for China swept over his praying soul. Strong men ought to stand together. He would charter a plane, fly the Pacific, and visit China again in the person of that upstanding man.

Such thoughts mingled with his prayer without disturbing it, and when he had finished praying he touched the button of his telephone again. Miss Smith's voice answered, irritatingly weak. She would not last long, he thought with momentary contempt.

'I want to speak to Mrs. Lane,' he commanded. A moment later the buzz told him that his wife waited.

'Emory? Have we anything on for tonight?'

'I half promised we'd go to that opening of the Picasso——'

'Cancel it! I feel that I need some relaxation in view of all that's ahead of me. Let's have dinner at the Waldorf: I'll order a table—and then we'll go to see something at the theatre. What's that new musical? *Night in Peking*?'

'I'd enjoy that. And I'll get the tickets.'

Emory's silvery voice was complacent and sweet. She was always ready to fall in with his wishes. When he had told her he wanted her to enter the Church with him, she had scarcely hesitated a moment.

'I've been thinking about it. I believe a solid religion will be good for you, William,' she had said.

'What do you mean by that?' he had demanded.

'Life isn't enough for you,' she had replied with her strange thoughtfulness. She seemed to think a good deal without letting her thoughts oppress her, or him.

'It will be good for you, too, I think,' he had said.

'Why not?' she had replied, with one of her graceful smiles.

He was very effective that night. There was no fiasco whatever. He must have been successful at something or other at the office, Emory thought, one of his big plans, perhaps, which he would tell her about afterwards. He was all of a piece, this man. Power flowed from him or, locked in him, wrecked his peace of mind and made him impotent. As always he made her his instrument and she did not rebel. Why, indeed, should she? He gave her all she wanted now in the world, which was luxury, which was beauty. Her wants were few but huge, and for beauty money was necessary, plenty of money, a mine of gold, the source inexhaustible. Only William possessed the golden touch nowadays. The old inherited capitalism was almost over, but he was the new capitalist. He had found the fresh source in the need of the people to be amused and to be led. And he led them—he led them into green pastures.

The staff perceived as soon as it congregated for the ferocity of the day's work that there was to be no idleness. William reached the office early and even the least of them understood at once that it was going to be one of his good days. Whatever thought of weariness, whatever listlessness of the night before that any one of them had felt was gone in the instant. Today the utmost would be demanded of them mingled with excitement and some terror. It was doubtful that they would all be at their jobs by night. On William's good days inevitably someone was fired. The weaker members decided not to go out to lunch. William himself never ate lunch.

'Miss Smith,' William said, 'give me all the recent dispatches from China. I want to study them.'

This news from behind the circular desk was telegraphed through the offices and gusts of relief followed. Focus upon China meant focus upon Lemuel Barnard, who had just returned to make his report of the Chinese situation.

The first assistant editor thoughtfully started his search for Lem who at this time of the morning might still be anywhere but certainly not at his desk. Telephone messages began urgently though cautiously to permeate the city. The receptionist in the main entrance, Louise Henry, a pretty auburn-haired girl from Tennessee, stayed by the telephone as much as she dared. She had left Lem somewhere between midnight and dawn at a night club. Shortly before noon, she found him where no one expected him, in bed at his hotel room and asleep. Louise woke him.

'Lem, get over here quick. He's been studying your dispatches all morning!'

'Oh hell,' Lem groaned and rolled out of bed.

At one o'clock William was delayed. Miss Smith brought in an envelope which she recognized as coming from her employer's divorced wife and which therefore she was not to open. She took it in at once to William, though fearful as she did so, for he had left orders that he was not to be disturbed. By then Lem was waiting out in the hall with Louise.

'I don't want to interrupt,' Miss Smith began.

'Well, you have interrupted,' William said.

'This——' Miss Smith faltered. She put the letter on the desk and went out.

William saw at once that it was from Candace. He did not immediately put down the map he was studying. Instead he discovered what he had been looking for, an old camel route from Peking into Sinkiang, and then he put down the map and took up the envelope. So far as he had any contact with Candace she had not changed. The heavy cream paper she always had used when he knew her as his wife, she continued to use. The fine gold lettering of the address simply carried the name Candace Lane instead of Mrs. William Lane. When he slit the envelope and took out the single sheet it contained, she began the letter as she usually did.

'Dear William,

'I have not written you for a good many months because until now there has been nothing to write. You hear from the boys regularly, I hope, and I live here in the same idle way. Today though there is something to write. I am going to be married again. I suppose this would not interest you, except I think I ought to tell you that I am going to marry Seth James. He was in love with me long ago when I was just a girl, before you and I were engaged. We began being friends again after Father died, and now it seems natural to go on into marriage. I expect to be happy. We shall keep on living here. Seth has always liked this house. But we'll have his town house, too. As you probably know, his paper failed, and he lost so much money that he has only enough to live on now and not enough to venture into anything else except maybe another play. But he says he will enjoy just living here with me. We will be married on Christmas Eve. Will and Jerry approve, by the way. It's sweet of them.

'Good-bye, William.

'CANDACE'

The letter was so like her that for a moment William felt an amazing twinge of the heart. Candace was a good woman, childish but good. He had an envious reverence for sheer goodness, the quality his father had possessed in purity, and which he sometimes longed to know that he had. This longing he hid in the secret darkness of his own heart, among those shadows of his being which no one had ever penetrated, even Emory, for whom he felt something more near to admiration than he had ever felt towards any human person. She met him well at every point of his being. Her mind was quicker than his own and he suspected, without ever saying so, that it was more profound. She filled his house with music. Yet, though quite independent of him, she never talked too much, she never led in any conversation when he was present, she deferred to him not with malice as so many women did to men, not with the ostentation which made a mockery of deference. He believed that she admired him, too, and this gave him confidence in himself and in her, although her admiration was not flat and without criticism as Candace's had been. Yet even Emory did not have the pure goodness of which he had been conscious in his father and now perceived unwillingly in Candace.

His eye fell on the letter again. Christmas Eve? He was leaving for China the day after Christmas. This made him remember Lem Barnard. He buzzed long and steadily until Miss Smith came to the door, her pale eyes popped in the way he intensely disliked.

'Tell Barnard to come here,' he commanded. 'I suppose he's about the office?'

'Oh yes, sir, he's been here for hours——' She liked Lem, as everybody did.

William did not answer this. He frowned unconsciously and drummed his fingers upon the table. Within fifty seconds Lem Barnard shambled in, a huge lumbering fellow, over-weight, and wearing as usual a dirty tweed suit. A button was gone from the coat and he needed a haircut.

'Sit down, Lem,' William said. He opened a folder on the desk before him. 'I have been reading over your recent dis-patches. China is going to be very important to us now. We have to have a policy, well defined and clear to everybody. There must be no confusion between editors and reporters. You are to find the sort of news that fits our policy.'

The veins on Lem's temples swelled slightly but William did not look at him. He went on, ruffling the edges of the typed pages as he did so.

'These reports you've sent in for the last three months have been very troublesome. I've had to go over everything myself. There has been little I could use. This is not the time, let me tell you, to bring back gossip and rumours about the Chiangs —either husband or wife.'

Lem exploded, 'I've only told you what Chinese people themselves are saying.'

'I don't care what Chinese people are saying,' William retorted. 'I never care what any people say. I am interested in telling them what to say.'

He tapped the sheets with the tips of his fingers. 'If I were interested in what people say my papers would soon degenerate to gossip sheets. Do you know why they succeed? Because they tell people what to think! You're clever, Lem, but you aren't clever enough. People don't care to read what they already think or what any people think—they know all that well enough. They want to know what they ought to think. It is a spiritual desire, deep in the heart of mankind.'

He stopped and surveyed Lem, sitting huge and gross upon a straight-backed wooden chair. Lem overflowed the narrow

404

seat and it was obvious from his clouded eyes and purplish cheeks that he ate and drank too much wherever he was. He was a disgusting sight.

'Man is a spiritual being,' William said sternly. His enunciation was incisively clear. 'Man seeks truth, he wants divine guidance, he craves security of soul. In all your dispatches remember that, if you please.'

Lem swallowed once again his desire to fire himself, to bawl at William, to cry and howl. He could not afford it. His wife was in an expensive insane asylum. He bit his tongue for an instant and tasted the salt of his own blood. 'Just what impression do you want me to give?' he then inquired in a sultry, gentle voice.

'Our people will now want to believe in the Chinese,' William said. 'They will want to trust the Chinese leadership.'

Lem closed his bloodshot eyes. Against the lids he always saw Chinese faces, the starving, the homeless. War had been going on in China already for five years but nobody here had taken it seriously. Even the Chief here couldn't seem to believe it. Then he thought of his poor wife again, steadily and for a whole minute. Whenever he got angry with William he thought about her. He had been happy with her for two years and she had gone everywhere with him in China. He had met her there in Shanghai, a beautiful White Russian girl, and he had suspected there were things she had never told him and never could tell him. But she had been a wonderful wife and had spoiled him for anybody else.

One morning when he had awakened in the old Cathay Hotel, Lem had found her bending over him with his old-fashioned razor, and he had known that she was about to kill him. He had one instant of horror and then he saw that of course she was mad. She had never been sane since. He had brought her to America himself, sleeping neither by night nor day. She tried to kill anybody who was with her and he could leave her with no one. He put her into an asylum near San Francisco. She never knew him when he went to see her. She always called him something else, names of men he had never heard of. But the bills were terrible every month and if he couldn't pay they would throw her out. It was not every place that would take such a violent case, they told him.

He had to stop seeing the Chinese when he shut his eyes. He had to see just Anastasie. He opened his eyes and said to William in the gentle and sultry voice, 'Chief, I wish you'd go to China yourself. I wish you'd just go and see. You haven't been there for a long time. You ought to go and see what it's like now. Then you'd know——'

'I have already decided to go,' William replied. 'I am going to see the Old Tiger.'

Chungking was a city set upon a hill. The sluggish yellow waters of the river wound around it and the tile-coloured flights of steps led upwards. There was nothing about it that was like Peking. Everything was at once familiar and strange. There were no palaces, no shining roofs, no dignity of marble archways and wide streets. The streets were crowded between grey-brick houses and fog-dampened walls. The cobble-stones were slippery with water and slimy with filth. The people were grim-faced with continuing war and constant bombing. They did not look like the tall handsome people of the north. William was alarmed and dismayed when he thought of these people as the allies of America. What had they to give as allies? They were a danger and a liability. Yet Chiang must be held, he must be compelled, he must be supported.

The American car driven by a uniformed Chinese carried him at once to the Old Tiger's house outside the city. It was reassuring to enter something that did not look like a hovel. The air was chill and damp, as everything was, but from the hall he was led into a square room where a fire blazed.

'Please sit down,' the manservant said in Chinese.

The words smote William's ear with strange accustom. He had not spoken a single Chinese word for years, but the language lay in his memory. He felt syllables rise to his tongue. Perhaps he would be able to speak with Chiang in his own language. The Old Tiger spoke no English. No one knew how much he understood—probably more than he was willing for anyone to know.

The door opened and he looked up. It was not the Tiger who stood there, but a woman, slender and beautiful, her great eyes filled with ready pathos, her exquisite mouth sad. She put out both her hands.

'Mr. Lane. You are America, coming to our aid at last!'

He felt her soft feverish palms against his and was speechless. He did not know what to do with a lovely Chinese woman, one who looked so young, who spoke English naturally. He had never seen this sort of Chinese woman. The ones in Peking had bound feet, unless they were Manchu, but Chinese and Manchu alike they had been alien to him, except the old amah who had been only a servant—and except the Empress.

This beautiful woman with imperial grace sat down and bade him by a gesture to be seated.

'My husband is delayed but only for a moment. We have had bad news from the front. Of course, now everything will be righted, since America is joining us. I grieve for the sad event of Pearl Harbour, but, really, I do believe it was necessary to awaken the American people to our world danger. I do not think only of China—I think of the world. We must all think of the world.'

The door opened again and she broke off. A slender Chinese man in a long robe came in. It was the Old Tiger. Impossible indeed for anyone else to have those bold black eyes, that stubborn mouth! But he looked fragile. Was this the man who for fifteen years had conquered warlords and killed Communists? The Tiger put out his hand and withdrew it quickly as though he hated the touch of another's hand, and the act revealed him an old-fashioned Chinese, unwillingly yielding to a foreign custom. With an abrupt gesture he motioned to William to sit down again and himself took a chair far from the fire.

'Does this American speak Chinese?' he inquired of his wife.

'How can he?' she replied.

'I must confess that I understand a little, at least,' William said. 'My childhood was spent in Peking.'

The Old Tiger nodded vigorously. 'Good—good!' His voice was high and thin. When he spoke to his soldiers he was forced to shriek.

William contemplated his ally, this bony bald-headed man who was the master of millions of Chinese. Tiger was a good name for him. In repose he looked like a monster cat, soft and safe, except for the eyes where ferocious temper smouldered. He was old China, he hated the new, he was rooted in the past. Enough of his own childhood knowledge remained with William for him to know exactly where the Tiger belonged. Had there been no revolution among the Chinese people he would have ascended the Dragon Throne and become a strong successor to the Old Buddha. He would have made a spectacular figure there, wrapped in gold-embroidered imperial robes, the Son of Heaven. And the Chinese people, William thought, would have been better off. What were they now but a scattered herd? People needed to worship and when they were given no god, they made themselves a golden calf. There was tragedy in this man, deprived of his throne because of the age in which he had been born. A strange respectful tenderness crept into William's mood. He leaned towards the Old Tiger.

'I have come here to know how we can help you. There are two ways in which I myself can be of some use. I can influence millions of people. I can tell them—whatever you want me to tell them. I can also report to my government.'

He spoke in English and the beautiful woman translated rapidly into a Chinese so simple that he could understand it. The Old Tiger nodded his head and repeated the short word signifying good, 'Hao—hao——' It was almost a purr. Not the soft purr of a cat, but the stiff, throaty rasp of a wild beast.

The beautiful woman seemingly effaced herself between the two men. She became an instrument, mild, almost shy. William all but forgot her as he pressed his arguments with the Tiger. But she was neither mild nor shy. A supreme actress

408

by natural gift, she took his English words and remoulded them into her fluent Chinese, stressing this word, muting that. When she perceived that he understood something of what she was saying, she varied her dialect slightly, slipping into a sort of Fukienese, excusing herself with adroitness.

'My husband comes from Fukien, and he understands that language better than Mandarin. It is essential that he grasp your every word.'

William could make nothing thereafter of what she said. He did not want to believe that she added meanings of her own. There was no reason why she should. He was ready for the utmost gift.

One hour, two hours went by. Suddenly the Tiger stood up.

'*Hao!*' he cried in his thin sharp voice. 'It is all good. We will do these things. I will command my men. I shall not rest until the yellow devils are driven into the sea.'

He folded his hands, this time without pretence of foreign custom, nodded twice to William, and went out of the room, his step silent and swift.

William was left with the beautiful woman. She put one soft pale hand upon his sleeve. 'Dear Mr. Lane, your coming is an answer to prayer. I believe that. I believe so much in prayer, don't you? Every morning my husband and I pray together.'

Tears came to her eyes and she took a little lace handkerchief from her sleeve and wiped them away. 'You know China.' Her voice was a whisper now, broken with her tears. 'I can speak to you. You see my husband. He is so strong, so good, he is really good. He wants to save our people not only from the present enemy but from those who are far worse. You understand me, Mr. Lane. I am sure you do. But my husband must be helped. He has not had the advantage of education. He has many impulses. I try to control them through praying with him, Mr. Lane. What I cannot do, God will do.'

William listened with rising sympathy.

'You have a very responsible work to do,' he said. 'Perhaps you are in the key position of the whole world.'

His voice was grave and he meant it to be so, and she looked at him sorrowfully. Her big black eyes were shining and the tears were gone. Her hands were outstretched to him again.

'You must help me, promise me you will help me!'

He took her hands in his own. 'I promise.'

A week later, after incessant flying, from the dried sands of the north-west to the green provinces of the south, hours broken only by descents into cities where he sat out long feasts given in his honour, he went southwards and then across the mountains and seas homeward. Wherever he went the beautiful woman had gone with him, and with them was always a third, a general usually, whom they picked up from the region and who could give them the latest news of the war. She translated for William as she had for the Tiger, giving him a continuing drama of a brave poverty-stricken people, patriots who wanted only guns in their hands, a few tanks and planes, to become invincible.

'Like your own Washington,' she urged. 'Like Jefferson, like Lincoln!'

He might have distrusted her eagerness, but she was always ahead of his mood. She knew when to let tears fill her eyes, but she knew also when to make her eyes hard and her voice firm. She knew when to show anger at a subordinate, when to be a queen and when to be a woman. Watching her he felt a new regret that the Phoenix Throne, too, had been destroyed. She would have made an empress fit to sit beside the Tiger on the Dragon Throne. People feared her, that he perceived, and he admired her for it. There must always be some whom the people fear.

At the end of the week he felt convinced that because of her it was safe to uphold the Old Tiger. Without her there might be treachery; with her there was no danger. When they parted at the final airport she used her tears again.

'Dear America,' she breathed. 'Give her my love. Give everybody my love! Tell them I spend my life to teach my people the lessons that I was taught over there!'

He reached Washington exactly on schedule and made his report and took the next plane home. It was snowing softly when he got out of the plane. The chauffeur was there to meet him. When he stepped into the car he found Emory, looking very pretty in a silver-grey frock and hat.

'This is good of you, Emory,' he exclaimed.

'Not good of me. I've missed you terribly.'

He crushed her shoulders in his arm and kissed her. She smelled of a delicate perfume, clean and warm, and he was grateful for all that was his, his wife, his home, his business, his country.

'I'm glad to be back. China is hell now.'

'Is it, William? Then do you feel your trip was wasted?'

'No, far from it. I made them feel that America is behind them. I made them promises that I must see fulfilled. My work is cut out for me, Emory, I can tell you. I've got to shape public opinion to support those two people who are all that stand between us and defeat in Asia.'

'Don't tell me now, William. You look fearfully tired.'

'I hope we haven't any guests tonight.'

'No, of course not. Just you and me.'

He sighed and relaxed as much as he could. Everything had a new meaning for him. He felt as he never had before the value of being an American. The big car gliding over the great highways, the smoke-stacks of the factories, the lifted outlines of the city beyond, this could only be America. If China was hell, this was heaven, and it was his own. Nothing must be allowed to destroy it or bring it down to dust, now or ever. Holding Emory's hand in his, he dedicated himself afresh and with all his heart to his own country.

Upon reflection, even after a night's sleep, William felt that his mission to China had been a successful one. He had performed it in the quiet private way he liked to do large things, simply flying across the world alone in a plane for which he had paid a fabulous sum. The money was spent as he liked to spend money, by himself alone, for an end chosen by him but which would affect the world. The world knew nothing of it and would never acknowledge its debt to him, perhaps, while he lived. But some day, when historians were able to penetrate the shades of the past, they would see that through him, perhaps above all men, the war which might have been lost was won. Let others pour their energies upon the small tormented countries of Europe. He would save China, and by saving that vast territory the enemy would be foiled. He commanded Emory to invite no guests, accept no invitations. For two weeks he must stay at the office, coming home only to sleep. During that time he would give directives to his entire staff. Those who could not obey with efficiency he would discharge at once. His whole organization must concentrate now upon his directives. Techniques must be worked out for the papers, compelling simplicity, subtle argument, plausible presentation, every visual aid, every mental persuasion.

At the end of the first day he fired four persons, among them Miss Smith and Lem Barnard. Miss Smith was nobody. He ordered the office manager to have another ready for his dictation tomorrow morning. But Lem was difficult to replace. The Chinese would not tell a foreigner things unless he had charm, although charm was something William did not care for in his own office. It was then that he thought of Jeremy. Jeremy might do very well with the beautiful woman, even with the Old Tiger, if he were accompanied by someone to buy his tickets and take care of his baggage and see that he got his stuff on time. Besides, it would move Jeremy out of the office. When he did not show up it was a bad example. Acting instantly, with that abrupt complete co-ordination which was the source of his extraordinary energy, he pressed a buzzer.

It was near the end of the day and there was a slight delay, which made the blood swell into his high forehead. The delay, it seemed, when he demanded to know the reason, was because Miss Smith had not waited for his going home as she should have done. She had gone for her cheque at once and had actually left half an hour ago. He was tempted to fire the office manager but was too impatient to stop for it. In a few minutes he heard Ruth's sweet, somewhat childish voice. It sounded unusually faint.

'Ruth—that you?'

'Oh, William.' Her voice was stronger. 'How wonderful to hear you!'

'Jeremy there?'

'No—he isn't—yet, William.'

'Where is he? He wasn't in the office.'

'William, he isn't—he's not quite well. I think he'll be back in a day or so.' She had begged Emory not to tell but maybe she had been wrong. Maybe William had to know.

'I have a job for him if he can get here by tomorrow. How do you think he'd like to go to China for me, as my personal representative?'

To his astonishment William heard his sister sob. He was fond of Ruth without having any respect for her, because she depended on him. Something was wrong with her marriage, of course, but he had never cared to go into it. Personal things took too much time and every hour counted in these terrible days. Now he had to inquire.

'What's wrong?'

'Oh, William, I'm afraid you have to know. I didn't want to bother you. Jeremy is in a sanatorium.'

'What sort? Is he sick?'

'Oh, William, no! Well, yes, I suppose it is a sickness. He was drinking too much and after you left he—Oh dear, he just went to pieces!'

'Nobody told me.'

'I didn't want them to. I kept hoping he'd. . . .'

He thought quickly while her voice babbled into his unheeding ear. This would give him the excuse to end everything with Jeremy. He would treat it as an illness.

'Ruth, I wish you would stop crying. I want you to know that I feel very sorry and I want to help you. I am going to give Jeremy unlimited leave of absence. He doesn't need to feel that he has to come back at all. But I want you to be independent. He wouldn't take a pension from me, of course,

413

but I am going to set up a trust for you and the girls. Then whatever happens to him you'll be safe.'

'Oh, William, darling——' her voice, still half sobbing, was breathless. 'I wouldn't think of——'

'Be sure he stays there long enough to get in good shape and let me know when he comes home. We'll get together. Good-bye. I'm frightfully busy——'

He thought for a moment and decided to send Barney Chester to China. He was a smart young Harvard man, only a few years out of college. Barney would listen to him.

He rose, refusing to acknowledge weariness, and went down the elevator to his waiting car. It was nearly ten o'clock and snow was falling. Sitting in the darkness of his car, staring steadfastly ahead, he saw the snow fly at him in little daggers of silver against the windscreen. Around him were the darkness and the cold, the people still plodding along the wet streets, their heads held down against the wind. But he sat in warmth and safety, secure in himself and his possessions. All that he was he had made himself and all that he possessed he had earned. He had come from China, obscure and unknown, a shy and gawky youth, and what he was he had achieved without help. Yet America had given him opportunity. In England his birth alone would have condemned him. Even a title could not have hidden it. He smiled against the darting silver daggers which could not reach him. Here people had forgotten where he was born and who his father was. Where could that happen but in America? . . .

In the morning he woke inexplicably depressed again. There was no reason for it, except, he decided, that his conscience was stirring because he had not told Monsignor Lockhart about China. He had not even called him on the telephone, afraid that he would be tempted by the priest's quiet voice to yield time he could not spare. It was not as if he needed counsel. He had already determined what he must do. Now, however, there was no reason why he should not allow himself the luxury of some hours of spiritual communion.

This musing took place long before his usual hour for rising,

414

but he felt wakeful and he took the receiver from the telephone at his bedside and called for Monsignor Lockhart.

The priest's voice came as usual, 'I am here, William.'

'I have wanted to see you ever since I returned, Monsignor, but you understand.'

'Always.'

'I count on that. But this morning?'

'Whenever you wish. I am in my study.'

He had planned to go back to sleep. It was still dark. Yet it might be interesting and even stimulating to get up and make his own way by foot to that huge gold-lit room. Their minds would be clear and quick.

In twenty minutes he was walking over fresh snow on the streets. He had never been out at this hour and the city seemed strange to him. The people he was accustomed to see were still in their beds. But the streets were not entirely empty, especially the side street he took from one avenue to the next. Two or three people were there, slouching along, one a woman who passed him and then stopped when an old man whose face he could just see in the approaching dawn held out a filthy hand without speaking. William went on. He made it a habit never to see an outstretched hand. His generous cheque went annually to the Community Chest.

'A cup o' cawfee fer Gawd's sake,' the old man muttered.

William went on and the dirty hand brushed his arm and fell.

'Damned capitalist!' the woman shouted at his back. 'Wants us to starve!'

A policeman suddenly rounded the corner.

'Did I hear somethin', sir?' he inquired.

William considered for a moment whether he should nod in the direction of the woman and then decided that he would ignore her.

'Nothing, except that old man asking for a drink.'

'They will do it,' the policeman said apologetically.

William gave the slightest inclination of his head and went on. Five minutes later he was inside the priest's warm and handsome home.

'You look hopeful,' Monsignor Lockhart said.

'I do not feel hopeful at all,' William retorted.

He finished a good English breakfast, while he talked, kidneys and bacon and buttered toast with marmalade. The coffee was American and delicious. A man came in and took the silver tray away, and closed the door softly.

'Yet I feel hopefulness in you,' Monsignor repeated.

'I am hopeful to the extent of thinking that it is possible to hold China. It is my belief that we should allow England to take the lead in Europe but we must take the lead in Asia, now and after the war. Since only China is a free country, it is there we must concentrate our power.'

'Very sound,' Monsignor said. 'I take it you do not mean permanent power.'

'Certainly not permanent in the sense of eternal,' William agreed. 'I hope a complete American victory will have been won somewhere this side of eternity.'

Monsignor's face was benign, although he wore this morning a lean weary beauty which showed hours of thought and perhaps prayer. William allowed himself a moment's wonder at this man who attracted him so much.

'You are tired,' he said abruptly.

The priest looked startled and then his face closed. 'If I am tired I am unworthy of my faith. It is true that the Church has great and new problems. In Europe our priests are facing oppression which we have never known, never in our agelong history. The gravest reports come to me from Austria. We have reached the age of anti-Christ. There is a demon in the people.'

'Then it is no private ill that I see in your face?' William said.

Monsignor Lockhart's fine brows drew down. 'What private ill is it possible for me to have?' he retorted. 'The affliction of the Church is my affliction. I have no other.'

William gazed at him, forgetful for the moment of their friendship. Monsignor seemed suddenly remote and cold. He was reminded of the temples of his childhood, where the gods sat aloof. No, it was not a god of whom he thought. It was the palace of the Old Buddha again, looking down upon him, a foreign child.

416

Monsignor dropped his lids. 'We understand each other. Let us proceed from day to day, watchful of each hour's history.'

He rose for the first time without waiting for William to signify that he was ready to go, and he put out his hand in the gesture of blessing. A deeper gravity came over his stern face. 'Many are called but few are chosen,' he said simply, and making the sign of the cross upon his own breast he left the room.

Throughout the day William carried with him the vague alarm of the priest's words, holding it upon the fringes of his mind.

He buzzed sharply for the new Miss Smith and did not look up when she came in.

'Dictation,' he said.

He dictated steadily for an hour, letters, finally a long directive for Barney Chester. Then he dismissed Miss Smith and buzzed for his news editor.

'That you, Barney? Come to my office. I'm sending you to China immediately as my personal representative.'

He spent the next two hours outlining to a silent and rather terrified young man exactly what he expected him to do in China.

'In short,' he concluded at the end of the two hours, 'I shall expect from you the most detailed reports of what American diplomacy is doing, in order that I may be kept informed here at home. At the same time I expect you to maintain confidential relationship with the Old Tiger and with—her.'

'Yes, sir,' Barney Chester said. He was a pale dark young man, very slender and smart. William liked all his young men to look smart. Actually Barney had a somewhat soft heart which he daily denied. Certainly before the stern, grey-faced man behind the circular desk he would have been alarmed to allow the slightest hint of a heart to escape him. This was the best paying job a man of his age could have anywhere in the country, anywhere in the world, probably. Lane paid his men well and worked them hard. He wished that his wife Peggy were not expecting their second baby. He had counted on asking for his delayed vacation when the time came so that he could take care of Barney Junior. There was no one to look after him, except a servant. It did not occur to him to mention such humble difficulties to William, who was still giving orders.

'Be ready to leave the day after tomorrow. I'll see that you get priority on the plane.'

'Yes, sir,' Barney said.

XII

IN the house now grown shabby with the years and which Henrietta never thought of renovating, Clem sat reading the newspapers. The season was summer, the first summer after the war ended. Clem had barely survived the atomic bomb dropped upon two Japanese cities  Like many other Americans, he did not know that atomic bombs existed, until on the fifth day of August, a year ago, he had opened a newspaper, to discover with agony and actual tears that the bomb had already been dropped and hundreds of thousands of people he had never seen were killed. Although he, like other Americans, except the handful, had nothing to do with this act, he felt it was his fault. He got up blindly, the tears running down his thin cheeks, and went to find Henrietta. When he found her upstairs making the bed, he had been unable to speak for weeping. He could only hold out the newspaper, pointing at the head-lines. When she saw what had happened she put her arms around him and the two of them stood weeping together, in shame and fear for what had been done.

For weeks after that Clem had been so nearly ill that she told Bump to trouble him about nothing. Clem asked very few questions any more. He was working with all his diminishing energy upon The Food, and he steadfastly refused to see a doctor or have any X-rays taken of his now permanently rebellious digestive organs.

'Don't bother me, hon.' This was his reply to Henrietta's pleas and despairs.

The big man in the White House was dead and a little man had taken his place. Clem went to see him immediately to preach for the last time his human gospel of food for the starving. The little man twinkled and smiled and took time to describe the United Nations plan for world food and somehow sent Clem away thinking that he had converted a President of the United States, but nothing happened.

In the spring Clem had talked of going to the San Francisco Conference to explain about how the starving people of the world must be fed if things were to go right. The Communists mustn't be the ones to get the upper hand, but they would unless people had food to eat.

Henrietta had persuaded him against going. She knew now that people even in New Point were laughing at Clem. He was called crazy, a fanatic, nobody listened to a man who had spent his life on one idea.

She hated people because they were laughing at Clem. She drew him into their house, kept him busy, worked with him on his formula, anything to shield him from the cruel laughter of people who were not fit to tie his shoe-laces.

On this summer morning when she was getting the breakfast dishes washed he sat reading the paper in the kitchen. Suddenly she heard him cry out.

'Hon!'

'Yes, Clem?'

'We've lost the war!'

'What on earth do you mean? The war is over.'

She left the sink, her hands soapy wet, and stood reading over his shoulder.

'We've said we ain't going to help the subject peoples. It's the beginning of the third World War.'

'Oh, Clem, it's not as bad as that!'

'It is. They're all looking at San Francisco and what we've said there can't be unsaid. "There comes a tide in the affairs of men. . . ."'

He got up abruptly and went downstairs into his laboratory and she went on washing the dishes.

It was not until March 1950, that Clem went to see William for the third and last time. By then so much of what he had foreseen had already come to pass that he thought he could convince William. Surely now he would believe that Clem was right. The Communists were ruling China and people were starving again by the tens of millions. Yusan was able to get word out about it. Old Mr. and Mrs. Fong were dead.

Yusan was the head of the family. Peking was full of Russians all giving advice. Meanwhile Manchurian food was being traded for machinery.

'If America could get food to us——' Yusan wrote. The letter was on one tiny slip of paper in a small filthy envelope without a stamp. Mr Kwok, now the head of a prosperous restaurant in New York, had brought it himself to Clem, and Clem had gone back with him to New York without telling Henrietta that he had made up his mind to go to William for the last time and beg him to tell the Americans that maybe they could still save China and the world if they would only understand. . .

Three days later Henrietta saw Clem coming up the brick path to the house, dragging his pasteboard suit-case. He could not reach the door. She saw him crumple upon the path and she ran outdoors and lifted him up.

He had not fainted, he was conscious.

'My legs just gave up, hon,' he whispered.

'You get in here and go to bed and stay there,' she cried, fierce with love.

But nobody could keep him in bed. He would not go to the hospital yet, he told Dr. Wood. Now more than ever he must finish his formula, now that William wouldn't listen to him. So Henrietta heard how Clem had gone to William and how been denied.

'I'm just tired for once,' Clem said.

He was up again in a few days and at his formula again, experimenting over the gas-ring with a mixture of dried milk and beans, fortified with minerals and shredded potato. Henrietta did not cross him in anything now. There was no use in pretending that he was not ill, but she was helpless. Clem would not have the doctor.

It became a race. He almost stopped eating and drinking and she kept by his side a cup of tea into which she slipped a beaten egg and a little sugar He drank this slowly, a sip now and then, and so sustained his life

By summer they both saw he could not win. One morning he was struggling to get out of bed. His night-shirt fell away from his neck, hollowed into triangular cavities. His ears looked enormous, his eyes were sick.

'Clem!' she cried. 'You've got to think of me for once.' It was her last appeal.

'Don't I think of you, hon?'

The strength was gone even from his voice. It sounded empty and ghostlike.

'You aren't getting up,' she said. 'You're staying right there until I can get Doctor Wood.'

He sank back on the pillow, trying to smile. 'You've got me —down,' he whispered.

She made haste then to the telephone, and found the doctor.

'I'll come as soon as I——'

'No, you'll come now,' she shrieked. 'You'll come right now, without one moment's delay! I think he's dying.'

She flew back to the bed-side, the wide old-fashioned double bed where they had slept side by side in the years since she had given up everything to be his wife. He was lying just as she had left him but when she came in he opened his eyes drowsily and smiled.

'The doctor is coming right over, Clem. Don't go to sleep.'

'No—I don't want to.'

They stayed in silence for a moment, she holding one of his bony hands between hers. No use wasting his strength in talk!

But he began to talk. 'Hon—the formula as far as I've gone——'

'Please, Clem.'

'Let me tell you—it's all written down on that little pad in the upper right-hand pigeon-hole of my old desk. Hon—if I can't finish it——'

'Of course you can finish it, Clem. You just won't rest long enough. I'm going to take you to California, that's what I'm going to do. . . .'

She was talking to keep him quiet and he knew it. As soon as she paused he began again.

'I think I've made a mistake using the dried milk, hon. There'll be people in China, for instance, who won't like the

422

taste of milk. I don't know why I didn't think of that before. I ought to have, growing up in China——'

He stopped suddenly and looked at her in terror.

'Hon—hon——' He was gasping.

'Clem, what is it?'

'The most awful pain here——' He locked his hands across his belly, and sweat burst from him and poured down his face.

'Oh, Clem, what shall I——'

But it was not necessary for her to do anything. He dropped away into unconsciousness.

Three hours later in the hospital in Dayton, Dr. Wood came out of the operating room. Henrietta had been sitting motionless for more than an hour, refusing to expect either good or ill. Her years with Clem, being his shadow, had taught her how to wait, not thinking, not impatient, letting her mind busy itself with the surface her eyes presented to her, the people coming and going, the bowl of flowers on the table, the branches of a tree outside the window.

'I imagine you are half prepared for what I must tell you, Mrs. Miller,' Dr. Wood said.

He was a kindly middle-aged man, so obviously a small-town doctor that anybody could have guessed what he was. His strength was in knowing what he did not know and when he had seen Clem's ash-white face upon the pillow this morning he had simply said briskly, 'We'll get this fellow straight to the city hospital,' and had sent for the ambulance.

While it screamed its way through the roads to Dayton he had sat beside Clem, with Henrietta near, and had said nothing at all. In the hospital he had taken Clem immediately into the operating room, and had stayed with him while a young surgeon operated.

'I have not prepared myself,' Henrietta said quietly. 'I have only waited.'

'He has no stomach left,' Dr. Wood said gently. This strong woman's face looking at his made him feel that it was no use holding back one iota of truth. 'He should have been operated on long ago. An old condition, he's a worrier, of course—and it's turned suddenly malignant.'

'Not a worrier, exactly,' Henrietta murmured. Her heart had stopped beating for a long tight moment and now began again very hard. 'He simply takes the whole world as his own responsibility. He starves with every hungry man, woman, and child, he crucifies himself every day.'

'Too bad,' Dr. Wood said. 'That sort of thing is no use, you know. One man can't do it all. I suppose you told him so often enough.'

'No, thank God, I never did,' Henrietta got up.

'They won't want you just now——'

'I'll just go anyway,' Henrietta said. 'They can't keep me away from him.'

She did not stop to ask how long Clem would live. However long it was, she would stay with him and never leave him, not for a night, not for an hour, never at all. She walked into the door from which Dr. Wood had come, and nobody stopped her. . . .

Clem lived for not quite a week. She was not sure that he knew she was there all the time but she stayed with him just the same. He might come to himself in spite of what the doctors and nurses said.

'It's really impossible, Mrs. Miller,' the night nurse said. 'He's so drugged, you know, to keep him from pain. He must have suffered terribly for a long time.'

'He never said he did,' Henrietta replied. Was it possible that Clem had suffered without telling her? It was possible. He would have been afraid that she would stop him before his work was done, in that fearful race he was running. How could she not have seen it? She had seen it, of course, in the tightness in his look, his staying himself to lean upon his hands on the table, hanging upon his shoulders as though they were a rack—a cross, she told herself. She kept thinking of Clem upon a cross. Plenty of people thought him a fool, a fanatic, and so he was, to them. But she knew his heart. He could not be other than what he was. He had been shaped by his parents

424

from their simple minds and tender hearts, from their believing faith, their fantastic folly, their awful death. The hunger of his own childhood he had made into the hunger of the world.

'Hon,' he had often said, and she would hear those words in whatever realm his soul must dwell, 'Hon, you can't preach to people until you've fed them. I'll feed them and let others do the preaching.'

It was like him to choose the harder part. Anybody could preach.

'You must eat something, Mrs. Miller,' they said to her.

So she ate whatever it was they brought, as much as she could, at least. Clem would want her to eat, and if he could drag himself out of the darkness where he slept he would tell her, 'You eat, now, hon.'

They fed him through his veins. There was nothing left of his stomach. 'The surgeon could scarcely sew it together again,' the nurse told her. 'It was like a piece of rotted rubber. How he ever kept up!'

'He always had strength from somewhere,' Henrietta said.

'Didn't you know?' the nurse inquired. She told the other nurses that Mrs. Miller was a queer, a heavy sort of woman. You didn't know what she was thinking about.

'I never felt I could interfere with him,' Henrietta said.

'Stupid,' the nurse told the others, for wouldn't a sensible woman have made a man get himself examined, if she cared about him? She might have saved his life.

'I suppose I could have saved his life,' Henrietta said slowly. 'But I understood him so well. I knew there were things he cared for much more than life. So I couldn't interfere.'

This was as much as she ever said.

'I'd say she didn't give a hoot for him,' the nurse told the others, 'except anybody can see the way she sits there that she's dying with him. There won't be anything alive in her after he's gone.'

Clem died at two o'clock one night. He never came back to consciousness. Henrietta would not allow it. Dr. Wood came several times a day and that evening he was there about

425

ten o'clock, and he told her that Clem would not live through the night.

'If you want me to, Mrs. Miller, I can leave off the hypodermic and he'll come back to himself enough to know you, maybe.'

'In pain?'

'I'm afraid so.'

No use bringing Clem back to pain; that would be selfish. One moment was nothing in comparison to the years that she had lived with him and the years that she must live without him. She shook her head. The doctor gave the hypodermic himself and went away.

Clem died quietly. She knew the instant of his going. She had sat in her usual place, not stirring, had refused at midnight a cup of beef broth the nurse brought in and took away again. Soon after midnight she felt the sense of approaching death as clearly as though she too must partake of it. With every moment that passed she felt a strange oppression growing upon her. At two o'clock it was there, and she knew it. Her flesh received the blow, her heart the arrest. His hand lay in hers, light and cold, and she leaned upon the bed, her face near his. No use touching his lips. A kiss was no communication now. Better to remember the living acts of love that once had been between them than to take into her endless memory the last unanswered gift! He had been a perfect lover, not frequent, never pressing, but sweet and courteous to her. Direct and sometimes brusque he had been in daily life, too busy to think of her often, and yet she knew he kept her always with him as he kept his own soul. Yet there were the rare times, the hours when he made love to her, each perfect because he won her anew, never persuading, leading and never compelling, flesh meeting and always more than flesh—and when it was over his tender gratitude.

'Thanks, hon. You make love very sweet.'

She would never hear those words again! She had not thought of that. The tears which had not come came now, slow and hot.

'I'm afraid it's the last, Mrs. Miller,' the nurse said. She was standing at the other side of the bed, her fingers on Clem's pulse.

Henrietta stood up. Her heart was beating so fast again that she was dizzy. Her knees were trembling.

'Could you just—turn away—a minute——'

The nurse turned her head and bit her lip. However often they died, it was always terrific. You couldn't get used to it.

Henrietta bent over Clem and laid her cheek against his. She put her lips to his ear and said very clearly, reaching with all her heart into the space between the stars:

'Thank you, my dearest. You've made love very sweet.'

It was the last time in her life that she ever spoke the word, love. She buried it with him, like a flower.

After Clem was dead, there was nothing to do but keep on until what he had wanted to do was done. This was all she had. Now that he was gone, it was astonishing how little else was left. Even his face seemed to fade from her mind. There had been few hours indeed when he had been hers undivided. Most of their companionship, and she now felt their only real companionship, had been when he talked to her about his work, his plans, and finally his dream, his obsession.

Clem had been her only lover, the only man who had ever asked her to marry him, the only man she could have married. Her alien childhood had shaped her. She was far past middle age now, a woman remote and alone. Bump remained nearer to her than any human creature, and he was kind enough, but always anxious and now aghast at the burden that Clem's death had left upon him. He said the markets had to be sold and Henrietta agreed. She had no heart for the big business they had become and without Clem's idealistic genius, there was nothing to hold them together.

It was not difficult to sell. In each of the huge self-serving concerns there was a man, usually the one Clem had put in charge, who was willing to buy her out. Her terms were absurdly low and she put no limit on the time for payment. For a while she tried to stipulate that Clem's ideas were to be kept, that people were to have food cheaper there than they could buy it elsewhere. This too she was compelled to give up.

It took genius to be so daring, and she found none. To Bump she simply gave the market in Dayton, and after some thought she gave him, too, her house, when after six months she made up her mind to go to New York with Berkhardt Feld, the famous German food chemist.

This aged scientist had left Germany secretly one day when he saw Hitler strutting like a pouter pigeon before a dazed mass of humanity who were anxiously willing to worship anything. Fortunately he was quite alone. He and his wife had been childless, a fact for which he never ceased to thank God when he understood what was happening in Germany, and then his wife had died. He had mourned her desperately, for he was a lonely man and Rachel had been his family and his friend. When he saw Hitler he stopped grieving and became glad that she was dead. It was easy to pack his personal belongings into a kerchief, hide in a pair of woollen socks the formula that represented his life work, and in his oldest clothes to take to the road and the border. People had not reached the point yet of killing any Jew they met and he saw contempt rather than madness in the careless glances cast at him as he went. He had money enough to get him over the border, and in France he found royalties from his last scientific work, *The Analysis of the Chemistry of Food in Relation to Human Character*.

From Paris he had gone to London, had been restless there because it was still too near Germany, and friends had got him to New York. Here, gratefully, he sank into the swarm of various humanity and spent almost nothing while he worked in the laboratory of a man who was a chemist for a general food company, a man named Bryan Holt who knew Berkhardt Feld as a genius. He found a room for the old man in a clean, cheap boarding-house and gave him a desk and a small wage as his assistant. If they ever discovered anything together he would be generous and divide the profit that came from it. Since he belonged to the company, however, it was not likely that such profits would be enormous. Dr. Feld cared nothing for money, except that he would not owe anyone a penny. He paid his way carefully and did without what he could not buy.

Henrietta had found Dr. Feld first through finding among Clem's papers a letter which he had written to Bryan Holt, trying, as Henrietta could see, to get the young scientist to help him devise a food cheap and nourishing that could serve as a stopgap until people became sensible enough, as Clem put it, to see that everybody got food free. There had been no time for an answer. Clem had died the week after he had written this letter. Ah, but in the letter she found her treasure, the voice of Clem, the words which she had longed to hear and yet which he did not speak to her because she had not allowed him to come back in pain. Here was the reward for her love, when she had denied even her crying heart. Clem knew he was dying, long before she had been compelled to believe it, and he had written to the young scientist:

'I am in some haste for I am struck with a mortal disease and may die any time. This does not matter. I have been very lucky. I have discovered a basic truth in my lifetime and so it will not die with me. What I have spent my life to prove will be proved because it is truth. Though I lie in my grave, this is my victory.'

Clem victorious! Of course he was, for who could destroy his truth? Here was the command she knew and prepared as of old to obey.

To Bryan Holt then Henrietta decided to go when she had given Clem's few suits to the Salvation Army, and had found herself possessed of an astonishing amount of money in more than twenty banks in various cities where money had been paid into Clem's accounts from the markets. His records were scanty but very clear indeed were certain notes on The Food, as he called it. The Food was half chemical, half natural, a final mingling of bean base with minerals and vitamins, which if he could get a chemist to work it out with him might, he had believed, make it possible for him to feed millions of people for a few cents apiece. This was the final shape of his dream, or as William had once called it, his obsession. It might be that the two were the same thing.

The first meeting with Holt had not been promising. Holt had not answered Clem's letter because it sounded absurd. He was respectful before Henrietta's solid presence, her square pale face and big, well-shaped hands. She had immense dignity. He tried to put it kindly but she saw what he meant. This young man was not the one she sought, but there would be another. Clem, though he had died, yet lived.

'Many people thought my husband was unbalanced,' she said in her calm voice. 'That is because he was far ahead of his time. It will be twenty-five years, much more if we don't have another war, before statesmen realize that what he said is plain common sense. There will not cease to be ferment in the world unless people are sure of their food. It is not necessary that you agree with my husband and me. I am come only to ask you questions about his formula.'

Bryan Holt wanted to get rid of her, though he was polite since he was almost young enough to be her son. So he said:

'I have a very fine scientist here working with me who has come from Europe. He will be more useful to you than I can possibly be.'

With this he had summoned from a remote desk a shambling old figure who was Dr. Berkhardt Feld, and so by accident Henrietta found her ally. When she had talked with Dr. Feld for a few hours she proposed to find a small laboratory for him alone, with an apartment where he could make his home. Then if he would teach her to help him, building upon her college chemistry, which was all she had, she would come to him every day and they could perhaps fulfil Clem's life work.

To Dr. Feld this was heaven unexpected. None of Clem's ideas were fantastic to him. They were merely axiomatic. It would not be too difficult to find the formula which Clem had begun very soundly upon a bean base, a matter perhaps of only a few years, by which time it might be hoped the wise men of the world would be ready to consider what must be done for millions of orphaned and starving.

'Then, then, *liebe* Frau Müller,' Dr. Feld said fervently, making of Henrietta as German a creature as he could, 'we will be ready perhaps with The Food.'

The tears came to Henrietta's eyes. She thanked Dr. Feld in her dry, rather harsh voice and told him to be ready to move as soon as she could go home and get her things.

That decision made, she began to clean away what was left in the house of all her years of marriage to Clem. Among the things she would never throw away was the red tin box of Clem's letters and with them the old amulet which he had given her. It was still in the folded paper in which he had sent it to her. She opened the paper and cried out as though he were there, 'I always meant to ask you about this!'

How much of him she had meant to ask about in the long last years she had expected to have with him, years that would never be! She cried a little and closed the box and put it into her trunk to go with her to New York. Some day, when she could bear to do it, she would read all his letters over again. So much, so much she would never know about Clem because he had been busy about the business of mankind!

On the night before she left, she invited Bump and Frieda to supper, that she might ask something of Bump. She did not mind Frieda, a lump of a woman, good-hearted, stupid, and kind.

'I wish you would tell me all that you can remember of Clem when you first saw him on that farm. He never could or would tell me much about it.'

She soon saw that Bump could not tell her much either. 'He was just about the way he always was,' he said, trying hard to recall that pallid, dusty boy who had walked into their sorrowful small world so many years ago 'The thing I do remember was that he wasn't afraid of anybody. He'd seen a lot, I guess. I don't know what all. But I always took it that he'd had adventures over there in China. He never talked about them, though. He pitched in right where we were. The Bergers never beat him up the way they did us. He even stopped them beating us, at least when he was around. When he decided to leave the others were afraid to go with him. They were afraid of the Aid people catching them again and things were tough if they caught you. I was afraid, too, but after he was gone, I was more afraid to stay. I don't think he was too

431

pleased to see me padding along behind him, though. I've often thought about that. But he didn't tell me to go back.'

There was nothing more, apparently. Clem's outlines remained simple and angular. After Bump had gone she studied again the notes Clem had left about The Food. If she went on trying to do what he had wanted to do then perhaps she could keep his memory with her, so that she would not forget when she was old how he had looked and what had been the sound of his voice. . . .

It did not occur to Henrietta to find her family and tell them that she was in New York. She had not even thought to tell them of Clem's death, but they had seen the announcement in a paragraph in the New York papers. Clem was well enough known for that. William had telegraphed his regret and Ruth had sent a floral cross to the funeral. Her mother was in England and it had been some weeks before a letter had come from her saying that she never thought Clem had a healthy colour and she was not surprised. Henrietta must take good care of herself. It was fortunate there was plenty of money. If Henrietta wished, she would come and live with her, but she could not live in the Middle West. New York or Boston would be pleasant. Henrietta had not answered the letter.

Now that Clem was gone she was lonely again, but not as she would have been had he never come. He had shared with her and did still share with her in memory her alien childhood which no one could understand who had only been a child here in America. Without loving China, without feeling for the Chinese anything of Clem's close affection, she was eternally divided in soul and spirit. It occurred to her sometimes in her solitary life that this division might also explain William. Perhaps all that he did was done to try and make himself whole. The wholeness which she had been able to find in Clem because they understood one another's memories, William had found no one to share. Perhaps he could not be made whole through love. She would go and see Candace. Upon this decision she went to the laboratory as usual.

Dr. Feld, observing the large silent woman who worked

patiently at his command, mused sometimes upon her remoteness and her completion. She needed no one, even as he needed none. They had finished their lives, he in Germany, she—where? Perhaps in China, perhaps in a grave. What more they did now was only to spend the remaining time usefully. He wished that he could have known the man who had left behind him these extraordinary though faulty notes. She had told him that her husband had only had a few years of education and no training in science.

'His knowledge must have been intuitive, dear madame,' he had replied.

'He was able to learn from human beings,' she said. 'He felt their needs and based his whole life upon what he found out. He called it food, but it was more than food for the body. He made of human need his philosophy and religion. Had you met him you would have thought him a very simple man.'

'So is Einstein,' Dr. Feld said.

They did not talk much. When they did speak it was about Clem or the formula. He explained the peculiar, almost atomic vitality of vitamins. 'The source of all life is in the atom,' he said solemnly. 'God is not in the vastness of greatness. He is hid in the vastness of smallness. He is not in the general. He is in the particular. When we understand the particular, then we will know all.' When he really talked he spoke in German. She was glad that she had taken German in college and had kept the language alive in her reading.

One summer afternoon she took off her big white apron and reached for her hat and coat. 'I'm going away early today, Dr. Feld, to see someone I know.'

He looked surprised and pleased. 'Good—you have friends, dear madame.'

So Henrietta went away and rode the subway uptown and walked to Sutton Place.

She found the doorway in a quiet street, in a row of black and white houses with white venetian blinds. The slanting sun shone into the street with glitter and shadow. The door opened promptly and a little maid in black and white asked her to come in, please, her voice very fresh and Irish. She followed her into a square big room, immaculate in white and gold. The maid tripped away. Henrietta sat in a vast gold satin chair and a moment later Candace came in, looking soft and still young, her eyes tender and her hair a silvery gold. Her full sweet mouth smiled and Henrietta felt a fragrant kiss upon her cheek.

'Henrietta, this is the dearest thing you could have done. I never expect any of William's family to—— Sit down, please, and let me look at you. I cried so when I heard about Clem. I ought to have written but I couldn't.'

She was in a violet chiffon tea gown, long and full and belted with silver. She was very slender again and more beautiful than ever.

'Let me look at you,' Henrietta said. 'Are you happy, Candy?'

Candace blushed. 'I am happier than I've ever been in my life, happy the way I want to be happy.'

She put her hand on Henrietta's. 'When I was with William I was happy, too. It is so easy for me to be happy. But then I was happy mostly by myself. Now I am happy with Seth.'

'I know,' Henrietta said. She did not take Candace's hand because she did not know how to do such things and Candace understood this and stroked her hand and took her own away again.

'I don't blame William,' she said gently. 'I won't even let Seth hate him. William needed someone who could understand him. Seth and I of course have grown up in the same world.'

She smiled at Henrietta brilliantly and softly. 'You must come and visit us, dear. We don't live here much. We live at the old seashore house.'

'Where is Seth working?' Henrietta asked.

'He doesn't work any more except on his plays,' Candace said sweetly. 'He says William galvanized him in college or he never would have worked.' Candace laughed her rich youthful laughter. 'Seth is so amusing. He says William shaped his life. First he influenced him to work for him and

434

then he influenced him to work against him. Now, Seth says, he's not going to work at all because he's really freed himself of William. We're both very wicked, I dare say.'

'It isn't wicked to be happy,' Henrietta said.

Candace pressed her hand again. 'How glad I am to hear you say that! I used to tell William so but he didn't know what I meant. I tell the boys that now, but they're William's sons, too. They're terribly proud of him.'

Henrietta said, 'Tell me about yourself.'

Candace held up her hand. Her face so illumined from within, turned towards the door. 'Wait! I hear Seth.' She rose and went to the door and called and he came.

Henrietta saw a tall, grey-haired man, with a handsome determinedly quizzical face. He was the one she remembered and she put out her hand.

'How good of you to come,' he said. 'Candy and I don't expect favours.'

'I am fond of Candace. I wanted to see if you were good enough for her.'

'Don't make up your mind at first sight,' he begged. 'My weaknesses are so obvious.'

She smiled politely, not knowing how to answer nonsense and he looked at Candace.

'My love, I've had nothing to eat or drink since luncheon.'

'Oh—I'll ring for tea.' Her violet skirt flowed across the silvery grey carpet and she pulled a black bell-rope, hung as a decoration by the marble mantelpiece.

They had tea then, a happy plentiful affair at which Henrietta sat loyally silent and faintly smiling, enjoying the warmth of the web these two wove about them, into which they wrapped her, too. They were mirthful without cruelty, and gaily frank with her.

'Your mother, darling,' Candace said to her, 'has been cultivating England, as you know. She's used up all the available relatives—— She's simply astonished everybody. Seth, where's the letter we had from Lady Astley?'

Seth pulled open the drawer of a mahogany escritoire, and tossed an envelope into her lap.

435

'You don't mind?' Candace inquired, eyes brimming with laughter.

'I know Mother,' Henrietta said.

Candace opened the pale blue writing paper, and began to read aloud:

'What we cannot understand here in England is why Mrs. Lane isn't the mother of the President. I think she doesn't understand it, either. She's a joy and a treasure. She makes us laugh our heads off and then we can face these Socialists. Really, she's a good sport—we like her. There's something English about her if you know what I mean—something quite frightful. She's so sure she's wonderful. There'll always be England and that sort of thing—and of course there always will. It's wonderful to think that it's in America, too. We'll quite hate to see her leave. God help us, it's odd, but the American Queen Mother hates Labour, too! She calls herself Republican. William the Son is a Republican, she says. What's a Republican, dear? Mind now and tell me when you write.'

'How wicked we are to read this aloud,' Candace said looking with laughing rue at Seth, sunk in his chair and smoking his pipe.

'Nonsense,' he said. 'Henrietta knows we like the old gal. God how I envy the old! They had the world all straight, heaven and hell, God and the devil, peace and war, good and bad, moral and immoral, stuffed hungry and rich and poor——'

Candace joined in the chant.

'Young and old——'

'Black and white——'

'Gold and silver——'

'East side, West side, and never the twain shall meet——'

'King and subject——'

'City and County——'

'Capital and Labour——'

'Union and non-union——'

'Capitalist and Communist——'

'White man, black man——'

'Stop,' Candace said, 'we're making Henrietta dizzy.'

'No, you're not,' Henrietta replied. 'You're just making me laugh. Bless you both for being happy. Now I've got to go.'

They let her go, clamouring for her return, making her promise that she would come to spend a month with them at the seashore house. She would not, of course, but she could not tell them so, lest they keep her to make her promise, and then she went away, back to the subway and downtown again to her little hole in the wall.

It was long past twilight. Dr. Feld might still be working but she did not go to see. When she shut the door upon that splendid foolish happiness she stepped from moonshine into darkness. She was so accustomed to loneliness that she could not quite understand why the loneliness was deeper than it had been before, since she had found out exactly what she wanted to know, that Candace was happy and that none of them owed a debt to her any more through William. Then she remembered that neither Seth nor Candace had asked her where she lived or what she was doing. It had not occurred to them. They were not cruel, they were not even selfish or unthinking. They were simply ignorant, Candace naturally so, Seth perhaps wilfully so. He had returned to the world into which he had been born, and Candace had never left it. For them no other existed. They had never known, could never know, what Clem had always known.

It occurred to her later, after she sat trying to study a chemistry text, that perhaps that was why Candace had never understood William. William knew too, another world. She let the book fall to the floor and sat for a long time, pondering this astonishing fact: Clem and William, so utterly different, were alike!

William Lane was no longer a young man. When he saw his two sons, both married and with children of their own, his grandchildren, he felt alarmingly old. On the other hand, his mother was robust and alive, though in her eighties, and so he

437

was still young. He had come to the point of being proud of her, though frequently irritated by her increasing irresponsibility. Now, for example, when Ruth was in such trouble with Jeremy, who had become a really hopeless sot, his mother was gallivanting in England. He complained of this to Emory who listened with her usual grace and then made a wise suggestion. He depended very much on her wisdom.

'Why not cable your mother to come home and live with Ruth?' Emory said.

'An excellent idea,' William replied.

Mrs. Lane received the cable the next day. She had been staying at a big country house in Surrey, where the tenants at Christmas-tide had gathered in the real old English way to drink the health of the lord in spite of government. There was something about English life that made her think of Peking and she would have liked to spend the rest of her life in England except that the Socialists were spoiling everything. There was no reason for an American to endure the austerity upon which Sir Stafford Cripps insisted, especially an American woman. She would have stayed longer, however, with her friend, the Countess of Burleigh, had not she received William's cable. Jeremy, it appeared, had been taken to a special sort of hospital and Ruth needed her.

Mrs. Lane shrugged her handsome heavy shoulders when she read the telegram the footman brought her. She was having a quiet tea with the Countess, just the two of them. The Countess was old too, and always looking for diversion, and Mrs. Lane had been diverting her by a long visit.

'I cannot understand why my children still insist upon my returning to them at every crisis in their lives,' she now complained to the Countess. 'One would think that at my age I might be allowed my freedom. But no—William, it seems, feels I must come home. My elder daughter is of course absorbed in her grief—I told you she lost her husband—and so my poor youngest child turns to me. Her husband has been taken sadly.'

'What's wrong with him?' the Countess inquired. She had been a music-hall star in her younger days and she continued to look very smart in spite of a tendency to palsy, and she talked with the youthful Cockney twang that she pretended she used on purpose.

'I fancy he's been drinking too much again,' Mrs. Lane replied.

'Ah, if it's that,' the Countess said decisively, 'then you're rahhly in trouble, my deah. I know poor Harold was the same—would have his little tipple, he would, and he ended that way. Nothin' to do about it, neyther. I used to rampage a bit and he'd get frightened at first. In the end, poah deah, it only made him drink more. I had to let him drink himself to death, I rahhly did.'

This was not encouraging, and Mrs. Lane took her way homeward by plane as soon as she could get a seat, which she was able to do very soon, to the surprise and annoyance of the man who had already engaged it. She knew how to use William's name in secret places.

She found Ruth alone. Emory, who had come to meet her at the airfield, went with her. Ruth began to weep when she saw her mother in the hall standing still so that the maid could take off her coat properly, and Mrs. Lane, regarding her daughter's tears, saw that Ruth cried as a middle-aged woman exactly as she had as a child, almost soundless and with bewildered pathos. She put out her stout arms and wrapped Ruth in them. 'There, there,' she said. 'Everything is going to be all right now. I've come to stay with you. You need me more than Henrietta does. Where is Henrietta?'

'I don't know,' Ruth sobbed. 'I can't think about anybody but Jeremy. Oh, Mother, why does he—the doctor says it's a symptom. Something is still making him unhappy—but it's not me, I'm sure. I do everything he wants me to.'

'Nonsense,' Mrs. Lane said, pulling her daughter along firmly in the circle of her right arm as she moved into the drawing-room. 'Men like to get drunk—some men. That's all there is to it. It's not any woman's fault.'

Emory kissed Ruth an inch or two off the cheek. 'William feels quite desperate, too, dear Ruth. We all want to help poor Jeremy.'

439

'He was so deceitful about it, Mother——' Ruth cried. 'He went off to the office every day apparently to work and instead he took a room at his club and just began, and went on, all by himself. When he didn't come home, of course we had to find him. He had locked the door and they had to break it down. He was unconscious. I had Doctor Blande go and get him. They took him straight to the hospital. I haven't even—seen him. Doctor Blande says I mustn't just now.'

She began to cry again. Mrs. Lane sighed and Emory sat, quietly beautiful, looking at these American relatives. She knew why Jeremy had gone off. It was his revenge upon William, the revenge of a weak man upon one invincible. She had sympathy for the weak, but she was prudent enough to cast her lot with the invincible. William was right to be invincible in the sort of world there was now. It was the only chance one had for survival. She was invincible, too, at William's side. She pitied Ruth and felt a new admiration for William's mother, sitting solidly and without tears.

'Ruth, there's not a bit of use in your crying now that I'm here,' Mrs. Lane said. 'I'm sorry for you. Your father was a saint. You're used to good men. William, too, is so good. It's natural that a man like Jeremy should be a trial to you. But you belong to the family, and you'll be taken care of. My advice is to let Jeremy stay right where he is until William tells you what to do. Maybe you ought to let Candace know, so she can go to see him.'

Ruth shivered. 'Oh, I can't! She'd think it was somehow our fault.'

'Then she's very silly,' Mrs. Lane said loudly. 'The trouble with Jeremy is that he was brought up to be spoiled. He can't live up to William's standards. Now you go and wash your face and brush your hair. You'll feel better. There's nothing you can do for Jeremy, not a thing. We may as well have a bite of something to eat and go to a *matinée*! It will take our minds off our troubles, Emory, why don't you come with us? That's a handsome frock you have on. I've always liked that shade of yellow, especially with jade. That's handsome jade, too.'

'William brought it from China,' Emory said. 'Madame Chiang gave it to him for me.'

'She has wonderful taste,' Mrs. Lane said. 'What a pity the Communists have taken over!'

They were alone, for Ruth had left the room as obediently as though she were a little girl. Mrs. Lane leaned towards Emory. 'Jade looks nice with dark hair and eyes. William ought never to have married Candace. She was a blonde, you know. He always liked brunettes best. The Chinese wear a lot of jade. Of course they're always brunette. Some of the Chinese women have very beautiful skin. It reminds me of yours. I used to know the Old Empress Dowager. In fact, we were almost intimate. She had that sort of skin, very smooth and golden. She wore a lot of jade. William always liked to hear about her. I took him to see her once, by special permission.'

'He has told me that,' Emory said.

'Nobody could forget the Empress,' Mrs. Lane said with complacency.

Ruth came in, looking pretty again. Her short curly hair was almost white and very becoming. They went away at once since it was already late, and they found the theatres so crowded that they could only get seats at a new musical.

At the dinner table that night Emory described to William the effect of the afternoon and he listened gravely. They seldom had guests nowadays. Since the war they had fewer really distinguished visitors from abroad and not many Americans were interesting enough to be invited for a whole evening.

'I shall advise Ruth to get a divorce,' William said with decision. He had grown very handsome with the years. The discontent which had marred his face from childhood was almost gone.

'Oh, can you?' Emory murmured mildly.

'Certainly, why not? She's not a Catholic,' William replied. 'Moreover, at her age she will certainly not marry again. For my own part, I shall be glad to be rid of Jeremy.'

Emory did not reply. They sat in comfortable silence. She

was glad that she need not live now in England. How ghastly might her life have been in such penury as Michael and his family endured! He was trying to make the farmlands pay, for the government was threatening to take over Hulme Castle if he could not. The only really safe and comfortable spot now in the world was America.

This thought moved her to an unusual idea. 'William, what would you think of a cosy family dinner now that your mother is back, something to gather us together again in these troubled times? After all, there's nothing quite like family. I think it would comfort your poor sisters and impress the children you know. We needn't ask the grandchildren.'

William's heavy eyebrows moved. He pushed aside his salad. He had never liked salads, which he called food for rabbits. 'I am going to Washington next week to insist on more arms for Chiang. I gave my promise to him—a promise I hold sacred, in spite of what's happened in Korea.'

Emory evaded this. William had grown amusingly dictatorial in these past few years. 'Why shouldn't I just telephone them tomorrow night? After all, it's family. One needn't be too formal.'

William reflected, then consented. 'Very well. But tell them to be prompt. Will's wife is always late.'

Emory rose at once and walked with her long lingering step across the floor. 'I'll telephone Henrietta first.'

None of them would think of saying he or she could not come, unless Henrietta declared she had to work in her absurd laboratory. She would tell her that she needn't dress, at least.

'You mean we aren't to dress?' Henrietta inquired over the telephone. 'But I have a quite decent black gown. I had to get it when Clem was given an award in Dayton—for the citizen who had done the most for the town during the war.'

'Oh, then we'll dress,' Emory replied. 'William always does anyway.'

So she had telephoned to everybody to dress, and therefore it was upon his family in its best trappings that William looked the next evening, after he had said his usual grace before the meal. The dinner was excellent, hearty without being heavy. Emory understood food as Candace never had and she had no qualms about dismissing a careless cook. She never allowed herself to become involved in the domestic situation of any servant, a fault which had been very trying in Candace. They had once endured abominable omelets for nearly three years because the cook had a crippled son. In the end William had dismissed the cook himself one Sunday morning over a piece of yellow leather on his plate.

Tonight the *bouillon*, the *soufflé*, the roast pheasant, and the vegetables were all delicious. He did not care for sweets but Emory had a Russian dessert that he had never tasted before, flavoured with rum. 'It is a pity,' he remarked, 'that our relations with the Russians cannot be confined to their sweets.' Everybody laughed and even Emory smiled.

His mother was looking very handsome in a lilac velvet, trimmed at the bosom with a fall of cream-coloured lace. No one would dream that she had ever been the wife of a missionary in China. She had kept her stout figure in spite of her age, and her visit to England, prolonged as it had been, had given her an imperial air, enhanced by the pile of white curls on her head, which he liked. He was proud of her and, the dinner over, he led her to the most comfortable chair in the long drawing-room.

'You're looking well, Mother.'

'I am in splendid health, thank God,' she replied in a resonant voice. 'I've had no chance at you, you naughty boy. Oh, I know you've been too busy for your old mother.' She leaned over the edge of her chair while the others were settling themselves. 'Now, William, I want you to have a talk with Henrietta. She is living all by herself somewhere way downtown in the most miserable little apartment. It doesn't look right for your sister.'

'What is she doing?' he asked. He knew vaguely from Emory that Henrietta was still working on one of Clem's absurd notions and his eyes fell on her as he spoke. She was sitting in her characteristic repose.

'She's working at some laboratory with an old Jew. I don't know what she's doing. Clem was a queer duck, if you ask me.'

At this moment Henrietta raised her dark eyes and smiled at them. She was gentler than she used to be, though even more withdrawn.

'I want a word with you later, Henrietta,' he called.

She nodded and her eyes fell.

Ruth was very pretty in spite of her troubles. He had time now to look at each one of his family. She had gained some weight—eating, probably, to take her mind off Jeremy. Of all of them Ruth looked the most like his father, her features delicate and her bones fine. Yet there was nothing in her face of that spiritual quality which he remembered with reverence as being his father's habitual expression. Her two daughters were nondescript young matrons, he thought. They looked like all the modern women, flaring blonde hair, wide painted mouths, a clatter of thin bracelets and high heels. He supposed they were well enough and certainly they need not worry him now that they had husbands.

He had taken no more relatives into the business, not even his own sons. He wanted to be free to dismiss incompetents like Jeremy. Not that his sons were incompetent in any way. Both of them were successful men. Will a lawyer, Jerry a surgeon. They were married and he had three grandchildren, two of them boys. He did not know his son's wives very well and had even been accused of passing them on the street without recognizing them. He had grumbled a good deal when Jerry married an ordinary trained nurse while he was an intern. William had a theory that it would be better for all young people if they were married in the Chinese fashion by their parents, in order that one could be sure of what was coming into the family. When he had said this to Emory she had gone into fits of laughter. 'You are the most unrealistic of men,' she had declared. 'Don't you know yet that you are living in modern America?' He did not know what she meant and was too proud to say so.

His sons and Ruth's daughters seemed on the best of terms with Emory. She sat among them and behind her coffee

444

table, appearing, he thought with self-congratulation, entirely happy. Her darkly regal head was bent while she busied herself with cups. She wore a coral-coloured gown of some sort that he did not remember having seen before. The full skirt flowed round her like a calyx, and she had on her diamonds.

It was all very pleasant and he did not remember ever having been quite so happy before. Everything was well with him, and it was dawning upon him that perhaps even the war had been good for him in its own way. The world needed leadership as never before. He must not allow himself to think of retiring, however much Emory hoped for it. Monsignor Lockhart had said to him only last week that the new war in Asia might be the beginning of mankind's most titanic struggle. Within the next years——

'William,' Emory said. 'Your mother wants to know what you think is going to happen in China. Why don't you tell us all?'

So he began, sitting in his high-backed arm-chair. 'A very strange new China, not at all what you and I remember, Henrietta, in old Peking. You would like it less than ever, Mother. I don't suppose Ruth remembers. . . .'

They listened to his picture of Communist China, no one interrupting him except his mother, who put in small cries of horror and interjections of outrage.

'But how repulsive, William!' And at the end, 'I'm glad your father isn't here to see it. He would want to go straight over there—though as I always said, what one man can do I don't know. "You're wasting yourself," that's what I always told him.'

'One man can do a great deal,' William said.

She heaved a mighty sigh and shook her head.

'Not any man, of course,' William said, 'but one who knows, one who has faith in God, has infinite power.'

His mother looked rebellious. 'Your father always thought he knew, too, William. He was always so sure that God told him what was best. I don't know that there's any difference between then and now.'

445

'There is a great deal of difference,' William said gravely. 'Now we really do know.'

Emory, scenting the dissension always possible in the presence of her mother-in-law, chose a lighter substance for talk.

'William says the Old Tiger's wife is very beautiful, though she's Chinese.'

'So was the Empress Dowager,' Mrs. Lane said promptly. 'The Empress was not Chinese exactly—Manchu, of course, but it's almost the same—and she was very beautiful. I shall never forget her. She had long eyes, very long and brilliant. She had a temper, as any woman worth her salt has. Her mouth was very red—of course she painted. Her skin was wonderful and smooth and white as anybody's. I never felt it was really her fault that things went as wrong as they did. She was so charming, and always perfectly lovely to me. I took William to see her—do you remember, William?'

'I can never forget,' William said.

'Powerful, wasn't she! With such charm, too!'

'She killed an extraordinary number of people.' This was Henrietta's voice coming so quietly that it seemed almost indifferent.

'Oh, well,' Mrs. Lane said, 'we don't know what provocation she had.'

'It is never right to kill people,' Henrietta said with what Mrs. Lane felt was her childish stubbornness.

William answered his sister. 'It is sometimes necessary. In order that the end may not be lost, the means must sometimes be very severe.'

'Then the end is lost,' Henrietta said. She lifted her head when she said this, and Emory felt that the family was really very difficult. They seemed determined to disturb life. She turned to the younger men.

'Will, why don't you and Jerry and the girls open the doors into the music room and roll back the carpet? I'll play for you and we can watch you dance.'

Under cover of the music and the rhythm of brisk feet swinging into new intricate steps, William went to Henrietta.

446

'Let us go into my library. I would like to know what you are doing.'

She rose almost obediently and followed him, her black-robed figure upright and dignified. Since Clem's death she had not cut her hair and now, almost entirely white, it was long enough to be coiled around her head and held at the back with a silver comb. Emory's eyes, from the piano, followed the tall figures. It was surprising how much William and Henrietta looked like each other. Yet they were utterly unlike. Henrietta was espousing poverty for Clem's cause. Emory had learned much about that solitary laboratory and the old scientist who worked there. And yet perhaps there was a likeness between William and Henrietta. A great deal of character and spiritual energy could be stubbornly bestowed upon something chosen and the chosen substance was changed, transubstantiated, and so deified.

Emory understood this without in the least partaking of it, kindly cynical as she was to the core of her heart, sadly agnostic, while she bowed her head. America was her country now and this her family. Her parents had been killed by one of the final buzz bombs. They had gone up to London, thinking it safe at last, and then the new horrible bombs began to fall. Poor Michael, in Hulme Castle, was still trying to make the land produce those impossible harvests under the cruelly critical eyes of the incredible government the British people had chosen for themselves after the war! William said he would never go to England until it fell. It might be a long time, it might be never. Her hands flew over the keys. She played as beautifully as ever, with a natural rhythm which she could suit as easily to a rhumba as to a waltz. Nothing made any difference so long as the music went on, the music and the dancing.

'So you see,' Henrietta was saying behind the library door which was so heavy that it shut out the music, 'I shall simply keep on with Clem's work until I succeed in what he wanted to do.'

William was too stupefied to speak. He had thought Clem

447

a fanatic and a fool while he lived, and in so far as he had given any thought to him since his death it was to believe that Henrietta was better off alone. When he thought of Clem now it was still as the pale boy whom he had first seen in Peking in a silly quarrel with a Chinese, an affair no more dignified today as he remembered it than it had been then. He had been repelled by Clem as a pale young man in a collar too big for him, after he had become Henrietta's husband, and there was that final folly of the day when Clem had come to his office with his absurd proposals and without any appointment. Clem never learned anything. His life had been all of a piece, all nonsense except that he had made some money for Henrietta. William had never acknowledged Clem as part of the family and he did not do so now. Careful for once of his sister's feelings, he made no reference to Clem. He spoke to her entirely for her own good.

'If, as you say, you have had by chance a respectable fortune left to you it seems madness to consume it on any idea so fantastic. If people were given food, which is, after all, the one basic necessity, most of them would never work again.'

Henrietta tried once more. 'You see, William, it is not only that they should not be allowed to starve. I believe, and Clem did, too, that unless people are fed they will rise up against any government they happen to have. The government that first understands the anger in the hearts of hungry people will be the one that wins. People feel they ought not to have to starve for any reason whatever. Dr. Feld says that Hitler's promises of food were the first steps to his power.'

William was walking restlessly about the room and she kept watching him. 'The idea is so fantastic,' he was repeating. 'Think of feeding the people of China! It can't be done.'

'It's got to be done,' she said. 'And there are the people of India and all the other peoples.'

'Fantasy, fantasy,' William muttered.

She contradicted him flatly. 'Not fantasy, William, but purest common sense. Do you know why you can't see it? Because you and Clem worked at opposite poles. He believed the world could get better only when people were better. He

448

believed that people themselves could make a good world if only they were free from simple misery. That was Clem's faith. Yours isn't that. You think people have to be compelled from the outside, shaped, ordered, disciplined, told what to do. I don't know where your faith is—I suppose you have it, for in your own stubborn way, William, I can see you are working for the same thing Clem was.'

William was suddenly violently angry. 'I deny the slightest resemblance to him! Henrietta, I tell you——'

He raised his clenched hands and saw that they were trembling and dropped them. 'Clem was a dangerous man, a menace, or might have been if he had been successful. He worked at the very roots of our nation to destroy us. I don't like to say this, Henrietta—I don't forget you are my sister—but now that he's dead, you had better know the truth.'

Henrietta remained calm. 'Well, William, we don't understand each other. We never did. But some day it will be proved that Clem was right. That is my faith. And when he is proved right, William, you will be defeated, you and with you the Old Tiger and his beautiful wife and all the rest of your kind. How wrong that Old Empress was whom Mother continues to worship!'

'Henrietta, you're talking very wickedly.'

'I dare say.'

She was so calm, so immovably stubborn, that for a moment he felt quite sick with rage, exactly as he had so often felt when they were children together in China. But he managed to follow her into the hall and help her on with her wrap, a black wool cape. For she was determined to leave him and, so far as he could see, to leave them all. She would not allow him to tell the others that she was going.

'No use disturbing them,' she said in her short fashion.

So he let her out of the door himself and then stood at a window watching her. She did not call a cab. Instead she began to walk down the street, her bare head held very high and the wind blowing hard and her cape flying out behind her. It was a clear night, and he could see a strip of stars above. At the far corner she stopped for a bus. He could still see her waiting there, and he would have continued to watch her except that one of those miserable creatures came shambling up to her. Under the light of the street lamp William saw her open her handbag and take out money and give to the beggar, thereby encouraging, he thought bitterly, all such persons everywhere. He pulled the curtains together across the window and trembled with anger. He had been angry with Henrietta all his life, and with that fellow Clem!

He stood behind the curtains, thick and velvet, and summoned his old arrogant spirit. He would not suffer fools! He closed his eyes, and waited. No reassurance rose to meet his soul's demands. He wished he had not thought of Clem. He saw him again now. Inside his brain, inside his closed eyelids, he saw Clem, that boy, intrepid in the Chinese street, ready to fight. Clem marching unbidden into his office. The fellow had no breeding, never knew his place. Dead, luckily! He had the world to himself, now that Clem was dead.

He opened his eyes, he heard faintly the music that Emory made and mingled with it the soft movement of dancing feet. He turned away from the window. Then he felt the familiar chill upon his heart. The old childish doubt of himself, the profound eternal doubt that had haunted him from his earliest memory, fell upon him again, this time so heavily that he felt too tired to shake it off.

What if he had always been wrong? The vague shape of victory—was it he? Or was it Clem? His imagination, diseased and tortured by his soul's perpetual uncertainty, lifted Clem from the grave, brought him back to life, clothed him in the dark garments of doubt and fear.

Could Clem be right? If so, then he himself was wrong and being wrong was doomed. But was Clem right? How could he ever know?